Quintin
Jardine
THE BAD FIRE

HEADLINE

First published in 2019 by
HEADLINE PUBLISHING GROUP

1

Cataloguing in Publication Data is available from the British Library

978 1 4722 5579 2 (Hardback)
978 1 4722 5581 5 (Trade paperback)

Typeset in Electra by Avon DataSet Ltd, Bidford-on-Avon, Warwickshire

Printed and bound in Great Britain by Clays Ltd,
Elcograf S.p.A.

HEADLINE PUBLISHING GROUP
An Hachette UK Company
Carmelite House
50 Victoria Embankment
London EC4Y 0DZ

www.headline.co.uk
www.hachette.co.uk

This is for my lovely wife, Eileen,
whose essence is unchanging.

Then . . .

Threat and danger come with the territory I patrol, the place where I make my living.

It's the nature of my work. Scottish criminal defence lawyers are guided by a professional principle that we can't pick and choose our clients, and I have to adhere to that rule, difficult as it may be on occasion. Some of the people I have represented in court have been as utterly reprehensible as the crimes of which they have been accused, but even beasts have a fundamental right to the best defence available. Sometimes that's been me, Alexis Skinner, Solicitor Advocate. Sometimes I've gone home and stepped straight into the shower to wash off the taint of the creep I've been doing my level best to return to society.

It wasn't always like this. When I left Glasgow University with my brand-new law degree (Honours), I wasn't bound for the high court, or any other level of the justice game. My first port of call was Scotland's top corporate law firm, Curle Anthony Jarvis. It was headed at the time – still is – by my dad's friend Mitchell Laidlaw. (Everyone knows my father; my father knows everyone. I'm sure that if Lloyd George was still around, they'd be acquainted.) Don't go thinking, though, that I was the teacher's pet; Mitch is a tough dude, and with him, the reputation of the firm is head and shoulders above any other consideration. My success as a corporate lawyer was down to my ability and the hard work that made them shedloads of money. And I was successful; the youngest partner in the firm's modern era, and winner of a couple of legal awards along the way. I was a rising star, with a glittering and lucrative future set out before me.

Occasionally I would stare at the ceiling and ask myself, 'Alex, why did you do something so profoundly fuckin' stupid as walk away from all that?'

But I know the answer. It was my dad, wasn't it?

I have met, but not for long, a couple of people – men, simpletons – who asserted that the legal avenue I chose at the beginning of my career was an act of rebellion against an authoritarian upbringing. Nothing could be further from the truth. My father, Sir Robert Morgan Skinner, QPM, remains the coolest guy I know. Yes, he had a ferocious reputation as a serving police officer. He scared the shit out of some very hard men. But at home he was Huggy Bear. My mother died when I was four, and he raised me to adulthood on his own. There were a few 'aunties' along the way, and one had some clothes in his wardrobe for a while, but he remained resolutely single until I was grown and flown. There are those who would say that he might have been better staying that way, for in the last twelve years he's had three marriages, to two women, and another unfortunate relationship that did him no good at all, but he has settled down now, for good, I am certain.

He is growing older gracefully. I am thirty-one, which makes him mid fifties, but he has the look and bearing of a younger man. He acts like one too, and that worries me. He's always had a tendency to draw trouble, and I suspect that in times past he's gone looking for it. He has an image of impregnability, but he's been shot, and sustained a near-fatal stab wound in a random attack; and he has a cardiac pacemaker installed as a result of a condition called bradycardia, which makes the heartbeat drop suddenly and without warning, in his case to zero. Not long ago, he was mugged in a garage by a Russian thug. It didn't end well for the guy, but not before Dad had sustained a heavy blow to the head. He said it was nothing, but Sarah, my stepmother, confessed to me that it's had an aftermath: occasional but severe headaches and a couple of dizzy spells.

When I was young, I wanted to be a teacher when I grew up, as my mother had been. Somewhere along the line that changed, and I wanted to be a cop. The motivation for my switch was Pops' girlfriend, Alison Higgins, who was a detective inspector. She showed me that women could be significant players in a service that was evolving rapidly, moving away from the sexist, bigoted outfit that my father had joined, emerging as one where merit was rewarded and where the glass ceiling, while it still existed, was moving higher and higher. He was one of the drivers of that change, and so it was only natural that I expected when I announced my future career choice, with the unshakeable self-assurance of a fourteen-year-old, that he would beam with delight and support me.

'Like hell you will!' he barked at me across the dinner table. To say that I was taken aback, that's putting it mildly. I couldn't remember him ever raising his voice to me in anger, not even when I was at my most wilful – and I had been wilful, after Mum's death and again as puberty crept up on me, a period of my life that her sister, Aunt Jean, had helped me through. It wasn't only the vehemence of his reproof that startled me; there was something in his eyes that I had never seen before.

One of his team in the CID Serious Crimes squad, Mario McGuire, a detective constable on whom I had a small crush, had told me a story about being in the room when 'the Big Man' (Mario was huge himself) had interrogated a suspect in an armed robbery. 'He never said a word, Alex. He sat there and looked at the suspect, stared at him across the table, never blinking, drilling holes in the guy with those eyes. It went on for minutes: Christ, I was scared, and I was sitting next to him. He never moved, never lifted a finger. The prisoner, who was no pussy, let me tell you, tried to stare him out, for maybe thirty seconds, but he couldn't hold it, couldn't look at him. The tension built and built until you could have cut in into blocks and built a house with it, until finally the prisoner threw both hands up and said, "Okay, okay, Ah was there! But Ah jist drove, mind. The other two had the shooters." Then he told us where to find them, gave us a full statement and earned himself a couple of years off his sentence in the process.'

I had doubted that story – Mario was one of my father's fan club, and I thought he was exaggerating – but that look, that glare made me a believer.

That's not to say I was as compliant as the armed robber. I fired back at him. 'It's what I want, Pops! I want to be a police officer and you can't stop me.'

He may have scared himself more than he alarmed me. In an instant, the fearsome detective superintendent was gone and Huggy Bear was back. The glower became a smile, and he winked. 'Actually, love, I think you'll find I can,' he said. 'But I'd rather it didn't come to that, and here's why. I've been a cop for about fifteen years, and in that time I have seen awful things, some of them so bad that I've done my best to un-see them. Every instinct I have as a parent makes me want to protect you from that.'

'You don't protect Alison,' I pointed out.

'That's not the same: Alison had made her choice before I met her.'

'What would Mum say if she was here? She'd have supported me, I'll bet.'

He laughed. 'I'll tell you exactly what she'd have said. "No way, Josita. The pay's crap and the hours are worse." She'd have said the same about teaching too.'

'Life isn't about money or convenience,' I protested.

'Don't knock either of those', he countered. 'But it's more than that. Very soon now, I'm going to be head of CID, chief superintendent. By the time you leave university, there is every chance that I'll be an assistant chief constable. If you were on my force, you'd be very difficult to manage. People are human; your line managers would struggle to know how to handle you. Do they favour you in the hope of finding favour with me? Or do they go out of their way to make life hard for you to show everyone else that there's no special favours on their watch? It would be one or the other for sure.'

'I could handle that,' I promised.

'I'm sure, but I couldn't. If I thought you were having special treatment, I'd have to intervene for the sake of fairness to your peers. If it was the other way, do you really think I'd stand by and let some sergeant with an attitude pick on my wee girl? He'd be on the night shift in Pilton before he knew it, then his successor would make you teacher's pet and I'd have to intervene again.'

'There are other forces. I could join Strathclyde.'

'You take sauce on your fish supper,' he retorted, 'not vinegar. You're east coast not west coast,' he explained. 'And I'm not having you walking a beat in any of the choicer areas through there. Kid, I have no doubt that you would be an excellent police officer, but the odds are stacked against you. On the other hand, if Grandpa Skinner was still alive and you were having this conversation with him, his eyes would light up – as much as they ever did – and he would welcome you into his profession with open arms and a promise of a partnership in his firm before the ink was dry on your practising certificate.'

'Did he do that with you?' I asked.

'Yes, but family law, worthy as it is, had no attractions for me. For you, on the other hand . . .'

'Grandpa's firm doesn't exist any more.'

'No, but there are others, and much bigger. For example . . .'

And that was the start of a process of persuasion that led me to the modern high-tech office of Curle Anthony Jarvis, the success I achieved there and the stellar future that was set out before me. Unfortunately, while we can fight our genetic inheritance for a while, long term it's always going to win.

My father and I share a low boredom threshold, and as for my mum, from what I've learned, hers was practically non-existent. She got bored putting on her knickers, which was why they came off so frequently – a trait I have not inherited, I rush to say.

The process began at my last awards dinner. It was sponsored by a business magazine, and I had been chosen by a panel of 'experts' as 'Young Dealmaker of the Year', because I had led the legal team in the acquisition of a whisky distiller by a Chinese client of CAJ. The shiny statuette was presented by the finance minister in the Scottish government. She was fulsome in her praise as the flashes popped, and then it was my turn to make the obligatory speech of thanks. I hadn't intended to say much, beyond thanking Mitchell Laidlaw for giving me the chance to shine, and paying tribute to my team. I did that, and that's when I should have exited stage left and sat down; but I didn't. I'd had a couple of drinks, and I was in a bad place with Andy Martin, my off-and-off love interest. He had stood me up with an excuse that I hadn't bought for a second, telling him so in direct terms.

The mood carried over. 'I should be prouder of this than I am,' I continued, brandishing the bauble. 'But I can't be, because it's ugly, probably made in Vietnam by a kid earning fifty pence a shift, and because it represents another step in the colonisation of my country, something to which we have become accustomed over the centuries.' As cheers rang out from a drunk SNP table at the back of the hall, I pointed to the base of the trophy. 'It says here,' I continued, 'on this wee plaque, "Scottish Business Awards". With every passing year and every big deal like this one, that becomes less and less true. Just saying.'

Mitchell Laidlaw couldn't look at me as I rejoined the firm's table. A couple of the more senior partners did, and they weren't happy. They couldn't say anything, though: my dad had taken Andy's place in chumming me. He stood as I reached my chair and drew it back for me. For a second I had a flash of dread that I had embarrassed him, for as long as it took for him to kiss me on the cheek and whisper, 'Spot on, baby, spot on.'

The dinner was a Friday event; I spent the weekend alone, worrying about the reception I would have in the office on the following Monday morning, not least at the partners' weekly meeting. As it transpired, nothing was said, but when I went back to my work area, I found that some comedian had pasted a photo of Mel Gibson, hair wild and face painted blue and white, on the wall behind my chair. Also, on my desk there was a copy of the Saturday *Scotsman*, a newspaper I never read, folded to display a report of my 'outburst'. It identified me as the chief constable's daughter, and carried a quote from an anonymous 'spokeswoman' commenting that it was simply 'Alex being the Alex that we all know and love'. The firm's PR consultant was female, so I pretty much knew who the author was, and also that she would not have dared say anything that hadn't been authorised by Mitch himself. The thing that annoyed me was that it wasn't true: I had never done anything but toe the official line, I had never spoken out of turn, and until then I had never shown anything but utter respect for the clients who paid our fees. My impromptu speech had surprised me as much as it had surprised anyone; it had come from a place I didn't know existed and it had shaken me.

I determined that it would be a one-off and that I would put it behind me. I threw myself into my work and continued to complete my projects on time or ahead of schedule. Month after month I was at or near the top of the confidential profit-per-partner table that the firm's management maintained. The *Braveheart* jokes stopped, and my views and comments on practice affairs were sought more than ever before. My star continued to shine.

But not at home. Professionally I was successful, but privately I was a mess. My relationship was in the crapper, I was lonely, and I could do nothing about it but spend hours in the Sheraton health club, punishing my body on treadmills, cross trainers and strength machinery.

I couldn't even talk to my father about my feelings. He had his own issues at the time. The politicians were determined to force through the unified Scottish police service to which he was instinctively opposed, and his then wife, Aileen de Marco, was leading the charge. It's the only battle he ever lost. Change happened, he couldn't go along with it, and he walked away from the job that had been his life for all of mine.

Without knowing it, when he did that, he unlocked the door of my cage.

He broke the news to me over dinner. His sadness almost broke my heart, and yet when I woke next morning I felt happy that he had been strong enough to take the decision. It took me a couple of days to realise that I also felt happy for myself.

It took another couple for me to realise why. For the first time since I was fourteen years old, I had a career choice that in theory was limited only by my aptitude and ability. I had been brought up by a cop, among cops; now that the constraint of a chief constable father had been removed, I could be one myself. I had my degree, and I could take it where I wanted.

The euphoria didn't last long, and reality bit. Although Dad had taken himself out of the game, I had grown up with most of the people who would be the big players. Worse, the team captain would almost certainly be Andy Martin. Topping all that off was the unfortunate truth that I wasn't fourteen any longer, but a little more than twice that age, racing towards thirty at an alarming speed. If I joined the service, there was a fair chance I'd be the oldest person in my training college class, by several years.

The cage door slammed shut again, with a clang. I went back to work the next day, doing my damnedest to let nothing show, but it was a struggle. I felt lethargic and I knew very well that I was sliding down the profit-per-partner table, hour by hour. In an attempt to shake myself out of it, I decided to call my father; he was still a chief, head of the Strathclyde force against his better judgement, but as he had told me during that fateful dinner, he felt like a man on Death Row whose lawyer had finally given up on him.

'I wouldn't abandon him to the needle,' I murmured as I picked up my phone. My mouth fell open, I gasped, and that cage door swung open again. 'No, you wouldn't, would you,' I exclaimed, with a beatific smile that I didn't even try to hide from my colleagues.

I knew in that moment what I wanted to do: I would be a criminal defence lawyer. I wasn't fooling myself: it required a completely different skill set from that which had served me and CAJ so well. But it didn't matter to me whether I would be any good at it. For the first time in my life, I understood what it was to feel a sense of vocation.

I went straight to Mitch Laidlaw's office and told him of my decision to leave the firm and go into private practice. He's a thoughtful and courteous man, so he didn't laugh in my face, but after a couple of 'mmm's he asked, 'Do you really want to spend the rest of your career defending drunk drivers in the sheriff court?'

'My ambitions are a little higher than that,' I replied. 'I'm going to become an advocate with rights of audience in the high court.'

'You can do that within this firm, Alex,' he said. 'I've been considering adding that string to CAJ's bow for some time now, having counsel in house, and moving away from employing them as the need arises. Complete the training, and I'll transfer you to the litigation department. You can replace Jocky Scott as senior partner there when he retires.'

'I'm sorry, Mitch,' I replied, 'but I don't want to do civil law. I want to establish a criminal practice.'

That's when his mouth fell open and he stepped out of character. 'What?' he gasped. 'You're going to hawk yourself around the detention cells like the famous Frances Birtles and the rest of that crew?'

I smiled at his surprise. 'Think of it as me setting up in opposition to my father. He locks them up, I'll get them out.'

He fell silent for another minute, before saying, 'Then God help the Crown Office. The prosecution's in for a hard time.'

My partnership agreement specified six months' notice, but as I'd expected, Mitch put me on gardening leave as soon as I had handed over my existing work; I didn't have a garden, but that stuff is complex and confidential and couldn't be left with someone who was heading for the exit.

'You do know,' he ventured, 'that the qualifications include experience of a solemn procedure trial in the sheriff court?'

I didn't. 'How do I—' '—get that?' I was about to ask but he cut me off.

'As it happens, I have a friend who has a solemn trial in Glasgow Sheriff Court next week. It's a corporate fraud charge, and he's in need of a junior with relevant experience. I can fit you in there, I think, and maybe into a few others along the way. You'll have to work your nuts off, mind,' he warned.

'I would if I had any,' I remarked. 'Just one thing,' I added. 'Don't tell my dad. You might not have tried to talk me round, but he would for sure, if he knew.'

I was halfway through the application process when I did tell him. To my surprise, he didn't question my choice at all.

He was so calm about it that I thought Mitch must have broken his promise, but he reassured me about that. 'He never said a word. Truth is, love, I've been expecting this since that awards dinner; this or something like it.'

'So I have your blessing?'

He laughed. 'If you told me you were training as a pole dancer you'd have my blessing. Go for it. The high court needs you, Alexis. And who knows, now that I have time on my hands, you might find that once you're established, you have a really cheap investigator.'

Actually it began with me doing some cheap investigating for him, but that's another story. However, he was a huge help to me in developing my new career. I didn't trade on his name, but I couldn't avoid being his daughter and I have no doubt that it helped me. I did use him as an investigator whenever he was free, but only on work that justified his involvement. But as my practice grew, so did that requirement. Eventually I decided that I was asking too much of him, and that I should blood someone else.

Unfortunate choice of phrase, Alex.

One

B y Scottish standards, it was an unusual summer. It had survived the first fortnight in May, continued into June, and was threatening to extend into July. Edinburgh's city-centre shoppers were sweltering, the nation's golf courses were turning brown in spite of their automatic watering systems and beach car parks were earning a small fortune for local councils all around the country.

'Get you,' June Crampsey laughed, as Bob Skinner walked past the open door of her office on the way to his own, dressed in shorts, sandals and a close-fitting blue T-shirt. 'Not even the directors of our parent company in Spain dress like that. Nice legs, by the way,' she added. 'I don't recall ever seeing them before.'

He paused. 'Don't you start,' he replied. 'Trish, the kids' carer, said I look like the guy from *Baywatch*.'

'Which version? David Hasselhoff or Dwayne Johnson?'

'I like to think she meant the younger one.'

'Could you do me a selfie?' the managing editor of the *Saltire* newspaper asked. 'I'm thinking of doing a photo feature in the next Sunday edition on unusual office attire.'

'This doesn't count as an office day for me; I was here all

day yesterday, remember, Sunday or not, talking to Spain about the UK expansion programme. Sarah's car's had a recall, so I drove her to work, then thought I'd come in to check my mail.'

She looked at him afresh. 'I don't see room for a phone in that skimpy outfit.'

'Left it at home, didn't I? The heat must be getting to me, for I'm finding that I quite like being out of touch, from time to time. I don't think I have been in years, since even before we all started carrying mobiles, or had them wired into our cars.'

'That explains why your daughter was up here looking for you half an hour back. She asked if you'd call in on her if you showed up.'

'I thought she was due in the high court this morning.'

'The trial's been postponed, she said. The prosecution have offered her client a plea deal.'

Skinner chuckled. 'Which means that the Crown Office doesn't think it can get a conviction. Okay, I'll go down and see her.'

'Don't forget that selfie,' she called after him.

He stepped into his own office; unlike that of his colleague, it looked towards the morning sun. The high-rise block was faced in glass that was meant to be heat-reflecting. It seemed to be doing its job, although the air-conditioning system was working full blast, ruffling the correspondence in his in-tray. Skinner was a part-time executive director of InterMedia, a family-owned company that was the proprietor of the *Saltire*, as well as titles and radio stations across Spain and Italy. He had been doubtful about the post when it had been offered by his friend Xavi Aislado. After a career in the police service, it had been a radical departure, but he had been persuaded – not least by the substantial salary – to give it a go. To his surprise, he had risen to the challenge, to the extent that while his contract specified one day a week, he spent at least three in his office, and had become effectively the managing director of the *Saltire*, as the board's British presence.

He spent fifteen minutes reviewing his mail, physical and electronic, and acting on it where urgency was required, then headed for the stairs that led to the office suite he had secured for his daughter as her legal practice grew to the point where it could no longer be run from home or from a law library.

'Bloody hell!' Alexis Skinner laughed as her father appeared in her doorway. 'Why didn't you just put on budgie-smugglers and be done with it?'

'You can talk.' She was dressed in a sleeveless white blouse and a light blue skirt. 'It's well seen that you're not on parade in the court. Have you got a result?'

She nodded.

'You don't look delirious about it.'

'I'm not. My client and his wife had a physical confrontation, and she wound up in a coma. Attempted murder was never going to stick, given that she came at him with a carving knife; her prints were all over the handle and only one of his on the blade. But he did whack her after he had disarmed her. He says it was to subdue her, and I went with a self-defence plea on that basis. On Friday night the advocate depute rang me and said she'd take a plea to serious assault if I dropped self-defence. I told her to piss off and this morning they asked for a continuation that will almost certainly lead to the indictment being withdrawn.'

'Great, you did get a result.'

'Try telling that to Jack McGurk, the SIO on the case. Medical evidence says that he hit her three times, with his fist, but what it doesn't say is whether he did that before or after he'd taken the carving knife off her. As I said, he put his hands up and admitted to hitting her once after she'd dropped it, and that was a glancing blow; his story was that the two disabling blows were struck when he was in fear of his life. Jack doesn't believe that. Jack's theory is that he beat her unconscious in a fit of rage after she confronted him about an affair, then slashed himself across the shoulder and put her prints on the knife.'

Skinner frowned. 'But he can't prove it.'

'No chance. It's his version against my client's; reasonable doubt wins every time.'

'So what's your problem?' her father asked.

'I believe Jack's theory too. I've spent enough time with my client to know that he's a fucking psychopath; also, I have seen the previous convictions that the jury couldn't be shown, including one for an assault that was serious enough for him to do eighteen months in a Young Offenders Institution. Despite all that, we have a woman in a chronic vegetative state, and the guy who put her there will be discharged.'

He shrugged. 'As an ex-cop, kid, I agree with you. But it isn't your fault. It's Jack's, for being too soft on the guy and failing to secure a confession. It's the examining medic's, for not being able to tell a self-inflicted wound from a real one. Either that, or you're both wrong and it happened exactly as your client described. Either way, you have done your job to the best of your ability and should be as proud of yourself as I am.'

Alex winced. 'I hear what you're saying, Pops, but professional satisfaction is as much as I can muster. I have too much sympathy for the woman, whatever the truth of it. Her brain isn't dead, but it's massively damaged. Even if it did happen as Reilly – my client – says it did, it's a hell of a price to pay.'

'You're not having second thoughts about your career switch, are you?' Skinner frowned.

'No, I'm not,' she insisted. 'When I went down this road, I knew that moral questions might arise. This is the first of them, that's all I'm saying.'

'Does it make you reconsider the offer that was made to you, to spend some time in the Crown Office as a prosecutor?'

'No,' she replied firmly. 'I'm not ready for that yet. But it might make me think about representing victims of crime.'

'I know plenty of those,' Skinner murmured. He paused. 'Is that why you wanted to see me, to get this off your chest?'

'Partly, but there are a couple of other things. Firstly, there's Uncle Jimmy's memorial service on Thursday. Is Sarah going with you?'

'Unless a last-minute job comes up that can't be delayed, yes, she is.'

'Can I tag along with you?' she asked.

'Of course. It won't just be Sarah alongside me. June Crampsey's going too, and her father, Tommy Partridge. I'll have a row reserved for us; there'll be a place for you.'

'How about Andy?' she murmured. 'If he shows up, will he be welcome?'

He frowned. 'Last I heard, Sir Andrew Martin was in America, lecturing and licking his wounds after his monumental fuck-up as the first chief constable of the national police service, or Holyrood's Folly, as I like to call it. I doubt that the death of Sir James Proud got too much coverage in the US media, so he may not even know about it. He's not on the guest list, that I can tell you. I know because his successor asked me to approve it on Chrissie Proud's behalf.'

'How is Lady Proud?'

'She has vascular dementia and Alzheimer's,' Skinner said. 'It hasn't registered completely with her that Jimmy's dead. Maybe I should give her his fucking dog back, as a substitute.'

Alex laughed. 'Come on, you and Bowser are getting along fine, and the kids love him.'

'The kids don't have to clean up after him when we walk him.'

'You could trust them to do that, surely.'

'Like hell I could. And our village being what it is, the first time James Andrew neglected to bag a turd, the family would be named and shamed on the Facebook news group.'

She smiled at the thought. 'I assume that you'll be speaking at the service.'

Skinner shook his head. 'No. I was asked, but I declined.'

'You what?' she gasped.

'I said no. I'm history. Maggie Rose is the chief constable, and she served under Jimmy. It's her place, not mine.'

'But she didn't know him,' she leaned on the verb, 'not like you did. You were his friend as well as his deputy. You spoke at Alf Stein's funeral, but you weren't nearly as close to him,' she added.

'I was a serving officer when Alf died. Love, near as dammit everybody who'll be in St Giles' Cathedral was Jimmy's friend. It's best that Maggie does it; she should have her place.'

'I flat out don't believe you. There's another reason for you refusing. And don't try to tell me you don't like public speaking, or you don't believe in God.'

18

'I'm not going to try and tell you anything. Subject closed. You can tag along with Sarah and me, and if Andy Martin does show up, I will shield you from him.'

'I don't need shielding!' Alex protested.

He winked at her. 'Maybe not, but I'll do it anyway. Now, what's the other thing you wanted to ask me?'

'It's about my next visitor,' she said.

'What's he supposed to have done?'

'Nothing, as far as I know. He called and asked for an appointment, but he refused to tell Clarice what it was about. Normally she'd have insisted he tell her, but there was something about him, she said, that stopped her from doing that. She just slotted him in for five o'clock today.'

Skinner shrugged. 'So why are you quizzing me?'

'Because his name is David Brass: the same as that blogger who was murdered in Haddington a few weeks ago – Austin Brass, the guy who was a thorn in the flesh of the police with that website of his. Brass Rubbings, wasn't it called? You were involved in that investigation. Is there a connection between them? Big coincidence if there isn't.'

He nodded. 'Yes: David is Austin's father. I met him a couple of times during the investigation. As a matter of fact, you can blame me for the contact. I gave him your card and suggested that he give you a call.'

'My turn to ask you. What's he supposed to have done?'

'Nothing at all. You were talking earlier about representing victims of crime. This could be your chance.'

'Are you suggesting that I help him raise an action against his son's killer?'

'Not at all,' Skinner said. 'It's not related to that . . . well, I suppose it is eventually. I don't want to get into it. It's best that you hear the whole story from him than second-hand from me.' He grinned. 'I should warn you, though. There won't be a hell of a lot of money in it.'

She wrinkled her nose. 'Thanks a bundle, Pops. I don't just have my own mouth to feed. There's Clarice, my PA, and Johanna, my associate.'

Her father raised an eyebrow. 'Don't give me that; you're doing all right. Not like CAJ, but okay. Johanna, she feeds herself by handling the sheriff court work that you don't fancy.'

'Will you sit in on the consultation?' she asked.

'Hell, no. You don't need me. It's best that you hear him out, then make your own judgement on whether you can help him. Besides, I don't plan to spend the whole day here; the weather's too good for that. I'm going to the beach, kid – with Bowser, of course.'

Two

'If I didn't live in an apartment, I might get a bloody dog myself,' Alex grumbled as she gazed through the glass at the sun-bathed city. 'If I did, I might spend less time in here.'

'You wouldn't say that if it was chucking it down outside,' Clarice, her assistant, countered. 'Besides, time is money, isn't it?'

'Not necessarily. I do a lot of productive thinking when I'm on the move. I'm like my father in that respect.'

'As far as I can see you're like your father in most respects. I'd only met him the once before this morning, but looking at the two of you, you're definitely from the same pod. Okay, you're prettier than he is, and you don't have that thousand-yard stare he shows from time to time, but in attitude, you're identical.' She paused. 'He's pretty fit too, for a middle-aged gentleman,' the matronly brunette mused, 'in those shorts and that T-shirt. Something of a FILF, as my daughter-in-law might say.'

'Stop right there, woman,' Alex laughed. 'My stepmother's a pathologist. She works with dead people, but if she heard that, she might make an exception for your kid.'

'I'll bear that in mind. Still, it's been worth your while to stay in the office today. You got a result for your attempted murder, and two new clients. A corporate fraud trial; that'll go on for weeks, won't it?'

'If it gets that far,' she conceded. 'I haven't seen the prosecution case yet, only the complaint that's been made by the alleged victim's solicitor.'

'Your old firm? Curle Anthony Jarvis?'

'Yes, and that's an added complication. If the indictment goes so far back that the complaint covers the period when I was in the corporate department there, I might have to declare a conflict of interest.'

'Is that likely?'

'I don't think so. The client was given my name by Jocky Scott, the senior litigation partner at CAJ: not directly, but through his wife when she rang Jocky to raise merry hell about him reporting her husband to the police. He wouldn't have done that if he hadn't been sure I could take the case.'

'So, you see, it hasn't been such a bad day. Your man Reilly is out from under an attempted murder charge, but you'll still collect a fee, and this one will be potentially ten times that – and not from legal aid either.'

'Neither was Reilly. He's a dentist, remember?'

Her prediction that the Crown would drop the case had been proved correct just after two p.m., when Serena Colley, the advocate depute who had been leading for the prosecution had called to throw in the towel. 'You've been lucky in this one, Alex,' she had said. 'You took a chance turning down the serious assault plea. If my boss had listened to me and let it go to the jury, there was a fair chance we'd have got a conviction.'

'Outside chance, at best,' Alex had countered. 'But no

chance at all that the appeal court would have let an attempted murder verdict stand. The evidence wasn't there.'

'Maybe not, but it would still have left a mark on the bastard, professionally. I don't hear any triumph in your voice, by the way.'

'No comment.'

There had been an ironic chuckle on the other end of the call. 'Reilly won't be doing your next implant, then.'

'Fuck off, Serena. Take it like a woman.'

DI Jack McGurk had called her an hour later. They were friends, but for a year and more their only contact had been professional. 'Congratulations are in order, I hear, Alex.'

'Or commiserations, depending on which side you're on.'

'Mmm.' His disappointment had been almost palpable. Strangely, she felt pleased that he had been able to make the call in a civilised way. A month before, a 'not guilty' verdict in a drugs trial in the high court in Glasgow had been followed by an email from Brendan Yeats, the DCI in charge, so vicious that she had considered forwarding it to Police Standards. 'Alex, do you ever regret a verdict?' McGurk had asked, in sorrow, not anger.

'Honestly, no, but I don't celebrate either. My first duty is to the court, not the client. If I had felt that Reilly'd had no other option but to plead guilty to attempted murder, that's how I'd have advised him. If he'd refused, I'd have told him to find another advocate, because I won't present a defence I can't believe in. But your case wasn't rock solid, Jack. The Crown Office let you down. They should have gone with serious assault and countered my self-defence claim with an excessive force argument.'

'Hey, maybe I can get them to continue on that basis?'

'Not now. They've told the judge they're withdrawing. Move on, mate; that's what I'm doing. In fact, by coincidence, I have another dentist coming to see me at five. This one's retired.'

'What's his problem?'

'I have no idea.'

'As long as it doesn't involve what's on his laptop.'

A shiver of dread at that prospect ran through her. She had decided privately that if she was ever asked to take a paedophilia case, she would find herself otherwise engaged.

She checked the time on her phone, her ear registering the sounds of Clarice shutting down her computer for the night, and of Johanna, her associate having an argument on the phone in her small office. It was ten past five; Mr Brass was late. She decided that she would wait until five thirty, then change into the gear in which she had walked to work that morning, and run home, across the Meadows and then through Holyrood Park. It was five minutes short of that when she heard a soft 'ping' as her outer office door opened.

She greeted him in the reception area: a stocky man, carrying a briefcase, mid to late sixties, she estimated, no taller than she was, with rounded shoulders, long arms and big hands. He was unsmiling and there was a sadness in his eyes.

'My apologies, Ms Skinner. It's so long since I've come up from Kelso. I thought the traffic would have been lighter at this time of day, but it took me by surprise when I had to join the city bypass.'

'That takes everyone by surprise. Its peaks are unpredictable; I'm fortunate in that I rarely have to use it. Come through to my office, Mr Brass, and tell me what my father thinks I can do for you.'

Surprise registered in his eyes. 'Sir Robert told you?' he exclaimed.

'No, he didn't. When I mentioned your name as my five o'clock appointment, he admitted that he'd given you my card, but he refused to tell me what it's about.' She ushered him into her office and to a seat at her conference table. 'I know your son was murdered a few weeks ago. Are you considering an action against the man who's been accused? It'll be months until he's dealt with, even if he pleads guilty, as I hear is likely.'

'No,' David Brass replied. 'That idea never entered my mind. My son isn't the only member of my family to have died an unnatural death. I'm here to talk to you about Marcia, his mother, my former wife.'

'What happened to her?' Alex asked, settling into her chair.

'She took her own life, nine years ago. She was accused of shoplifting clothes from a supermarket called LuxuMarket, in Kilmarnock. She denied it, vehemently, but she was prosecuted, and the media gave her a hard time. She was a target, you see, a local councillor, and a vociferous one. She made more enemies than friends on the council, but her constituents loved her. She was a constant irritant to the powers that be, which means Labour, on the West Coast Council.'

'I notice you called her your former wife, not your late wife,' she observed.

'Your father really has told you nothing. Marcia and I were divorced. It was how we celebrated the Millennium, she used to joke, although it was a little after that. It was my fault more than hers. I wasn't the most faithful husband, but none of my flings ever came to anything and we remained on good terms, held together by our son to an extent.' A less likely Lothario Alex had never seen; she did her best to banish the thought from her expression.

'What were her politics?' she asked. 'What party did she represent on the council?'

'She was an independent.'

'How did she die?'

'She took an overdose. She was a hospital manager; the investigating officers determined that she stole a lethal dose of morphine from the pharmacy.'

'This all happened nine years ago, you say. What brings you here now?'

'Marcia maintained that the shoplifting charge was a frame-up, from start to finish, and so did Austin.'

'Your son ran a blog that focused on police misconduct. Did he ever use it to advance that theory?'

Brass shook his head; for the first time she realised that it was disproportionately large. There was something simian about the man. 'No, he was more discreet than that. Not least because he was warned off by the supermarket's very aggressive owner. We made a fuss after Marcia's suicide, of course we did. But the media were, well, frankly disgraceful; they played a part in her death, no doubt about it. The local paper ran a front-page lead under the headline "Shamed councillor facing theft charge". It assumed Marcia's guilt and told the whole story, leaked to them no doubt by the police.'

'Not necessarily,' Alex pointed out. 'It could just as easily have been the supermarket.'

'Given its attitude, that wouldn't surprise me,' Brass conceded. 'We fought back, of course; I wrote to several newspapers but none of them published my letters. Austin went to one of the tabloids and suggested in a comment to a journalist that the supermarket was responsible for her suicide by its intransigence. That got some coverage, but LuxuMarket's owner replied by threatening to sue him to within an inch of his life, or words to that effect.' His eyes narrowed. 'That's when he decided to set up the blog,' he continued.

'My son didn't have a bitter bone in his body until his mother died. The change in him was instant; he blamed the police as much as LuxuMarket. They had made him cautious, but he saw the police as open targets. He abandoned a very successful career as a child psychologist and began to pursue and investigate complaints against them, always intervening on the side of the aggrieved. He found cases easy to come by; they were all over the media. He went to the people involved and set himself up as an advocate on their behalf. Where a complaint was spurious, he realised that carly on and gave it up. But where there was something in it, he did a little investigating and then went straight for the jugular. In the early days of the blog, he copied his posts to all the Scottish news desks. After a couple of spectacular successes, well covered by the red-tops, his fame spread and people with grievances began to approach him, rather than the other way around. He was even approached by the police on occasion, by serving officers who knew of something that wasn't right but couldn't do anything about it internally, for a variety of reasons.'

'Going back to the accusation,' Alex murmured, 'you said that Marcia denied it vehemently.'

'Absolutely, from the beginning. She protested her innocence from the outset. When she was charged, she said that was how she intended to plead – and then the procurator fiscal had a private word with her solicitor. He told him that there was more than enough evidence to convict, and that if she went to trial, the sheriff would be likely to impose a custodial sentence, precisely because she was a public figure. On the other hand, if she pleaded guilty, there would be a modest fine and that would be it.'

'What did she do?'

'It didn't get that far. The day before the pleading diet, she was found dead.'

'Did she leave a note?'

'No.'

'Was there any hint that she was about to take her own life?'

'None. On the contrary, she told Austin the night before she died that she intended to go to trial.'

Alex frowned. 'Did the police treat her death in any way other than suicide?'

'Not that I could see. The investigating officer was the man in charge of the shoplifting case.'

She gasped. 'You're joking. That's . . . it's irregular at the very least.'

'It was nine years ago,' Brass pointed out, 'in a different policing environment.'

'I don't care if it was in the reign of Queen Victoria,' she retorted. 'Given the possibility that the death was linked to the prosecution he was driving, that should never have been allowed. Do you know the officer's name?'

'Terry Coats; he was a detective sergeant at the time, later detective inspector. Mind you, Austin did have a measure of revenge. He did an exposé on the man in Brass Rubbings a year or so back, and Coats was held to account. He resigned from the force shortly afterwards. I believe he was briefly a suspect in Austin's murder.'

'That much I do know,' Alex said. 'My father had a run-in with him. You're correct, he was a suspect, but he was eliminated very quickly.' She paused. 'How did the Terry Coats piece come about? Was Austin watching everything he did, looking for evidence of any wrongdoing?'

'No, he was very careful about Coats. The fact is, he was tipped off by a very senior officer that it was worth taking a look at him.'

'Was that a coincidence, or did that officer share his doubts about the accusation against Marcia?'

'I can't honestly say, although I suspect that if it was the case, Austin would have told me.' He paused, but only for a second. 'No, it's not possible,' he decided. 'Before he ran the exposé on Coats, he cleared it with me. I noted that it didn't refer back to his mother, and he said no, that he didn't want to be seen as less than objective, not until he had one hundred per cent proof of a conspiracy. Then he would act.'

'This person who spilled the beans on Coats. Do you know who it was?'

'I believe so. If I'm right, she's dead.'

Alex nodded; she sat silent for a while, considering everything that he had told her. 'Mr Brass,' she continued, 'this is a very sad story and I sympathise with you for the losses you've suffered. But what do you want me to do? Why are you here?'

He gazed at her across the width of the table; his eyes were kind, but as sad as any she had ever seen. 'I would like to see justice done, for Marcia and for Austin. Her death triggered the circumstances that led to his murder. If she hadn't died, he would never have started that blog of his, never have been working on the story that got him killed. He'd have had a quiet and fulfilling career and the world would never have heard of him. But he didn't. To my shame, I encouraged him to start Brass Rubbings and backed him financially until it started to generate revenue. It was very popular. It didn't take long until its readership was large enough to attract advertisers.' He wrung his massive hands and winced. 'I should have seen the danger in what he was doing, though. I should have realised that he might attract the attention of dangerous people, both within the police force and beyond.'

'You couldn't have anticipated what happened to him,' she said.

'I should have. I was blinkered, I didn't realise the potential consequences. For example, I never knew, until your father told me, that someone died as a result of the piece on Detective Inspector Coats. It identified a man, a confidential informant to whom Coats was closer than he should have been. Not long after it appeared, the fellow was found murdered. If I had known that, I would have put a stop to the blog there and then, but I didn't until it was too late for my son.'

'This is about your conscience, isn't it?' Alex suggested. 'As much as it's about justice.'

'I suppose it is,' Brass admitted, 'but it's about my anger too, over Marcia and the way she was . . . what's the phrase? Framed, fitted up, for that shoplifting.'

'You think she was?'

'I'm persuaded that she was, Ms Skinner. I don't know who did it, or why, but I don't think they did it without help. I suspect that Strathclyde Police, Mr Coats in particular, colluded with it.'

'That's a big accusation, and it brings me back to my question. What do you want me to do about it?'

The man drew in a deep breath and closed his eyes. For a moment, Alex thought that he was meditating, but in fact he was simply composing himself, finding the right words, for his eyes opened and he replied. 'I want you to take Marcia's case. Even though she's dead, even though it's years in the past, even though the supermarket in question no longer exists. I want you to reopen the investigation and clear her name.'

'You want me to treat her as a living client?'

'Precisely.'

'The problem with that is that she isn't,' she exclaimed, 'and unfortunately dead people don't qualify for legal aid.'

'That isn't a problem, Ms Skinner. I'm not Warren Buffett, but I'm wealthy enough; I can afford your fee.'

'And my associated costs? I might need to employ an investigator, and I tell you now, it will not be my father, not on a case that might involve police corruption as you suggest.'

'That too. This means a great deal to me, Ms Skinner.'

'Call me Alex, for God's sake,' she retorted. 'I'm still struggling to see where I would start on this. It's ancient history, the case never came to court and the chances are that the investigation files have been destroyed.'

Brass picked up his briefcase and snapped it open. 'That may be, but I have a copy. Austin came by the papers through a contact who had a down on Mr Coats and who had his own doubts about the quality of the case against Marcia.' He took out a thick folder and laid it on the table. 'It's all here. The complaint by the supermarket, witness lists, statements, all that stuff. All of it bogus, I believe.'

'Again, do you know who that contact was?'

'Not by name, but my understanding was that he worked in the procurator fiscal's office.'

'Let me see the papers, please.' He slid the file across. She opened it and began to study.

'This appears to have come from the procurator fiscal's office,' she murmured. 'This is the charge sheet. It alleges that she stole a matching jacket and dress, value one hundred and sixty pounds, from the premises of LuxuMarket Limited in Kilmarnock.' She moved on and read in silence for over a minute. 'This appears to be a statement by the store manager, Mrs Hazel Delaney. It alleges that the items were hidden in a plastic bag that Ms Brown . . . Ms Brown?'

'Marcia reverted to her maiden name after our divorce,' he explained. 'Not because she was at odds with me, but because she was very combative in her council role and didn't want me or my dental practice to suffer because of her.'

'I see. The statement says that she failed to present the bag at the checkout, that she was observed by store security and stopped in the car park.' She flicked through the file. 'There's a statement by one Zaqib Butt, describing that. It says her groceries were in five bags and the clothes were in a sixth, hanging on a hook on her trolley.'

'That's right; I know it all by heart. It describes the contents of the bag.'

Alex looked at the guard's deposition. 'Matching dress and jacket in peacock blue,' she read, 'from the LuxuMarket Regency range.'

'Size?' Brass interjected.

'Size twelve.'

'Exactly. Marcia was a biggish woman. She was a size sixteen, although she would only ever admit to being a fourteen.

If she was going to steal something it wouldn't have been that many sizes too small for her; maybe one out of vanity or optimism, but no more.'

Alex nodded, fully engaged in the story for the first time. 'What did she say about the bag on the hook?'

'She told me that after she cleared the checkout, she was distracted by another shopper, a constituent who wanted to nobble her about some complaint or other that he had against the council. She left her trolley at the exit and went across to speak to him for a few seconds. She believed that was when the bag was put on the hook.'

'Why didn't she see it? Usually these hooks are below the handle and pretty visible.'

'This one wasn't. There was a hook there, but others on the sides of the trolley. The bag was on one that was out of her sight. If you look in the file, you'll find a photograph that Detective Coats took when he arrived.'

'Coats was actually at the scene?' she exclaimed. 'Shoplifting is a uniform job as a rule.'

'Delaney, the store manager, called the station commander, and Coats turned up. He said it was because Marcia was a councillor and the police thought it might be a delicate situation.'

'How did she know to phone the commander?'

'I can't say for certain, but I have my suspicions.'

'Those being?'

'This is where it gets tasty.' Brass leaned back stiffly on his chair. 'When Austin began to investigate, after his mother's death, he went through her papers, her notes, everything. He found a diary entry that referred to a fellow councillor, an opponent, a Labour person. It was underlined and had three exclamation marks after it, a typical Marcia sign that she was not best pleased with that person. Austin approached one of her allies on the staff of the council, and established that a week before the LuxuMarket incident, Marcia and this person had a blazing row in the councillors' sitting room.'

'Did he find out what it was about?'

'No, only that there had been voices raised and fingers pointed, threats made on either side. There was nothing in Marcia's notebook that offered a clue to the business.'

'The name of her enemy?'

'She's called Gloria Stephens. She's still on the council; in fact she's its leader, as she was then. With Marcia out of the way, she went from strength to strength; she pretty much runs the district now.'

Alex nodded. 'Okay, David. If I'm reading this right, your suggestion is that there is a connection between their argument and Marcia's arrest. How could that possibly happen?'

'Very simply. Councillor Stephens has a daughter, Vera. She was on the staff of the supermarket, an assistant manager. Her responsibilities included the clothing range. At that time, she was engaged to a police constable, who was a regular golf partner of Terry Coats. Austin believed that Vera Stephens set the whole thing up at her mother's behest, and that it was her fiancé who advised her to make the complaint directly to the station commander.'

'What's the cop's name?'

'If I ever knew, I'm afraid I can't remember. We didn't know about him until Austin started to investigate.'

'If it was that carefully set up,' Alex pointed out, 'surely the constituent who distracted Marcia must have been involved too. Do you know who he was?'

Brass sighed. 'No,' he admitted. 'That's the damnable thing. Marcia couldn't remember his surname; his forename was Adrian, that she did recall.'

'Did Austin try to find him?'

'He did, but without success. That of itself was significant. He went through the entire electoral roll for the West Coast Council, but couldn't find a single registered voter called Adrian, first name or second.'

'What about the security man, Mr Butt? Was he interviewed?'

'Only by the police and the fiscal. When Austin tried to speak to him, he was told that he had resigned from his job.'

'I assume that Marcia had a solicitor. What was his name? Is he still in practice?'

'She did, but no, he isn't. His firm, Black and Grey, still exists but he retired four years ago. His name is Cedric Black, but I have no idea where he is these days.'

'Do you know if the firm holds a file on the case?'

'They did, but they refused to release it to Austin; they may have been scared by LuxuMarket's aggressive posture. Austin believed it had been destroyed because it showed that Black had made no real effort to put together a defence for Marcia.'

'We'll see about that.'

Brass offered a small smile. 'Does that mean you'll take the case?' he asked.

'I'll explore it,' Alex replied. 'But you need to know this. The only way it will be reopened will be if I find evidence of criminality. Nine years on, even if you're right, the chances are that tracks will have been covered well and truly; what I'm saying is don't build your hopes up.'

'I understand that; I've always understood it. What more do you need from me?'

'Initially, I need a letter of instruction from you. If I have to require access to the records of Black and Grey, I'll need to have the authority to go to the Law Society to force it. I may need access to Austin's papers on the subject as well.'

He frowned. 'Austin's files are quite extensive; I had them moved to my house in Kelso after he died. Do you want me to bring them all up here?'

'I don't need you to bring anything up. I'll ask my investigator to go to you if it becomes necessary.'

'Do you know who that will be, if not your father?'

Alex grinned. 'Oh yes. I have the very woman in mind.'

Three

'I don't know whether to thank you or yell at you, Pops,' Alex said, settling into a garden chair and uncapping a bottle of sparkling water. It was early evening, but the heat was still in the day as they looked out across Gullane Bents. The beach car park was full, and dozens of bathers could be seen on the edge of the incoming sea, with several paddle boards beyond them, their owners taking advantage of the rare opportunity to dispense with their wetsuits.

Skinner smiled. 'I'll know when you've made up your mind, then,' he replied amiably. He raised an eyebrow slightly as he glanced at his daughter. 'Your hair's a mess, by the way.'

She ran the fingers of both hands through her mass of loose curls and shook them back into shape, casting a mock glare in her father's direction as she did so. 'Thanks for that,' she chuckled. 'I had the top down all the way out from town. What's the point in having a convertible if you can't convert it?' She paused, frowning. 'From the quiet around here, I'm guessing the kids are on the beach.'

'Apart from the baby, yes. Sarah's upstairs putting our wee Dawn to bed.'

'Who's in charge? Ignacio?'

'No, he's up in Perthshire with his mother. Didn't I tell you? He started a holiday job at the weekend, in his stepfather's hotel. Trish wanted to go for a swim, so she's riding shotgun on them.' He laughed. 'The fact is, they're all looking after Mark. Jazz is part fish, and Seonaid's competent too, but Markie, he swims like a brick.'

'Probably because he hasn't found a computer program to teach him.'

'You may have a point there. The boy is a genius in that respect.'

Alex sipped her water. 'You okay with Ignacio being up there?' she ventured.

'With his mum?' he retorted. 'How could I not be? What right do I have to be anything *but* okay? I missed the first eighteen years of his life. Mia Watson and I had a one-night stand twenty-odd years ago; she ran off to Spain straight afterwards, before she even knew she was pregnant, never told me when she did know, had Ignacio, and lived a very illicit life there until she was forced to come back.'

'None of that was your fault.'

He held her gaze. 'You think? If she'd stayed, she might have faced criminal charges. That wouldn't have been good for me, for you, for anyone.'

'Are you telling me you tipped her off?' she asked him quietly.

He nodded, almost imperceptibly. 'I tipped her off. I told her to run and not stop. My Achilles heel, my one dark guilty secret . . . no, I have more than one, but only that one bothers me, because I never went after her. I wrote her off as bad news, along with the rest of her stupid, useless criminal family, and I shouldn't have done that. There was always much more to Mia than any of that crew. "Mia Sparkles", she called herself on the radio station, and she did, too; sparkle, that is.' His smile came from nowhere and gave him away.

'Bloody hell!' Alex gasped. 'Ignacio's a genuine love child; you actually fell in love with her. I never realised.'

'Rubbish,' he protested, snapping back to the moment. 'I didn't.'

'Yes you did; it was written all over your face.'

'Maybe,' he conceded. 'Maybe I did. But I loved you more, and I knew that I couldn't disrupt your life. If I'd done that, your mother would have reached up from down below and ripped my heart out.'

His daughter stared at him. 'From below? Surely she'd have sent a dove from heaven to whisper in your ear and put you straight.'

He beamed at her. 'I remember very little about my great-granny Skinner. She was early nineties when I was born, and she didn't quite make it to the hundredth birthday card from the Queen. But one thing sticks in my mind. My dad took me to see her one day, out of duty more than anything else. She still lived on her own, and she gave him tea and me ginger beer; I was only four, but from time to time I still have its taste in my mouth. I was bored, and I started to play with an ornament she had on a side table. It was an Indian thing, a prayer wheel, I think, and I picked it up and started to spin it. Then this skeletal hand clamped on my wrist – for a woman of ninety-five, her grip was remarkably strong – and she drew me to her and hissed in my ear, "If you break that, boy, you will go to the bad fire!" By that time, I was going to Sunday school, and our church was authoritarian, to say the least. I knew all about the concepts of heaven and hell and I understood exactly what she meant.'

'What an old witch,' Alex murmured. 'That explains why you never told me much about her, and why her photograph always stayed in a drawer. So,' she continued, 'that's where you think my mum is? She went down there?'

'It was a joke, love, but if such a place as the bad fire exists, I reckon Myra Graham Skinner might prefer to hang out there than with the angels.'

'In that case, I'm glad I don't believe in it,' she said. 'I wouldn't want to run into too many of my former clients.'

'I doubt that you'd meet David Brass there. I'm guessing that he's the reason for this unscheduled visit.'

'Your guess is spot on. You knew I wouldn't be able to turn him down, didn't you?'

'I'd have been surprised if you had,' Skinner admitted. 'What's your gut feeling?'

'All my instincts say that he's right. Marcia Brown was set up. I've read the official file; he said that a sympathetic person in the fiscal's office slipped his son a copy. Did he show it to you?'

'No. I didn't want to get involved, not then. I was too wrapped up in finding Austin's murderer. Also, at that time, I couldn't be objective about Terry Coats.'

'What was it with him?' Alex asked. 'You never really explained what that fuss was about.'

'He was playing away games. When he became a person of interest in the Austin Brass murder, it all came out, and as Noele, his wife, was a DS on the investigation team, it was inevitable that she would hear about it. For some reason he thought I was responsible for that. The one person he should have blamed was himself, and I had to explain that to him, firmly.'

'What's your take on him now? Could he have framed Marcia Brown?'

'What does the prosecution file tell you?'

'Nothing that implicates him in a stitch-up. If there was one, okay, he might have been complicit, but equally he might just have done a sloppy job. He did make it to detective inspector, though, so he must have been an effective officer generally.'

Skinner nodded. 'He was, but he was also a risk-taker. He walked in shady places, cultivated contacts on the other side, and built his reputation by putting them at risk. Did David tell you who turned Austin loose on Coats; who gave him the information that was used on Brass Rubbings and finished his career?'

'A senior officer was all he said.'

'It was Toni Field, his chief constable, my predecessor in Strathclyde. She couldn't have nailed Coats through the normal procedures because she had no basis for a complaint, so she used Austin to do her dirty work. There's no harm in you knowing that when your investigator interviews him, as I assume they will.'

'Yes,' she nodded, 'Coats is bound to be on the list, along with half a dozen other people.' As a cloud passed overhead, casting a sudden shadow across the garden, she seemed to mimic it by frowning. 'The more I think about this, Pops, the more I'm beginning to feel like a prosecutor. If we prove Marcia's innocence, we have to prove someone else guilty.'

'Guilty of what?'

'Perverting the course of justice, or something similar. What should I do, Pops? Should I begin there and work backwards?'

'You should do nothing; let your investigator set the priorities.' He looked away, across the bents, and saw a group of four, three children and an adult, making their way in his direction. 'The peace is about to be breached,' he announced, rising from his chair. 'You staying for supper?'

'Sorry,' she replied as she stood too. 'I've got a date.'

'Another lawyer?'

'Worse, a banker. Nobody you know.'

'I do tend to avoid them. Back to the case: anyone in mind for the investigator role?'

'I'm thinking Carrie McDaniels,' she said. 'That's one reason why I'm here, to pick your brains about her. Do you think she's up to it?'

Skinner stretched his back as he considered the question. 'Who would your alternative be?' he ventured. 'One of a string of ex-cops who would do a routine job but wouldn't really give a fuck. Carrie's capable, she's not as brash as she used to be, and she knows the ropes. She should do; I showed her where most of them are. Yeah, go for her.'

Four

'Are you remembering you have a meeting in Chambers Street at ten thirty?' Clarice Meadows asked her boss. 'About Mr Paton, your arsonist?'

'Don't say it like that!' Alex protested, standing framed by the doorway, clad in the tracksuit and trainers in which she had walked to work. 'You make it sound like I employ him. No, I haven't forgotten; I have a clean blouse in my wardrobe, hanging beside my suit. I bought it yesterday lunchtime.'

She liked her new assistant; she was two years short of her fiftieth, and had been recruited from the civil service, where she had worked since the birth of her second child, who had just turned twenty-one. Her career change had been prompted, as she had explained at interview, by the way the service had become factionalised, with an unofficial elite being created by the patronage of ministers, and a culture of secrecy that she abhorred. It had been accelerated when she had expressed that view directly to the Environment Secretary within earshot of the First Minister's chief of staff. She had brought an air of stability to Alex's office; regardless of her title, she was effectively the practice manager, and made sure that her boss and Johanna DaCosta, the associate, were always on time for meetings and

43

court appearances, and fully briefed. There was something maternal about her too that Alex liked and, although she would never admit it, needed.

'How was your date?' Clarice asked, almost coyly.

'Ondine's always good,' she replied.

'That wasn't what I meant, and you know it.'

'Satisfactory.' Alex shrugged, and smiled. 'Okay, I might as well get it all on the record. James Hayes and I met when I was at CAJ. He's thirty-seven, just gone through his second divorce and I have no intention of being his third. We had an enjoyable dinner, we talked about old times, and somewhere along the line I decided that I didn't want to have sex with him, so when we were finished, I got the bill, he got a taxi and I walked down the Royal Mile and home. You know how it is: you look at him, you think about it, you ask yourself, "Would it be memorable?" You decide "Nah", so you don't bother.'

'Mmm.' Clarice pursed her lips. 'Sometimes I wish I did know how it is. Mr Meadows and I celebrated our silver wedding the year before last. There are times when I wish I could put him in a taxi and go home, and I'm sure he would say much the same. Memorable? Sorry, boss, I can't remember that far back. But I do believe this: when the most lovable thing about a husband is his dick, you've made the wrong choice. Now,' she said abruptly, 'about your arsonist. Are you fully briefed for that meeting, or is there anything else you need to know?'

'I'm up to speed, as far as I can be. I'm not going along there to talk about a plea, I'm afraid. The psychiatric reports, ours and the prosecution's, which you haven't seen, are unanimous in diagnosing Mr Paton as suffering from a serious personality disorder. He's schizophrenic.'

'Jekyll and Hyde?'

'Both of those people. The man who was caught on CCTV setting the fire that burned down his child's school after he was dropped from the rugby team isn't the Mr Paton who walks around normally, sings in the church choir and does the *Saltire* crossword every day. He's another person entirely, and if the Crown's allegations are true, that wasn't his first fire. The garage that screwed up the service of his car three years ago, that was burned out too, as was his doctor's house when he was fifteen and his mother died. There's no way the man's fit to plead.'

'What'll happen to him?'

'Maybe he'll go to the bad fire,' Alex murmured quietly.

'Eh?'

'Sorry, bad taste irony. I was just thinking about something my dad said last night. Paton'll be sectioned and transferred into the custody of the state as a psychiatric patient. Most likely he'll go to the hospital at Carstairs.'

'For how long?' Clarice asked.

'Until he can be safely returned to society. That could mean never; the parole system has no locus in there.'

She checked her watch; it showed eight fifty-six. 'My nine o'clock will be here any minute. Show her straight in when she arrives, okay? Then there is something you could do for me. Find out all you can about a business called LuxuMarket. Mr Brass's wife was done for shoplifting there, but it's a new one on me. A supermarket in Kilmarnock; beyond that I know nothing. I'm told it's closed down, but does that mean it's gone bust or been acquired by someone else? Who owned it nine years ago? Who owns it now? What was its planning history? You should find that out from the West Coast Council. Also, I need as much as you can get me on its leader, Councillor Gloria Stephens, public life and private. If you can put together a timeline of her career, I'd like to know what she was doing nine or ten years ago.'

Her assistant nodded, then turned at the 'ping' triggered by the office entrance door opening. Alex's eyes followed, taking in their visitor as she stepped through: a fair-haired woman, her face showing signs of sunburn, a little shorter than Alex herself, in the same age bracket, dark eyes narrowed, and tight-lipped. She wore a business suit and carried a black folder.

'Carrie,' Alex called out. 'Welcome and thanks for being on time. I'm on a tight schedule.'

'Me too,' the newcomer replied. 'You're lucky I could fit you in, given that you only called me at seven last night.'

'Then I'm all the more grateful,' she said, trying to keep her instant irritation from showing in her eyes. Her father had warned her that Carrie McDaniels could be abrasive as he had outlined her CV: a claims assessor with an insurance company, coupled with service in the Territorial Army military police in locations including Afghanistan, before giving everything up for the precarious life of a private enquiry agent.

'Come through to my office,' she continued. 'Clarice, if you could let me have your first findings while Ms McDaniels is with us, that might be helpful.'

She led the way to her room, unzipping her tracksuit top as she stepped inside, instantly recalling that she was wearing only a sports bra underneath and closing it again. *Not that informal, Alex,* she thought.

'Welcome again,' she said as she took a seat at the conference table. The folder that David Brass had given her was there, as she had left it the night before. 'Since we both seem to be tight for time, I'll dispense with the standard offer of coffee and get straight to business. I've been asked to put some heat into a very cold case, and I'm going to need an investigator, to conduct a series of interviews, explore anomalies and see where they go. It'll require initiative, as long as I'm kept aware of everything that's happening, as it happens.'

'This sounds like a job for your father,' McDaniels observed, 'or is it below his pay grade?'

'Probably above,' Alex retorted. 'I get a discount. This isn't one he'd feel comfortable with, for various reasons.'

'In that case, can your client afford me?' McDaniels un-zipped her folder, took out a small leaflet and laid it on the table. 'That's my schedule of fees and expenses.'

'I know what you cost: I didn't only ask my dad about you. It won't be a problem, unless this thing lasts much longer than I envisage. How busy are you? Can you take this on?'

'What's the location?' the investigator asked.

'I can't say for sure,' Alex admitted. 'The incident that triggered this whole thing took place in Ayrshire, but the people involved may have moved away from there by now. Some may be dead; the woman at the centre of it all certainly is, which is why we're here.'

Carrie McDaniels' expression changed, as reservation gave way to engagement for the first time. 'What is this?' she murmured. 'Is it a homicide?'

'My client might argue that it was, of sorts. He would argue that his ex-wife was hounded to her death. You and I, we can be more objective than that.' Alex pushed the folder across the table. 'The story's in there; read it for yourself. You'll want to make notes as you go, for you can't take it away. It's a copy of a prosecution case file and I only have my client's word about how it came into his possession.'

'Are you saying that it might be stolen?'

'I'm not saying a damn thing, Carrie; the person who gave it to my client's son might have had the authority, but to keep myself in the Lord Advocate's good books I have to assume that he didn't. I have a meeting at the Crown Office at ten thirty, and I intend to take it with me. I'll return it, in the hope that they'll give it back and legitimise my possession, but just in case they don't, read through it quickly and thoroughly and get as much as you can out of it.'

'Can't you take a photocopy?'

'Not until I have it in my own right.'

'Okay,' McDaniels agreed, 'but my clock starts ticking now.'

'As far as I'm concerned, it started ticking the moment you walked into this office. You can use my associate's room; she's in the sheriff court this morning. I have a few things to clear up here before I head up to Chambers Street.'

The other woman nodded and picked up the file. 'Once I've got to grips with it, I'll have an idea of what I need to do. I'll draw up a schedule, work out the time commitment and give you an idea of approximate costs and expenses.'

'What about your other clients?'

'Thanks for assuming they exist,' Carrie chuckled. 'That's not a problem. I have an associate too; he's a retired cop, name of Charlie Johnston, stolid but thorough.'

'Ha,' Alex exclaimed. 'I know Charlie. He started in the job on the same day as my dad. He never looked like reaching the second rung on the ladder, but as Sir Bob is fond of saying, if you don't take any risks you won't make many mistakes.'

She was still smiling as her office door closed and she turned to her in-tray to check the morning's mail. It was almost empty when Clarice Meadows knocked and walked in.

'A little progress,' she announced. 'Nothing yet on Councillor Stephens, but . . . I have a friend in the Labour Party central office that I know from my civil service days. I've spoken to him about her, and he's promised to ask around and report back.'

'Will he be discreet?'

'The soul thereof. That party is so fucking toxic now that everything is done in behind-the-hand whispers that can never be pinned down to anyone. He knows the woman only by reputation, and that isn't good, but he's going to ask people who work for her on the basis that he's been asked to put together an action group on global warming and he's sounding out potential candidates.'

'What about LuxuMarket?'

'That was much easier,' Clarice said. 'It's all online, start to finish. It even has a Wikipedia page, although what sort of anorak took the time to set it up, I cannot imagine. LuxuMarket was the trading name of a company registered as LX Retail Space plc. It was founded in nineteen ninety-nine, with a single outlet in Kilmarnock. Initially it traded as LX; the LuxuMarket branding was developed later. It traded successfully, with continuous growth until it was acquired seven years ago by a venture capital company, which turned it into a household products warehouse. The takeover was a cash deal, rather than equities, worth eight million, so the founder must have walked away happy. Eighty per cent of the equity of LuxuMarket was held by an offshore investment trust called Abuelo Incorporated. Wikipedia isn't forthcoming about who owns that, as it's registered in the Cayman Islands, but it's assumed to be

Scottish capital because of the location of the store.'

As she finished, she saw that Alex was frowning. 'What's up?' she asked, curious.

'Did you say Abuelo?' Alex retorted.

'Yes.' Clarice spelled the word letter by letter, watching a smile play at the corners of her boss's mouth. 'I believe it's Spanish for grandfather.'

'It couldn't be,' Alex murmured. 'It couldn't be,' she repeated, as the smile turned into a broad grin. 'But I'll bloody bet that it is.'

Five

'What does it feel like to have one surname for your first eighteen years, then having to get used to another?'

Ignacio Centelleos Skinner Watson pondered the question for a few seconds before replying. 'You could ask my mother the same thing. Women in Britain change their names when they marry, do they not?'

'Touché,' Cameron McCullough acknowledged. 'It isn't normal for a boy your age, though.'

'Not normal perhaps, but I am not unique. Wasn't Elton John called Reg for the first years of his life? I could have kept the name on my identity card in Spain. I didn't mind being Ignacio Centelleos Watson, but I did feel like an outsider. I've never heard of anyone else called Centelleos, not even in Spain, and there are absolutely no Watsons. Having taken Skinner as my first surname gives me a proper sense of identity for the first time. When you've grown up without a father to acknowledge, and without even knowing who he is . . . I must leave you to imagine what that feels like.'

'I suppose.'

'So now I have a father,' Ignacio continued, 'and he is an

51

important man. More than that, I have a stepfather and so is he.'

McCullough laughed; the restaurant was empty, and they were alone. 'Not many people would call me important, son. They'd call me a few things, but not that.'

'Why not? You own radio stations, you own this hotel. You own part of a football club. That makes you important.'

'Does it? Ownership itself, it doesn't matter. It's what you do with your property that determines how people think of you. That's if they know it's yours. I've never put my own name over the door anywhere. Everything I have is tied up in companies. I'm invisible.'

'In that case, your cloak is failing. I have only been here for a few days, but I've seen the way people look at you; not only the staff, the customers as well. They know who you are, and you have their respect. Me, the young waiter, the boy who clears the tables? They don't even know I'm there.'

His stepfather winked at him. 'Apart from the women. I've seen the way they look at you too, the way they eye you up.'

'Now you make fun of me, Cameron.'

'No, I don't. I'm serious. You don't realise it, but there's something about you that draws attention. It's no mystery where it comes from either; it's your dad. He and I have never exactly played on the same team, but I respect him, not least because he has power. Okay, you could give it another name – magnetism, authority – but whatever it is it comes off him in waves. I've only ever met a couple of people who came close to matching him; one of them is dead, and the other your father put away for life. You've inherited it, son, and you've got your mother's genes in you as well; that's a hell of a cocktail. Mia Watson's recklessness and Bob Skinner's ruthlessness.'

'You make it sound as if I'm a bomb waiting to explode,' Ignacio said.

'You have done already, remember, although that was your mother's fault more than yours.'

'What are you telling me, Cameron?' he asked.

'Be aware of yourself. Don't be reckless, like your mother can be, and don't be as cruel as your father can be.'

'Cruel? My father? You don't know him!' the young man protested. 'I see him at home with the kids and with Alex, my sister. He couldn't be more gentle.'

'But you don't see him at work,' McCullough countered. 'Bob Skinner only gets to gentle when he's worked through all the other options.'

'You don't like him, do you?'

'That's the bugger of it: I do.' He hesitated. 'Has he ever talked to you about me? Like really talked to you?'

'No,' Ignacio admitted. 'When I said I was coming here to work in the summer, he was a little hesitant at first, but not for long. What could he tell me?'

'Stuff: rumour, legends, all about me, none of them ever proved, fewer of them true than false, and most that weren't fiction were really down to Goldie, my crazy sister, God rest her. I have always been a legitimate businessman, Ignacio. Before I'd even finished qualifying as a chartered accountant, I inherited and ran my father's building business. It was nothing when he died, but by the time I was twenty-five, it was the biggest in the east of Scotland, and I'd already started branching out, taking stakes in other businesses and growing them. I've always had good judgement, had the courage to back it with cash, and over the years I have made a hell of a lot of money. I still do. But alongside me there was fucking Goldie, who saw business in a completely different way. She got into all sorts of stuff – drugs, money laundering, you name it. The police called it organised crime; the press couldn't, but the stories spread. I was even arrested once: someone disappeared, a quantity of Class A drugs was found, and I was charged. The truth was that Goldie thought she could get by without me, and set me up, but she bribed the wrong people. The cases against me collapsed, and finally I brought her under control. Ignacio, if I was everything the police said I was, I'd have made her disappear, but I didn't. We reached an understanding that held good until she died.'

'How much of this does my father know?' his stepson asked.

'Well that's the thing. He was a cop; in his heart he still is. But he was never part of any force investigating me. He was fed the official version – Grandpa McCullough, major player in organised crime – and he had no reason to doubt it. I think he does now, but I can never have a conversation like this one with him. Thing is, I did know about some of the stuff that Goldie was up to – never the detail, but enough, my sources being far more reliable than the police had – and I did nothing about it. I can't ever tell Bob that. It's better he still believes the old stories.'

'Why are you telling me?' Ignacio's question was a challenge.

'Because I'm married to your mother; you're my stepson. She knows all about me; she could tell you at any time, so I might as well do it myself.'

'You trust me that much?'

'Yes, I do, not least because you are your father's son, and however wary he may be of me, and I of him, I know this for sure: if I had to pick one man in the world to fight a battle for me, it would be him.'

Six

'Now that you're had some time to study and consider the file – which I now have officially, by the way – what's your feel for it?' Alex Skinner asked her investigator. They had reconvened in her office for a working lunch, fetched by Clarice, who had no qualms about KFC.

'I don't have one, not yet,' Carrie McDaniels confessed. 'My assumption is that you've hired me to establish her innocence, so that's how I'll proceed.'

The solicitor frowned. 'No, don't assume that,' she countered. 'My father knows David Brass, he likes the old guy, and yes, that's where he's coming from. He could have handled this himself, but for two things. It could turn into an investigation of improper police conduct, even malpractice by the Crown Office, and he wouldn't want to do that, not with his background. Added to that, he has history with Terry Coats over something that came up during the Austin Brass murder investigation.'

'Do tell.'

Alex smiled. 'It doesn't leave this room, but given Coats being the top name on Austin's target list because of his mother, he was asked for his whereabouts at the time of Brass's death. The account he gave wasn't accurate; when CID checked it out, they found that he wasn't at work but with a lady friend.'

'So?' Carrie made a face as she interrupted. 'Granted, he should have come clean, but these things happen. When I worked in the insurance company, for a while I was shagging a manager in my department. He was married and we got caught, but it was seen as a private matter that didn't compromise us at work. Why should Coats be grinding axes and how does your old man come to be involved?'

'Reasonable questions. I don't think Coats' horizontal jogging caused him any work problem, but his wife happened to be a DS on the Brass inquiry team. She had to be stood down for a while while his real alibi was checked out, and she had to be told why. My dad's connection? He's still involved with the cops in an occasional mentoring role. It's the only way that Maggie Rose, the chief constable, and Mario McGuire, the DCC, could keep him on the team. He led Sauce Haddock, almost literally, to Coats' illicit bedchamber door. When Terry's wife found out, she kicked him out, and he turned up at my father's home in Gullane looking for a fight.'

'I take it he got one?' McDaniels asked. 'I've seen your old man in action.'

'He did. Pops would probably have calmed him down, given him a drink and sent him on his way repentant, but he made a lot of noise and took a swing at Ignacio, my half-brother. Pops walked in on it and poleaxed him.'

'And now he's predisposed to cast Coats as a villain?'

'Not necessarily, but that's how it would be seen.'

'You're saying that I have to be seen to approach him with an open mind?'

'Approach everyone with an open mind,' Alex said. 'To skip back to your earlier assumption, I've undertaken to establish the facts of the matter. If they exonerate Marcia, or even establish reasonable doubt that should have been clear to the Crown Office, that'll be enough. If it turns out she was guilty as sin, so be it.'

'What about the circumstances of her death?'

'No,' Alex said firmly. 'That would be a separate investigation, and one for the police. Stick to the brief. How will you go about it? Do you need to see Brass?'

'I don't think so. You've told me as much as I need to know about him, and the Crown Office file has given me the facts. I'd prefer to be impersonal when I look at this, and for all you say you're only interested in the truth, I reckon you want it to favour him. It'll be better if I steer clear of him. I plan to begin with Marcia's solicitor, Cedric Black. As David Brass told you, he's retired from his firm, but I've run him to ground. He lives in Millport, and spends his time playing golf all along the Ayrshire coast. I've spoken to his former partner, Mr Grey. He was very evasive about the Marcia case until I threatened him with the Law Society. He did a complete about-turn and has now arranged for Black to see me, tomorrow morning. I'm looking forward to it. I've never been to Millport.'

Seven

'If an autopsy wasn't done, I'd be wanting to know why not,' Professor Sarah Grace Skinner declared. 'The first responders, medical and police, would have been bound to have seen it as a suspicious death. How old was the victim?'

'Fifty-nine, I think.'

'Did she have any adverse medical history?'

'Not that her ex-husband knew about. She played badminton to a good standard, he said, and she celebrated her fiftieth birthday by running the London Marathon in three minutes under four hours. I'd be happy if I could do that,' Skinner added.

'Who were the first responders?' his wife asked.

'I don't know. The file from the fiscal's office that David Brass was given only dealt with the criminal complaint. Marcia's suicide was a separate investigation. There was never any sort of inquest or public hearing, as there would have been in England, in a coroner's court.'

She speared a lightly curried prawn from the bowl in front of her. 'Look, Bob,' she said slowly, 'have you any reason to believe this woman's death was anything other than suicide?'

'None at all. She died from a massive overdose of morphine.

David says that the police decided she had stolen it from the hospital where she was a manager.'

'There you are then! There must have been an autopsy if the cause of death was determined so precisely.'

'But how thorough would it have been? The pathologist had an apparent suicide victim – with an empty bottle found by her side, I would guess. Tests would confirm lethal levels of morphine in her system. Come on, Sarah, let's say you're presented with a victim whose cause of death is seemingly obvious, and you confirm it immediately. How much further are you going to look?'

'I don't know,' she replied. 'I can't speak for whoever did the job. I don't know what his or her workload was that day.' She chuckled. 'Don't go all *Silent Witness* on me. If it looks like a duck, it walks like a duck and it quacks like a duck, then ninety-nine times out of a hundred it's a fucking duck.'

'Agreed, but one time out of a hundred it might be a guy with a fist up its arse, trying to make you believe that it's a fucking duck. My question is, would the original pathologist stop once he had an answer in line with the presumption, or would he carry on looking for an alternative? I don't believe you would simply have sewn her up and stuck her back in the fridge. Did whoever Marcia's pathologist was do that?'

'If you're that curious, ask someone who might know the answer.'

'I might just do that,' he murmured. 'I might indeed.'

Eight

In common with most of those from the eastern side of Scotland, Carrie McDaniels was stirred by the grandeur of the Firth of Clyde and its islands. Great Cumbrae and its only town, Millport, were reached by a small roll-on roll-off ferry, the shortest route between it and Largs. She had heard enough radio weather bulletins to know that the area could be windswept, and so she was grateful for the continuing heatwave as she watched the vessel approach its slipway.

The strait between mainland and island was narrow and the journey took little time, but even as she drove down the ramp, Carrie knew no more about her destination than she had on leaving Edinburgh. As she followed the slow-moving electric Nissan in front of her, she had a broader view of Largs and Hunterston beyond, but it was not until the road took a long curve that Millport revealed itself – not so much a town as two or three ranks of houses gathered around two long continuous bays, which gave it shelter and an outstanding view to the south of Little Cumbrae, and beyond, the great and spectacular island of Arran.

The Nissan peeled off into the drive of the third house they reached, making her the leader of a small convoy. In a city she would have speeded up instinctively, but instead she held her steady pace, taking in the scenery. The beaches were less busy than she had expected. Her great-aunt had told her stories of her own holidays here when they, the cafés and the tennis courts had been thronged even in weather that varied most summers between bleak and hostile, and where the most popular items in the small community's shops were windbreaks and mallets to hammer their poles deep into the sand. But those had been the days before mass air transport had taken holidaymakers off to hotter and more reliable places, and also when there had been more accommodation for rent, before the affluent professionals of Glasgow had taken it off the market by acquiring second homes.

She had expected more people, she had expected the Crocodile Rock, Millport's only landmark, but she had not expected the palm trees that lined the second beach she reached as she followed the instructions of the voice of Apple Maps. They took her by surprise and for the first time she drew an impatient beep from the car behind. Annoyed, she flicked him a one-finger salute, but picked up her pace, moving on past the original jetty, where her great-aunt might have disembarked, and beyond, following the directions that her Bluetooth speaker recited until she was in West Bay Road, where it announced, 'You have reached your destination.'

She looked to her left, appraising it. No holiday home, surely; a substantial two-storey grey sandstone villa looking imperiously down a long garden with bay windows on either side of a double storm door, which stood open. She pulled her key from the ignition, unclipped her seatbelt and stepped out of the car. As she did so, she realised that the vehicle that had been behind her, the one whose driver had run out of patience, had pulled into the driveway.

'Miss McDaniels.' Its owner, a slender man in a pale blue short-sleeved shirt, exclaimed as he approached. Her first thought was that he must have taken early retirement, until she noticed that the skin around his elbows was beginning to lose its elasticity, a sign of ageing that she had seen in her vigorous father. 'Cedric Black. I'm sorry, both for my bad manners on the road back there and for not guessing it was you in the queue back in Largs and introducing myself. I had a very early dental appointment this morning down in Stewarton. I've gone to the same practice for thirty-seven years; my long-term dentist retired a few years ago, but it's never occurred to me to look for someone closer to home.'

'No worries,' she said, accepting his handshake. 'I've always meant to come here to see the place for myself.' She added a smile. 'Plus, I'm on expenses.'

'That's good. It means I don't need to feel guilty about not meeting you on the mainland. Come on in; hopefully my other half will have coffee on the go.'

He led her up the long pathway to the front door. As they approached, it was opened by a woman in shorts and a halter top. 'You cut it fine, Ced,' she called out. 'Come in, Miss McDaniels. There's a table in the back garden if you'd like to talk there, but it's baking hot.'

'Indoors will be fine, Mrs Black,' Carrie said. 'I'd always thought I was daft buying a car with air con, until these last few days.'

'Same here. It's not Mrs Black, by the way; Mrs Morgan, Eileen. Ced's widowed and my husband's living with another man these days: his cellmate in prison. He was one that Cedric couldn't get off. I had no idea what a long firm fraud was until Skip got eight years for setting one up very badly.'

Carrie was taken aback by her openness. 'Skip?' she repeated.

'His real name is Jeffrey, but he was always known as Captain Morgan, after the rum. Inevitably, that was shortened to Skipper, then further to Skip.'

She was fascinated. 'Does he know about you and Mr Black?'

'Hell yes. He's relieved; it means he'll have some money left when he gets out. He was afraid I'd have sold our house and spent the lot.' She pointed to a door at the end of the hallway, through which Black had disappeared as they spoke. 'Go on through there; it's Ced's study. I'll bring you coffee, unless you'd prefer something cool.'

'Iced coffee would be great.'

'So shall it be.'

Like the rooms to the front, Cedric Black's study also had a bay window, overlooking a landscaped garden with a central water feature. It was more of a man cave than a work room, with a pool table and a wall-mounted TV. There was a desk, but Carrie suspected it was used rarely.

Her host had taken a chair by the window and offered her its twin. 'So,' he murmured, 'the ghost of Marcia Brown has risen.'

'Are you surprised?'

'Not in the slightest. I've been expecting it for the last nine years, truth be told.' He paused. 'Earlier you said you were on expenses. Who's paying them?'

She frowned. 'Can I tell you that?'

'I'm not asking you who your client is, although I have a shortlist of two. I'm asking who's your instructing solicitor. No confidentiality applies to that relationship.'

'That's true. It's Alexis Skinner.'

His eyebrows rose and his lips pursed. 'Indeed? The Crown Princess?'

'Eh?' Carrie exclaimed.

'That's what a couple of friends of mine at the Bar call her,' he explained, 'the Skinners being Scotland's royal family of crime-fighters, and her being the heir to the throne. She's using you to do her leg work this time, is she? I know that Sir Robert has given her some help in the past.'

'He's a busy man, and Alex's practice is growing.'

'And he doesn't want to upset his friends on the force and in the Crown Office.' Black stopped short and grinned. 'It's all right,' he said. 'I may think so; you couldn't possibly comment.'

'A shortlist of two,' Carrie ventured, moving the conversation back a notch. 'Let's assume we both know who one is. Who's the other?'

'I'm thinking of Joan Brown,' the solicitor replied. 'Marcia's sister.'

'She had a sister?' she exclaimed, unable to disguise her surprise.

He nodded, then paused as his partner nudged the door open and came into the room, carrying their refreshments on a tray. She laid it on a table by the window. 'I've given you ice in a glass,' she said, 'in case you change your mind and prefer your coffee hot.'

'Thanks, Eileen,' Black said, then added, suddenly, 'Joan Brown. You remember her, don't you? You and Skip introduced her to Catherine and me, one night we were out for dinner as a foursome. Must be what, seven years ago?'

'Yes, that's right,' she agreed. 'It was in Rogano; the night Skip's credit card bounced and I had to use mine. Her sister was a client of yours, a councillor who was caught nicking stuff from a supermarket and killed herself rather than face the music. Joan was taken aback when she realised who you were. I thought she might have made a scene; she blamed everyone involved in that incident apart from her sister. She didn't, though; she was icily polite, as I remember.'

'How did you come to know her?' McDaniels asked.

'Through Skip. He had an electrical goods business in Shettleston at that time; she was his office manager. She was a teacher really, but had had her fill of lazy, disinterested teenagers. The business went bust not long after that, he moved on to another flawed enterprise and she went back to teaching, I assume. He never mentioned her again.'

'Would he know where she is?'

'He might. At the time I suspected he was sleeping with her, although I could never catch him out. Not that I tried too hard, mind you. My daughter worshipped the ground he walked on; if I'd made a fuss, it would only have upset her.'

'Would he talk to me?'

Eileen Morgan laughed. 'You're an attractive woman; of course he would! He's in Edinburgh Prison if you want to pay him a visit. Coffee's getting cold,' she added. 'You won't need the ice in a minute; I'll leave you to it.'

'Ms Skinner didn't tell you about Joan?' Black asked as the door closed.

'No, she didn't,' McDaniels admitted, opening a notebook as she spoke. 'That can only mean that nobody told her, for Alex is very thorough. It probably means nothing, but I will need to interview her. Councillor Brown and her husband were divorced by the time of the case. It may be that her sister was closer to her than anyone, other than her son Austin, and he's dead.'

'Yes, I read about his death; the trial of his alleged killer must be due very soon. It wasn't connected to his mother's case in any way, was it?'

'No,' she replied. 'Not at all. It was linked to another miscarriage of justice, as I understand it.'

'Does that mean you're convinced that Marcia's was too?'

She smiled. 'No, it means that I'm getting ahead of myself. Alex's instructions are to approach the case with an open mind. How did you feel about it at the time?'

Cedric Black watched as she poured coffee from a cafetière over the ice. As she added milk, she was aware that he was giving himself thinking time. 'That doesn't really matter, Carrie, does it? Yes, my client protested her innocence and insisted that she was a victim of a vindictive rival. Her son was as vociferous as she was; he was almost out of control. But the only way to overcome the Crown's case against her would have been for counsel to prove either that the key witnesses were liars, or that an unknown person, who was never seen, had added the bag of stolen clothing to her trolley while she was distracted by someone who chose that precise moment to lobby her, and who was never seen either.'

'Adrian.'

'Yes, the mysterious Adrian. I tried my best to find him, believe me, and I think the police did too, but no trace of him was ever found. The Crown case would have been that she had simply made him up as part of a spurious defence. Without actually producing the wretched man in court, counsel would never have been able to overcome that.'

'Did you advise her to plead guilty?'

'Not directly. But I'm sure you know, because Austin knew – and if your client isn't Joan Brown, it can only be his father, and it's bound to be in your notes – that a couple of days before Marcia was due in court, I had a call from the procurator fiscal, Bobby Hough. It was a warning, really, not a threat. Bobby had nothing against her personally. In fact, she was his local councillor and he had voted for her. He told me that he had seen the sheriffs' rota for that day, and that the one we had drawn was a notorious hard-liner, who would have imposed a custodial sentence for sure if we had gone to jury trial with an unwinnable defence. I relayed that conversation to her, word for word, but I didn't advise her. She told me to thank Bobby for his concern but that she would take her chances. The only hope I could give her was that if the sheriff ignored sentencing guidelines, any prison sentence might possibly be overturned on appeal, but I added that it was unlikely. That was the last conversation we had. The next day I learned that she'd been found dead.'

McDaniels peered at him over her glass. 'Can you remember your instant reaction when you were told that?'

'Very clearly. I was afraid that she'd reflected on my bluntness and decided in the heat of the moment to top herself. Then I found out how she'd done it and realised that she had to have planned it in advance. Between my phone call and her death, there hadn't been time for her to go to the hospital and steal the drugs she used.'

'I see,' she murmured, making a note in her book. 'Can I ask you about the police investigation?' she continued. 'I'm told that Detective Sergeant Terry Coats responded in person to the call from LuxuMarket. Did it strike you as unusual that a ranking CID officer would be the first on the scene, rather than the nearest uniforms?'

'If that was the case, then it might have, but I wasn't aware of it. I was told that a PC Parker was the first respondent.'

'Vera Stephens, the daughter of Councillor Gloria Stephens, was engaged to a police constable. Was that him?'

'Yes, that emerged after the event, but the police attitude was "So what?" I did pursue it for a possible – but very risky – defence of impeachment. Marcia's assertion was that she was deliberately distracted by this Adrian person, allowing Vera Stephens to attach the so-called stolen goods to her trolley. It collapsed when the police were persuaded that the woman was in another part of the store when the incident happened, and we were unable to prove otherwise.'

'Was Councillor Stephens ever interviewed?' she asked.

'By the police, no,' Black told her. 'I tried. I went to her office at the council chambers. When I told her why I was there, she gave me a two-word response, the second being "off". Not the nicest woman I've ever met; she bore a grudge, too. Up until then, Black and Grey had represented the West Coast Council on a variety of matters. From that day on we never received another instruction.'

'To get to the heart of it,' McDaniels said, 'the basis of Marcia's case was that she and Stephens had a furious argument, and that Stephens used her daughter to set up the theft charge as a way of getting rid of her, or at the very least discrediting her. That's correct, yes?'

The solicitor nodded agreement.

'Did you believe that? Do you believe it now?'

He hesitated. 'Again, I have to say it doesn't matter what I believe. You're right, that was her assertion and most of it would have formed the basis of her defence in a trial. Counsel would never have attempted to impeach Vera Stephens herself, not without absolute proof. The argument would have been that the clothes were put there by an unknown person, a constituent with a grudge, perhaps.'

'What about them being the wrong size?'

'Easily countered, I'm afraid. Marcia was short-sighted and the labelling was in small print.'

'Okay, but I'm going to press you,' Carrie insisted. 'Did you believe her?'

Black sighed. 'To be honest, no. The fact was, Marcia could be just as difficult and confrontational as Gloria Stephens. I only took on her defence at the request of David Brass. He was my real client; I represented him during their divorce, sorting out the property split. She was a real bugger then, I can tell you, excuse my language.'

She smiled. 'Excused.'

'If I read this right,' Black went on, 'David is so upset by Austin's death that he's raised Marcia's case in his son's memory rather than in hers. To be frank with you, Carrie, the best thing you and Alex Skinner could do for him would be to persuade him to forget all about it, and let mother and son rest in peace.'

Nine

'Nice one, Maggie,' Skinner murmured.

'I still think it should have been you doing Jimmy's eulogy,' Chief Constable Margaret Rose Steele replied, crisp and neat, clutching her uniform cap in her hands. Without it, the grey strands in her red hair were more noticeable, he observed. Her job came at a personal price, as he knew well.

He shook his head. 'No, it's not my place any longer. Besides, I hate bloody theatre, and that's what this is.' He glanced around St Giles' Cathedral as the congregation filed out, loose chairs scraping on the ancient stone floor. 'There'll be nothing like this for me when I peg it. Sarah knows and Alex knows what I want, and nobody will persuade either of them to do otherwise.'

She winked at him. 'Not even your ex, the prime minister in waiting?'

'Aileen?' he grunted. 'For all her Italian Catholic heritage, she's a bloody atheist. It won't even occur to her to have a wingding like this, for me or anyone else. Nobody asked Jimmy, you know, nor Chrissie either, not that she'd have understood the question, poor old lady. The justice minister decreed it should happen and wouldn't listen to anyone who suggested it might be over the top.'

'You being one of them?'

'I sent a message,' he admitted, 'through my friend the Lord Advocate, but it was ignored. Bugger him.'

'Seconded,' Steele whispered, 'but I never said that. Sarah's looking well,' she observed briskly. 'Alex too.'

'Thank you, Mags. You'll note they raced each other to the exit. Sarah has someone on the table, and Alex has a meeting with a client, one of your customers, an alleged embezzler.'

'Have we got a solid case?'

'She doesn't think so. It came from the financial crimes unit in Gartcosh. I'm wary of these people; they can do the numbers, but they're not so good when it comes to mundane stuff like intent. If I was still involved, I'd recruit a few football referees and promote them up the ladder. They're always fucking right.'

'Hey, you are still involved,' she reminded him. 'You promised Mario and me that you'd act as a mentor for rising stars, like you did with Sauce Haddock not so long ago. As a matter of fact, I have someone in mind.'

'Oh yes? Who would that be?'

'Someone you know. Lottie Mann.'

'Are you serious?' Skinner exclaimed. 'Lottie would eat me if she thought I was trying to mentor her.'

'Mario doesn't think so. In fact he put it to her and she was all for it. She's just been promoted to DCI, Serious Crimes West, in place of Sandra Bulloch. For all her success, she's young in the rank, and she doesn't have Dan Provan to guide her any longer.'

'I heard that she does, even though he's retired.'

The chief constable laughed. 'Domestically she does, but Dan was seriously old school as a cop.'

'And I'm not?'

'Of course you're bloody not! You modernised the service, more than anyone I ever served with. Lottie has a new DS, Dan's replacement; his name is John Cotter, and he's newly promoted as well, transferred down from Aberdeen. He has great promise; he's the sort who would benefit from your oversight and wisdom.'

'Bullshit. He's a kid who's been fast-tracked; you're worried that it's maybe a bit too fast and that he's going to take Lottie's eye off the ball. You want me to introduce him to the real world.'

'More or less,' Steele admitted.

'Okay, but not to the detriment of my other work. When?'

'When something appropriate comes up. Don't worry. I won't involve you in anything that looks like it's going to be twenty-four seven, long-running. We'll need to work out a remuneration package, of course. As we agreed, the theory is that you're a special constable, to put a warrant card in your hand, but we don't expect you to do it at a PC's pay grade.'

'I won't be doing it at any pay grade, Mags. I'm drawing a police pension; if I took on any sort of paid work for you lot and it came to light, some tosser would be bound to make an enormous issue of it. Worse still, another tosser might post it on social media and that would compromise me with the *Saltire*. We'll call it *pro bono* – not that there's too many bastards in your outfit that speak Latin.' He looked around the great cathedral, feeling its history overwhelm his cynicism and seep into his bones, thinking of John Knox and Jenny Geddes, and all the others from his nation's past who had created their legends under its arched roof.

He shook himself. 'Time we were both off. You've got a country to protect, and me, although I wouldn't speak at Jimmy's memorial, I still have to walk his bloody dog!'

Ten

Carrie McDaniels was no stranger to prison security procedures. In a former life, as a member of the Territorial Army military police, she had been ordered to collect serving soldiers from civilian jails and deliver them to their barracks. She had always had a male companion, but the missions had all been uneventful, their charges being sober and contrite by the time they arrived. Most had been in their first year of service, young men – and on one occasion a young woman – who had believed, wrongly, that they had an image to project, then protect. The fact that they had been remanded to prison rather than being stuck anonymously in a police custody cell for the night was likely to lead to their discharge from the service, but she had never allowed herself to feel sympathy for them. She had seen enough on foreign postings to know that a reckless soldier was far more dangerous to those around him than to any enemy.

Her Majesty's Prison Saughton was as impressive as any she had visited. Its secure public entrance was of fairly recent construction; visitors were tightly marshalled and efficiently searched for contraband. She was no exception, even though her visit was for a specific purpose and had been arranged at short notice. Experience told her to leave most of her possessions locked in her car – her phone, her wallet, her make-up, even the prized Rolex watch that had been a gift from a departed boyfriend – taking with her only her identification and her notebook. She placed them in a tray for X-ray, then walked through the scanner gate before being patted down by a female prison officer.

As soon as she was cleared, another woman in uniform, at least ten years older than the first, came towards her. 'Ms Daniels? I'm Roberta Forrest, assistant governor; Bobbie. Come with me and I'll take you to see Morgan.'

'Thanks. This is all very official,' Carrie remarked, ignoring the slip-up over her surname. 'I was expecting just to go into an open visiting area.'

'This is official. Your request for a visit to Prisoner Morgan was made through Alexis Skinner's office, so you will be treated as if you were the lady herself . . . or her father, for that matter. He was a regular visitor, over quite a few years. I imagine he's sunning himself somewhere exotic these days.'

'In sunny Gullane, normally, from what Alex has told me. I've met Mr Skinner professionally too; he'll never be one for the quiet life.'

'Sir Robert now, I believe.'

'Yes, but he's almost shy about it, so Alex said. He discourages people from using the title.'

As they spoke, Bobbie Forrest led the visitor along a series of narrow corridors, connected by solid metal doors, each of which she unlocked then secured behind them. Carrie found herself hoping that in a fire emergency there would be an automatic override. Eventually they arrived at a small room with a window on to a courtyard; it was the first sight of daylight since they had left the prison entrance. Inside, two men waited, one light-skinned, the other dark, larger and younger, in prison officer uniform. Jeffrey 'Skip' Morgan looked to be in his late fifties; he was clad in russet trousers and a green sweatshirt, the mark, Carrie recalled from an earlier visit, of a long-term prisoner.

'Prisoner Morgan,' the assistant governor announced. 'You still consent to this meeting, Skip?' she asked.

'Absolutely, ma'am,' he replied, in a smooth accent that hinted of a privileged education. 'It's my pleasure.'

'In that case, I'll leave you to it. Skip, Ms Daniels is an investigator, but we'll afford you privacy, as we would if Ms Skinner was here herself. Officer Brathwaite will wait outside; when you're finished, he'll call me. Ms Daniels, are you happy with that, or would you prefer Officer Brathwaite to be in the room?'

Carrie smiled. In addition to being the best part of thirty years older than her, Morgan was no taller, and his flabby jowls suggested no physical threat. 'I'll be fine,' she said.

As the door closed behind the assistant governor and the guard, Morgan appraised his visitor. 'Nice to see you,' he began, breaking the short silence. 'I confess that I've never heard of Alexis Skinner, and I don't have the faintest idea what either of you want with me.'

'That being so, why did you agree to this visit at a moment's notice?'

He smiled. 'That's very simple. I've got a parole hearing in three weeks. It's in my interest to be the most co-operative man in this prison. How can I help you?'

'I'm hoping that you can put me in touch with someone who used to work for you, a woman called Joan Brown.'

For the first time, his expression changed, the mix of curiosity and self-confidence giving way to sudden concern. 'Joanie? Why? Is she in trouble? Is her nephew after her? You're not representing Austin Brass, are you?'

'You know about him?'

'I know he's a boy on a mission who won't stop until he finds someone to blame for his mother topping herself. It took Joanie long enough to get over that, if she ever did. I wouldn't want him stirring things up and putting her back to square one.'

'You don't have to worry about Austin, Mr Morgan. You're behind the times; he's dead. He was murdered a few weeks ago. The man accused of killing him is in this very jail, but he's in the remand section, so your paths won't have crossed.'

Morgan gave a soft whistle. 'Are you serious? I haven't heard a whisper and the grapevine in this place is usually pretty good. The man on remand wouldn't be a police officer, would he? Austin Brass was obsessive about police misconduct after Joanie's sister died. There are a couple of people in here that he brought down and who were jailed as a result. They're pretty much in solitary. Even if they made them part of the protected population, there could be guys in there who would have a go at them. It wouldn't surprise me at all if one of his targets turned on him.'

'No,' Carrie said. 'The man in the remand wing isn't a cop. If he was, I'm sure you'd have heard about that on your grapevine. We would like to talk to Ms Brown, though, if you can help us. It's about her sister's case; my boss, Ms Skinner, has been asked to take a look at the evidence against her.'

78

'Why come to me?' Morgan's eyes narrowed very slightly. 'I had nothing to do with it. Neither did Joanie for that matter, not directly.'

'Possibly,' she admitted. 'But I didn't know of her existence until yesterday. I need to talk to her, just in case she has insight that nobody else has.'

He nodded. 'I get it. You've been talking to Ced Black. He sent you to me.'

'Not quite. It was your wife who suggested I talk to you. She seems to think that your relationship with Ms Brown might have been more than professional.'

'Delicately put,' he chuckled. 'I suspect she was a little more specific than that. How is she, by the way? Are she and Ced getting along?'

'They seemed very happy,' Carrie replied blandly. 'Was Eileen right? Can you put me in touch with Joan Brown?'

'Not directly,' he replied. 'I have a number. I can call it and give her yours; if she wants to talk to you, she will.'

'How much does she know about her sister's death?' Carrie asked.

'Good question. More than she ever told me, I think. She was well on board with Marcia's conspiracy theory, that's for sure. She thought there had been stuff going on that had made her an embarrassment who had to be removed. Ced Black thought it was all bluster, but Joanie bought into it, one hundred per cent.'

'Was she implying that her sister's suicide was faked, as well as the theft?'

Morgan snorted. 'Implying? She flat-out believed it. She even thought that Ced Black was involved.'

'You don't believe that, do you?' Carrie exclaimed.

'Put it this way. There is nothing about that whole business that I would rule out one hundred per cent.'

Eleven

'Morning, Roy.' Skinner greeted the newcomer as he stepped into the coffee shop, beckoning him towards the corner table that he had commandeered. 'I'm pleased you could join me. In fact, I'm pleased you're still here. You must be due for retirement pretty soon.'

'That's being negotiated.' The Crown Agent scowled. 'I was due to go last year, until we had a new Solicitor General, a political appointee who didn't know her bottom from her elbow, and the Lord Advocate asked me to stay on for a while to keep the train on the tracks. The word is she's giving up. If the rumours about her successor are true, I can see the same thing happening again. I feel like a hamster on a treadmill, Bob.' As he took his seat, he called out his order to the barista: a latte and a Danish. The venue, on King George IV Bridge and close to his office, had been Roy Pettigrew's choice. 'You're a fine one to talk about retirement, though. I've just reviewed the file on that murder out in Haddington. Your fucking spoor was all over it. You and big Mario McGuire: which of you can't live without the other?'

'I get along without him very well,' Skinner sang softly in

reply. 'I may take an interest on occasion,' he continued, 'but only when I'm asked.'

'I've heard you also take an occasional interest in the security service.'

Skinner glanced across at the counter, where Pettigrew's latte was being prepared. 'Amanda Dennis has consulted me on occasion,' he admitted, 'and I do have an informal connection. I haven't heard from her in a while, though.'

'Probably because you're too busy being a media typhoon.'

'That would be tycoon, would it not?'

Pettigrew looked at him over the rim of his spectacles. 'I choose my words carefully, Big Bob. You and the *Saltire* are a big wind blowing through the Scottish media, they're saying.'

'Perhaps,' Skinner conceded, 'but not always kindly. The *Saltire* was the best newspaper in Scotland long before I got involved with its owners.'

'Maybe, but now it's the most influential. Which makes me ask: this unexpected invitation to morning coffee, is it off the record?'

'Strictly off. It has nothing to do with the newspaper. I'm not editorial.'

The Crown Agent peered at him anew. 'I never thought, my friend, that I'd accuse you of being naïve, but that day has come. You might not be a member of the reporting staff, but you're a main board director of the owners, and your office, I'm told, is next door to the managing editor, who reports to you. Anyone who sits down with you informally has to ask how confidential the chat might be. I know cops are more secretive than most, but even they talk to other cops.'

Skinner nodded. 'I hear that, and I repeat. This is strictly off the record. It's not a hot topic, not at all; it flows from the

Austin Brass murder that you mentioned a minute ago, but it's nothing to do with it. Austin's father, David, has asked me if I'll take a look at a shoplifting case involving his former wife. It happened in Kilmarnock, nine years ago, but it never got to court—'

'Because she killed herself. Yes, it crossed my desk briefly, because the woman was a local councillor and when she died the fiscal shat himself. I told him to man up, view the death as the post-mortem report said it was, a straightforward suicide with no added extras, and decide whether to have a formal inquiry, or classify it and close the file; that's the norm in such cases, as you're aware.'

'I know that,' Skinner agreed. 'But in this case, the local newspaper ignored sub judice rules and really went to town on her, blackened her name to the extent that it might have been a factor in her death. The Brasses, son and father, never forgot it, and never gave up on uncovering what they saw as the truth. With Austin's death, the dad's picked it up again.'

'How deep are you digging?' Pettigrew asked, after a pause as his coffee and pastry were delivered.

'I'm not . . . well, not really. I've referred him to my daughter, and she's looking into it. She's looking at David Brass's conspiracy obsession, but there's another side of it that I thought I'd cast an eye over. Given that it happened a decade ago, where would the fiscal's report on the suicide lie right now?'

'Almost certainly it'd be in an archive . . . such as it was.'

'What about the witness statements?'

'Same place, not that there would be likely to be many with a suicide. The person who found the body, and the attending police officer.'

'And the post-mortem report?'

'The paper report might not exist any more; it won't be in the Crown Office files, of that I'm sure.'

'Where else could it be?' Skinner asked.

'I suppose it's possible that the pathologist kept a copy, although unless the circumstances were exceptional, I'd say it's unlikely.'

'If they did, who would have it?'

The Crown Agent sipped his latte and nodded satisfaction. 'Let's see . . . The death was in Ayrshire, so I'd be looking at Glasgow. You might have a word with Professor Scott, in the new super hospital through there. Mind you,' he added, 'it'll cost you more than a coffee and a bun with him.'

Twelve

McDaniels had expected that Zaqib Butt would be a hard man to find. His employer of the time, LuxuMarket, no longer existed as a trading entity, and according to the Crown Office file he had been a short-term employee, hired on an initial six-month contract to cover the maternity leave of another staff member. She had entered the name into the Facebook search bar with no expectation of success, but to her surprise, one name had popped up. His location was Motherwell, and his page carried a full CV which listed all his employers, including 'LuxuMarket, Kilmarnock'. She had contacted him through Messenger asking for a meeting on a confidential matter, and he had agreed without question.

Mr Butt had come up in the world in the nine years since his brief foray into on-site security. He was now the managing director of a steel stockholding company on the outskirts of what had been one of the largest burghs in Scotland. The ever-reliable Apple Maps plotted her course, but it could do nothing about the traffic. Glasgow and Edinburgh were linked by a motorway, but it was at least a lane too narrow for the throng of Friday-afternoon commuters. There was nothing for it but to crawl patiently with the rest, grateful yet again for her air con, listening to the melodious Mark Knopfler and contemplating what she had learned in her brief investigation into the sad and lonely death of Marcia Brown.

Her lawyer thought she had been guilty, it was clear, but her elusive sister was, it seemed, convinced of a conspiracy, up to and including murder. Carrie had no expectation that Butt would add much clarity to the picture, but he was another box that had to be ticked, and she was pleased that she would be able to do it so quickly. Butt was in the diary, then Terry Coats. She disliked working weekends; they were for her father and for quality time spent with one of a small list of men. She was not a woman for commitment, not for a while at any rate, a trait she had sensed that she shared with Alex Skinner. Coats, however, had insisted on a Saturday-morning meeting, in his office at the airport.

Following Coats on her list was Hazel Delaney, the former LuxuMarket boss, scheduled for the following Monday morning. Social media had become a great boon to the detecting business, she acknowledged. LinkedIn had led her straight to the woman, who had crossed the country after the sale of the business to become general manager of a radio station in Dundee. She was looking forward to that visit, after a quick look at its website; its star presenter was Mia Sparkles, a name she recognised from her primary school days when she had been the top disc jockey in Edinburgh until her sudden disappearance from the airwaves, leaving thousands of disappointed kids behind her. Carrie liked to believe that her feet were squarely on the ground, but even she could be star-struck on occasion.

Mark Knopfler had given way to Corinne Bailey Rae when Apple Maps, to her relief, instructed her to leave the motorway. She followed its guidance through a place called Holytown, which looked to be anything but, past a sign for a crematorium – for some reason those always gave her the creeps – then on for a mile or so until she turned into an industrial estate. A signboard stood at the entrance, listing half a dozen companies. WZB Stockholders was third on the list.

The unit that the business occupied was much larger than she had expected; steel stockholding was a business of which she had heard and about which she knew nothing, but it had no bearing on the purpose of her visit. A single-storey black-walled office building sat in front of the massive shed, with a parking area alongside in which one car stood out from half a dozen others: a silver Mercedes S Class with a personalised number plate that bore the company's three initials. *Advertising on wheels*, she thought.

She checked her Rolex as she walked towards the office. Four forty-seven, and Butt had made it clear he would be leaving at five on the dot. 'Sorry,' she exclaimed to the young clean-shaven Asian man who greeted her. 'Can you explain to Mr Butt that the motorway was a real nightmare? I left in plenty of time, but it was like there was a pilgrimage of sorts out there.'

'No need to explain to him,' he replied. 'I know the M8. I'm Zaqib. A pilgrimage of sorts,' he repeated. 'That would be a good title for a book. Come on through.'

He led her into a spacious, well-furnished office, dominated by a glass wall that looked out on to the shed, which was piled high with slabs of steel and girders, beneath overhead cranes. She counted five men and three women on the stock floor, each wearing overalls and a yellow hard hat, as they operated cutting machines. In each of the four corners of the roof, fans were located; even through the thick glass wall she could hear that they were going full blast, against the heat, she assumed.

'Is this all yours?' she asked. 'You're very young, if you don't mind me saying.'

'I don't mind a bit,' Butt replied. 'I'm twenty-nine years old and it bigs me up. But it's one reason why you didn't see any personal photos on Facebook. This is a very competitive business, and if my rivals could use my age against me, they would.'

'Still, you've come a long way in a relatively short time. Nine years ago you had a short-term contract at LuxuMarket.'

Zaqib Butt smiled. Involuntarily she checked his left hand for a wedding ring and saw none. 'That wasn't what it seemed,' he said. 'It was a vacation job. My dad was a minority shareholder in the holding company. He fixed it up. When the business was sold a few years later, he set me up here.'

'Is he involved in running this business?'

'Only if I ask him for advice, but I don't do that very often. He knows nothing about the steel industry; always was a retailer. Mind you, he offers me advice whether I ask him or not. He's back in Pakistan just now, for good, I like to hope, but no such luck.' He glanced at a wall clock; it showed six minutes to five. 'I'm sorry to rush you, but I really do have to be out of here sharpish. I have a golf tie at Lanark at six. What is it that you want to ask me?'

'It's about your time in Kilmarnock, and a shoplifting case in which you were cited as a police witness. I'm looking into the incident on behalf of a client.'

Butt frowned; the openness in his expression was replaced by concern. 'I remember it,' he admitted, 'but only because the lady who was accused took her own life rather than face the court. That was a great pity, I thought. If she stole something, it was hardly worth dying for. The goods in her basket that she had bought and paid for already were worth almost a hundred pounds – groceries, drink, household goods. The clothing in her bag, it was shit, a suit off the sale rail that had been discounted down to twenty-five quid or something around that.'

'Are you sure about that?' McDaniels asked. 'The charge against her said it was worth over a hundred and fifty.'

'That was the regular price. I saw the red discount tag sticking out of the bag when I stopped her. Now that you force me to think about it, I remember wondering why the police were involved. I had only been there for a couple of weeks, but I had caught a couple of thieves already. All that happened to them was that they were photographed and barred from the store, because the stuff they had nicked was worth less than thirty pounds. That was store policy; they threatened to prosecute everyone caught stealing, but they only did it if it was more than that.'

'Did you query it with anyone?'

'I told my father after she had died. He said he asked the store manager, Mrs Delaney, if there was really a need to prosecute, but she said that her hands were tied by established policy, and that was that decisions were based on the price of the stolen goods. She didn't think they had been discounted.'

Carrie felt her excitement rise. 'Did you tell any of this to Ms Brown's solicitor?'

'I was never asked,' Butt replied, 'by him or anyone else other than the cop who interviewed me. I was told I might be a witness if it went to trial, but it never did, did it?' He checked the wall clock again.

'Sorry,' she promised, 'I'll be quick.'

'It's okay,' he insisted. 'Let's deal with this. You've got me worried now.'

'Thanks. Part of Ms Brown's defence would have been that she was distracted on her way out of the store by a man called Adrian, who claimed to be a constituent of hers. Can you confirm that?'

'No, not as such, but she mentioned it as Geoff, the other security guard, and I were taking her back to the office. I did remember seeing her trolley near the exit, though, before it all happened.'

'Did you tell the police?'

'I can't remember. It was a while ago; I can't remember much of the detail.'

'The other security guard: I've never heard of him. There's no mention of him in the file.'

'There wouldn't have been. He saw nothing. I called for backup after I'd stopped her.'

'So you were the only person who was there when the security alarm was triggered?'

'Yes.' Butt paused for a moment. 'The alarm was never triggered, though. It was broken.'

'Eh?' McDaniels exclaimed. 'Then how did you know to stop her?'

'I was told to, by another staff member.'

'Ah, I'd forgotten that. The corroborating witness's statement was on file: Alicia Malcolm.'

Butt looked at her. 'I really can't remember who called out to me. Alicia was a checkout girl, that I do recall. It could have been her, I suppose, who told me to stop Ms Brown . . . Whoever it was, I remember clearly that she called out to me, "Boy, stop that one, she's nicked a suit."'

'Do you remember a woman called Stephens on the staff?'

He grinned. 'Her, yes. Geoff called her Zeppy because she had ti—' He stopped himself, but Carrie had heard the one about racing airships half a dozen times in her part-time army career. 'Not much older than me, but full of herself and a nasty little racist as well. Vera, she was called, Vera Stephens.'

'Could it have been her, not Alicia?'

'Nine years ago? I can't say. For all I know, it could have been you.' He looked at the clock for a third time. 'Is that us?' he asked, 'Because really . . .'

'Yes, that's great, thanks,' McDaniels said. 'Mr Butt, Zaqib, would you be prepared to speak to the police about this again?'

'Absolutely!' he declared. 'That woman died because I stopped her. I don't want that on my conscience.'

Thirteen

Skinner became aware mid afternoon, from a news flash on the *Saltire*'s in-house information system, that there had been a multiple fatality on the westbound M8 motorway just before its link with the M73. His regret over the four reported deaths was accompanied by pity for any commuting motorists heading for Glasgow, and by the realisation that Professor Graham Scott would have his hands full and was unlikely to be responding to his voicemail any time soon.

In fact he was just leaving Aberlady, with Gullane Hill in sight, when his ringtone sang out over his car's Bluetooth system, and the information screen showed a Glasgow number. He pushed the receive button. 'Graham,' he said, 'I didn't expect to be hearing from you today.'

'Oh, I'm not finished, Bob,' the pathologist replied. 'It's taken longer than anyone anticipated to cut the last two bodies out of their vehicle. They're on their way here now; that'll be me and the team tied up until midnight. I've just taken a break from the second one: a girl in her early twenties. I'm told the boyfriend was driving, clocked at a hundred and twenty-eight by the police. Fucking thing went airborne and took out a couple of innocent Belgian tourists in a car in front. The police

92

haven't released any names yet, but the boyfriend was an English Premier League footballer. Your news desk and all the others will go crazy when they find out. My God, the whole world's gone crazy; the boy was driving a Lamborghini, and it was less than a week's wages to him. What are they going to do about it?'

'Not a fucking thing, chum,' Skinner assured him as he pulled into the nature reserve car park to continue the call. The road was busy and he had no wish to wind up on his wife's mortuary table. 'Supply and demand; you've got agents falling over themselves to supply players to the top clubs, and able to demand ridiculous money because the global television market is apparently insatiable.'

'But that's not why you called me earlier,' Professor Scott said wearily.

'No, it's not. It's a fit of curiosity on my part, actually.'

'It was ever thus,' Scott chuckled.

'Maybe,' Skinner admitted. 'My daughter's been asked to look into a nine-year-old shoplifting involving a local councillor from Ayrshire. The accusation led to the woman's suicide.' He paused. 'That's what the fiscal decided it was, at any rate.'

'You have doubts, I take it.'

'I wouldn't go that far. It was an unexplained sudden death, maybe not suspicious at first sight, but if I'd been investigating it there would have been certain questions I'd have wanted answered, the main one being was there any likelihood, possibility even, that the drugs that killed her might not have been self-administered. Is that routine for your guys?'

'It bloody should be.'

'Who would keep the records of that autopsy? The Crown

Office doesn't have that much detail, only a summary of the fiscal's findings, and they're archived.'

'We'd have them if they still exist; my department, that is. Ayrshire, you said?'

'Kilmarnock,' Skinner volunteered.

'In which case, the post-mortem would almost certainly have been done there, by two pathologists since it was for the fiscal and corroboration would have been required. Going back nine years, I'd have no idea who'd have done it, but I can find out. What was the subject's name?'

'Marcia Brown. She was divorced and went back to her maiden name. It's possible, I suppose, that she was listed as Marcia Brass.'

'Brass?' Scott exclaimed. 'Any relation to the dead blogger, Austin Brass, the guy who made life hell for quite a few police officers?'

'She was his mother.'

'Then I know of the case. The guy approached me, what, must be eight years ago. I'd just been appointed to Glasgow, and he wanted me to get him a copy of his mother's autopsy report. When I found out that it was a suicide, I told him he'd have to go to the fiscal. He said he'd done that but all he was given was a single-sheet summary; he wanted the whole thing, photos, the lot. I told him he'd need a court order for that, and even then he would still have to get it from the fiscal, because it had fuck all to do with me. That was true then, but data storage has got a lot more rigorous since then, and I do have oversight of everything in the west of Scotland, just as your Sarah has in the east.'

'If I said I wanted to see the full report,' Skinner ventured, 'would you still tell me to get a court order?'

'Too fucking right,' the professor replied. 'I'd be in breach if I didn't. Talk to your daughter, but I doubt that you'd get such an order, not without very serious grounds.'

'I was afraid of that.'

'How severe is this itch that you're trying to scratch, Bob?'

'It might keep me awake tonight.'

'Then maybe, since I'm the custodian of the data, I can review it myself and give you a hypothetical overview together with my observations. By that I mean if it wasn't kosher I'll tell you, and you can take it from there.'

'If you can do that, Graham, it would be great. No rush; she's been dead for nine years.'

'Nah, my curiosity's pricked now. As soon as I've finished with the poor girl on my table, I'll get on to it.'

'What about your Belgians?' Skinner asked.

'They're in no hurry either. I can keep them overnight, to give the police time to complete identification and inform their consulate. I'll get back to you soonest. Give Lady Skinner my regards.'

Fourteen

'Lady Skinner indeed!' Sarah Grace snorted.

'Don't turn your nose up so high,' her husband laughed. 'Your American blood might set you against honours, but it doesn't stop you wearing that very nice gold brooch that goes with the title.'

'I only wear it because you bought it for me,' she protested.

'Pull the other one. You never wear anything you don't like. For example, you never wear the green earrings I bought you for your last birthday. What have you got against them anyway?'

She looked at him in his garden chair, a dark shadow against the glare of the sinking sun. 'You'll think I'm crazy if I tell you.'

'You spend your working life up to your elbows in dead people's organs, intestines and waste products. I think you're crazy anyway. Go on, prove it.'

'Booker T,' she said, unable to see his confusion because of the sunshine but knowing it was there.

'Uh? You've made your case, now try to show me the thought process behind it.'

'Booker T,' she repeated, 'and the MGs, a great American band famous for one tune and one tune only; it was called "Green Onions". Every time I look at those dangly emeralds, that's what they remind me of, and when I do wear them, I have this mental picture of green onions hanging from my earlobes.'

'Fuck me!' he gasped.

'Later,' she murmured, 'but let's enjoy this wonderful evening for a little longer. This weather cannot last. It mustn't last. Did you see the colour of the golf course when we took Bowser for his walk earlier? Even with the sprinkler system and all the hand watering the greenkeeping staff are doing, it's turning brown. Our garden, the bents over the wall, so are they. I know the council has banned barbecues, but people are just going where they can't be seen and ignoring that. There will be a fire, for sure.'

Bob laughed. 'And if there is, it'll be a bad one.'

'Yes, it will. What's the joke about that?'

'Nothing really. I was thinking about my great-granny and about a discussion I was part of the other day.'

'Your scary great-granny?' Sarah asked. 'The one you get it from.'

'My great-granny was much scarier than me, trust me on that.'

'I wish I'd met her.'

'You don't; you're not that crazy. What are you going to do with the earrings?'

'Alex likes them. We've talked about how to break it to you, since you gave them to me.'

He shrugged. 'As long as they don't wind up stuck in a box in a drawer, I don't mind whose earlobes they hang from.' He broke into a tuneless whistle with a faint resemblance to the 'Green Onions' tune. It was overridden by music from his wife's phone as her news alert tone sounded.

She looked at the screen. 'Wow!' she whistled. 'One of the fatalities in that accident through in Glasgow this afternoon: it's—'

'Yeah, I know,' he said, silencing her as his own phone sounded, glancing at it and taking the call. 'Graham, hi. I didn't expect to hear from you tonight.'

'I said "soonest", and I meant it, even more now. Bob, I don't want to talk about this over the phone. Can we meet? Ten thirty tomorrow, my office in Glasgow?'

'Sure,' Skinner said, 'but why the secrecy? I'm sure your phone's not being monitored, Prof; I'd probably know if it was.'

'It's something I need to show you rather than tell you. I think you have a murder case on your hands.'

Fifteen

'You want to talk to me about a nine-year-old shoplifting case?' Terry Coats laughed. 'That's what all the mystery was about? We could have done that over the phone rather than waste your time hacking out to the airport on a Saturday morning, not to mention the cost of the car park. Pause for a fart on your way back, and it costs you an extra couple of quid.'

'I took the tram,' Carrie McDaniels replied dryly. 'I also took a commission from a solicitor client, and that's why I'm here. I'd rather be sunbathing in Holyrood Park like the rest of the city.'

'You might as well; I barely remember the case. Are you sure it was me? I was a DS then, and usually that sort of complaint was handled by uniform.'

'You know what, Mr Coats? I think you're bullshitting me. I think you're hoping that I'm a silly woman who'll take confusion for an answer and go away. You barely remember it? How would you know that when you haven't even asked me what the name of the accused was?'

The man looked out of his office window, sighed and then turned back to his visitor. 'Okay, have your moment. Tell me who it was.'

'I think you know already, because you're right, there can't have been too many shoplifters in Kilmarnock who had the personal attention of a high-flying detective sergeant. We're talking about Councillor Marcia Brown; the late Councillor Marcia Brown, because she committed suicide shortly before she was due in court. You remember her, Mr Coats, you remember her only too well, because ever since she died, her son and her ex-husband have been trying to find out the truth about the business. You remember the son, too, Austin Brass, because when he started to investigate you personally, beyond his mother's case, his persistence got you kicked out of the police force.'

Coats reddened. 'I wasn't kicked out!' he snapped. 'I resigned because I'd had enough of the jealousy and back-stabbing.'

'You resigned rather than accept a posting to the wilds of Argyllshire. That's the version I heard; also that you were so upset by Brass's interest in you that you were briefly a suspect in his murder.'

'You never told me who your client is,' he growled, 'but I think I can guess. It's Alex Skinner, and you've been talking to her old man.'

'Not about this I haven't. Sir Robert has nothing to do with it.' She stopped and took a mouthful of the coffee that she had bought in an airside outlet before heading for Coats' office in the security section of the airport. 'Look, Terry,' she continued, 'I'm ex-police, of sorts; nothing as exalted as you were, but I understand the job. When I took this commission on, I didn't really have an open mind. I expected to find a thorough police investigation, a case that was rock solid, and a classic tale of self-inflicted death by guilt. But I haven't. I've interviewed two people, and I've found that a half-decent lawyer who'd done a proper job for his client instead of assuming her guilt would have torn the prosecution apart.'

'Wait a minute,' Coats shouted, rising to his feet. 'You can get the fuck out of here right now!'

McDaniels raised a hand. 'No, you wait a minute. I am not saying that you did a shoddy job, or were part of anything, but I'm beginning to suspect that woman was set up. I'm only at the beginning here, and I've no idea where it'll take me, but I need you to help me by telling me everything you can remember about the case.'

The ex-cop still bristled with anger, but he resumed his seat. 'I remember next to fuck all about the case,' he said, more calmly. 'Her death, though, that's all too clear in my memory. If you really have police experience, you'll know that you never forget a body.'

'That isn't part of my remit,' she replied. 'I've been asked to determine if the police case was flawed. It'll be up to Alex's client to give her further instructions after that. Can I begin by going back to the first question? How did you get involved?'

'Through the station commander,' Coats told her, 'a uniform chief inspector called Mason, Shereen Mason. She rang me and said she'd had a shout from the manager of LuxuMarket about a thief they'd caught. There was a plod on the scene, but he was nervous about it because she was a local councillor and making a big fuss about being stitched up.'

'It's a long shot, but can you remember the name of the plod, the PC?'

'Funnily enough,' he retorted, 'now that you ask me, I can.

It was Spidey; Police Constable Peter Parker. Everyone in the station called him Spidey, for obvious reasons.'

'Not obvious to me,' Carrie admitted.

'In that case, you've got no kids and don't go to the movies much. Spider-Man, aka Spidey, is a comic book character, a superhero, and his real name is Peter Parker. Things like that, you can never escape. There was a legend about a traffic cop down in the old Dumfries and Galloway force whose name was Clark Kent, gospel truth. The local wide boys found out and he kept getting bogus calls to phone boxes; they'd to take him off the cars eventually and put him in Special Branch. Anyway, Spidey, he told the store manager to call CI Mason. Why her directly, and not just his sergeant, I don't know, but he did. Mason asked me if I would do her a favour, get down there and write it up, so that if there was any political heat, she could say it had been dealt with at a high level. I agreed, as long as she signed off the report to the fiscal.'

'She didn't. I've seen the Crown Office file. Her name isn't on it, just yours.'

'What a bitch!' he exclaimed, shaking his head. 'Fucking typical of the woman. You're telling me that she hung me out to dry, just in case something like this ever came up?'

'That's a reasonable conclusion. Whatever, Chief Inspector Mason called you after the store manager called her, on Spidey's advice, and you went to the scene. Alone?'

He frowned. 'I guess, because I'd have assumed Spidey was there.'

'Was he?'

'Now you mention it, no, he wasn't.'

'What did you do?'

Coats paused, gazing at the wall behind McDaniels as he

searched his memory. 'I took statements from the two security guys – don't ask me what they were called, but one of them was an Asian kid – from the store manager, from the checkout girl, to confirm that the stolen items weren't with the stuff she'd paid for, and obviously from the woman Brown herself. She said it was a stitch-up. She was effing and blinding about another councillor called Gloria Stephens having set it all up. I put that to the store manager, who said it was all nonsense, as you'd expect.'

'When you arrived, did you see the stolen clothing?' McDaniels asked.

'Obviously.'

'Where?'

'In the room where I interviewed Brown.'

'Did you check the size against her own?'

'No, but I didn't see the need. She could have been stealing the stuff for her sister. Size wasn't relevant.'

'How did you know she had a sister?'

Coats' face darkened. 'She identified the body, after the suicide. They were twins, identical.'

'They were?'

'Yes. Spooky.'

'I can imagine. Did you interview the security guys in any depth?' she continued.

'I took statements to confirm they were witnesses to the theft; that was enough.'

'From both? But only one of them was there at the time, Zaqib Butt, the Asian kid. The other was called from another part of the store after Ms Brown had been apprehended.'

He frowned. 'Are you sure?'

'Zaqib Butt is. He's also sure that when he stopped

103

Councillor Brown, there was a discount sticker on the clothing, pricing it below the level at which the shop would have prosecuted. Your statement makes no mention of that; it quotes the item at full price.'

'Then there couldn't have been a discount sticker.'

'Not when you saw the clothing, no. But between her detention and your arrival, anyone could have removed it.'

Coats eyed her with undisguised cynicism. 'Do you have anyone in mind?'

'Vera Stephens, for one.'

'Who the hell is Vera Stephens?'

'Councillor Gloria Stephens' daughter. She was an employee at LuxuMarket at the time. Then there was the checkout girl. If you'd pressed him, Zaqib Butt would have told you that it was her who told him to stop Marcia Brown. You assumed that the security alarm went off, but it didn't. It was broken.'

'I assumed no such thing. I was told that it had been activated.'

'Told by whom?'

'By Spidey, when I found him, eventually. Yes, he was there right enough.'

'Good, that's established, but when did he arrive? Before or after you? Can you say with any degree of certainty?'

Coats frowned and shook his head. 'No, but the store manager made the call to Mason on his advice, remember.'

'Can it be proved that Parker was actually there when the theft took place?'

'Not fucking now it can't! But why would he be involved with something like I think you're suggesting? A false accusation?'

'Because he was engaged to Vera Stephens, Councillor

Gloria's daughter, the LuxuMarket employee nobody told you about.'

He stared at her, sinking into his chair. 'Sum it up for me,' he murmured. 'I get what you're saying, but put it into words for me.'

'My pleasure,' Carrie said. 'I'm suggesting that Marcia Brown could have been falsely accused of shoplifting as a result of a plot executed by Vera Stephens, the daughter of a bitter council rival, with the active co-operation of her fiancé, Constable Peter Parker, and possibly a third party . . .' She paused. 'Try to recall this. When you and Spidey finally met up, was he in police uniform?'

'Now you mention it,' Coats said, 'he wasn't. He was in plain clothes.'

'In that case . . . Marcia Brown's defence relied on her story about being waylaid by a constituent called Adrian, with a complaint about a council matter. Adrian was never traced, but now I believe he could have been Peter Parker.'

'Dressed as bloody Spider-Man?' Coats exploded desperately.

'Dressed as a civilian. Come on, Terry. Drop your guard and think as a cop. On the basis of what we both now know to be true, were you fooled or were you not?'

He buried his face in his hands, and rubbed it, vigorously, then threw back his head. 'It's possible, goddammit,' he hissed. 'It's possible. And then she died.' He paused. 'It couldn't have been Parker that waylaid her, though; not if he was going to be a possible witness against her.'

'True,' McDaniels admitted. 'Do you know if he's still a serving police officer?' she asked.

'He may well be,' he replied, 'but not in Scotland. A few months after the LuxuMarket incident, just before I was promoted and posted to Glasgow, he got married and emigrated to Adelaide. The word in the station was that he'd been accepted for the South Australian Police Service. Natural, I suppose; Australia's notorious for its bloody spiders.'

Sixteen

As Skinner had anticipated, the death of a Premier League footballer in a shattering car crash dominated the Saturday-morning news media. As always, the *Saltire* story was sharpest and carried the most detail, possibly because of the head start that he had given June Crampsey in one of those hypothetical discussions that never took place.

Heading for Glasgow along a less crowded M8 with his youngest son in the passenger seat beside him, he frowned as he thought of the families of the girlfriend and of the Belgian tourists, who had been reduced to bit players in some of the coverage. 'Also among the dead were,' he growled, repeating the words of the radio news announcer.

'What's up, Dad?' James Andrew asked. A strapping lad a few days off his eleventh birthday, he had threatened rebellion when his father had insisted that he use his booster seat but had yielded when given the choice between that and missing out on a visit to the city's spectacular Riverside Museum.

'Respect, son. There was once a poet and wise man named John Donne, who said, "Any man's death diminishes me because I am involved in Mankind." Understand?'

'I think so. When I went to the Jesus and Me club at the

church, I remember the minister saying that we are all equal in the eyes of the Lord. You're saying why are they talking about the footballer as if he's more important than any of the other people who were killed.'

'That's it. What about you, what are you saying?'

'I'm saying that it doesn't matter if you have a Champions League winner's medal, you can't take it to heaven.'

'A shade blunt, perhaps, because the footballer isn't un-important, but you're on the right lines.'

'Am I supposed to believe in heaven, Dad?' the boy asked, taking Bob by surprise.

'Many people would say you are,' he replied. 'I prefer to tell you to make up your own mind once you've had time to consider the question. There are many visions of heaven; I think we each have to choose the one we find most realistic.'

'Have you chosen one?'

'I know what I believe, yes. But I'm not going to tell you what it is, not yet. I don't want you adopting a belief system just because it's mine.'

'But you believe that when you die and Sarah dies,' James Andrew persisted, 'you'll meet up somewhere?'

'I hope so.'

'If you do, and if you meet up with Alex's mum as well, won't it be . . . awkward? What if they don't like each other?'

'That is not something I have ever considered,' Bob admitted.

'Would they have liked each other?'

'Honestly? I doubt that very much.'

'If Alex's mum had lived, would she have been my mum?'

'She might have been another boy's mum, but he'd have

been different from you. But then again, if she hadn't died, she and I might not have stayed together, Sarah and I might still have met and . . . well, here you'd be.'

'But . . .'

He laughed. 'Jazz, stop right there. Let's resume this conversation in five years. Quit thinking like a teenager until you actually are one.'

He drove on, steadily and carefully, switching to the M74 motorway and approaching their destination from the south side of the river that cuts Scotland's largest city in two. The car park at the Queen Elizabeth II University Hospital was as busy as Skinner had expected, but Graham Scott had given him directions to the staff section, where he announced himself through a microphone and waited as the barrier was raised by unseen security staff.

He had been to the mortuary section before and had no intention of taking an eleven-year-old. Instead he led his son to the nearby café, bought him a mineral water and an apple, and told him to amuse himself with his iPad. He trusted Jazz to stay where he was until he returned, but as an added precaution he identified himself to the reception staff, told him that he had a meeting and asked them to keep an eye on the boy.

As he'd expected, Graham Scott was ready and waiting for him in his office. 'This had better be good, chum,' he told the professor, smiling. 'Whatever it is, from the sound of you last night, it seems to have made your weekend.'

'It has,' the pathologist replied, 'and it hasn't. What I've found shames a member of my profession, on two grounds, incompetence and possibly corruption as well: a man called Archie Banks, a peripatetic beyond retirement age who was commissioned by the procurator fiscal to do the Marcia Brown autopsy because there was nobody else available.'

'I know the name,' Skinner volunteered. 'Sarah encountered his work in her early years here. She was unimpressed; called him a horse doctor if I remember right.'

'God help the horse. The fiscal has a lot to answer for; he let Banks sort out his own corroboration, and he used a student, Marguerite Swanson. Her name features very briefly in the report. I had my doubts that she was ever in the room, so I checked with her – she's qualified now. She was present, but not close up. Banks let her observe, not participate; she remembered that, and also that there was very little to see.' Scott opened a file on his desk. 'That's the report to the fiscal, and that's her corroborating signature below Banks's, but she told me she had no part in its preparation. Look at the dates, of the post-mortem and the report.'

Skinner peered at the page, then with a sigh of exasperation took a pair of reading spectacles from his pocket and perched them on his nose. 'They're the same,' he observed. 'He did the PM and signed off on it on the same day. Quick work, but so what?'

'I'll get there. The report says that the examination was also witnessed by Detective Sergeant Terry Coats, but his signature is not present.'

'It fits, though; we know that he attended the suspicious death call-out.'

'As it turned out,' Scott said, 'he wasn't suspicious enough. Banks's finding was that death was due to a massive overdose of liquid morphine, self-administered, that the dose was too great to have been accidental, and that the victim undoubtedly ended her own life. That's what he reported and that will have been enough for the fiscal, I am sure.'

'It was,' Skinner confirmed. 'It was signed off as suicide. So, Graham, why am I here?'

'Because the stupid bastard signed it off on the blood analysis alone! That would have been done very quickly, and it was enough for him. What he didn't do was what any competent pathologist would have done. He didn't wait for the result of the stomach contents analysis!' He took a second page from the folder and, clearly agitated, thrust it at his companion. 'Look what it says! It notes the presence of rice, curried lamb, banana yoghurt, coffee, and a significant amount of red wine, but not a trace of morphine! It can only mean that the fatal dose was injected. According to the capsules and the packaging found with the body it was fucking Oramorph, Bob, the kind that the patient swallows. Why would anyone intending to kill herself bother to inject the stuff, even if she was half pissed? She wouldn't, Bob, she wouldn't have. She'd have fucking swallowed it, as you're supposed to!'

'But the stomach contents do indicate that she was drunk. Can you say with any certainty that she didn't do just that?'

'I can say with certainty that a fatal dose of morphine was injected into the bloodstream. The police report, and Detective Sergeant Coats, wherever he is now, will have to tell you whether a syringe was found at the scene. Possibly more than one, or she'd have had to reload, given the size of the dose. That, by the way, would have been practically impossible; she'd have been unconscious before she was finished, most likely. She had help, for sure, and she wasn't a willing victim.'

'Proof, Graham,' Skinner insisted. 'Proof.'

'Yes, and I can show it to you.' He turned to his computer

and swung it round. 'The one thing that was done right was the photography of the body. Marguerite Swanson did it, she told me, with a digital camera, and the images were stored on a memory stick. It was in the file when I opened it. I've studied them, I've enlarged them, I've improved the definition as much as I can. Now look at these.'

He went to his keyboard and clicked, bringing on to the screen an image of a woman's upper torso and shoulders, and the lower part of her face. He zoomed the image, focusing on the left shoulder then the right.

'What can you see, Bob?'

'Bruising,' Skinner whispered. 'On the upper arms below each shoulder.'

'And the shape?'

He peered at the screen, trying to focus, until finally he gave up and put on his spectacles. 'General bruise on the right,' he murmured. 'On the left, yes, definite finger marks.'

'Exactly. This person was gripped and held, with great force, causing immediate bruising. If death followed soon afterwards, and it did, the marks would remain. I believe there were two assailants; that she was held down and forcibly injected with the dose of morphine that killed her. I would testify to that effect in a criminal court. I can't prove it, but I would also suggest to a jury that from the shape of the marks on her upper arms, if we had clear images of her armpits, that's where we would find the injection site or sites. This was never a suicide, my friend. As I told you, this was a premeditated homicide.'

Skinner nodded. 'I'll buy it. Okay, Graham, it was worth my while coming through.'

'What are you going to do about it?' the professor asked.

'It's been nine years; it can wait for a few more hours. Right now, I'm going to take my son to the Riverside Museum. At some point after that, I might just pay a call on a lady of my acquaintance.'

Seventeen

Carrie was pushing her luck, she knew it. Undoubtedly, the sensible, responsible thing was to do nothing precipitate until she had interviewed Hazel Delaney, the LuxuMarket manager, in Dundee on the following Monday, as she had intended. However, as her father had told her when she was sixteen and he had caught her *in flagrante* with the married woman next door, she had been born with no sense and even less responsibility. It featured nowhere on her CV, but her recklessness had led to the end of her career in the Territorial military police. A headlong rush through an open door in Kabul when she had been ordered to hang back had brought her face to face with two Taliban intruders and had cost her colleague his life.

She had her case already: David Brass and his dead son had been right all along. She was sure that Marcia Brown had been framed, set up as a shoplifter by a conspiracy involving Vera Stephens and her fiancé. A call had been placed to the South Australian police headquarters in Adelaide, asking for confirmation that Peter Parker was indeed a member of that force, and requesting a phone call whenever he was next on duty.

She knew that she should wait, that she should go nowhere near Councillor Gloria Stephens until she had all the facts assembled, until she was in a position to report everything to Alex. There was only one more question to which she needed an answer. Perhaps Hazel Delaney could supply it. Perhaps Spidey could be scared into telling her the whole story, in the hope of saving his Australian career. But perhaps not, in either case: probably not.

There really was only one person who knew the answer, and she was holding a constituency surgery that afternoon, advertised on the West Coast Council website, in her office in Newmilns. Carrie had driven straight there from Edinburgh Airport, and a shaken Terry Coats. Her blood was up, and she hoped to put just as big a scare into the councillor.

She found the small office easily. It was above a row of small shops, faced by a public car park that might have been busy through the week but was empty on a day when most of the townspeople had probably headed for the nearest beach. The door that she confronted bore a glossy image of a smiling Gloria Stephens, on a campaign poster; she opened it and stepped inside, into a waiting room where three people, middle-aged women, sat on a long bench. They were faced by a man behind a desk, burly, grim and unsmiling. Carrie had a flashback to her first year in secondary school, and a humourless maths teacher who had earned the dislike of the entire class.

He stared up at her as she approached him; his eyes were dull and disinterested. 'Here to see the cooncillor?' he drawled.

She smiled back at him. 'I hope so,' she replied, but drew not a flicker in return. Instead he slid a piece of paper towards her.

'Name, address and the reason for your visit,' he growled.

She leaned over the desk and took her pen from its slot in her notepad. 'No' there!' the gatekeeper snapped. 'You'll mark it.'

'I won't be the first,' she retorted. 'Where, then?'

He shrugged and returned his attention to that day's *Metro*.

McDaniels took a place at the end of the bench and began to fill the form on her lap, using her notepad as a support. Adopting the name Daniella Carrington, her favourite subterfuge, she recalled the name of the street that had led her into Newmilns and used that, adding the number thirty-seven. Beneath her bogus credentials she scrawled, 'School catchment areas', then handed her submission back to the custodian, who accepted it without a glance. As he did so, a door opened behind him, and a man emerged. His expression did not suggest that he was a satisfied constituent.

One of the waiting three rose to her feet, but she was waved back down by the man behind the desk, with a terse 'Haud on.' He stood up himself, and vanished into the room behind, taking Carrie's information form with him. He was gone for less than a minute; when he returned, he ignored the waiting trio and pointed to her. 'You next.'

'Sorry,' she murmured to her companions as she stood. 'Don't know why.' She walked past the man into the inner sanctum.

The Gloria Stephens who faced her from a chair behind a larger desk than the one outside was an older version of the one in the welcoming photograph; older and considerably less friendly. Her hair was still auburn, well cut and carefully arranged, but she wore much less make-up and there were no laughter lines around her eyes.

'Which paper are you from, hen?' she asked in a smoker's rasp. 'Or have you got a hidden camera in your bra?'

'I don't know what you mean,' Carrie protested.

'Save it,' Stephens snapped. 'Daniella fucking Carrington indeed! If there was anybody with a name like Daniella fucking Carrington in my ward, I'd have known about her long ago. As for the address, the number you gave me, it's a shop. Once again, what paper are you from and what the hell are you playing at?'

Knowing there was no point in further pretence, Carrie settled into the low-slung chair facing the councillor and opened her notepad. 'No newspaper, no hidden cameras.' She took a business card from the pad and handed it over. 'My name's Carrie McDaniels and I'm a private investigator. I've been hired by an Edinburgh solicitor advocate, Alexis Skinner, to look into the death nine years ago of a fellow councillor of yours, Marcia Brown. She killed herself after being accused of stealing from a store in Kilmarnock. Councillor Brown claimed at the time that she was the victim of a conspiracy. The enquiries I've made, and the sources I've spoken to, lead me to believe that was true. It appears that Marcia may have been set up by your daughter Vera with the help of her boyfriend at the time, a serving police constable name of Peter Parker. Their motive is less clear, but I've been told that you and Councillor Brown had a blazing row in your room in the council offices just before it happened. It'll be for my client, Ms Skinner, to decide what to do about it, but she's an officer of the court, so she won't really have much choice but to ask for a formal police investigation. Before we get to that stage, I feel it's only right to give you a chance to tell your side of the story, if you have one.'

Hatred flowed across the desk in waves. 'That is fucking nice of you,' Gloria Stephens growled. 'Okay, this is my side of the story. There is no fucking story. Whoever's been talking to you has been telling you very large porkies for one reason alone: to smear me. I've been at this game for a long time, and I've left a lot of jealous and bitter people in my wake. You might have met a couple of folk who've strung you along, but once your so-called sources have to put their hand on a Bible, or a Koran, you'll hear fucking different. That's if they've got any hands by that time. Marcia Brown? Well named, she was; a reckless, vicious pile of shite driven by one thing and one thing alone, and that was pure fucking insanity!' She paused, leaning forward, icy grey eyes drilling into Carrie, 'I don't know what drives you, lass, but if you think you can walk into my town, and my office, and threaten me without there being any consequences, you have made a very dangerous mistake.' She pushed herself to her feet. 'Now get the fuck out of here, before I get big Ronnie outside to show you out through a window!'

Carrie McDaniels had been threatened before, in military situations, and in the course of her work, but she could not recall anything resembling the cold stab of fear that pierced her as the dumpy woman glared at her. It was all she could do to maintain her dignity and to walk from the room, rather than breaking into a run.

Her panic did not subside until she was back in her car, safely locked within. When she was calm once more, she took out her phone and dialled her client's mobile number. When it went to voicemail, she stifled a moan but recovered herself. 'Alex,' she said to the recorder, 'hopefully you're in Edinburgh this weekend and you'll pick this message up very soon. I know it's Saturday, but I'd like to update you on my investigation.'

She checked the Rolex once again. 'Since I don't know where you live, I'm going to head for your office; since you share it with a newspaper, I assume the building will be open. With a bit of luck, I'll be there by five thirty.'

She drew another deep breath, fastened her seatbelt, switched on the engine of her Renault and drove steadily out of the car park. Rather than return to the M77, she decided to head in the other direction, towards Strathaven, where she would have a choice of heading for East Kilbride and on to the M8 or simply staying on the A71 heading for Edinburgh. Until then, the road was straight, and it was quiet; the Clio had plenty of poke for its size, and so she put her foot down.

She was through Drumclog before she became aware of the car behind her, a black Ford Mondeo that was travelling as fast as she was. She thought no more of it until the driver reached out of his window and placed a flashing blue light on the roof, flashed his lights and turned on his indicator.

'Bugger!' she murmured as she pulled over.

Eighteen

'Do you remember those, Dad?' James Andrew Skinner asked as he stared up at the brightly coloured tramcars.

Bob shook his head. 'No, they were being taken out of service when I was born,' he told his son. 'They tried replacing them with trolley buses, great big heavy things that used the overhead power lines. The problem was that they pulled into the kerb, while the trams ran on rails. They were silent, and that was dangerous, because people couldn't hear them coming. If they stepped off the pavement . . . well,' he grimaced, 'squish. They called them "the Whispering Death". Grim, eh? It didn't take long for the city council to realise they were a bad idea and take them out of service. Everything was buses after that.'

'Why did they take the trams away?'

'That's a good question, Jazz. I don't really know the answer, truth be told. Grandpa Skinner told me that they were very popular; they were a distinctive part of Glasgow culture. Also, there was a huge network of them, running all over the city, to places with wonderful names like Auchenshuggle.'

'Ocken-what?' the boy tried to repeat.

'Auchenshuggle.'

120

'Ocken . . .' He laughed. 'I can't even say that.'

'That's because you're a Gullane boy. Me, Ah'm fae Motherwell.'

'Is that why you speak like that?' Jazz asked.

'It's my curse, son; an accent that's never left me in thirty-five years, not completely. You can take the boy out of Motherwell, but you can't take Motherwell out of the boy.'

'Mum says that about New England, where she was born.'

'Copy her accent, not mine; that would be my advice. Come on,' Skinner said. 'Let's go and visit the Tall Ship, then head back to Edinburgh. I need to call in on someone on the way back home.'

'Who?'

'Your uncle Mario; Mario McGuire.'

'How do you know he'll be at home?'

'I texted him from the hospital. He's expecting us around three thirty.'

Father and son were both fascinated by the history of the *Glenlee*, the steel-hulled three-masted ship moored at Pointhouse Quay, adjacent and complementary to the great Riverside transport museum. Built in Port Glasgow and launched five years before the death of Queen Victoria, she had sailed the world in a colourful cruising career before becoming a Spanish naval training vessel, when she had been named *Galatea*. She had come close to celebrating her centenary by being scrapped, but had been rescued by the Clyde Maritime Trust and towed back to Scotland to become one of its most notable landmarks.

'I hope you remember all that,' Bob told his son as they drove away from the museum car park, in search of the expressway and the connection with the M8. 'You're bound to be asked what you did on your holidays when you go back to school.'

'I will,' Jazz promised. 'I have all the brochures and I've got lots of photos on my phone. How long is it until we go to Spain, Dad?' he asked.

'Three weeks. I wish it could be sooner, but that's when Mum can take her holidays.'

'Will Ignacio still be working in Perthshire?'

'Yup. He's there all summer; at least that's the plan.'

'Could I go and work there when I'm old enough?'

'When do you reckon that will be?'

'When I'm sixteen?' he ventured.

'I'd sooner get you a job in Spain when you're that age.'

James Andrew's eyes shone. 'Would you do that, Dad?'

'I will do it; as long as you keep working on your Spanish with Ignacio.'

'Can we speak Spanish now?'

'Sì.'

Father and son conversed in slow, clumsy but functional Spanish all the way to Edinburgh. Although Bob had owned property in Catalunya for over twenty years, he had never set out to master the language until his appointment to the board of InterMedia had made it a necessity. He had become fluent in Castellano and passable in Catalan. In the former, he had been supported by his oldest son, who had been born and raised in Spain, and Ignacio was only too pleased to help his half-brothers as well. Mark absorbed knowledge like blotting paper and had impressed everyone by watching *Roma* without subtitles. Jazz was making progress beyond his years, had begun French at primary school, and his father was determined that he would add conversational German at secondary.

One language that was not on his list was Italian, in which Paula Viareggio McGuire greeted them as Skinner arrived for his meeting with her husband. Mario had been his protégé, one of several young officers he had plucked out of uniform and trained as detectives. He had risen to become deputy head of the Scottish national force, success that pleased his mentor. McGuire and his bosom friend Neil McIlhenney, who had moved south to become a deputy assistant commissioner in the Met, had been two reckless young men. Their progress under Skinner's tutelage, together with the chief herself, Maggie Rose, gave him belief that his police career had actually been worth something.

'Hey, boys,' Mario exclaimed as he came into the hall with young Eamon, his son, perched on his shoulder. He was massive in shorts and a sleeveless blue shirt. 'Good to see you, Jazz. You a police cadet now?'

'I'm not joining the police, Uncle Mario,' James Andrew replied earnestly. 'I want to join the army.'

'Mmm,' the big man murmured, glancing at Skinner. 'What does your father say to that?'

'At the moment,' Bob told him, 'he says, "Your life will be your own, son, but you're making no such decision until you've done a relevant university degree – languages or business studies, or both." On that, James Andrew and I are agreed. Just about everything else is open to debate.' He glanced down at the boy. 'Can I park him somewhere while we talk?'

'Sure,' Mario said, setting his own son on his feet. 'Eamon, show Jazz your Lego. Maybe he can help you build something. Please, Jazz,' he added in a whisper. 'Bloody stuff's doing Paula's head in, and mine.'

The two boys had met before, and Eamon was star-struck.

He allowed James Andrew to take his hand as he led him towards his playroom.

The adults made for the kitchen. McGuire took a Peroni from the fridge, and without asking handed Skinner a zero-alcohol Heineken. 'Who's dead and who did it?' he asked. 'I know it's a crisis for you to dig me up on a Saturday.'

'Crisis, no. It's a cold case that was never hot, although it bloody well should have been. We thought we had heard the last of Austin Brass when the guy who killed him was locked up. But no, the bugger's reached out from beyond the grave.'

'No,' the deputy chief constable sighed. 'Not another bent cop uncovered by Brass Rubbings. Tell me it's not.'

'There's no indication of that, although one might emerge from the mess left behind by a seriously incompetent pathologist who allowed a very obvious homicide to be categorised as a suicide: Marcia Brown, Austin's mother. No fucking way did she kill herself.'

McGuire necked half of his Peroni, then shook his head and looked at his old boss with a grin. 'You don't do ordinary, Bob, do you. You take your laddie on a day out in Glasgow and come back with a previously undetected homicide. Any thoughts on what I should do about it, or you, for that matter?'

Skinner smiled back at him, took a sip of Heineken and winced. 'Oh, I know what *I* want to do about it,' he replied. 'I want your approval first, then your co-operation; that'll do for starters.'

Nineteen

Alex Skinner had never seen herself as the maternal type, and so the unexpected arrival of her new baby half-sister, Dawn, had taken her by surprise. She had looked at the child for the first time and had been overwhelmed. Tears filled her eyes, and if she had tried to speak, the lump in her throat would have struck her dumb.

They had the same father, but there was thirty years between them in age. Had she lived, Myra, her mother, would have been mid fifties. That conceded, Sarah, her stepmother, was looking over her shoulder at forty. She had been shocked when she had fallen pregnant. As a doctor, she should have known better, she had confessed to Alex, but with the surprise of her unexpected reconnection with Bob, things had been over-looked.

Since the birth, Alex had spent much of her free time in Gullane, ostensibly helping Sarah at weekends, when the children's beloved Bajan carer, Trish, was on her leisure time. She doted on Dawn, but not to the exclusion of her other siblings. In particular she spent more time with Seonaid than she had before. She had come through her nursery years and was well established in primary school, her literacy mastered, and showing signs already that one day she might follow her mother into the field of medicine. Her interest in Sarah's work was awkward in the sense that much of it could not be discussed with a seven-year-old, but it showed a remarkable imagination that could be focused on other areas.

Am I broody? Alex asked herself as she reached into the fridge for a bottle of orange and mango juice. Her sleep pattern was chronically awful; invariably she would waken after three or four hours with a dry mouth and a fully active mind. *Maybe I am*, she thought. *Maybe this wakening in the middle of the night is mimicking being a mum, four-hourly feeds and all that stuff.* Smiling, she weighed her breasts with her free hand as she put the bottle to her lips. Not insubstantial but no heavier than they should be. *But if it is, having a baby might not be the best way to cure it.*

'Mmm,' she whispered. 'Still, Alexis,' she asked herself, 'is this your life? Standing naked in the dark in your kitchen at three a.m.? Maybe this is it, for us single ladies. On the other hand, it could have been worse. You might have married Andy Martin.'

She let the thought fade away. The idea of comparing notes with Carrie McDaniels took its place. Another single woman, in the same age bracket. Did she experience nocturnal omissions too? On the other hand . . . She knew that Carrie had relationships with men, and yet, had there been a vibe, an unspoken suggestion that she might be open to offers? *Not my game*, she thought mischievously, *but if it was, she isn't unattractive.*

Guilt bit her on two levels: her moment of fantasy, and the fact that she had stood up her investigator without even knowing about it. She had spent late morning and all afternoon at

Gullane, waiting until her father and James Andrew returned from their Glasgow adventure. Her dad had been in a curious mood; she had sensed that something important had happened, but when she asked how his day had been, he had shrugged and said, 'Fine. The Riverside Museum was great, wasn't it, Jazz?' Her brother had nodded, but only after a glance towards him. Those two were keeping a secret: no effing doubt about it. It had amused her, and it still did; she was enjoying James Andrew's development, watching him absorb more and more of their father's habits and mannerisms.

It was only when she had returned to her car that she realised she had left her phone on charge in its socket. She had checked her voicemail, finding only one message, from Carrie, asking for a five-thirty meeting in her office. She had missed it by an hour. She had called her back, but it had gone unanswered. Instead she had sent an apologetic text, suggesting the following afternoon as an alternative, but there had been no response. She frowned as she thought about it. She was good at reading people – it was part of her skill as an advocate – and there had been an underlying tension in her investigator's voice. Without reading too much into it, she wondered whether the David Brass investigation might be less straightforward than she had expected.

She turned to replace the juice in the fridge; as she did so, the corner of her eye registered a flash, reflected in the kitchen window, a flash that came from behind her. She spun round and saw two men, and the knife that the one closer to her was brandishing, the knife that had reflected the light of the full moon. 'What the fuck!' she yelled instinctively as he approached, stepping around the island that held her hob and food preparation space. *Black fucking balaclavas!* she thought hysterically. *These guys are so fucking stereotyped!*

She threw the juice bottle at the nearer and more threatening of the intruders. He batted it away and closed on her, but rather than back off, she stepped towards him, grabbing the sauté pan that sat on the hob and swinging it at him back-handed. The Le Creuset had been a gift from Ignacio; that was the only reason she used it, for she found it heavy and hard to handle. For the first time she was grateful for its heft as it caught the man on the side of the head and sent him sprawling.

The second man did not react to his partner's fall; instead he stepped forward and moved towards her. He was bigger, more agile, and even without a blade he seemed more dangerous. Alex still held the pan, but that had been a one-off; all she could do was throw it at him and she did. The mouth in the black mask grinned as it missed. She took a step to the side and made to grab the biggest knife in her butcher's block, but she was clumsy, and it snagged.

He was almost on her when a figure, as naked as she was, burst into the kitchen with an improbable cry of 'Police officer!' He dived at the attacker from behind, catching him in the middle of the back, driving him downwards and face first into the door of a cupboard. 'Alex,' he called out. 'Gimme a towel, something, anything to tie this bastard up.'

She looked around, but there was nothing in sight that was big enough to do the job. For a moment, she was helpless as the two men on the ground struggled. Her attacker looked strong enough to fight his way free, but in the event the duel was ended when the first man climbed to his feet, unsteadily but with knife in hand, and slashed his companion's captor viciously across his lower back.

In a matter of seconds, both of the invaders were upright

and facing her, side by side, but by that time, Alex had armed herself with a long knife and a cleaver from the block, one in each hand.

'Just in case you think I'm only a girlie,' she hissed as her wounded protector pulled himself painfully to his feet, 'I promise you that I have been combat trained by an expert, and that if you put me to the test, at least one of you will not leave this room.' She waved the knife. 'This is for slicing Serrano ham; you won't believe how sharp it is until it takes your fucking head right off.'

The two men gazed at her, made a shared professional judgement, then turned on their heels and ran from the apartment.

Twenty

'Fuck's sake, Alex,' DI Harold Haddock exclaimed as he stepped inside the curtain that screened cubicle C from the rest of Edinburgh Royal Infirmary's Accident and Emergency Department, 'are you okay?'

'She's fine, Sauce.' The ground-out reply came from a man; he lay face down on a hospital trolley, frowning, teeth clenched as a green-clad doctor stitched a long gash across his lower back, just above his buttocks. 'It's me you should be concerned about; I'm the one who nearly had his arse sliced off.'

'You've been back in uniform too long, Inspector Montell. "Superficial knife wound", that's what the paramedic who brought you in told me. There's a guy two cubicles along who was brought in with his right ear in a bag. Just another Saturday night in Scotland's capital city; on scale of ten that cut's no more than a three. By the way,' he added, 'I didn't know you two were an item again.'

'We're not; just grown-up friends who both happen to be single at the moment.' Griff Montell winced. 'Ah, you wouldn't understand, Sauce, you're happy ever after.'

'I think I can work that one out, though. Who called who?'

'I did,' Alex replied. 'I'm not sure why; possibly because I'd

130

spent the day with my very young siblings and felt like some adult company. I'm glad I did.'

'Me too,' Haddock agreed. 'I'm more than glad. I ask again, are you okay? The paramedic said possible delayed shock, and that you might have a reaction later on.'

She looked up at him from her seat, knees hunched up in what seemed to him a defensive posture. Her hair was pulled back in a ponytail, she was dressed in a green sweatshirt and tracksuit bottoms, and she wore no make-up. Haddock had known her since his earliest days on the force, but he had never seen her so tired, gaunt or angry.

'I'm fine, Sauce,' she replied, tight-lipped. 'As you said, the doctor checked me over, but I have no physical injuries; only hurt pride and outrage. There will be no delayed reaction. Griff's right: he's the one with the damage. When you catch the bastards, make sure the arresting officers know they knifed a cop. I take it you haven't caught them yet.'

'No such,' Haddock admitted. 'Emergency services prioritised the ambulance when you told them that a police officer had been wounded, but the nearest of our cars were attending a club disturbance on Lothian Road and a mugging in Leith Walk. The pair must have been long gone by the time we got there. We didn't know from your call that it was a home invasion. The 999 operator had it down as a Saturday-night domestic.'

'It was that all right,' she growled.

'Is there anything you can tell me that might help us?'

'Physical descriptions, you mean? They were both wearing masks, so facially nothing. The one with the knife was stockily built, about five nine. His mate was at least six feet, moved like an athlete and could handle himself.'

'Bollocks,' Montell called out from the trolley. 'He was all mine.'

'Only after you went through him from behind like a Springbok flanker, and even then he wasn't done.'

'I still had him down, though. If only you'd had some proper tape in the kitchen.'

'If only you'd brought your handcuffs and your pepper spray.' She looked back at Haddock, who seemed mildly amused. 'One thing that might help. When you do catch them, the smaller one will have a very sore head, maybe even a fractured skull. I beaned him with a French sauté pan just before Griff drilled through his mate.'

'Thanks. I doubt that he'd be crazy enough to come to this A&E,' the DI suggested, 'but we'll check all the others. Which side of the head?'

'Right.'

'Okay. How about you, Griff? Did you hear anything said?'

'Nothing. I saw nothing that would help you either, except . . .' he paused as the last stitch was tied off and the doctor left, 'at least one of them's likely to have my blood on his shoes. I saw him step in it as they legged it.' His eyes narrowed. 'That was a wise choice; if they'd gone for Alex, cut wide open or not, I'd have held one back and let her take care of the other. Then it would have been open season on number two. As it is, when I do find them . . .'

'Don't go there, Griff,' Sauce cautioned him. 'I'm worried enough about what'll happen when the big fella finds out about this.'

'My father must not find out about this,' Alex snapped. 'You will say nothing to him, Sauce. I insist on that.'

His eyes widened; he gasped. 'You are joking, aren't you?

You want me to be the man who didn't tell Bob Skinner that his daughter was attacked by two hitmen who broke into her home? As it happens, by "the big fella", I meant DCC McGuire, who's known you since you were in the fucking Guides. I have to tell him, because it's my job. You think he won't tell your dad? Alex, these blokes would be better off handing themselves in to the United Nations than the police. Far safer.'

He broke off as the nurse who had admitted them came into the cubicle to dress Montell's stitched wound. The three kept silent as she worked. 'That's it,' she announced when she was satisfied. 'We want to keep you in overnight for observation. We're sorting out a bed for you.'

'Nurse,' Montell said, 'it's twenty past six; "overnight" is almost over. Find me something less revealing that I can wear until I'm reunited with my clothes at Alex's place, and we'll both be out of here.'

She smiled. 'Let me rephrase that. We want to keep you in for at least twenty-four hours. I'll be back soon.'

'Behave yourself, Griff,' the DI murmured. 'You know she's right; it may only be a three out of ten by our standards, but it's still a significant knife wound. Besides,' he went on, 'not even Alex can go back to Alex's place.'

'You what?' Her reaction was a second ahead of Montell's.

'You can't go back because it's a crime scene, and,' he added, 'because you wouldn't be safe there. Wind back to something I said before the nurse came in.'

'Specifically?' she demanded.

'Hitmen, Alex; I called them hitmen. Why do you think I'm here? I'm Serious Crimes; I wasn't called just because I know you, but because the judgement is that it's an incident that falls within my remit. When the specialist burglary team arrived at your place, just after the ambulance had left, it took them no time at all to realise it wasn't your usual housebreaking.'

'Why shouldn't it be?' Montell asked.

Haddock sighed. 'You're sedated, Inspector, so I'll make allowances for your slowness on the uptake. First and foremost, because Alex lives in a duplex on the seventh floor – or is it the eighth? – of a secure apartment block. Secure,' he repeated. 'Which of you locked up last night?'

'I did,' Alex replied.

'Did you use your security chain?'

'I always do.'

'Right. The burglary team assumed that, and they found that your door had not been forced. The lock – not a simple one – was picked, and the chain was undone by a magnet, certainly. They got up there in the lift, not a big risk at three a.m., after they'd gained access through the garage, using a reader to decode the touchpad. These were not casual housebreakers, Alex, they were professionals. It's a possibility – and I am only saying this because I know you're tough enough to cope with it – that they didn't do all that to take your diamonds, but to take your life.'

Twenty-One

'On no account do that, Sauce,' Mario McGuire instructed. They were in Haddock's room in the old Fettes police building; the remains of bacon rolls and two takeaway coffee mugs sat on his desk. 'Do not call Bob Skinner; leave that to me. You focus on the crime and forget the people involved. What resources do you need? I know you're tight, with Sammy Pye being off on paternity leave. No, don't ask me what I think about that,' he grumbled. 'Equal opportunity employer, my arse.'

'At the moment I'm okay for bodies, sir; I've got the two DSs, McClair and Singh, and Jackie Wright's worth as much as either of them.' Haddock paused for thought, then took a chance. 'Boss, is there anything about this that you're keeping from me? Anything you know that might help explain why someone would want to attack Alex?'

'If there was, you'd be the second to know it, Inspector. You're the SIO; I'd keep nothing from you. Why do you ask?'

'I'm curious about being told to stay away from the gaffer – from Sir Robert, I mean. I'm leading the investigation into an attack on his daughter. Shouldn't you be more worried about keeping him away from me?'

'That's part of my thinking,' the DCC admitted. 'I don't

want him getting close to the investigation. If he gets wind of possible suspects, he'd be better at finding them than you, and if that happened . . .'

'Come on, sir,' Haddock said, 'he's a retired chief constable. You're not suggesting he'd go vigilante on us, are you?'

'Rule that out at your peril.' McGuire picked up his coffee and took a sip. 'Tell you a story that's known to very few people. A long time ago, when I was still a DC and Alex was a student, she was kidnapped by a terror group, led by a guy who'd got close to her. There was a news blackout and only the basics were reported after the event, and after Alex was safe; what was never revealed was that when Bob caught up with them, it did not end well for the man.'

'What happened to him?'

'Bob did, and that's all I'm saying. I don't want history repeating itself, but if he finds these two before you, chances are it will. If it does, you will never know about it; they will disappear, and it will be as if they never were. Christ, man,' he exclaimed, 'when you do catch them, don't let me be in the same room with them, let alone him!'

'Understood. I brief you and you alone on the investigation, and you brief him?'

'As far as it's prudent to do so.'

'Have you given any thought to the possibility this might be terror-related?' Haddock asked. 'That someone might have wanted to make a statement and Alex might have been seen as an easier target than her father?'

'I won't discount it,' McGuire conceded. 'You can be sure that Bob'll be using his MI5 contacts for any whisper of that. I'll make sure that if there is any relevant feedback, you're made aware.' He drained his mug. 'Now I must go and pick up Alex from the Royal and give Montell a pat on the shoulder, for courage, and just for being there.'

'And then?'

'I'll take her to Gullane and break the news to himself. Hold on to your desk in around an hour; there could be a fucking earthquake.'

Twenty-Two

'What was Montell doing there?' Bob Skinner asked his daughter brusquely.

'Pops!' she shot back. 'Twenty years back, when Alison Higgins arrived with her toothbrush, did I ask you that?'

'As a matter of fact, you did once. I told you she was keeping me company.'

'Same answer. I was at a loose end; I called Griff, and so was he; we went for a meal in the Lookout up on Calton Hill, and then back to mine . . . for coffee.'

'How is he?'

'Scarred and angry, but he'll survive. I'm glad he's in uniform now; he's going to need a quiet life for a while.'

'I wish you'd gone to his.'

'What difference would it have made? They'd have come another night.'

'Maybe,' Mario McGuire agreed, his bulk making Skinner's small home office seem like a cupboard, 'but how did they know you were in last night? If they'd been watching you, they'd have known Montell was there.'

'I've been thinking about that,' she said. 'Just before midnight, my phone rang, the landline. I answered it and a man's voice said, "Sorry, wrong number", then he hung up. It must have been them, surely. Maybe you can trace them through the number.'

Skinner looked up at the sky, where three birds flew. 'They're seagulls, not pigs. It will either be a call box or a burner phone.'

'If you can find the call box, you might get them on CCTV.'

'Exactly,' McGuire commented, 'so my money's on the disposable SIM.' He frowned as he looked at her. 'Alex, you're a criminal advocate. Have you defended anyone lately who might have a grudge against you?'

'Nobody that I can think of. Without boasting, Mario, I'm rather good at what I do. If I take a case to trial, it's because I believe the Crown Office doesn't have an overwhelming case against my client. If it does, I try to strike a plea bargain. Usually that works out okay. Sorry, I don't believe I have any stalkers out there.'

'There's another side to it,' her father pointed out. 'Your guilty clients – and maybe some of those who're acquitted too – they all leave victims behind them. Have you ever been threatened by one of them?'

'If I had, I'd have reported it to the police. I wouldn't sit still for crap like that.'

'Maybe not, but can you think of anybody you've ever had concerns about, people who might harbour a grudge?'

She shook her head. 'It isn't like that, Pops. I've only ever heard of one advocate being threatened and he was a high-profile Celtic supporter who made the mistake of walking into a Rangers pub one night. Look, I am sorry. If Sauce's theory is correct – and yours, Mario – and these people broke into my apartment to do me harm, then I cannot see how it relates to anything in my professional life.'

'Honestly, kid,' her father exclaimed. 'I don't give a bugger what their motive was. We have to accept that they were after you, and my focus now is to keep you safe. You're staying here for the duration and you'll have police protection in the office and the court. Right, Mario?'

'Too damn!'

'No way!' she cried. 'Police keeping a general eye on me I will accept, but I am not staying here. My brothers and sisters live here. If I am attacked again, who knows how they'll do it? An IED, a grenade launcher? All three of us know that the Scottish criminal arsenal is pretty bloody formidable. You know I am right about this, Father.'

'Yes,' he sighed, 'I do.' He scratched his head. 'I suppose I could park you with Grandpa McCullough. Whatever the truth about his reputation, nobody fucks with him.'

'Too far away. Besides, Ignacio's there.'

'True again. How about Griff's place? I'm sure he'd have you.'

'Yeah, and then he'd want me to stay there for good. No thanks. Besides, he'd be no bloody use as a bodyguard. The way he is at the moment, I'd be protecting him.'

'As a police officer, he could be armed,' McGuire volunteered.

'No thanks,' Alex replied. 'I don't want that.'

'Fair enough,' Bob said. 'Leave it with me. There's a solution somewhere; I'll find it.' He turned to McGuire. 'Mario, thanks for looking after my kid. I'll check in on Haddock regularly to see how he's doing.'

'The hell you will. He has his orders: he doesn't share with you at all, only with me. You don't involve yourself in this investigation, Bob.'

'You are fucking joking, aren't you? As soon as you leave here, I'll be pushing certain buttons with my friend in London.'

McGuire laughed. 'As I told Sauce you would. Any worthwhile feedback you get you can pass to him – through me. If you're in the mood to go chasing people, you can satisfy it through that thing you reported to me yesterday.'

'What's that?' Alex asked.

'David Brass's ex,' Bob replied. 'I did a bit of digging, looked at the autopsy report with Graham Scott. It wasn't a suicide.'

'No kidding? From the look on your face it wasn't an accidental overdose either, so you're saying . . .'

'She was murdered. Held down and injected with morphine. Graham's sure of it and so am I.'

'Why wasn't that discovered nine years ago?'

'SFU.'

'Somebody fucked up. Jesus!' she whispered, and not in prayer. 'Could that relate to the shoplifting thing? Carrie McDaniels asked me for a meeting yesterday afternoon, but by the time I got her message it was too late. I tried to get in touch with her last night, but no joy. I need to try again,' she said anxiously. 'Whether the murder is related or not, she needs to be aware of it. So does David.'

'She needs to back off altogether,' McGuire said. 'It's a police matter now. An investigation will be set up, and it'll be taking a look at everything that was happening in Marcia Brown's life at that time, not just her predilection for petty pilfering. Everything McDaniels has done up to now will need to be reported to the inquiry team.'

'Who's the SIO?'

'A recent client of yours: DCI Charlotte Mann.' He smiled and nodded towards Skinner. 'With a mentor,' he added. 'I knew there was no point in asking him to stay out of it, so I didn't even try.'

'First things first, though,' Skinner declared. 'Let's get our priorities sorted out. The most immediate is Alex's short-term security, the second is me briefing Lottie Mann, and the third is getting in touch with Carrie McDaniels. Alex, you can do that while I make a call about priority number one; I have just had the brainwave to end all brainwaves. When it comes to bodyguarding you, my first two choices would be Mario here, and Neil McIlhenney. They're not available, so it takes me to the third name on my list.'

'Who is it?' she asked.

Bob grinned. 'Let me make that call first.'

'Who is it?' Mario repeated.

The grin became a chuckle. 'DCC McGuire, you probably don't want to know.'

Twenty-Three

'Who was that?' Dan Provan asked, glancing up from the sofa, where he sat beside young Jakey Mann, each with a game controller in hand. 'There was a lot of "sir-ing" going on, whoever it was. Not that useless divisional commander, I hope, interrupting our hard-earned Sunday.'

'Our?' Lottie Mann laughed. 'Hard-earned? Are you telling me you regard three lectures a week at the Jackton police college as hard work? From what you've told me, you spend more time in the gym there than you do in the classroom.'

'I've got to embrace my new persona, Lot.'

After over thirty years of police service, most of it spent in Strathclyde CID – for whose senior command he had developed a level of cynicism that bordered on contempt – a lifestyle that if not self-destructive had shown little concern for his long-term welfare, and a broken marriage, Detective Sergeant Provan had been persuaded to take a sabbatical to visit his daughter on Australia's Gold Coast. The man who returned had been so radically different that even Mann, who had spent most of her own service under his guidance, even after she had risen above him in the ranks, was astonished, and barely recognised him when she met from the airport. The boozy cynic had become a fitness fanatic, with horizons broadened and a new set of ambitions, none of which related to continuing his police career. He had taken the retirement package that had been his right for several years, and had been signed up immediately by the senior command of the new national police service to share his experiences and imbue the professional education of a new generation of detectives with practical policing common sense.

'Operate by the book, always,' he told his students. 'That's your job. But never be afraid to edit it when the need arises.'

His relationship with Lottie had changed almost as much. As a young detective she had looked up to him, even when he cut corners and did some extreme editing of the rule book. She knew that she was twice the cop for him than she would have been without. She had always liked him, and yet there had been something else too, something living just beyond her imagination. It had fallen into place after the Australian metamorphosis: she had feelings for him that went beyond admiration. When Dan accepted that he felt the same things that she did, the realisation had astonished them both.

Their relationship was still based on fellowship more than on physicality. They had tried that, shyly, a few times, always on neutral ground, with Jakey in the care of his aunt. It had been good, but in truth, sex had never been a driving force for either of them. There was talk of moving in together – Dan's house was bigger than hers, and mortgage-free – and there was a tacit agreement that it would happen. They had gone as far as to take Jakey to meet the head teacher of the primary school that he would attend, without putting a date on the move.

'Embrace it as hard as you can,' she replied, 'and one day it might be able to beat a pre-teen at a video game.'

'Don't wait up,' he muttered. 'Have you seen how

complicated these things are? I had trouble with that tennis ball that went in slow straight lines; I'm right out my depth here. Jakey,' he pleaded, 'gie's a break, son. Is there no' a handicap system or something like that?'

The boy laughed and exploded another mutant with a rocket.

'You going to tell me who it was?' Dan asked again, as the carnage continued.

She dropped on to the sofa beside him. 'It was the DCC.'

'The big DCC? McGuire?'

'Himself. He called to warn me that wee John Cotter and I are heading up a major new investigation. Suspicious death.'

Provan frowned. 'Then what are you doin' here? Should you not be on your way to the crime scene?'

'There is no crime scene. It's an old case where some new evidence has been uncovered. We're to give it top priority, I think because there's politics involved.'

'Holyrood?'

'No, local level; the West Coast Council. That's all I know; he said we'll get the briefing, me and Cotter, tomorrow morning, my office ten o'clock.'

'No' exactly a sense of urgency. Bugger it,' he snapped as he failed to dispatch a titanic orc. 'Who's doing the briefing?'

'This you're going to love. Bob Skinner.'

Instantly he forgot about the video game, turning to catch her gaze. 'You are havin' one, aren't you? Skinner? Sir Bob himself? Has he no' got a home to go to?'

'It seems not,' she agreed. 'Big Mario only said that it's something he came up with on his own time, spin-off from some client business that Alex has been doing. It may be related to it, it may not; that's for us to determine.'

'But Skinner's doing the briefing? Not the fiscal, not a serving officer?'

'That's the thing, Dan. Technically he still is. The chief's made him a special constable, with a roving brief. He neither gives orders nor takes them; his role is that of an adviser or a mentor, however I want to see it.'

'Do you have to see it?' Dan asked her. 'Can't you just thank him and send him home?'

'Yes,' she replied. 'The DCC made it clear that he's only there with my agreement. The term that was used was mentor; if I feel that I don't need one, least of all the most overbearing, forceful personality in the history of Scottish policing, I can thank him for his information and then ask him to go away and let me get on with it.'

'But you're no' going to do that, are you?'

'No, I don't think I am. I like big Bob, and I value his judgement and his experience. As well as all the things I called him before, he's also by a country mile the second best detective officer I ever knew.'

'The best being . . .'

She leaned towards him and kissed him on the cheek. 'You, my darling man, who else but you?'

'Nice of you to say so, but that man's seen things I'm glad Ah haven't. If he's prepared tae advise you, ye'd be daft not to let him, not least since you've got a new spare wheel. Will this one last any longer than the last two?'

'I hope so. Your two successors just weren't up to the job.'

'They'd a hard act to follow, mind,' Provan murmured.

'Granted, but the first one, the newly promoted woman from Traffic, she couldn't have followed an ice cream van, and the second one, he was an Irish joke. I'd never really believed in the Masonic connection in the old Glasgow force, but a month working with Detective Sergeant McFee put me right about that. There's no other way he could have got stripes on his arm.'

'And the new boy? Young John frae FurryBoots City? How is he going to do?'

'This'll be his first big test,' Lottie said, 'but so far the signs are good. He's got an honours degree, and he realised that it wasn't going to do him any good in the transport police. Best of it was, you know they floated the idea of merging the railway plods with our crew, and forty-plus per cent of them quit? John Cotter did the opposite. He made the switch the day the policy was announced; he was promoted in Aberdeen within six months, and transferred to Glasgow three months after that.'

'Who's his fairy godmother?' Provan asked. 'These young superstars have usually got someone in the hierarchy looking out for them.'

'Nobody that I've heard of. My chief super was vague about him when he posted him to me. "Don't break this one, DCI Mann. He could be precious," was all he said.'

'A couple of ways you could take that. The other is that he could go running tae his rep at the first harsh word.'

'My first impression is that he's a goodie. Young, late twenties, keen and full of ideas.'

Provan frowned. 'In that case, do you think it's a good idea having Skinner around him?'

'Why shouldn't it be?' she countered.

'One of the things I've learned already from this college job is that there are folk coming into the job who have no clue of the history and traditions of the service. They know eff all about the service as it used to be, when we had eight chief constables, no' just the one. That's the norm to them; they're more civil servants than they are cops, and they're gonna regard the likes of Bob Skinner as exhibits in some polis version of *Jurassic Park*. If your boy Cotter's one of them and he lets Skinner know it, well . . .'

He paused, then beamed beatifically. 'On second thoughts, go for it. Kids like that think Ah'm a dinosaur too. If yours is one of them, it'll do him no harm tae find out just how terrifying a tyrannosaurus must have been up close and personal.'

Twenty-Four

Not once had Clarice Meadows regretted her decision to leave the civil service, not for a single second. She was free of politics both office and national, the two having become increasingly interlinked in her experience; she had a congenial workplace in the city centre, and with thirty years of accrued pension rights transferred into her employer's more-than-adequate workplace scheme, she felt secure for life.

She had never been a clock watcher by nature, but she had spent her working life surrounded by them, and by desks that were regularly empty on Mondays, given the resigned attitude of management to ad hoc sick days. She enjoyed working until a task was complete, not only to Alex Skinner's satisfaction but to her own. To her surprise, she had discovered that she even acquired a certain buzz from being called on Sunday.

She had been in the garden with Sandy, her accountant husband, watering their desperately dry lawns, when her mobile had vibrated in her pocket. Her left eyebrow rose slightly when she saw Alex's number, and she felt a quick flash of excitement.

'Clarice?' Her boss had sounded tentative, less than her usual confident self. For an instant Clarice suspected that she might have the same hangover that was keeping her daughter in her room with the curtains drawn tight against the sun. 'I'm sorry about this, but there's a . . . situation. I have to be somewhere so I can't handle it myself, and it isn't something that Johanna's been involved in, so I'm wondering. Could you give me a hand?'

'I'd be delighted. Sandy's off to the bowling club . . .' the lie came spontaneously, to put Alex more at ease, she told herself, 'and our Janice will be best avoided until about five, so it's no problem. What do you need doing? Do I have to go into the office?'

'No, that won't be necessary. Do you have Carrie McDaniels in your contacts list? Carrie the investigator?'

'The woman who came in the other day about the Brass affair? Military type? AC/DC? Yes, I have her. Mobile number and her address; you said she works from home.'

'I need you to run her to ground. She called me yesterday and asked for a meeting in the office at five thirty, but I didn't get her message until it was too late. I tried calling her last night and again today, but she's been on voicemail herself ever since. I really must speak to her, but right now, short of leaving yet another message, there's nothing I can do.'

'Urgency on a scale of ten?'

'Off the scale.'

'No problem, Alex. Leave it with me; it's as good as done. What do I tell her when I find her?'

'Tell her to stop what she's doing and get in touch with me, urgently.'

'Do you need her to come and see you?'

'No, because I don't know where I'll be.'

'Sounds mysterious. Boss, are you okay?'

'I've been better, but yes. Thanks for this, Clarice. There'll be a bonus.'

'A bottle of something with bubbles will be perfectly fine.'

'Thanks, you're a darlin'.'

'It might need to be two bottles,' Clarice murmured now, as she walked up the Royal Mile. She had expected no miracle from her call to McDaniels' mobile. At best a drunken mumble, at worst the 'subscriber is unavailable' message that she heard.

'Magic! Her voicemail's full or her battery's dead. Help me here, woman?'

Her contacts book was comprehensive; it had a landline number, email address, a Facebook listing and a WhatsApp notation. The landline call went to message after a few seconds of ringtone; not immediately, as it would have done if the number had been engaged. Clarice left her name and number, then delved back into her phone and sent three messages, the first an email, the second a WhatsApp chat contact, and the third using Facebook.

That done, she picked up the garden hose once more and went back to watering. When the parched grass finally felt squelchy under her feet, she checked her phone. None of the tries had been acknowledged, and most significantly, the WhatsApp icon showed that its message had not reached its target. One way or another, Carrie McDaniels was off the reservation.

Faced with no other option, but determined to keep her word, she had picked up her car key.

'Where you off to?' The mumble had come from the garden chair.

'Duty calls.'

'Above and beyond the call, if you ask me.'

'I don't. Make our daughter a fizzy drink and tell her the longer she lies there, the worse it'll get.'

Summer Sundays in Edinburgh attract more motorists to the city than its car parks and meters were ever intended to cope with. Eventually she had found a slot in the underground facility beneath Dynamic Earth, leaving her a long uphill trudge towards McDaniels' address.

'It's bloody Sunday,' she muttered, realisation dawning as she passed John Knox's House, searching for the number she had noted. 'What if this really is an office? What if Alex was wrong? What if this has been a complete waste of bloody time?'

'F2,' she read. 'Second bloody floor.' She trudged up two flights of worn stone stairs, making a mental note to renew her gym membership, now that she no longer had access to the lavish civil service facilities.

Carrie McDaniels' door was varnished. There was a peephole just below eye level. She peered through it, hoping to see some sign of movement, or even light. Crazily she began to hum her old Elvis Costello favourite 'Watching the Detectives', then burst into laughter.

When it had subsided, she pressed the doorbell, and heard a loud chime from inside. She waited, her ear close to the door, listening for signs of movement. Hearing none, she lifted the letter box and called through it, 'Ms McDaniels. Carrie. It's Clarice Meadows from Alex Skinner's office. Alex needs to speak to you, urgently.'

'You lookin' for Carrie?'

The voice came from halfway up the flight of stairs above her. Its owner was a skinny young man with long greasy hair, clad in shorts and a T-shirt with a slogan that the basic

152

knowledge of Norwegian that she had gleaned in one of her civil service postings told her was extremely offensive. She doubted that he knew, but chose to let him carry on in ignorance until he met a Scandinavian tourist in the street.

'Yes, I am, actually,' she replied. 'It's a business matter, quite urgent.'

'She's no' in,' he assured her. 'Hasnae been in a' day. Ah'd have kent if she was. She plays her music far too loud; fuckin' Indian stuff. She telt me she got to like it in the army. Ah tell her if she plays it any louder they'll be able to hear it in fuckin' India, but she taks nae notice.'

'When did you see her last?'

'She was in last night, when Ah got in frae ma work.'

'What time?'

'Two thirty. Ah work in a pub on the Cowgate, just doon the road. Ah finished at one then hung on for a drink wi' the staff. So, aye, it would be about two thirty.'

'Did you speak to her?'

'Well, no. Ah never actually saw her like, just heard her movin' aboot.'

'Were her lights on?'

'How the fuck wid Ah know? That isnae a glass door ye're standin' at, is it? Ah,' his mouth fell open, 'haud on. Ah had a fag after Ah got in. Ah don't smoke in the hoose, ma granny doesnae like it – it's her place, ken – so Ah wis hingin' oot the back windae, and naw, her light wisnae on. Ah could still hear her, mind. That's a', though. Ah certainly never heard her this mornin', and Ah would have. Mind you, Ah never woke up till hauf eleven.'

Clarice maintained what she hoped was a pleasant smile. 'Do you have any idea where she might be now? Does she have a favourite hang-out? Does she have a boyfriend, a girlfriend even?'

'FucktifAhknow,' he replied, unwittingly copying the name given to a Yugoslav footballer by a legendary Scottish radio commentator who had misheard his assistant. 'Ah can gie ye her faither's number, though.'

'You're a friend of her family?' she exclaimed, taken aback.

'Naw, Ah've never met him, but Carrie gave me a card wi' his contact details; for emergencies, ken. Haud on and Ah'll get it.' He grinned. 'That's as long as ye're no' a debt collector, like.'

'Do I look like a debt collector?' Clarice boomed.

'These days, who looks like onything?' he chuckled, re-tracing his steps and disappearing through a blue front door on the landing above. He reappeared after a few minutes brandishing a sheet of paper. 'Sorry,' he said as he descended, 'Ah'd a hell of a job findin' it, then Ah did ye a copy on my printer. Ah'd tae wait a minute for it tae boot up.' He handed her the information, then carried on downstairs. 'Nice meetin' ye.'

She looked at the sheet of paper. It was a copy of a calling card, for personal use rather than business. 'Peter McDaniels MA, 17 Skylaw Place, Musselburgh,' she murmured. There was no mobile number, only a landline. Checking her phone, she saw that the signal strength was poor inside the old stone building, and so she waited until she was back on the Royal Mile before keying it in. The number rang four times, then went to message mode. 'Hello, this is Peter,' a cheery voice announced. 'I'm out right now. If you're a friend, leave a message; if you're a former pupil, leave a threat.'

She framed her message in her mind, then launched into it. 'Mr McDaniels, my name is Clarice Meadows. I work for a client of your daughter and I am trying to get in touch with her.

She's not responding to her mobile, nor is she at home, so I am wondering if she's with you. I'd be grateful if you'd call me back when you pick this up.'

She walked slowly back down the historic thoroughfare. As it narrowed, the crowds grew thinner and the atmosphere became less oppressive, but the heat had reached continental levels and she began to be sorry about being in the sun too long. She walked in shade where she could, until she spotted the familiar Starbucks logo and stopped off to buy a bottle of sparkling water.

Outside, she stepped into the shade of an alleyway and checked her phone once more. No missed calls showed. She tried Peter McDaniels again, but received the same reply. She had no idea whether there was a Mrs McDaniels. It was entirely possible that there was and that the pair were enjoying the relative coolness of the Costa Brava, or that there was not and that father and daughter were enjoying a day at the seaside.

Clarice hated to abandon a mission, she hated to leave a task unfulfilled, but she feared that she had no option but to call Alex and report failure. She was on the point of making the call when she decided that there was one last card in her hand. She returned to the car park, and programmed Skylaw Place Musselburgh into Apple Maps. After all, she was on the east side of the city, and the bypass would take her home in reasonably quick time.

Peter McDaniels lived in a new estate that was actually on the fringes of Wallyford; she supposed that the developer, a major housebuilder that had been expanding its brand across East Lothian, had determined that Musselburgh, with its famous racecourse, its ancient golf links and its boarding school, was a more marketable address. Skylaw Place was a cul-de-sac, a mix of detached and semi-detached properties; number seventeen was one of the former. Clarice sighed when she saw that there was no car in the driveway. There was a garage, but its up-and-over door was raised slightly and she could see that it was unoccupied. 'Maybe he's a bloody cyclist,' she muttered.

Parking space was limited; to avoid blocking thc road, she pulled her nearside wheels onto the pavement as one or two others had done, and stepped out, exchanging her air condition-ing for the full glare of the sun. The house had no border to the front; a path bisected a small lawn, leading to the front door. She had almost reached it when a car, a red vehicle with plastic side panels, swung into the driveway.

She stopped and waited as the driver switched off the engine and stepped out. He was tall and silver-haired; his face was lined but he had a healthy tan; his legs, revealed by his shorts, were thick and sinewy and his grey eyes were clear. If she had been forced to guess his age, she would have taken a stab at early sixties, but she recognised that could have been up to ten years too low.

He stood by the car, appraising her, but with a smile. 'You have a slightly bewildered look about you,' he began. 'Are you lost, or are you going to tell me I've won the Postcode Lottery? If you are, yes, I'm Peter McDaniels.'

'I'm not lost, Mr McDaniels, and I'm sorry not to be bearing great news. I did try to phone you, but obviously you were out and I wasn't given a mobile number. I'm looking for your daughter Carrie, and I hope you can help me.'

The expressive eyes showed a flash of concern. 'Maybe we can help each other,' he murmured. 'But first,' he added, 'I've been daft enough to buy frozen stuff at the supermarket, on a day like this, and it needs to go in the freezer, pronto. If you'll allow me to take care of that, then we can talk.'

She stood aside, giving him access to his own front door, then offered to help him by carrying some of the bags she could see on the back seat of his car as he returned to open it. 'Thanks,' he said, handing her two of them. 'Follow me.'

He led her through the house and into the kitchen. As they passed through the hallway, a single glance told her that no woman lived there.

She watched as he packed away his groceries. 'I thought,' he said, 'that today of all days, Tesco would be quiet. Wrong. Tesco is never quiet. Nightmare as always. Now,' he continued as he finished, 'to complete the introductions . . .'

'Of course,' she replied. 'I'm Clarice Meadows' – in her surroundings it occurred to her for the first time that her name sounded like a Cala housing estate – 'and I work for Alexis Skinner. She's a solicitor advocate and your daughter's doing some investigative work for her.'

He nodded. 'I've heard of Alex Skinner. Carrie's mentioned her in the past – and her formidable father – but not recently. She doesn't discuss her client business with me; she's pretty good at confidentiality, always has been. Did she give you my number?'

'No, I was given that by her upstairs neighbour.'

McDaniels senior grinned. 'Young Barclay? The little unwashed, Carrie calls him. A good barman, she says, and an idiot in every other way, but there's no harm in him. Now, to business. You're looking for Carrie? Well, the truth is, that makes two of us. She was supposed to be here for lunch – indeed, she was supposed to bring it with her – but there's been no sign of her. Her phone's off too, but I guess you've been trying that yourself. Can I ask, though, why the urgency on your part?'

'I'm not one hundred per cent sure,' Clarice admitted. 'All I know is that Alex asked me to contact her, tell her to stop whatever she's doing on the brief, and get in touch with her.'

'On a Sunday?'

'Exactly,' she agreed. 'They were supposed to meet last night but it never happened. Carrie left a message saying she'd be at Alex's office at five thirty, but she was busy and didn't pick it up until too late. She wasn't able to contact her after that, and today she passed the task on to me.'

'She'll turn up,' he said. 'As it happens, she was out of town last night.'

'She was?'

'Yes. She's a big Gregory Porter fan, and last night he was singing at the Sage in Newcastle. What's happened, she'll have given up on Ms Skinner after half an hour or so and belted down there. She'd booked herself into the Malmaison, across the river, and intended to drive up this morning to be here for lunch. If I know her, she had a couple last night, overslept and left much later than she'd meant to. Her phone battery will be flat; she always forgets to take her charger. That's why I don't have one,' he added. 'The things are so bloody unreliable. Would you like a cup of tea, Ms Meadows? Chances are before we finish it she'll pull up outside, full of apologies and Coca-Cola.'

'She couldn't have come home last night? I ask because Barclay said he heard movement in her flat about half past two.'

McDaniels frowned. 'Was he sure about that?'

'He seemed to be; he said he was sure he heard her moving around, even though there were no lights showing.'

'Now that does worry me. My daughter would not walk away from a hundred and twenty quid hotel booking; if the boy's right – and he's not that big an idiot – I've got a problem, I'm afraid. I need to check this out right away.'

'But what about Carrie?'

'We have each other's keys. If she arrives here, she can let herself in, and be annoyed about me for a change.'

'In that case,' Clarice declared, 'I'll come with you.'

'You don't need to do that,' he said. 'You have better things to do, surely.'

'Not many,' she replied. 'The bowling club afternoons can drag on well into the evening. And besides, as dear old Magnus used to say, I've started, so I'll finish.'

Twenty-Five

'Where are we going?' Alex asked her father as he drove along the coast road past the Seton Sands holiday complex. He was at the wheel of her car, having insisted on using it.

'You'll see,' he replied affably.

'Bloody man . . . You are so damned annoying when you go all mysterious on me. It's even more extreme this time, given that you wouldn't even tell Mario. Gimme a clue, go on.'

'Okay, if you insist. I'm taking you to a friend of mine, someone you've never met.'

'Someone you feel safe leaving me with, given that two guys may have tried to kill me last night?'

'One hundred per cent.'

'Then who the hell is he? What the hell is he? Is he ex-special forces? Is it that security service guy, Clyde Houseman? He was SBS, wasn't he?'

'Yes, he was, and no, it isn't. Ex-special forces guys are ten a penny; I could have hired a couple of them. The problem with that is that for all I know, the two guys who broke into your place were ex-special forces too.'

'If they were,' she countered, 'they didn't live up to their billing. Once I'd armed myself, they thought better of it and headed for the door.'

'Tactical withdrawal. The truly elite know when not to push their luck.' He smiled. 'That said, they didn't sound top drawer. Plus, special ops soldiers blow doors off their hinges; they don't pick locks as a rule.'

'So?' she persisted. 'This friend of yours, if he isn't one of them, what is he?'

'He's an academic,' Bob said.

She gasped. 'An aca-fucking-demic! If these fellows find out where I am and give it another try, what's he going to do? Set them an exam?'

'They will not break into his place. My friend is uniquely qualified. Do you think for a moment that I would entrust your safety to someone if I had the slightest doubt that he was up to the job?'

'No,' she conceded. 'I don't.'

'Then be patient.'

He drove on, past the empty ground where once Cockenzie Power Station had stood, then through Prestonpans, taking the roundabout marked by a pub called the Levenhall Arms, but still known as Mrs Forman's, then braking slightly as a red Citroën Cactus with a Toyota hybrid in close pursuit took their ground.

'Cool it, people,' Skinner whispered. 'If I was a traffic car, you'd be done.'

'Hey!' Alex exclaimed. 'I think that's Clarice's car, the Toyota. What's she doing here?'

'Whatever it is,' Bob said, 'I'm not chasing her to find out.'

He carried on, past the racecourse and then Loretto School. The convertible's hard top was down, and he began to regret not having put more sunscreen on the crown of his head, given the closeness of his recent haircut, but carried on regardless. Musselburgh became Joppa, Joppa became Portobello, and eventually, after the unsightly Seafield, Portobello became Leith.

He crossed the river, and took the first turn on the right.

Alex's forehead furrowed. 'Isn't this the place where Mario and Paula used to live?' she asked, looking upwards at a high-rise block.

'It is indeed. Same place, same duplex. It belonged to Paula's family, but they sold it when she and Mario moved to Cramond. It was bought by an investment trust. My friend is the tenant, officially, but he happens to own said investment trust. One of the attractions is that the place still has all the security that befits a deputy chief constable, just as I have in Gullane. The real benefit you will meet in a moment.'

He parked in a visitor space, led her into the building, and took the lift. There was only one apartment on the seventh floor, and its door was open, almost framing an enormous man, so big that he blocked out any light that might have been coming from within his home.

'Alexis,' Bob said, 'may I introduce your host, my friend Dr Dominic Jackson.'

Twenty-Six

'Was I seeing things, or did I nearly take my boss out?' Clarice Meadows asked herself aloud. A glance in her rearview confirmed her suspicions but told her also that it was Bob Skinner at the wheel, not Alex.

She had no time to dwell on the incident, for Peter McDaniels continued to regard the thirty m.p.h. speed limit as no more than advisory, and she had to work to stay on his tail. He led her back the way she had come, but instead of turning into the Dynamic Earth car park, he headed beyond it to another just short of the St Mary's Street junction. They were able to park side by side, the afternoon visitors having begun to head for home.

'That's where Carrie leaves hers,' he explained. 'She leases a space over there. Where she lives it's the easiest option, and she can offset some of it against tax.'

The walk was half the distance but every bit as steep; McDaniels was long-striding, and Clarice was out of breath by the time they reached their destination, wishing she had done the sensible thing and left him to it. 'Chances are this has all been in vain. She'll be sitting upstairs in her living room and young Barclay will have imagined the mystery intruders; probably had one too many after work.'

If that's the case, Clarice thought, *wouldn't he have seen her car in the car park?* But she said nothing, simply returning his smile.

Two minutes later, Peter's optimism had evaporated; he had rung his daughter's doorbell three times, without an answer. He reached for his keys.

The door had two locks, a night latch and a five-lever Chubb Mortice below. He slid in the Yale key first, and when he turned it, the door opened under the slightest pressure. 'She must be in the toilet,' he exclaimed hopefully. 'She never leaves the Chubb unlocked, not even for a quick trip to the shops.'

They stepped into the flat, into a narrow hallway. The bathroom faced them; its door was ajar, and the toilet was not in use. 'Carrie?' McDaniels called out, but the name echoed around the empty apartment. He went into the only bedroom, then the kitchen, and finally into the living room. Clarice waited in the hallway until he called to her.

'Come and see. She's had burglars.'

She followed him into the reception room. It was small, but there was an alcove – once a bed recess, she guessed – big enough to accommodate a bureau with a fold-down front, a chair and a filing cabinet, on top of which there sat a printer. The room was in a state of chaos. The lower drawer of the filing cabinet was open, as were the doors of the bureau. Papers were strewn over the floor, a chair lay on its side, the television had been turned through ninety degrees, and the drawer of the Blu-ray player was open.

'The bedroom and the kitchen are the same,' he said. 'The place has been gutted.'

'Has anything been stolen that you can see?' Clarice asked.

'Yeah. Her laptop. And her iPad. Bastards.' His face twisted and she saw a different side of Peter McDaniels. 'And that damn clown upstairs heard them and did nothing! Wait till . . .'

He turned and strode from the room, with Clarice following instinctively, out of the flat and up the stone stairs to the landing above, where he pounded on the blue door. 'Barclay!' he shouted. 'Are you in? It's Peter McDaniels, Carrie's father.'

'Haud on! Haud on!'

The cry came as the door was opened as far as its security chain would allow. 'Minute! Minute!'

The chain was freed; the young man stood there in boxer shorts and a green shirt. His hair was tied back, and for a moment, Clarice had a vision of Dylan, the *Magic Roundabout* rabbit. 'Mr McDaniels, where's the fuckin' fire?' he wailed.

'You might be the fire, son. Carrie's flat's been burgled, and from what I'm told, you heard them and did nothing.'

For a second, Barclay squared up to his visitor, then thought better of it. There might have been forty years in age between them, but it would still have been a mismatch. 'How was I tae ken?' he moaned lamely, looking at Clarice for support. 'It was the middle o' the fuckin' night.'

'Exactly!' McDaniels boomed. 'It was the middle of the night.' He paused. 'Let's go inside,' he said. 'There's no point in doing this in front of the neighbours.'

'Well naw, wait a minute,' Barclay protested, but he was brushed aside.

Clarice followed the two men. The layout of Barclay's flat was different from the one below. It was an attic flat; the ceilings were lower and the floor space was restricted, but when she counted the doors off the hall, she saw one more. The place smelled stale, as much in need of deodorant as its occupant.

He led them into the kitchen; the window was open, but for all the height of the building, most of the view was of the rear of another tall tenement in Jeffrey Street below. 'See? Ah wis just hingin' out, ken. It wis that fuckin' hot.'

'But you heard noises?'

'Aye.'

'What kind of noises?'

'Stuff gettin' moved aboot like.'

'And it never occurred to you as odd that Carrie might be moving the furniture at half past two in the morning?'

'Well mibbe, but—'

'Did you hear voices?'

Barclay frowned. 'I might've; no' words, but voices mibbe.'

'Male voices?'

'Mibbe.'

'But you never thought to check, or to phone the police?'

'Naw, Ah never did.'

'Because you didn't want to disturb your granny?' Clarice suggested.

He seized the question like a lifebelt, turning to look at her as she stood in the hall, just outside the kitchen, putting her exceptional sense of smell to work.

'Aye, aye, that's right,' he agreed. 'She's auld, ken; needs her sleep.'

'I hope we're not disturbing her now, with all the noise Peter was making. I'll just check on her, shall I?' She moved towards the only door in the hallway that was not slightly ajar.

'Naw, naw!' Barclay yelled. He made a sudden rush for her, trying to thrust Peter McDaniels aside but failing, and finding himself instead in the grip of two remarkably strong hands.

Clarice opened the door, and as she did so, the smell that she had separated from the rest of the funk in the apartment intensified, becoming distinctive, becoming something that she had encountered once before, as a much younger woman, visiting a farmer friend of her father who had been forced to put down an aggressive Rottweiler, and who had buried it not quite deep enough.

She stepped into the room. It was lit by a window in the sloping ceiling, propped half open for the constant ventilation that she realised was very much needed. The room was furnished: a dressing table, a wardrobe, a chest of drawers, a commode chair and a bed, made, and with something lying on top of its quilt, rather than beneath.

It could have been taken for an ordinary parcel, but for its shape, but for the fact that it was between five and six feet long, wrapped in discoloured sheets and bound tight with wide brown tape, and that it was, unquestionably, the source of the smell.

Clarice had been around Alex Skinner, and her father, for long enough to know to step back out of the room immediately and close the door. Barclay was still in the kitchen, still restrained in McDaniels' powerful grasp. His face had gone ashen, and he stared at the floor.

'What?' Peter whispered.

'Hold him,' she replied; then the fear in his face registered. 'It's not Carrie,' she added, 'for sure. I've got this, I'll deal with it.'

She closed the kitchen door and went into Barclay's living room, which was only marginally tidier than the one below.

She took out her phone, opened her contacts at the letter A, and made a call. It was answered almost immediately. In the background she could hear seagulls, normal when Alex was at Gullane.

'Clarice, have you run her to ground?'

'No, I haven't,' she replied. 'But I've found something else, and I'm going to need the police; not the bobby on the beat, you understand, but someone a little more senior and a little more specialist. And a pathologist, and a doctor; a psychiatrist, possibly. There's a situation, and dammit, I'm afraid I've come out without one of your business cards, for there's a young man here who most certainly needs you.'

Twenty-Seven

'This will be your room,' Alex's host said, opening its door. 'The previous owners used it as guest quarters, I believe. I've never used it for anything, but it's clean and the bedding is brand new, like everything else in the place. It's *en suite*, and there's a small fridge and a kettle, so you'll have complete privacy. We don't even need to see each other, if you don't want to. I'll fit a bolt on the inside of the door if it makes you feel more comfortable.'

She smiled, imagining how much use that would be against a man of his size. 'If my father thought I'd need a bolt on the bedroom door,' she chuckled, 'I wouldn't be here.'

He stood aside, allowing her to step into a large, well-lit bedroom, facing east. The curtains were drawn back; the building was taller than its neighbours, giving her a view of North Berwick Law, twenty miles away by crow-flight. 'This is beautiful,' she murmured, sincerely. 'You and I have at least one thing in common, Dominic. We both like high living. My place is a duplex too; my view is the Salisbury Crags.'

'Which makes it remarkable that you were burgled,' he remarked.

She looked up at him, unsmiling. 'They weren't burglars. I think we both know that.'

He nodded. 'Yes, your dad told me. Do the police know why you were targeted?'

'No, they still have to figure that out. The obvious place to start looking is my client list, but Sauce and I agreed that it's unlikely to lead anywhere. Without flattering myself, I've never had a dissatisfied client. I never tell them things I don't believe myself or make them promises that I have any doubt about keeping.'

'Sauce?' Jackson queried.

'Detective Inspector Harold Haddock, aka Sauce, because that's what we put on our fish and chips in this part of the world.'

'Ha, I should have guessed,' he laughed. 'Yes, I've heard of him; he's a rising star, they say, on a fast track that he's laid out for himself.'

'That's the boy. He is favoured, you're right, but only because he's exceptionally good at his job. Many another guy would be back in uniform, given his . . . domestic arrangements.'

'Those being?' he asked, intrigued.

'His partner is Cameron Davis, known as Cheeky. She's named after her grandfather, a man with a reputation.'

'But no convictions.'

'You know him?'

'No, but if I'm guessing right, I've heard of him. If Grandpa McCullough is everything they say, he's extremely clever, for he must have contracted that side of his business out. Everything you'll find his signature on is legitimate. His late sister Goldie, on the other hand, was a hoodlum, pure and simple.'

'You sound as if you knew her,' Alex suggested.

'I met her,' he admitted, 'a long time ago. She had a con-nection with somebody I knew.' He glanced through the window, towards North Berwick. 'Yes, a long time ago. So Sauce Haddock is Grandpa McCullough's son-in-law,' he mused.

'In a manner of speaking. And Cheeky's his heir.' She grinned. 'Which means, now that I think about it, that my half-brother Ignacio is Cheeky's step-uncle, his mum being married to Grandpa. I wonder if she and Sauce have figured that out. It's weird that our family should be intertwined with his.

'What do you think?' she asked suddenly. 'If you met Goldie, do you think Grandpa was really in charge of everything? The police did. My ex was deputy chief on Tayside and he spent a lot of time trying to nail him.'

'Mmm. The man who used to be Andy Martin,' Jackson remarked quietly. 'I think he was probably wasting his time. Cameron McCullough is a very successful businessman. He's also a very clever man, so why put everything at risk by getting involved in organised crime when he was making just as much money legitimately? Did he know about his sister? Undoubtedly, for everyone in Dundee did. Did he protect her? Probably. Did he restrain her from time to time? Possibly. Did he ever allow her to launder money through his businesses? Absolutely not.' He paused. 'Come on, let's go upstairs, out on the deck. It's too nice a day to be stuck in the house.'

Alex let him lead the way; the deck, as he described it, was slatted wood over the roof of the building, L-shaped, facing south and west, looking up towards the city of Edinburgh and its great landmark, the castle. She waited as he produced a second patio chair from a storeroom. 'You seem to know a hell of a lot about the activities of the McCullough family,' she ventured as he handed her a spritzer, taking a soft drink for himself. 'Is that your day job? Are you a journalist? Do you write investigative stuff for the *Saltire*? Is that how my father knows you?'

'No to all four questions. My day job? I'm a psychologist; that's what my doctorate's in. I teach at Heriot-Watt. My speciality is criminal behaviour.'

'You're a profiler?'

He smiled, faintly, almost shyly. 'I have been used as such.'

'By the police?'

'Not yet, but I'm working on it.'

'MI5?'

'No, they're more involved in prevention than detention, I think.'

'And the last question? How do you know my father so well?'

'We're former business associates, you might say.'

'You were a cop?' Alex exclaimed.

'No, I was a criminal. Bob put me away, for my own good as much as society's, he told me.'

She stared at him. 'He did? He never mentioned you, not to me, and yet he talked about his cases a lot. There was no point in him being discreet; most of them wound up in the papers, with his name attached. What did he lock you up for?'

'Murder. Three of them . . . although there was one I didn't do,' he added, watching as surprise and uncertainty registered on her face. 'I wasn't called Dominic Jackson then; that was the name on the fake passport I was using to escape when he caught up with me. I liked it, so I used it to register at the Open University and kept it when I was released. My birth name is Lennie Plenderleith.'

Alex gasped. 'You're Lennie Plenderleith? The Lennie Plenderleith? Of all my father's customers, as he calls them sometimes, you're the only one he speaks of with anything other than contempt.' She paused for a few seconds. 'In fact you're the only one he speaks of much at all. He's never mentioned Dominic Jackson, though.'

'I'm impressed by that; I assumed he told you and Sarah everything. I really am Dominic now. Lennie was a misguided twin brother who did things out of loyalty rather than pure malice . . . although he did have plenty of that. Did Bob ever tell you about someone named Tony Manson?'

'Yes, a while back; nowadays, very rarely. The man he never caught, he says.'

'Tony was the man Lennie worked for. He rescued him from a terrible family background – alcoholic parents, brutal older siblings – and took him under his wing. Tony wasn't a marginal case like Grandpa McCullough; he was organised crime, and Edinburgh was his. Bob left plenty of bruises on him, but he never put him away. Even so, he didn't lose too much sleep about it. Nothing was ever said, but there were lines drawn and Tony was smart enough to know not to cross them.'

Alex gazed at him. 'Are you saying that my father let a criminal go free?'

'No, I'm saying that Tony was very careful never to give him grounds to arrest him.'

'But Lennie gave him grounds, didn't he? More than once, from what he told me.'

Dominic gazed back. 'Yes, he did. Bob Skinner put Lennie Plenderleith away twice, the first time for assault. And you know who was behind that?'

'Tony Manson,' she replied. 'He told me that much, that he had an anonymous tip-off about potential trouble, though the voice wasn't very well disguised. But he didn't explain why Manson would do that.'

'He did it to protect me. Tony had an anonymous tip-off himself, that he was in someone's bad books. Lennie was a problem, though. By that time everyone was afraid of him, and so they should have been where Tony was concerned, because Tony was like a father to him. Therefore, before they came for him, Lennie would need to be removed.'

She whistled. 'You're saying that Tony Manson got you . . . sorry, Lennie locked up for his own good?'

'That's right.'

'And he died because of it?'

'Oh no, he took care of that threat by himself, through some hired help from London. Tony died because he became careless. He got in tow with a couple of con men, just before Lennie was due for release. One of them stabbed him to death; unfortunately for them, they didn't know about Lennie. It didn't work out too well for either of them, or for anyone else involved in that business.'

'Did that include Lennie's wife?' Alex asked tentatively. 'Dad said he pleaded guilty to her murder as well.'

'That's right, he did, but he didn't kill her.'

'So why the hell did his counsel let him admit to it?'

'Those were his instructions. There was some forensic evidence, enough to lay the charge. Lennie was already going away for two murders; a third wasn't going to make any difference. He pleaded to it because he was pretty certain that Tony Manson had done it, to stop Lennie finding out that he had been servicing her while Lennie was away.'

'Would Lennie have minded?'

Dominic sighed. 'That's the irony of it. That short spell in HMP Saughton was the great turning point in his life. In fact, it was the beginning of the end for him, and the birth of Dominic Jackson. It was the first opportunity he had ever been given to explore his own mind and to contemplate the reality of his sad existence. He came to see many things, and he realised that Tony Manson had stuck him in there for his own development as much as for protection, probably even more so. Tony could actually have told Lennie to go and kill his rival, and he would have, but I believe he knew that if he'd done that, he'd have been locking him into that life for ever. Would the newly evolved Dominic Jackson have gone Old Testament if he'd discovered that Tony had been having it off with Mrs Plenderleith? No, because he was leaving her behind too; that was his plan. He wouldn't have married her in the first place. Would Lennie have gone off on one if someone hadn't done for Tony already? I doubt it. He suspected it and he might have been disappointed in him, but a shouting match is as far as it would have gone.'

'I see,' she murmured. 'I'm still getting my head round the fact that my father knows all this, yet never mentioned a word about you to me, not until today, and that even then, he's left me to find it out for myself.'

'I must admit, I'm pretty impressed by that too, but here's how I see it. When your father caught up with me after Lennie killed those people – I'm making a distinction, because it was Dominic Jackson that he caught – Lennie had done everything he had to do; he'd ceased to exist. If Bob had been one minute later, I'd have been away, off to the other side of the world with my inheritance from Tony, and nobody would ever have found me. But he did turn up, on his own, ahead of the backup he'd called for, and he stopped me. He stopped me physically, something I thought nobody could ever do, not even that big bear McGuire. That earned my respect, and I believe that in the same way, I earned his; I was his biggest challenge and he came through it. What I didn't realise for a few years was that in stopping me, he gave me a chance at a proper life, one I wouldn't have had as an exile.

'The way I look at it now, Bob Skinner didn't just send me to prison, he sent me to university. It was a long course – twelve years – but I completed it, with his encouragement every step of the way, for he visited me at least every six months, and latterly more often. He asked me about my progress, but after a while he began to share stuff, too. His difficulties with Sarah, for example, he opened up about that. His thing with Aileen de Marco too; I told him, as a psychologist, that if he married her, he'd be back to me for counselling in a year, tops, and that's how it worked out. It cut both ways: once he asked me where I would live when I was released. I said I'd like to go back to Leith, but I never could, because that was where Lennie lived. He said that was bollocks, because as far as this place was concerned, he really was dead. He told me that after Tony died, he had cleaned up the entire city, and that anyone who might have cared about Lennie Plenderleith and what he might have done in the past was dead, in prison, or just plain gone. He even said that he knew of a place coming on the market that would be ideal for me.'

Alex laughed out loud. 'I might have known. Did he tell Mario and Paula who their buyer was?'

'Yes, he did, because he could see that he might be worried about a potential embarrassment, a red-top story about a senior police officer selling to a murderer. McGuire was okay with it, for his name never appeared on the title deeds. The property belonged to the Viareggio family trust, and now it belongs to mine, not to me. So here I am, back in Lennie's home town, a new man, an academic who just happens to be two metres tall but otherwise doesn't look or act at all like the man he used to be. And it's all down to your father, my friend.'

'Who trusts you enough to let you shelter his daughter,' she said. 'And I never knew. I thought that man had no secrets from me.'

'Everyone has secrets, Alex. Even you, I'll bet.'

She frowned. Yes, she had; a few things she had never told her father or anyone else, and never would. She was looking at the latest of them: she realised that she found Dominic Jackson intensely attractive, but knew in the same moment that she must say or do nothing about it, for the consequences could be explosive.

'How about Dominic?' she asked. 'Does he have any?'

'Not yet, it's too soon. But he will have, I'm sure.' He glanced at his watch. 'Are you hungry? I can knock something up.'

'Let me take you out, as a thank you. I'm not going to hide away from these bastards. I intend to go to work tomorrow, as usual. I have a full court diary this week.'

'Understood. I promised Bob I would take you there and pick you up. I don't know how he'll feel about us being seen in a restaurant, though.'

'I don't care how he'll feel. I won't be a prisoner; you of all people should understand that.'

'Yes, I do. Okay, if you want to cross the bridge, we can go to—'

He was interrupted by the opening bars of 'Baba O'Riley',

Alex's chosen ringtone. She looked at her screen. 'It's my PA,' she said. 'I must take this. She may have found my elusive investigator at last.' She put the phone to her ear. 'Clarice, have you run her to ground?'

Twenty-Eight

'You're telling me,' Sarah said, 'that for all these years, you've made the redemption of Lennie Plenderleith your personal project? The man nearly killed you.'

'Actually it was the other way round. I broke his arm and kicked him hard enough in the head to give him a severe concussion.'

'Then you charged him with three murders.'

'For which he has paid the debt to society that the court required and emerged a different man. He'll never be completely free, love. He's changed his name legally to Dominic Jackson but he's only released on licence, and he always will be. He'll have to comply with the conditions like anyone else. He has to meet regularly with his supervising person, for the first few years at least. He can apply for a passport, but its granting is discretionary. As it happens, he chooses not to, for now.'

'Who's his supervising person?'

'Who d'you think? Me.'

She laughed. 'Different class, man. But why? Of all those people, why this one?'

Their garden chairs faced each other; Bob looked across at

her. 'Because I saw myself in him; still do, always will. Lennie Plenderleith's background and mine were very similar: alcoholic mother, disinterested father, brutal older sibling, three of them in Lennie's case. The difference between us was our social circumstances. If they'd been reversed, I could have gone to work for Tony Manson and Lennie could have been chief fucking constable. If that had happened, I likc to think someone would have looked out for me, and so when he needed it, I looked out for him. I reached out to the prison service and let them know he was under my protection. I made sure that his applications for educational courses were processed quickly, and that he was given facilities to study. After a couple of years, the senior staff realised they were dealing with a very bright guy, and got with the project, so to speak.'

'What about the junior staff? Teacher's pet and all that. Didn't any of them give him a hard time?'

Bob smiled and shook his head. 'No, nor any other prisoners either. Let's just say that he had a certain magisterial authority, and nobody ever tested it. He was left alone, and he repaid his privileges by gaining an honours degree in psychology, and a doctorate, both from the OU, and finally a masters from Glasgow University, on day release. The governor of his last nick, Kilmarnock, actually used him professionally to help with a couple of problem prisoners.'

'You're proud of yourself, aren't you?' his wife said.

'I'm proud of him. And if any credit is due to me, yes, I'm proud of that.'

'Will I meet him?'

'I have no idea. There was a time when you were likely to have met him as a customer, but that's past. Socially we'll—'

He was interrupted by Sarah's mobile. 'Bugger,' she

muttered as she accepted the incoming call. 'Looks like work. Sauce, what can I do for you? I take it you're not looking for a four for bridge.'

'Sorry, Sarah, no,' Detective Inspector Harold Haddock replied. 'Are you available? I've got a situation in the city centre that needs the top pathologist.'

'Suspicious death?'

'Good question, one it'll take you to answer.'

'I've had one beer, so I won't drive, but my dear husband has been on the fizzy water; he can drive me.'

'Actually, I need to speak to him too. There's been a development on the situation with Alex. I might need to see her, and only he knows where she is.'

Twenty-Nine

'The lad's name is Barclay Potter, aged twenty-seven. He says that the body in the second bedroom is that of his grandmother, Mrs Alice McNeilly, aged eighty-seven, or whatever she was when she snuffed it. She was wrapped up tight in bedsheets, like Tutankhamun . . . a grandmummy, you might say. Barclay's not sure when she died. He swears that it was natural, that he didn't give her any help, but we'll need Sarah to confirm that, and to give us her best estimate of time of death. Whenever it was, he's been operating her bank account since then and using her pension to pay his bills. We'll do him for concealing a death, social security fraud, and murder if Sarah finds that the old lady didn't go naturally. He's a silly bastard; we've established already that he's her only living relative. The flat was the old lady's, unmortgaged, and even in its present state, that address is worth a tidy sum. He's her heir, whether she left a will or not.'

'Grandmummy,' Skinner growled. 'Who writes your scripts, Sauce? What else has the boy told you? And do you believe a word of it?'

'That's the thing, we do,' the DI replied. 'He's sticking to his story of hearing people moving around in the flat below – that's

182

another thing: he really does lean out the window when he smokes, because his granny won't allow it in the house.'

'The boy's in denial,' Dominic Jackson volunteered. 'He's made himself believe that she's simply asleep. He's going to need careful handling when reality bites; he'll be fragile. You should put him on suicide watch.'

'Thanks, we'll bear that in mind, Dr Jackson,' Haddock said. 'Would you like to be present when we interview him? I will need my arse well upholstered on this one. He hasn't got a lawyer yet, but a half-decent one will want assurances that he's mentally fit to be interviewed.'

'He has, Sauce,' Alex said. 'Got a lawyer, that is. Our Clarice is quick on her feet. I won't take it on, but he's agreed that Johanna DaCosta, my associate, will represent him. Clarice briefed her before the uniforms arrived. Where are you taking him? St Leonards?'

Haddock nodded. 'He's there now.'

'Don't interview him before she gets there. And yes, I agree that it would be wise to have Dominic present.' She turned to him. 'Are you up for that, Dr Jackson?'

The huge man smiled expansively; she felt a flutter run through her. 'My day gets better and better. Yes, I'll do it.'

'Thanks,' the young detective said. 'Your fee note will come to me, of course.'

'It should go to the city council social work department,' Skinner barked. 'An eighty-seven-year-old woman completely off the radar! Bloody ridiculous. But back to the intruders; you are certain it wasn't Potter himself.'

'Absolutely, gaffer.' Jackson raised an eyebrow at Haddock's use of the term. 'Carrie McDaniels' door was either opened with a key, which he didn't have, or it was expertly picked.

Barclay Potter couldn't pick his own nose unassisted. He heard them, and this is where it gets really worrying. It happened just before three o'clock, half an hour before you were attacked, Alex, and Inspector Montell was wounded.' Jackson raised another eyebrow. 'That's easily enough time to get from her place to yours.'

'Worrying on several levels,' Skinner observed. 'We know these guys were capable of getting into Alex's place without a key, but I doubt they needed one at Carrie's. What was taken, Sauce, that you know of?'

'Her computer and her iPad. Also her files were trashed; if they were looking for something there, it'll have gone too.'

'Agreed. Thing is, they went there specifically for those items. They knew where Carrie lived, and like I said, you can bet they had a key . . . that they got from her. Next thing they did was go down the hill possibly with the intention of silencing Alex.' He looked at Haddock. 'Carrie's been missing for twenty-four hours. She's either being held captive somewhere . . . or she's not.' He turned to his daughter. 'Kid, your brief from David Brass has become extremely fucking toxic.'

'David Brass?' Haddock repeated.

'We'll get to that,' his 'Gaffer' told him, 'but there's something else that you don't know, not you, Alex, something I wasn't planning to tell you just yet. Marcia Brown, the woman at the centre of the investigation Carrie was working on: she didn't kill herself; she was murdered.' He explained how Graham Scott's review of the autopsy file had uncovered basic errors and crucial findings that would have ruled out suicide had the negligent pathologist spotted them at the time. 'I've reported it to Mario McGuire; DCI Lottie Mann will open a full-scale murder investigation tomorrow, once I've briefed her.'

The DI grinned. 'Let me guess. You'll be along as an adviser.'

Skinner peered at him. 'The word is mentor, Sauce, but you get the picture.'

'Fine, but doesn't the Carrie McDaniels situation overlap with that, if she was investigating the Brown woman's death?'

'She wasn't,' Alex said. 'She was looking into an accusation of shoplifting that had been made against Ms Brown just before she killed herself . . . or didn't, as it now appears.'

'Investigating on your behalf?'

'Yes, I was instructed by Mr Brass. He's obsessed by it, as was his son.'

'Had she reported back to you before she went off the radar?'

'She was going to. She wanted a short-notice meeting at my office, five thirty on Saturday, but I didn't get her voice message until well after that, so I didn't turn up.'

'Do you know if she did?' Haddock asked.

She frowned. 'No, I don't.'

'It's important that we find out. What time did she leave her message? Do you know?'

'Two something, as I recall. I can check; I didn't delete it.'

The DI looked across at a woman who had been standing silently against Dominic Jackson's living room wall. 'Noele, we need to check with security at the *Saltire* building where Ms Skinner has her office to determine whether Ms McDaniels arrived for the meeting she'd requested. If she did, the search for her begins in Edinburgh. If not, we know that she disappeared sometime after leaving her voicemail.'

'On it, boss,' Detective Sergeant Noele McClair replied,

her ice-blue eyes flashing as she nodded. They had won her the nickname 'the Night Queen' among her Serious Crimes colleagues. 'Should we issue an appeal for sightings?'

'Soonest,' he agreed. 'We'll need a photograph; you can get that from her father, and while you're at it, ask him if he has any idea of his daughter's movements over the last week. Her laptop's gone, her iPad's gone, and she's gone. We need to know where she's been and who she's been speaking to. Somewhere she's tripped a wire.'

'Those names should all be in the file,' Skinner said, looking at his daughter.

'What file?' Haddock's eyes narrowed.

'The file David Brass gave me,' Alex explained.

'And where's that?'

'In my office.'

'When were you there last?'

'Friday. I see where you're going,' she said, 'but the building's secure, and it's a newspaper office so there are always people around. They couldn't have got in there.'

He sighed. 'Alex, these guys broke into your penthouse apartment in a secure building with multiple occupants, and you never heard a thing until it was nearly too late. They could have got anywhere they bloody well liked. At the very least, it has to be checked.' He turned back to the DS. 'Noele, make that your first priority, before you call on Mr McDaniels. Gaffer,' he said to Skinner, 'this has to be a single investigation, hasn't it? Carrie's disappearance, the break-in at her flat, the attack on Alex, and Marcia Brown's death.'

'That'll be the DCC's decision, Sauce,' he replied, 'but I'll be advising him to keep them separate until they come together. Apart from the geography, one crime in Ayrshire and the others in Edinburgh, Marcia Brown died nine years ago. The likelihood is we're looking for different perpetrators, and the motivation might be completely unrelated. One thing's for sure, though: while Noele sets about her tasks, we need to interrupt big Mario's weekend, again.'

Haddock threw him a questioning look. 'We?' He sighed. 'Aye, okay.'

Thirty

'This is serious, Sergeant, isn't it?'

'I'm afraid it is, Mr McDaniels,' Noele McClair affirmed. 'We've established that your daughter didn't show up at Saltire House for the meeting she herself had requested only three hours earlier. When DI Haddock and I saw you earlier at her flat, you told us that she was going to Newcastle on Saturday night for a concert. We've checked with the Sage, the venue; they've established that the seat she bought was never occupied. They'd have the ticket stub, and they don't.'

'How do they know which seat was hers?' As reality began to bite, Peter McDaniels seemed to be ageing before her eyes.

'They have a record of credit card purchases. More than that, though, we checked with the Malmaison. She didn't take up her booking.'

'In that case,' he said, 'something really is wrong. Our Carrie's careful with her money; she wouldn't miss something that was bought and paid for without a bloody good reason.' He frowned. 'Or a bloody bad one. Is there anything you can tell me?'

'Nothing positive. We're fairly certain that the intruders Barclay heard in your daughter's apartment were the same two men who broke into Alex Skinner's duplex a wee while later.'

'Eh? Was anything stolen from there?'

'No.' McClair decided to economise with the truth of what had happened. 'They were disturbed, but they were able to escape.'

'You're saying the same two guys ransacked Carrie's and Alex Skinner's place. How did they know to go there? Is there a source inside her office?'

'No, there isn't. The thing is . . .' She faltered, but McDaniels could see where she was headed.

'The two guys knew,' he continued, 'because they got it out of Carrie; her keys, the Skinner woman's address, and they went looking for everything that recorded her investigation.'

'That's what we believe.' McClair sighed. 'They even got into Saltire House and stole a file from Alex's office. She has CCTV and they were caught on camera, but they weren't bothered; they wore balaclavas, and they knew exactly what they were looking for and where to find it.'

'Does she not have an alarm system?'

'She does, and they were able to disable it. These men have considerable skill, or one of them has.'

'What have they done with Carrie?' McDaniels was on the edge of panic.

'We don't know. Our hope is that once they'd got everything they needed from her, they tied her up and left her somewhere she wouldn't be found for a while.'

'You'd better get out and look for her then!'

'That's partly why I'm here, Mr McDaniels. We want to make a public appeal for sightings, and for that we need a photo. Can you help?'

'Sure,' he replied, 'I've got loads on my phone. Give me your number and I'll send you one.'

She did as he asked. Within a matter of seconds, an image of a smiling, forceful woman appeared on her screen. At once she forwarded it to Haddock with a covering message.

'Do you want me to go on TV to make an appeal?' McDaniels asked. 'I'm up for it if you do. I won't be breaking down like most of those poor folk do. I won't be begging these bastards to let her go, I'll tell you. I'll be warning them what'll happen if they don't. I'm still in touch with a few of Carrie's friends from her days in the Territorial Army. A couple of them are regular soldiers now. They'd weigh in right away.'

'I don't think we're there yet, sir,' McClair murmured. 'Let's just start with an appeal for sightings, of Carrie or her car. Chances are she'll be found within the first twenty-four hours.'

'Could you not find her through her phone? Get a fix on that?'

'First thing we tried,' the DS replied. 'It doesn't exist any more. The SIM card's been destroyed, and the phone itself too most likely. The intruders were after all her IT equipment, anywhere she could have stored interview notes and other material about the investigation. We're hoping that anything there is will be backed up to the Cloud and we'll be able to access it.'

'You won't get much,' he said gloomily. 'Carrie's got a thing about Cloud storage. She doesn't trust its security; she backs up all of her work stuff on an external hard drive. Any chance they left that at her flat?'

'I'll check, but given their general efficiency, I doubt it.'

'What about her notebook?' he asked. 'She writes things down, then transcribes them afterwards. Everybody thinks IT these days, mini recorders and the like. Carrie reckons that if you go to interview someone and put a recorder in front of them, you might as well not bother. She thinks it's rude and counter-productive, so every meeting she has, she takes notes. These men wouldn't know that. I'm telling you, find her notebook.'

'They've got everything else, Mr McDaniels,' McClair pointed out.

'She might have locked it in the glove box of her car,' he persisted.

'We'll look when we find it,' she promised. 'First, can I ask you, has she said anything to you about what she was doing over the last few days?'

'Carrie doesn't break client confidentiality with anyone, not even me. I understand that; I didn't in my job either.' He frowned. 'The closest she's come . . .' He hesitated, searching his memory. 'Last time we spoke, she said that the job she was on was letting her see new parts of Scotland, places she'd never been to.'

'Such as?'

'Motherwell, that was one. Ayrshire, another. And Millport; she'd always wanted to go to Millport but never got round to it. She'd to go and see somebody there.'

'She didn't say who?'

'Oh no, she'd never do that.'

'Never mind, it's not a big place; my ex and I used to go there often. Anywhere else?'

'Mmm . . . yes, there was Dundee, that she mentioned. She's going there tomorrow.'

'She's never been to Dundee?'

'Oh yes,' McDaniels chuckled, 'often enough. But she told me she's never been to a radio station, so that'd be a first.'

Thirty-One

'What did Mario say?' Sarah asked.

'Not just Mario,' her husband replied. 'He consulted with the chief constable, and Maggie agreed that the two investigations should be conducted separately, with him as co-ordinator. Also, she approved my involvement in the inquiry into the death of Marcia Brown. She was a bit miffed that she hadn't been asked before, but she thought it was advisable to have outside oversight, given all the possibilities.'

'What did she mean by that?'

'Corruption, mainly. Was it negligence by Banks the pathologist, pure and simple, or was he bribed or otherwise induced to submit his shoddy report? Was there involvement by the police officers at the scene? According to the police report in the file Graham and I reviewed, there was no proper forensic examination carried out there; the woman was zipped straight into a body bag and sent to the mortuary, to be opened up the next day.'

'You won't get anything out of Banks, I can tell you that.'

'I don't expect to; my assumption is that he'll have a complete memory lapse.'

'He suffered that two years ago. He spent most of his time in a place he had in Dubrovnik; he had a cerebral haemorrhage while he was out there. I saw his obituary in a professional journal.'

'Damn the man!' Bob growled. 'Useless then, and just as useless now. Do you know a pathologist called Marguerite Swanson?'

'I know of her, but we've never met. She spent some time with my predecessor, Joe Hutchinson, in Edinburgh as an assistant. I was away in the US at the time. When I came back, she had moved on, to Birmingham, I believe. I can track her down if you need her, no problem.'

'Graham's already found her. He spoke to her about her role in the autopsy, which was minimal, as the examination itself seems to have been. She may need to be interviewed formally for the police investigation. If she's in Birmingham, maybe we can do it by video link.'

'We?' Sarah queried.

He laughed. 'Funny, Sauce said the same thing, in the same tone of voice.'

'They're dragging you back in, you know, Maggie and Mario, as they've always wanted to. She can call it . . . what was it? . . . "outside oversight", but you'll put just as much into it as you do with every investigation. And you'll be running the operation.'

'They won't drag me any further than I want to be dragged,' Bob promised. 'As for running the show, I will make damn sure that Lottie Mann thinks she is.'

'And that Sauce thinks the same with the Edinburgh investigation?' she challenged.

'He is,' Bob protested.

'Sure he is. An investigation into an attack on your daughter and you're going to keep your hands off it. Play me another tune, big boy.'

He sniffed. 'I admit that some co-ordination between the two investigations may be necessary, beyond that of the DCC. Because,' he added, 'I want to be within reach of these guys when they catch them.'

'It's more than just Alex, though, isn't it? You know Carrie McDaniels. That appeal we've just seen on the news: is there a realistic chance of finding her?'

He looked her in the eye. 'Since I first heard about Alex's break-in, I've been trying to make myself believe that they went there to throw a scare into her, no more than that. She's high profile as an advocate, and those blokes would possibly be aware that she's my daughter; any physical harm done to her would have drawn all sorts of heat. Yes, I put her with Dominic for her safety, but I don't think they'll go near her again. Carrie? She's an unknown, one of life's foot soldiers, literally in her case, even if she was only part-time. Safer to kill her than leave her alive.'

Sarah shuddered.

'Either way, love, you ask will we find her? Not if these guys are as thorough at their job as they've shown until now.'

Thirty-Two

After the visit from Skinner and the police, Alex and her host were left with no inclination to eat out. Instead she examined the contents of the fridge, and announced that she could 'throw something together'.

'Please do,' Jackson said. 'I can't remember the last time someone cooked for me in my own home. Come to think of it, I'm not sure anyone ever did. The late Mrs Plenderleith, poor lass, didn't know a soufflé from a suffragette. We never ate anything that didn't come out of a box.'

'Don't build your hopes up,' she warned. 'I didn't have a mother to teach me, and I've never done a cookery course. Everything I know in the kitchen came from my old man. And you know what they say about blokes' cooking: they call it goulash, they call it stroganoff, they call it Sloppy Joe, but at the end of the day it's all bloody stew.'

Alex's 'stew' was in fact a crisp salad of Chinese leaves, endives, tomato, sliced yellow pepper and chopped chives, crowned by smoked salmon and tiger prawns. In her perusal of the fridge she had seen no wine, only soft drinks and two cans of the spritzer he had given her earlier. 'You don't drink?' she asked as she worked in the kitchen with him looking on.

'No, I don't. I went for nearly fifteen years without, no choice, but Lennie never did drink much, so it was easy for Dominic to become a teetotaller.' He smiled. 'That's a damn silly word. Do you ever wonder where it came from?'

'Not for one second,' she replied cheerfully, 'but I have a feeling I'm about to learn.'

'One version anyway; it's attributed to a man named Turner, a crusader against the demon drink who was forever going on about total abstinence. Unfortunately, he had a speech defect and it came out as "tee-tee-tee-total". That's what Google says. I assume you're not one of those; I can go pick up a bottle of something if you like.'

'No, I'm fine. Our family aren't big drinkers either; I can live without. Our family,' she repeated, smiling. 'Half of it are too young to drink. Do you know, I am over thirty years older than my youngest sister? She was a surprise, they said. At their age you'd think they'd know what caused it. Mind you, my dad has previous; as witness my half-brother Ignacio.'

'I remember his mother,' Dominic said as he took the laden plate she handed him and carried it through to the dining table. 'She was the big name on Edinburgh local radio at the time. Tony Manson knew her, sort of, but I never met her. She was under the protection of a man called Perry Holmes, who had a particularly crazy brother. I'd have liked to have had a couple of counselling sessions with him, but Mia's uncle, Billy Spreckley, denied me the chance.'

'Those are names from my youth,' Alex said. 'Dad told me about them, but I'm sure he toned down some of the stories.'

'He'd need to.'

'I did meet Mia back then. Dad brought her to the house, in

Gullane; I was star-struck like the rest of them, but even I could see she was making a pitch for him.'

'Did you approve?'

'Not really. He had a very nice girlfriend at the time called Alison Higgins; I liked her. Unlike the rest of Edinburgh, I wasn't too upset when Mia vanished from the airwaves.'

'I'm told she's surfing them again.'

She paused for a forkful of salad. 'That's right. When she and Ignacio came back from Spain, and Dad and I learned that he had another son and me another brother, she got a job on a station in Dundee. Mia being Mia, she married the owner and wound up very solidly on her feet. Grandpa McCullough, he's omnipresent. The place where the Marcia Brown affair kicked off, a low-end supermarket in Kilmarnock called LuxuMarket, he was the majority shareholder until he was bought out.'

'Is that so?' Dominic murmured, then turned and pointed at an expensively framed landscape positioned on the wall so that no natural light would reach it. 'See that?'

'Yes, I've been admiring it. Who painted it?' she asked.

'I did. It's Loudon Hill, in Ayrshire, where Robert the Bruce gave the English their first good kicking. For quite a few years that was the view from my window in HMP Kilmarnock. Towards the end of my sentence, when I was doing my masters on day release, I went past the site where LuxuMarket had been, on my way to the station.'

'Does that mean you were there when the Brown incident happened?'

'Yes. I wasn't playing a major role in community matters at the time, you understand, but I do remember it being a one-week wonder in the local paper. The woman's name was splashed all over the front page. It said "allegedly" in small print, but the story went to town on her. Two weeks later, there was a small piece on page three reporting her sudden death.'

'God,' she gasped. 'You were almost a witness to the events.'

'Hardly,' he laughed, 'given my circumstances at the time, but I did know a lie when I saw one.'

'You think it was a stitch-up?' Alex asked eagerly.

'I was sure it wasn't. I devoured the local paper, and Councillor Marcia Brown was all over it, always on the attack. Her targets were the Labour Party and its leaders, and she never let up. Editorially the paper was always on the side of the West Coast Council, but Councillor Brown was good copy and they reported her, even though they always put her down. Balance was not a concept the editor seemed to grasp.'

'What made you think the shoplifting allegation was correct?'

'First, its timing. Second, the paper printed a photograph of the clothes she was accused of stealing; not the actual items, a store photo of the range. Marcia Brown herself was pictured in that paper almost every week; in most of the shots she was dressed differently from the week before. She'd never have worn clothing like that, Alex. She was a sweatshirt and denim woman. My theory at the time was that she stole that stuff to give herself a defence in a trial.'

Alex frowned. 'A couple of sizes too small,' she murmured. 'The suit was too small for her; that would have been part of her defence.'

'See? If you want confirmation of the way she dressed, ask her ex-husband. You can call him once we've eaten.'

She nodded. 'I should anyway. He may well have seen the appeal on the TV news, but he has no way of knowing that Carrie McDaniels was working indirectly for him.'

'Oh.'

She looked at him, noting his furrowed brow. 'What is it?'

'Tell me about Carrie,' he said. 'What sort of a woman is she? What's her background?'

'Mmm. Strong-willed, forceful, maybe a wee bit reckless; courageous, plain-spoken. She was a claims investigator for an insurance company, and also a weekend warrior. No, that's an inadequate description; what she did took her away for longer stints than that. She was in the Territorial Army military police and went to some dangerous places. Eventually she chucked the insurance company and the TA and set up on her own as a private investigator. The insurers still use her, and several lawyers.'

'All of that means she wouldn't have been an easy target, wherever she was taken,' he surmised. 'And yet she was taken, without fuss, without any reports to the police of a disturbance.'

'By the same people who broke into my place?'

'A fair assumption, but whether it was them or someone else, the people you met acted on information extracted from her. I can only hope for her sake that she didn't hold out too long. From what you've told me, she's a brave woman, but I didn't like the reckless part. I hope she had enough common sense to know that everyone has a breaking point, so there's no sense in taking too much pain.'

'But you doubt it?' Alex asked softly.

'I don't know her, but I fear for her. I fear for your client too, just a little. The balaclava boys got everything else out of Carrie, whatever it took; let's hope they weren't after his name as well.'

Thirty-Three

'Mr Brass is okay?' Haddock asked. 'You're sure of that?'

'As of half an hour ago,' Noele McClair assured him. 'I had a Kelso patrol car call on him to check. They told him there were bogus meter readers in the area and said he should call the police if he has any suspicious callers. I've asked them to keep an eye on the house at regular intervals.'

'Fair enough. It's a wise precaution, but no more than that. Even if these guys do have the report he gave Alex, there's no reason for his name to be on it. He and Marcia Brown had been divorced for a few years when she died.' The DI glanced at the clock in the CID suite and sighed. 'I reckon we're all clear to go home now.'

His sergeant grinned back at him. 'Are you not going to report in to Sir Robert first?'

'If I told you to fuck off, would you report me for workplace harassment?' he growled. Then he returned her smile. 'Actually, I will. The gaffer likes the old boy. He met him during the investigation into his son's death.'

'It's a bit ironic that the mother should turn out to have been murdered as well.'

'These things run in families; look at Mia McCullough –

Mia Sparkles as she still calls herself on the radio. Her lot was pretty much wiped out, so I was told by the Big Man. I tell you, his kids must have some bedtime stories.'

'I'll bear that in mind next time my Vicky has a sleepover with Seonaid,' McClair said. 'Talking of Mia Sparkles, I did some digging into radio stations in Dundee, and apart from a BBC presence, hers is the only one. I had a look at its website and its Facebook page. All the presenters are listed – Mia gets top billing, naturally – but there's only one other name: the station manager, Hazel Delaney. There's no biography on either site, but I did a search on LinkedIn and she showed up. There isn't a lot on her CV, but her last job before she went to the station did jump out at me: general manager, LuxuMarket, Kilmarnock. I think we can assume she's who Carrie McDaniels was supposed to be meeting tomorrow.'

'Maybe Carrie will turn up,' Haddock suggested. 'In this job, nothing's impossible. But if she doesn't, we will. Dundee can be our second visit tomorrow. First we need to go to Kelso. Alex told us she didn't read the file that Mr Brass gave her; she passed it straight on to Carrie. But he'll have read it; he's had it for nine years, so he probably knows it off by heart. Maybe he kept a copy. At the moment, he's the key to reconstructing Carrie's movements since she began her investigation.'

Thirty-Four

'What's Sir Robert like?' Detective Sergeant John Cotter looked up at his boss, who was at least four inches taller than he was. 'Old school?' The accent was English, from somewhere north of Teesside.

'There's a bit of that in him,' DCI Lottie Mann admitted, 'but not much. He's very much a twenty-first-century cop, rather than a holdover from the last one. Whatever school he is, he's the headmaster. I will never forget the first time I met him. It was a major crime scene in Glasgow, a shooting; I arrived to find the victim, my chief constable, with her brains on the floor and this big guy apparently in command. I didn't know him from Adam, so I told him to get his fucking arse out of there along with the rest of the civilians. He was chief constable through in Edinburgh then, but what I didn't know was that he'd just been put in temporary charge of Strathclyde by the First Minister and the police authority chair. I maybe had more sharp corners then than I do now; it could have been my arse getting out of there, but he was good about the misunderstanding.'

'The story in Aberdeen is that he went off in a huff because he was passed over for the top job in the new force.'

'They know fuck all in Aberdeen,' she retorted. 'He never wanted the job. In fact he opposed police service unification as loudly as he could, but it went through in spite of him, because the politicians reckoned it would save money. Maybe it has, but it doesn't make folk sleep easier in their beds – far from it, in some areas.'

'It doesn't bother me,' the DS said.

'And where do you live, son?'

The two detectives turned at the sound of the calm, even voice that came from the open doorway behind them. Mann smiled; Cotter gulped. 'The Merchant City, sir,' he replied.

'Right in the middle of Glasgow. Of course you feel safe and sound, with blue lights flashing outside your window all night. As a plus, you can walk a couple of hundred yards to your bank or your post office as well. I live in a rural community; we don't have a bank any more, the post office operates two hours a week, the butcher's closed, the baker has become a coffee shop as well, and as for the candlestick maker, he's absolutely shitting himself. Villages like mine feel like they're being abandoned, so taking away a sense of ownership of their policing couldn't have happened at a worse time. Most of your senior officers would agree with that, privately. Hi, Lottie,' he continued, seamlessly. 'How are you doing? Congrats on the promotion; I haven't seen you since it was announced. And how's your evil twin enjoying retirement?' He glanced at Cotter. 'As for you, Sergeant, why are you "sir-ing" me when we haven't been introduced?'

'Don't mind John,' Mann laughed. 'He's just naturally polite. I'm good, thanks; getting used to the rank and the extra money. Dan's fine too. He's loving it at Jackton, although he doesn't admit it. Now, Sir Robert, why the hell are you here?

Did you just fancy a visit to the Clyde Gateway? Surely not; it's grand, but not that grand.'

'Agreed. I prefer my police stations old and ugly, like Pitt Street in Glasgow, or Fettes through in Edinburgh. But I'm not sightseeing; I'm here with the approval of the top brass to brief you on a case that didn't even qualify as cold two days ago but is now very warm indeed.'

'It wouldn't have anything to do with the missing person appeal I heard on the radio this morning, would it, Sir Robert?'

Skinner stared at the little DS. 'Why should you think that?'

'I don't know really,' Cotter admitted. 'Probably only because it's a hot story. The press haven't dug into it yet, maybe because yesterday was a Sunday and the appeal was made late in the day, but I did a search for the name, and she showed up as a licensed private investigator. She disappeared on Saturday; you said that your case is only a couple of days old, so . . .' His voice tailed off under the gaze of his two seniors.

'Do you smoke cigars, DS Cotter?' Skinner asked.

'No, sir. Why?'

'Because you wouldn't be getting one for that, but you are close. Come on, let's all sit down and I'll fill you in.'

Mann nodded, directing them to her small conference table. 'Anyone want coffee?' she enquired. Skinner frowned back at her. She nodded. 'Of course you do. It's a machine,' she warned, 'and it's crap.'

'As long as that isn't literally true, it'll be okay.'

She exited, leaving the two men together. 'Transport cops, eh,' Skinner murmured. 'A strange career choice for an honours graduate.'

'So I discovered,' Cotter confessed. 'The recruitment people said it would let me see the country. I'm from North Shields, so that appealed to me. As it turned out, I got to see Aberdeen and points north of that, wherever the railways went. I'd been thinking about London, Birmingham, Bristol, maybe, even Edinburgh. With my degree, it let me make sergeant earlier than it might have, but the future was long and boring. I did think of a transfer, but my inspector told me that the national police service looked down on transport cops.'

'He was right, truth be told.'

'So I discovered, but when the talk of a merger happened, I took that as a change of attitude and applied for a move. They took me on, and here I am, posted to Serious Crimes and DCI Mann.'

'A whole string of bad luck,' she said as she returned with three plastic cups in a cardboard container.

'Cheers, Lottie,' Skinner said as he accepted his. 'Could have been worse. At least Provan was gone by the time he arrived. Nobody to lead him into bad ways. I am joking, John,' he added. 'Dan Provan was, not to put too fine a point on it, a fucking legend in Glasgow. Not a dark corner unexplored, not a rule unbent, but an absolute cop's cop. He'd have made the Carrie McDaniels connection, and he'll be impressed that you did when DCI Mann tells him over the *petits fours*. Carrie,' he continued, his face darkening, 'is known to me; I like her, but I fear for her.'

'She hasn't simply run away from a personal problem?'

He shook his head. 'No, Lottie, I'm afraid not. Carrie doesn't run. She's been taken, and I'm not optimistic about her turning up. But,' he added firmly, 'she is not why I'm here; not directly at any rate. She was working on an investigation, under instruction from a solicitor advocate, in turn on behalf of a client. Her brief was to investigate the circumstances of a shoplifting allegation made nine years ago against an Ayrshire councillor, Ms Marcia Brown. The case never came to court, because Ms Brown was found dead the night before she was due at a pleading diet. On the basis of a very firm report by the pathologist who carried out the post-mortem, the procurator fiscal determined, without the need for an inquiry before a jury, that she had taken her own life. He was perfectly entitled to do that, but what he didn't know was that the autopsy was flawed to say the least.'

'How did this come to light?' Mann asked.

'I got curious.'

'That tells me who the solicitor advocate is,' she said.

'I'm sure it does, but that isn't relevant. I know her client; in fact I sent him to her, as the case had been festering with him for years. It was toxic; indirectly, it cost him his son. When I looked at it, and considered the reported facts, I didn't buy that a person who had declared forcefully an intention to plead not guilty would take her own life the night before she had an opportunity to do that. At my request, Professor Graham Scott – whom you know, DCI Mann – dug the PM report out of the archives and examined it, word for word, line by line, photograph by photograph. He realised very quickly that its conclusion was one hundred per cent wrong, and that there's no way Marcia Brown killed herself.'

'The original pathologist, sir,' Cotter exclaimed. 'Was he plain incompetent, or could he have been corrupt?'

'A Provan-esque question, young man,' Skinner laughed. 'It's one that's going to be hard to answer, for the man in question went to Jesus a while back, but you can try. If you succeed, that's the point at which this investigation may overlap with the other, which is now tied into the disappearance of

Carrie McDaniels, and which is being conducted by a separate team based in Edinburgh.'

'Who's in charge?' Mann asked,

'Sauce.'

She nodded. 'Good.'

'You don't talk to him, though, not until you're told to. This investigation will be free-standing, and discreet.'

'Where do you suggest we begin?'

'The first thing you do, Lottie, is take a detailed statement from Professor Scott. The second is to find out everything you can about the victim. All I know is what I've been told by her ex-husband. You need more information, and if you can get it, a different perspective. Then you look at the officers who attended the initial suspicious death report. You're going to want to give them a hard time; you'll want to know why the fuck they didn't call in a forensic team, rather than jumping to their own conclusions and packing the victim straight off to the morgue.'

'Are they still on the force, sir?'

'I can only tell you about one, John, and he isn't. The only police name on the report is Detective Sergeant, later Detective Inspector, Terry Coats. He left the service under a small cloud two or three years ago, and he's now in security at Edinburgh Airport. You should be aware that his estranged, soon to be ex-wife, is a DS on Sauce Haddock's team. She doesn't know about Coats' involvement in this thing, and doesn't need to know, for now. That's it,' he declared. 'Questions?'

'Just one,' the DCI replied. 'What's your role?'

He smiled. 'The buzz word at headquarters is "mentor". I have a warrant card, that of a special constable, which means that I can do anything the chief constable or her deputy tells me to do, at any level. But this is your inquiry, Lottie. You don't report to me, formally; you simply tell me what's happening, and seek my advice, but not my instructions, when necessary. I'll decide when it's time to go to the DCC, and when to share information with, or seek it from, Sauce Haddock's investigation.'

'Are you involved in that in the same way?'

'No, but I have a personal interest in one aspect, so I'm not taking my fucking eyes off it. Is all that okay?'

'Do I have a choice?' Mann asked.

'Yes. If you feel strongly enough to complain to Maggie Rose, go ahead.'

'Bollocks to that. I like being a DCI. Will you need a room?'

Skinner shook his head. 'No, that would beg questions. If I need to, I'll bunk up with young John here. I've got lots of stories to tell him about the world beyond Thomas the Tank Engine.'

Thirty-Five

'That's appalling,' David Brass exclaimed. 'The woman is working on my ex-wife's case, you say. Surely her being missing can't be connected to that.'

'We have very strong evidence that it is,' Sauce Haddock assured him.

'If you say so. I'm sorry to be so ill-informed. I don't watch much television news these days,' he explained. 'I don't really keep up with current affairs at all. Like most of the country, I'm sickened by all that Brexit nonsense. Bloody parliamentarians! They had their orders, so why all the fuss about carrying them out? I never prevaricated in my job. If a tooth had to come out, out it came. All that apart, I don't see how I can help you; I've never met the lady, even though you say she was working on my business.'

'That's not why we're here,' Noele McClair said. 'It isn't only Ms McDaniels who's missing. Early yesterday morning, there was a break-in at your lawyer's office, and the file you gave Ms Skinner was stolen. The same night, Carrie McDaniels' home was burgled and all her computer equipment was taken. Given the fact that your ex-wife's case never made it to court, there's no other record of the investigation. In trying to piece together her movements last week, we're working in the dark. By any chance, did you copy the papers you gave to Alex Skinner?'

Brass sighed. 'No, I'm afraid not.' He ran his fingers through his sparse hair. 'What have I started?' he murmured. 'What you seem to be telling me is that if I'd let Marcia rest in peace, this woman wouldn't be missing.'

'We're not saying that at all, sir,' Haddock assured him. 'If you believe your wife was wrongfully accused, it was your right to look into it.'

'It's good of you to say so, but the real truth, I'm ashamed to say, is that I personally didn't give a damn. When we were married, Marcia was always a pain in the backside with her crusading politics. The cause of the month was always more important than me and our son. She divorced me because I had relationships elsewhere, and I was happy to let her. When the LuxuMarket business blew up, and she died, I was sorry, angry even, but not exactly overcome with grief. Austin was, though. He inherited his mother's obsessive gene, and he refused to accept the official version. He made a huge fuss about it, accused the police of conspiring with Marcia's enemies on the council, accused the store owner, accused everybody. He only stopped when he had a visit from the LuxuMarket owner. I wasn't present and Austin never told me exactly what had happened, but he was pretty chastened afterwards. All he would say was that there had been a threat of legal consequences. It didn't stop him, though; he took a step back from Marcia's case and started his blog, Brass Rubbings, uncovering and publicising other miscarriages of justice, police misconduct and misuse of public office. And look where that got him, eventually. He died, like his mother . . . thanks to his mother, damn her! That was when I dug out the file on Marcia and decided to have one last try at finding the truth. But I didn't do it for her; I did it for my son.'

'I see,' the DI murmured. 'But you did it, and a chain of events began that has led to the disappearance of your investigator and to related crime, including,' he added, 'an attack on Alex Skinner in her home.'

Brass gasped. 'My God, is she all right?'

'She was unhurt, but a colleague of ours who was with her at the time did sustain an injury. She's safe now, but it adds even more urgency to our investigation.'

'I'll bet. Her father must be incandescent.'

'He is,' Haddock chuckled. 'Alex is her father's daughter, though; she nailed one of the intruders with a heavy frying pan before the pair of them ran for it.'

'That's good to hear. I wish I could be of some help to you. These people need catching.'

'Maybe you can. The only clues we have to Carrie's movements come from something she said to her father about places she was seeing for the first time. Dundee we know about, but she also mentioned Motherwell. From what you can remember about the file, was there anything in it that might point there?'

The old dentist frowned, then shook his head. 'No, nothing comes to mind.'

'How about Millport?'

'Millport? She'd be seeing Cedric Black, Marcia's lawyer; my lawyer really, but he represented her when she was arrested. He's retired now, and lives there with his new lady.'

The detectives looked at each other. 'I suppose so,' the DI sighed. 'We don't have many possible leads.'

'If you see him, it'll likely be a wasted trip, though. Cedric always believed she was as guilty as sin. He only took the case on for me. Poor old Marcia, only two people really believed she was innocent. Her son and her twin.'

'Her twin?' McClair exclaimed.

'Oh yes. She had a twin sister, Joan. Didn't you know?'

Thirty-Six

'Sir Robert didn't hang around for long,' Cotter remarked as he drove away from the Queen Elizabeth II University Hospital.

'I didn't expect him to,' Mann said. 'He said he was only coming along out of courtesy to Professor Scott. He has a day job with the owners of the *Saltire* newspaper. It's not full-time, but it tends to keep him in Edinburgh.'

'Will we see much of him?'

'As much as I want. I'm not so proud that I'll turn down help from the best detective officer I have ever met.'

'Better than Dan?'

'For all I may say, even Dan would concede that, although maybe not before witnesses. What did you think of Professor Scott?'

'He's impressive, and he has a nice turn of phrase. He seems to be in absolutely no doubt that we have a murder case on our hands.' The DS hesitated. 'But guv, can we open a full-scale investigation on his word alone? Don't we need a second opinion?'

'Two things, John. One, don't ever call me guv. This is not the fucking Sweeney; here its ma'am, or boss, or gaffer, or Lottie, once we get to know each other a bit better, and I'll tell you when that is. Two, in the west of Scotland Graham Scott is the top pathologist, and utterly reliable. His opposite number through in Edinburgh is Professor Sarah Grace, who happens by sheer chance to be Lady Skinner. Yes, I could ask her to look at the report, but she'd agree with Graham's findings, Graham would be pissed off if he ever found out, and we'd have wasted time. Now, Sergeant, tell me: in the unfortunate absence of Dr Archie Banks, who either screwed up Marcia Brown's post-mortem examination or deliberately submitted an incorrect report to the procurator fiscal, Robert Hough, where do we begin?'

'With the second pathologist?' Cotter suggested.

'Sound idea, but she's not going to tell us anything she hasn't told Graham Scott already. We'll leave her for the moment and interview the only other witness, the former Detective Inspector Terry Coats. But before we do that, we'll do some advance research, by pulling his file from HR. That name has meaning for me. I never met Coats, but I made DI not long after him and heard some stories about him, not all of them to his credit. Dan knew him, though.'

'What did he think of him?'

'The words "fucking chancer" come to mind.'

Thirty-Seven

Bob Skinner was in a reflective mood as he stepped out of his car in the Saltire House car park. He glanced around as he pressed the lock button on his remote; it had become a habit with him after an incident when he had been attacked by a misguided thug with a score to settle.

Sarah had been right. He had been dragged back into what was potentially a major criminal investigation; although he was not in the lead, he had semi-official oversight. Alongside that was the disappearance of Carrie McDaniels, and the attack on Alex. He was sure that Rose and McGuire had asked him to focus on the Marcia Brown investigation to keep him away from Sauce Haddock more than anything else. 'As if,' he murmured.

He was still thinking of his former colleagues when his phone rang, so he was not surprised when Mario showed on the screen.

'Steady on,' he said as he took the call. 'I've only just briefed them.'

'It's not about that,' McGuire replied. 'Where are you?'

'Saltire House, just about to go up to my office.'

'Can it wait?'

215

'It can. Officially I'm not here today. Why?'

'I want you to meet me, down at Lauder. The Dalkeith divisional HQ has had a call from a business there; the commander had the foresight to advise me. This is being played close at the moment, but on the basis of what I've been told, I've sent Arthur Dorward and his forensic team down there, pronto. I want to see for myself before I do anything else, and I'd like you to meet me there. Can you?'

'You going to tell me what this is about?' Skinner asked.

'No, because I'm only guessing myself at this stage.'

'Okay, you've got me. Where am I going?'

'I'll text you a postcode; copy it into your satnav and let it take you there.'

'Will do. See you when I see you.'

Thirty-Eight

'Have you come up with anything on Marcia's twin?' Haddock asked as he drove past the new Tate Gallery that dominated the Dundee waterfront. 'You've been on that iPad for long enough.'

'I've come up with something I never expected,' McClair told him. 'Believe it or not, Marcia Brown has a Wikipedia page.'

'Unexpected,' he agreed, 'but not necessarily surprising. Austin probably set it up.'

'Possibly he did, but it was last edited two days ago, and sure as hell he didn't do that. The additional text says that the case against Marcia has been reopened, with the aim of proving her innocence. Who would know that?'

'Outside of Alex Skinner's office, only David Brass, and the people Carrie McDaniels interviewed before she disappeared. The only one of those we know for sure is the lawyer, Cedric Black, but he never believed in her innocence even when he was acting for her.'

'We don't even know for sure that Carrie has seen him,' the DS pointed out. 'Her father didn't actually say that she'd been there, only that it was on her list.'

'Does Wikipedia not tell you who did the edit?' Haddock wondered.

'It does,' she replied, 'but it's a code name: La Pucelle. That suggests the editor is French. How would that be?'

The DI laughed, flexing his fingers on the steering wheel as he took a turn. 'You should have listened harder in school. La Pucelle means "The Maid". That was what Joan of Arc called herself. Joan. Joan Brown, Marcia's twin sister, the only person other than Austin who believed in her innocence. David Brass told us she's a teacher. He never said what, but I'll bet it's either French or history.'

'There are thousands of teachers in Scotland. How are we going to find her?'

'The General Teaching Council. She'll be registered with them, almost certainly.'

'Will they co-operate?' McClair asked doubtfully. 'Won't they throw data protection at us?'

'They can try,' Haddock replied, 'and I'll throw obstruction of justice at them. Give Jackie Wright a call back at base and set her to work on it.'

They drove on towards the road that fringed Dundee on the west, until they came to a small industrial park. Their destination was visible at once, a flat-roofed single-storey building with a bright blue logo and the name Clouds above its main entrance. The face of a smiling woman almost filled a full-length window beside the double doorway.

'Is that her?' McClair asked. 'The famous Mia Sparkles?'

'That's her. There's been a bit of retouching, maybe, but she's glamorous, no doubt about that.'

'I wonder why she's never made it to television.'

'Probably because her husband doesn't own a TV station,' the DI surmised.

They parked at the side of the building and walked to the

entrance. Access was video controlled; Haddock pressed the buzzer and held his warrant card close to the camera as he identified himself and his colleague. As they stepped inside, they were greeted by the station output, filling the foyer, and by a silver-blonde middle-aged receptionist, who had definitely been retouched. McClair felt a stab of sympathy for the man; he wore subtle make-up, but his acne scars were still visible.

'Do you ever wish you could turn that stuff off and listen to PopMaster?' the inspector asked, jerking a thumb towards a Bose speaker at the junction of floor and ceiling.

'Every bloody morning,' the receptionist replied quietly. 'The rest of Dundee does; that quiz does serious damage to the national economy. How can I help you, Officers?'

'We'd like to see the station manager, Ms Delaney. Also the owner, Mr McCullough, but separately.'

'Hazel's here, I'll ask her if she's free. As for Mr McCullough, he rarely comes into the station.'

'Nonetheless, we'd like to see him,' Haddock repeated.

'I can let him know.'

'Please do, but first, Ms Delaney.'

'Give me a minute.' He rose from his chair, revealing his considerable height, left his booth and disappeared through a door to the right. When he returned a minute later, he was accompanied by a petite brown-haired woman who might have been a foot shorter than him.

'God,' Hazel Delaney exclaimed, 'they really are getting younger, Detective Inspector Haddock.'

'I have a portrait in my attic back home,' Sauce replied. 'You really don't want to see that. Ms Delaney, can I begin by asking whether you had a visit earlier today from a woman named Carrie McDaniels, or whether you're expecting her later?'

'Neither, and it's Mrs. She was due here at ten, but she didn't show up. That didn't surprise me; I listen to our news output. But folks, I can't help you. I don't know the woman, and I have no idea why she wanted to see me. She phoned on Friday and made an appointment, through my assistant here . . . isn't that right?'

The receptionist nodded. 'Yes, but she didn't say what it was about, only that it wasn't station business. She's lucky Hazel agreed to see her.'

'Why did you, Mrs Delaney?' McClair asked.

'I suppose I was intrigued. She said it was something to do with my former life, which wasn't very interesting.' She paused. 'Come on through to my office. We shouldn't do this out here.'

The room into which she ushered them had a window on either side; one was to the outside, and the other looked directly into a broadcast studio, in which a young male presenter was working.

'Do we have to be quiet?'

Hazel Delaney smiled at the detective sergeant. 'No way; you could shoot someone in here and it wouldn't be heard through that. It's triple-glazed, thick glass, with a two-inch vacuum between each layer.

'When does Mia Sparkles come on air?'

'Four; she does drive-time. Are you a fan?'

'When I was twelve. I lived in Lanarkshire, but I could get the Edinburgh stations on my trannie. And then she vanished, just like that.'

'If you should meet her before you leave here,' the station manager warned, 'don't ask her about that. It's off limits to everybody.'

'Apart from the owner,' Haddock suggested.

'Sometimes I wonder about that. To me, Mia's the boss's wife, so I keep my curiosity in check.'

'There was a connection between you and your current boss in your last job, Mrs Delaney, wasn't there? As we understand it, Mr McCullough was the majority shareholder in LuxuMarket.'

'That's true. Not one of his finest investments, but he more than washed his face when he got out, as I understand it.'

'How did you come to move here?' McClair asked.

'A vacancy arose and Mr McCullough offered me the job.'

'Did you have background in broadcasting?'

'No,' Delaney answered, 'but I don't need one. My title is station manager and that's what I do, manage. Mia's the output director; before her, when I came here seven years ago, it was Benny Young. He's on BBC local radio now, down in England.'

'About two years before you came to Dundee,' Haddock ventured, 'there was an incident in LuxuMarket. A woman was accused of shoplifting and was facing prosecution; her name was Marcia Brown and she was a local councillor, quite a figure in the town.'

'That? Is that what she wanted to talk about? I've spent the weekend going over my past life, wondering what I could have done to attract the interest of a private investigator. And all the time it was the Marcia Brown affair. Oh yes, I remember that, but only because the poor woman killed herself before the case got to court.'

'Haunted you ever since, has it?'

'I wouldn't say that, Inspector. I was very sorry when it happened, of course, but I've never felt guilty about it. The company's policy was very clear: above a certain value we went to court. If we'd made an exception for her, just because she was a councillor, it would have been used against us for ever more.'

'Ms Brown insisted that she was framed,' Haddock continued. 'She said the goods were planted on her after she had left the checkout.'

'They all said that, or something similar. As I remember it, an alarm was raised by a checkout girl and Ms Brown was stopped by a security officer.'

'Was LuxuMarket big enough to have its own security staff?'

Delaney grinned. 'They were shelf-stackers really. It was easier to recruit them if we gave them a more impressive title. Look, is all this not in the incident report?'

'It was, but that's gone missing with Ms McDaniels. All we have to go on is the recollection of Ms Brown's former husband.'

'Not the son? He made a hell of a fuss at the time. We were sympathetic, of course, but it got to a point when he had to be threatened with legal action if he didn't stop.'

'The son is no longer alive. He never did stop; now that he's dead, his father feels an obligation to him.'

'Are you telling me that the Marcia Brown case is now the subject of a police investigation?'

'No, we're not,' McClair assured her quickly. 'Our investigation is into the disappearance of Carrie McDaniels. We're trying to get an idea of her movements since last week. We knew about this appointment, and were hoping you might point us in the direction of other people she might have seen, or planned to see.'

Delaney whistled. 'That's a tall order; it's been nine years. I suppose she would want to speak to the security officer who stopped Councillor Brown. I can't remember his name, but he was a Pakistani boy, on vacation from uni. Then there was Vera

Stephens, our fashion buyer. That's right!' she exclaimed, as a sudden recollection came to her. 'Marcia had a beef with Vera's mother, the notorious Gloria, the queen bee on the local council, and she claimed that Vera had set her up on her mother's orders, to get her out of the way. Vera denied it, of course; she told the police she wasn't on the shop floor when the theft happened. She said she was in my office, in fact.'

'Was she?'

'To be honest, Inspector, I couldn't tell you. Vera's room was close to mine and she accessed it through my outer office. If she said she was there, she probably was, but I wouldn't necessarily have known. That's what I told the detective who investigated the theft.'

'Do you recall his name?'

She nodded. 'In fact I do. He was a detective sergeant, which I thought at the time was over the top for a shoplifting. He was a flash bastard, full of himself. I had the impression he might have been trying to pull me.' She glanced at McClair. 'You know the type, dear; a white mark on the third finger, left hand. His name was Coats, Terry Coats.'

The DS turned a vivid shade of pink.

Thirty-Nine

The postcode that Skinner entered into Apple Maps took him, as McGuire had said, to Lauder, then a little beyond, to a turning off the main thoroughfare, and half a mile along a slightly narrower road to a wide gateway. It was open, leading him into a gravel driveway with a rose garden on either side. The centrepiece was a square building with a facade that reminded him vaguely of the Taj Mahal, but which was marred by a tall, broad chimney towards the rear.

He spotted the DCC at once, standing beside his Range Rover, which was parked on the right, in the midst of four other vehicles, including a police car and a large van labelled Forensic Services. He manoeuvred his own as close to it as he could and stepped out. 'What the hell is this place?' he asked.

'It's called Eternal Meadow,' McGuire informed him. 'There's no point in having a gaudy sign out here, but that's the name on the website. It's a pet crematorium.'

'I've got a fucking dog I wouldn't mind bringing here,' Skinner muttered.

'I'm sure Bowser would be treated with respect, but I think they'd prefer him to be dead first. Come on.' The DCC led the way to the grandiose front of the structure, and through the main door into a reception hall with a plush purple carpet, a dozen upholstered chairs and a three-foot-high rectangular plinth in white wood, set against a curtained opening in the back wall. 'This is the chapel of rest,' he whispered.

'You're having a laugh!'

'No, seriously.'

A man and a woman stood in an open doorway; they were clad in matching dark suits and white shirts.

'This is Mr and Mrs McGough,' McGuire said, 'the proprietors.'

'Val and Michael,' the woman added, stepping forward and offering a handshake. 'Can we get on with this?' she asked impatiently. 'We need to be able to tell Charmaine's owners when we can reschedule their ceremony.'

'Charmaine?' Skinner repeated.

'A very fine Pyrenean mastiff bitch. A big animal; the coffin was a special order.'

'Where is she now?' he asked lamely.

'In the cool room, where else?'

'I can't imagine,' he said quietly. 'Mario, what's going on here?'

'Mrs McGough will explain,' the DCC told him. 'It was her who contacted us.'

'Yes, it was,' she confirmed. 'We've had a break-in overnight. Michael and I discovered it when we opened up this morning.'

'What was taken?'

'Nothing!' she exclaimed impatiently. 'Someone's cremated their pet illegally! Broke in and used our facilities.'

'How can you be sure?'

'Because the remains are still there. How else?'

225

'They couldn't have been left over from the last time the oven was used?' Skinner asked.

'The crematory, you mean. No, they couldn't; Michael and I collected and processed those on Saturday evening and sealed them in their casket. The crematory is cleaned thoroughly after every use. It was immaculate when we left it.'

'That was your last cremation? Saturday? Nothing on Sunday?'

'That's our day of rest. Our last client was on Saturday midday. Jolyon,' she added, 'a Staffordshire bull terrier.'

'Okay, I get it.' He was also beginning to get McGuire's concern. 'Apart from the cremated remains, did you find anything else?'

'Nothing, nothing at all. Apart from the remains, whoever it was cleaned up after themselves.'

'Why would they leave the remains? Why not take them and be completely undetected?'

'The crematory would have taken some time to cool, and they'd need to be finally processed – put though the grinder,' she explained. 'My guess would be the intruders were in a hurry, or they simply didn't know what they were doing; didn't know about that final stage in the process. People talk of ashes,' she explained, 'but they're not really. Tissue is vaporised by the intense heat; what goes in the casket is ground-down bone.' She sniffed. 'Gentlemen, how much longer are your people going to be? This really is interfering with our business.'

'I'm sorry, Mrs McGough,' McGuire replied briskly. 'We'll take as much time as we need to, but not a minute more. Bob,' he murmured, 'let's talk to Arthur.'

He strode past the proprietors and into the space beyond the chapel of rest, a much larger area with a higher ceiling. Skinner looked around; the place was stacked with what he guessed, despite their irregular shapes, were coffins of various sizes, some tiny, one very large, almost human size. Its top was open, revealing a pink satin lining; ready for Charmaine, he surmised. In the centre of the great room were two ovens, again of different sizes and capacity, both vented into a cylindrical pipe that rose up and through the ceiling. The door of the larger crematory was open; a blue-suited technician was crouching inside it sifting through a pile of light grey fragments, varied in size, while another, a red-haired man, stood outside.

'Well, Arthur,' Skinner called out, 'you and I have met in some strange places, but this one takes the biscuit.'

'Bakes it, more like,' the veteran Dorward retorted.

'What have you got there?' McGuire asked him. 'What was it?'

'You're looking at bones,' he replied, 'but they've been shattered by the heat, so it's difficult to say what they looked like before they had a couple of hours at two thousand degrees. Because of that, Mario, your guess would be as good as mine, were it not for one fact. I have never seen an animal, not even one of the pampered mutts this place deals with, that would wear one of these.' He held up a twisted piece of shiny metal. 'You couldn't tell now, but this was once a Rolex watch.'

The DCC frowned. 'How can you know that?'

'Amazingly, some detail on the back survived the flames; all that heat for all that time, but the name was still legible. So was the serial number; I photographed it and sent it to the office in Gartcosh, and asked them to check whether its guarantee had been registered. I've just had a call back; it belonged to somebody called Ben McNeish.' He gesticulated towards the pile of twisted remains. 'I'm guessing that used to be him.'

Skinner sighed, so loudly that his two companions looked towards him in surprise. 'No,' he said. 'For once you're wrong, Arthur. I know Ben McNeish; he's the stepson of a friend of mine. He's still alive, but he's not around here. He found himself a new career as a United Nations observer at elections around the world. At the moment he's in Papua New Guinea. Arthur,' he asked, 'is that the only ID we'll ever get?'

'The identification of DNA from cremated material is a forensic anthropologist's wet dream, but it can't be done, Bob, not yet. You'll have to rely on that watch. It's a few grand's worth, so somewhere there's likely to be paperwork to match the serial number.'

'You don't need it. Carrie McDaniels wore a Rolex. The first time I encountered her she didn't have it, but she was involved with a lad – Ben McNeish. Almost certainly,' his voice faltered; he was visibly upset, 'that's her.'

'The poor, poor girl,' McGuire whispered, shuddering. 'I'll get Sauce to check her apartment,' he said. 'The guys who dumped her here can't have thought it through or they wouldn't have left the watch on her.'

'Further proof, if we needed it, that they weren't thieves,' Skinner added, 'or they'd have taken it. You don't need to go that far, though; I can get a mobile number from Ben's mother. If he's within range of a cell, one phone call could confirm that he gave the watch to Carrie.'

The DCC looked over his shoulder, towards the doorway, where the proprietors stood, Val McGough and the silent Michael, looking on. 'Whatever they were, it's bad news for those two. Their place is now a crime scene. God knows what effect the publicity will have on their business, and there will be pub—'

He stopped in mid sentence, looking at his friend, and at the distant expression on his face. 'What's up?' he asked. 'You look as if . . . Nah, of course, you knew this girl; seeing that would upset anyone.'

'Yes, but it's not that. I was thinking of my great-granny, Mario. "The bad fire" was the threat she used to terrorise kids. It put me off Hansel and Gretel for life, mate; one story I never read to my kids, none of them. Maybe this is what the old witch meant.' He smiled, sadly and self-consciously. 'Sorry, guys. Arthur, what's your next move?'

'I'll need the full team down here.' Dorward sighed. 'There might be no victim DNA in there,' he nodded at the crematory, 'but the people who did this will have left some, as always. We'll need samples from the owners and everyone who's been here – not you, of course, that's on file – and we'll need in situ photography.' He looked up at McGuire. 'Is there any point in a pathologist?'

'I wouldn't say so. She should go to a mortuary, though, even though we won't be doing an autopsy.'

'No, we won't,' the scientist agreed. 'However, there is one thing they need to do, and it will not make your day, Deputy Chief Constable. They need to weigh her. Was Carrie McDaniels a big woman, Bob?'

'Average,' Skinner replied. 'Five six, five seven, solidly built, but fit, not gone to fat. Why?'

'Well, this isn't my field of expertise, but as I understand it, the remains of a person that size would be around three kilos in weight. I think we're looking at a hell of a lot more than that. I might be wrong, but that would be unusual: twice in one day, it would be impossible. I don't think those remains are Carrie McDaniels' alone; I believe she had a companion. We're looking at two bodies, gentlemen, not one.'

Forty

'I swear to God, boss, I did not know,' Noele McClair murmured. 'Nine years ago, when Terry was a DS in Kilmarnock, I was a probationer, stationed in Castlemilk. We'd been married for less than two years; it was him that persuaded me to join the force. White band round his finger indeed! A sign of things to come right enough. Since we split up, I'm starting to discover that Mr Coats played more away games than Celtic. That explains why he was so keen for me to use my maiden name at work, so it didn't tip people off that he was married.' She looked anxiously at Haddock. 'This won't take me off the investigation, will it?'

'Not as it stands. Bob Skinner must have known about the connection. He'd have spoken up if it was a problem. If Terry becomes a suspect, that might be a different matter, but we're nowhere near that.'

They were back in the reception area of the radio station. Hazel Delaney had asked them to wait there after their interview had finished, without explaining why. The answer became obvious when the double doors burst open and Mia McCullough strode in, followed by her husband. 'Sauce,' Cameron McCullough exclaimed. 'I hope you realise you're

231

getting special treatment. I have a standing golf game on a Monday afternoon, but I had a message that my granddaughter's other half was demanding to see me. I know you like to keep me at arm's length, but you know where I live; you've been there.'

'This isn't social, Cameron. It was either here or on our ground.'

The silver-haired man smiled. 'In a way, I'm pleased to hear that. I dread the day when you come to me and tell me I'm going to be a great-grandpa.' He jogged his wife's elbow. 'I don't reckon you'd fancy that either, love,' he chuckled. 'On you go and get ready for your show, while I answer the officers' questions, whatever they are.'

Mia gave them a cool look. 'Keeping it in the family, eh, Sauce?' she murmured, then strode off, tight and fit in her designer jeans and sleeveless cotton shirt.

'Let's go to the boardroom,' McCullough said. He led the detectives out of reception, along a corridor and into a chamber at the rear of the building. It was more of a den than a meeting place, with a wall-mounted television, two armchairs and a corner bar. There was a table, but it was small, with only four seats.

'How many directors do you have?' Haddock asked.

'Just the two: Mia and me. The third chair's for our lawyer – she's the company secretary – and the fourth, that's for Hazel when we invite her in to discuss management matters: ad sales, listener figures and so on. The business pretty much runs itself; it's popular and it's profitable. Cheeky's probably told you, Sauce, that she begged me to buy it, eleven years ago, when it was about to go bust. She liked it and reckoned it could be saved if somebody changed its programming and gave it wider appeal. She was right up to a point, but it never did more than wash its face until Mia turned up looking for a job. She's got class, and she has a history in the business. She's raised our advertising profile by a mile, and got us international attention, through the live listening facility on our website. I'm still astonished by the number of people who remember her from Airburst FM, and not just Edinburgh folk either.'

'I'm one of them,' Noele McClair admitted.

'Can we get down to business, Cameron?' Haddock asked. 'DS McClair and I are trying to find a woman who's gone missing. Your station has been covering the story.'

'I've heard it. You haven't volunteered a hell of a lot – name, rank and serial number, not much more. What's behind it? It's serious, I can see that if they have a Serious Crimes team looking for her. You can tell me, son; it won't leave this room without your approval.'

The DI pursed his lips and made a decision. 'On that understanding: Carrie McDaniels was investigating the circumstances behind a shoplifting allegation made nine years ago, in Ayrshire, against a woman called Marcia Brown. It happened in a supermarket in Kilmarnock called LuxuMarket. You owned the business at the time.'

'I suppose I did,' McCullough agreed, 'but I was an angel really.' He smiled. 'A business angel,' he explained, 'is a private investor who puts money into a small business to help it start up, then cashes in when it's established. LuxuMarket had been a cash-and-carry off-licence that had outlived its time. The owner wanted to sell, so he approached me. I had a look at it and decided the risk wasn't unacceptable, as long as it could be converted into a full-range food store and supermarket. It worked out, too. I ran it for a while, built up the business and sold out at a very tidy profit – on which I paid tax, in case you were wondering. That was seven years ago.'

'Around the time you offered Hazel Delaney the job here?'

'That's right. She impressed me in Kilmarnock, and I needed to make a change here, so it worked out. For her too; she'd just got married and her husband worked offshore, so it was handier for her to be in the east, near his base. Poor bastard; he was killed on a rig not long after that.'

'Do you remember the Marcia Brown affair?'

'The way it ended, I could hardly forget it, Sauce. Hazel told me about it. In fact, she consulted me about the decision to prosecute. With the woman being a councillor, she felt she needed my seal of approval. There were elections coming up, and if Marcia Brown had become chair of planning, or even leader of the council, there might have been repercussions. I couldn't see any chance of either, since she was an independent, and the theft was above our discretionary level, so I told her to go ahead.'

'Did she also tell you about Marcia Brown's death?' Haddock asked.

'Yes, she did.' McCullough gazed at him. 'Are you going to ask me if I felt guilty, son? Of course I bloody did! So did Hazel, so did everyone in the bloody store. One of the security lads who stopped her had to be counselled; health and safety insisted. The other just quit. Hazel needed counselling too; she was really cut up about it. And so was I; upset enough to get involved and order that the discretionary limit be doubled, but I never told anybody other than store management.'

'What about Vera Stephens? Was she upset?'

'Who?'

'The fashion buyer; Ms Brown accused her of planting the goods she was accused of stealing.'

'I've no idea who she was; I never met her that I know of. Like I said, Sauce, I was an angel, an investor, not a micro-manager. I knew the people in charge of each of the branches, but I wasn't familiar with the whole bloody payroll.'

'Afterwards,' McClair said, feeling the need to assert her presence, 'did Mrs Delaney keep you informed of the publicity about the case?'

'No, why should she? Look, Sergeant, when someone dies like that, she's going to leave unhappy family and friends behind, but at the end of the day it wasn't LuxuMarket's fault, and it wasn't my fault.'

'Are you telling me that you had no knowledge of the campaign carried on by Ms Brown's son to have his mother's case reopened? You didn't know about the accusation of a frame-up that he trumpeted to any journalist who would listen to him?'

'Of course not.'

'Then why did you threaten him?' she asked.

Cameron McCullough's eyes darkened, showing Haddock, if he had ever doubted it, why his fearsome reputation and rumour of his capabilities had persisted through the years. They said clearly, I am a dangerous man, and not to be crossed. They reminded him of Bob Skinner.

Nevertheless, McCullough's voice remained quiet, almost gentle. 'Listen, lady,' he replied, 'I'm sitting here being interviewed by the police, who have been after me since I was in my twenties. I'm doing it without a lawyer, because of your boss here, because my granddaughter loves him, and he makes her happy. So don't you go all Cagney and Lacey on me. Don't go throwing spurious accusations in the hope I'll collapse at your feet like some teenage corner boy.' He looked at Haddock. 'Sauce, what the hell is she on about?'

'Like I said, Cameron,' the DI said, 'this is a police matter; at the moment it's a missing person investigation, but we are deeply concerned about the lady. We've been told that Austin Brass, Marcia Brown's son, was warned to shut up and go away, and that the warning came from the owner of LuxuMarket. Brass took it seriously enough to take his tanks off LuxuMarket's lawn, but only ostensibly, for he never really gave up. I don't doubt the truth of what we've been told, and we have to put the question to you.'

'This would have happened when?'

'A couple of months after Marcia Brown's death.'

'A death,' McCullough observed, 'that you have never once described as a suicide. Is that part of your investigation as well?'

'No, it is not,' Haddock told him truthfully. 'As I've just said, this is a missing person investigation, no more than that. What do you say?'

'I say, Sauce, that less than a month after Ms Brown died, however she died, I went to Russia, where I had and still have business interests. I stayed there for four weeks. From there I flew to Singapore, where I met up with a lady whom you know very well: my granddaughter. She and I boarded a liner and went on a six-week cruise of the Far East, finishing in Hong Kong, where we spent another week before flying home via Los Angeles. It was her graduation present. Hasn't she told you about it?'

The DI sighed. 'She has.'

McCullough beamed. 'In which case, thanks, son, for being my alibi.'

Forty-One

The display on the monitor blinked for a second, and then a face appeared, that of a woman, her face half covered by huge round spectacles, with short dark hair cut back from her forehead, and long earrings that appeared to Lottie Mann to be matching cameos suspended on gold chains. She started as she saw herself admiring them in a small box on the lower right corner of the screen, seated close enough to John Cotter for the computer's camera to capture them both.

'Dr Swanson?' she began.

'That's me.' The face broke into a slightly amused smile. 'Is this how the police work these days?'

Mann grinned back at her. 'Skype saves a lot of time and money; we use it for non-caution interviews whenever there's distance involved and we can't bring the witness to us.'

'As a taxpayer, I'm glad to hear it. How can I be of service?'

'I'm DCI Charlotte Mann,' she replied, 'and this is my colleague DS Cotter. Thank you for agreeing to talk to us. We're investigating a suspicious death that took place nine years ago. It led to a post-mortem examination in Kilmarnock at which you were present.'

'Marcia Brown? Graham Scott called me last week to ask

me about that one. There wasn't a hell of a lot I could tell him, other than that Banks, the pathologist, was a dickhead. What's your interest? And what was suspicious about the death? The blood analysis showed fatally high levels of morphine, and Banks said he was signing it off as suicide.'

'Would it surprise you if I told you we now believe that Marcia Brown was murdered?' Mann asked her.

'Given Graham's suddenly renewed interest in it,' Swanson murmured, 'no, it wouldn't.'

'Did you have suspicions at the time?' Cotter interjected.

'I can't say that I did, but I was only a student, there as the legal requirement for a second pair of professional eyes – not that old Banks let me close enough to do anything other than photograph the victim and take the blood sample to the lab. Really, what he did was unprofessional at best, maybe borderline illegal, but like I said, I was only a student at the time, plus he'd promised me a hundred quid – which I never saw, incidentally.'

'There was a police officer present,' Mann resumed. 'Detective Sergeant Coats. Did you have any interaction with him?'

'Personally, no. Banks did when the guy handed over the stuff he'd brought from the scene: the empty morphine capsules and the boxes they'd been in.'

'How many?'

'I can't be sure, but a lot, more than enough to see the poor woman on her journey with no return ticket.'

'Do you remember him handing over anything else? Specifically, syringes?'

'I don't, but that's not to say he didn't.'

'Did Coats stay to witness the examination?'

'I think he was up in the viewing gallery, yes.'

'You were in the room?'

'Yes,' she agreed, 'but I wasn't assisting as Banks had told me I would. He made me stand well away from the table, almost against the wall. I was nothing more than a gofer, but to be honest, I wasn't too bothered. My presence was recorded, so I got to put it on my CV.'

'How long did the examination take?'

'Less than an hour. Looking back it was a shocking performance. It was as if everyone had decided in advance that it was a suicide: the police, the fiscal, Banks himself.'

Mann saw herself frown in the onscreen box. 'When he was finished,' she continued, 'did Banks say anything?'

'All I remember is him looking at the lab analysis of the blood, laughing and saying, "That confirms it, suicide," or words to that effect. Oh yes, he looked up at the CID man and said, "You can go now, Sergeant. I'll sign the fiscal report myself." I think that was all. I don't think he said anything to the other man at all.'

'The other man?' Cotter exclaimed.

Marguerite Swanson's eyes seemed to widen behind the large spectacles. 'Yes, didn't I say? Sorry. There was another witness present for the whole thing. In fact, when I arrived, he was already in the examination room, talking to Banks.'

'Who was he?' the DCI asked.

'I have no idea. He didn't have to identify himself to me, and Banks didn't bother to enlighten me.'

'Did you overhear their conversation?'

'If I did, it didn't stick. I mean, it wasn't a row or anything. It wasn't animated.'

'This fella,' Cotter ventured, 'could he have been police?'

The pathologist shook her head. 'I don't think so. He never spoke to Coats, not at all.'

'But he stayed for the whole examination?'

'Yes, until Banks made his pronouncement. Then he just nodded and left. Separately from Coats,' she added.

'Can you describe him?' Mann asked her.

'Not really. Older chap, but not as old as Banks, or as worn. Slim, well dressed; that's about it.'

The DCI sighed. 'Okay. Thanks for your help, Dr Swanson. We might need a formal statement from you at some stage, but if we do, I can ask an officer from your local force to take it for us. Are you sure that's all you can tell us?'

'Yes, I . . .' She frowned. 'Shit,' she whispered. 'Of course,' she said more loudly, 'there was the woman.'

'What woman?'

'She burst into the viewing gallery just as Banks made the Y incision. I heard her shout, "Why wasn't I informed?" Coats replied, "Because we're not required to, madam. Because you have no right to be here." Then he took her by the arm, firmly but not roughly, and escorted her outside. Banks waited until he came back before going any further. He wasn't bothered, though; he didn't even ask who she was.'

'What about the other man? Did he get involved?'

'That's the thing,' Swanson replied. 'Now that I think about it, I'm sure she was shouting at him.'

Forty-Two

'What do you have for us, Jackie?' Haddock asked Detective Constable Wright as he strode into the Serious Crimes suite in the building that had once been the headquarters of an autonomous police service. 'Sorry I didn't call you from the road, but I've spent the best part of the day behind the wheel, and to be honest, I wanted a break from business, knowing that this place was in your capable hands.'

She grinned. 'Can I have that in writing for when the next DS vacancy comes up? I've got quite a bit,' she added. 'For openers there's Marcia Brown's twin sister; Joan Brown teaches French and Spanish at Houndswood Secondary in Lenzie. She lives in a flat in Bearsden, she's fifty-nine years old, as Marcia would have been, and she's single. But if you're hoping to talk to her, you're going to have to wait. The schools have broken up for the holidays; when I tried her phone, I got an answering machine. I gave her an hour and tried again, but got the same result, so I asked for a call-in by the nearest patrol vehicle. The uniforms spoke to an elderly neighbour, who told them that Ms Brown's gone off to walk the Camino de Santiago with a crowd of friends. She had no idea when she'll be back. I suppose we could ask the Spanish police to find her and get her to contact us.'

'We will ask,' the DI agreed, 'but whatever "fuck off" is in Spanish, don't be surprised if that's what they tell us. Hundreds, no, thousands of people make that pilgrimage throughout the year. If you do the whole route, it takes a month. Did you leave a message on her phone?'

'Yes, boss.'

'Then the best we can hope for is that she checks her machine remotely and picks it up. What did you say?'

'That it had to do with a reopened investigation into her sister's death.'

Haddock nodded. 'That'll get her attention. What else?'

'I checked with Carrie McDaniels' bank and credit card provider. She drew out a hundred quid last Friday evening, but the ATM wasn't far from her home, so that gets us nowhere. However . . .' she paused, 'her Barclaycard was used at twenty past midday on Saturday to buy fuel in a petrol station in East Kilbride.'

'East Kilbride?' McClair repeated. 'I wonder what she was doing there.'

Wright shrugged. 'Buying petrol. You don't have to be doing anything in East Kilbride to make a fuel stop there. You pass through it on the way to anywhere south-west of Glasgow.'

'When she stopped there,' Haddock asked, 'was she alone?'

'That'll need to be checked with the filling station, assuming it has CCTV.'

'Most of them do these days. Are you on it?'

Wright peered at him from beneath furrowed eyebrows. 'Again, I've asked for uniformed assistance. I've given the East Kilbride office the registration number and the time of the purchase so it should be easy enough to find.'

'She could have had company that never got out of the car,' McClair pointed out.

'Let's see what the CCTV shows us, okay,' the DI snapped testily, regretting it at once. 'Sorry, Noele. I'm still smarting from being made to look a clown by Grandpa.'

'That's okay, Sauce. You weren't to know about the trip.'

He winced. 'That's the thing, I did. Of course Cheeky told me about it; I just never put the dates together. That's good work, Jackie,' he continued.

'I'm not done yet,' the DC replied cheerfully. 'We reckon Carrie's phone's a goner, but I checked with her provider, BT, and they told me that she backed up her personal data to their Cloud service. Her diary will be on it for sure.'

'And if we really get lucky,' McClair added, 'so will any notes she made of interviews and meetings.'

'Maybe so,' Haddock agreed, 'but we'll need to get access to find out.'

'Surely that won't be a problem.'

'It might, though; this isn't a criminal investigation, so data protection restrictions will apply. I can ask, but it might be better if I report to the fiscal and ask him to do it, lawyer to lawyer, for you can be sure any request will be referred to theirs. I'll do it right now, before they've all knocked off for the day.'

'You might want to hold off on that.' The trio turned to see DCC Mario McGuire framed in the doorway. 'Your rights of access have just improved. We've made a positive identification of remains that were discovered earlier on today, Carrie McDaniels is no longer a missing person. She's a murder victim.'

Forty-Three

'This is a first,' Sarah Grace declared, looking at the viewing window behind which her audience of three stood. 'For me and maybe for any other pathologist.' She pointed at a camera on a tripod, in the corner of the examination room in Edinburgh's city mortuary. 'Which explains why I am having this autopsy – if I can call it that – filmed. It's not unusual for us to be presented with the remains of fire victims, from houses, auto accidents and such, but normally there's more left than this: fragments of fabric, for example. The intense heat of a crematory vaporises all tissue and clothing, and reduces the bones to the condition that you see here.'

'Cut to the chase,' Bob Skinner exclaimed. 'Was Arthur Dorward correct? Were there two victims?'

'Almost certainly,' his wife replied. 'Post cremation of an adult you'd expect to have two to three kilos of remains.' She turned to the examination table on which the skeletal remains were laid out. 'We've weighed these and they come to around five and a half.'

'That's assuming these are human,' Sauce Haddock pointed out. 'This lot did come from a pet crematorium, and as I understand it, the oven was big enough to handle large animals.

Okay, okay,' he exclaimed, 'I know about the Rolex that's been identified as belonging to Carrie McDaniels, but I don't want you – or me, for that matter – to be asked that question by a top silk defence counsel without being able to answer unequivocally. We need to be able to discount any other possibility.'

'We can,' she assured him. 'I haven't begun my detailed examination yet, but I did take a look as we were putting the remains on the scale. There are other gold deposits apart from the Rolex.'

'Could they have come from the watch?' Noele McClair asked.

'No. They were attached to a charred piece of bone.' She reached out for a folder on a table close by and brandished it. 'Thanks to the very efficient DC Wright, I have Ms McDaniels' dental records. They show that she had gold fillings implanted into her lower wisdom teeth, not in Edinburgh but during a period of military service in Afghanistan. The field clinic was run by Americans, by the way; if it had been British, they'd have used amalgam, and I suspect there would have been nothing left. Your top silk defence counsel might persevere, but unless he can produce a dental vet who uses gold to fill the teeth of ponies, I'd say we were beyond reasonable doubt.'

'Sarah, you and I discussed this last night,' Skinner said, 'but for the benefit of the recording, can we talk about DNA recovery?'

'Yes. I know that Arthur Dorward suggested it was impossible to extract DNA from cremains, and in any normal circumstances he'd be correct. If the crematorium gives you an urn and says this is Granny, you have to take their word for it. However, these are not normal circumstances. The surviving skeletal remains were not ground into powder as they would be in a conventional human cremation. I'm not going to tell you that it's possible to get an identification from what we have here, but I will ask Arthur to give it a damn good try. Now, I will begin.'

McClair, Haddock and Skinner fell silent as she went to work, watching as she picked up each fragment and studied it, trying to fit together the pieces of the most bizarre jigsaw any of them had ever seen. She worked in silence for fully ten minutes before pausing and turning to look at them.

'This will take some time,' she announced, 'not less than an hour. You three might as well go get a coffee. There's a Caffè Nero round the corner in Blackwell's, the bookshop.'

They took her at her word, leaving the mortuary and climbing the hill that led towards the South Bridge. Halfway to their destination, Skinner paused at the building that had once housed the Infirmary Street Public Baths. As he surveyed it, his eyes seemed to glaze over, and his attention moved elsewhere. 'That place was a crime scene once,' he murmured, loud enough for his companions to hear him but in a tone that suggested he was talking to himself as much as to them.

'Major?' Haddock asked, breaking into his trance.

'Very,' he replied. 'An organised crime thing, around twenty years ago. The place was closed as the baths but was waiting for conversion into whatever the hell it's been since then. Somebody used it to torture a poor bastard to death. The pool was empty, but the high board was still there; the victim was dropped off it, then carried back up to the top and dropped again, and again, until there was no point in doing it any more.

I was called to the scene because of the gang involvement; the lad was Tony Manson's driver and someone was sending Tony a message.'

'Did you catch the perpetrators?'

'Of course.' He stared at McClair, unsmiling. 'It had a fairly bloody conclusion.' He winced. 'The whole thing was bloody, now I think about it. A couple of good things came out of it, though, one being it was the first time I met Mario McGuire. He was a plod then, until I had him seconded to my team.' He smiled faintly. 'The flash bastard turned up for his first day wearing a designer suit. I had to tell him that the name of the game was not to draw attention to yourself; rather the opposite.'

'Who was the victim?'

'There were a few at the end of the day, but the unfortunate high diver was a lad named Marlon Watson. I heard you bumped into his sister yesterday.'

'Sister?' the DI repeated.

'Mia McCullough. She was Mia Watson then . . . as well as Mia Sparkles, which she still is.'

'Is that why she disappeared?' McClair asked. 'Was she afraid they were after her too?'

Skinner laughed bitterly. 'I doubt Mia was ever afraid of anything in her life. No, she left for other reasons.'

'Those being?'

'Those being ancient history, Sauce.' He nodded towards the Caffè Nero sign at the top of the rise. 'Come on, you two. My body clock's telling me it's my coffee time.'

'It's always your coffee time, gaffer,' Haddock chuckled.

The two officers each ordered a flat white, while Skinner asked for a cappuccino with an extra shot. McClair chose an eclair, Haddock a slice of rocky road; Skinner had nothing at all. 'Is that how you keep the weight off?' McClair asked him. 'Strong coffee and no food?'

'I don't keep it off,' he retorted. 'I weigh eighty-nine kilos, give or take a few grams, and I have done since I was twenty. I eat what I like, I run, I play golf, and I have a kick-around with my Thursday football mates whenever I can, which is usually at least twice a month. Maybe the coffee helps, but it is what it is.'

'Terry used to play squash,' she said. 'He was okay, but every time he lost, he came home in a filthy temper. Eventually it just tapered off; I think he ran out of people to play with.'

'Squash is all about control, patience and self-discipline, I reckon. I played until I made ACC, then I just got too busy.'

'I'll stick to golf,' Haddock volunteered. 'I'm crap at everything else.'

They allowed Sarah the hour she had specified, and another ten minutes, before making their way back to the mortuary. When they arrived, she was still at work, but the relics on the table had spread to another and had taken on outlines that were almost recognisable as human.

'What you have here,' she announced when she was ready, 'are the remains of two people, definitely. I can't be certain that I've separated them completely, but I've managed it well enough for me to make the most basic determination. The bones on my right are those of Carrie McDaniels. Those on my left are those of a male, identity unknown. I've been able to determine this by piecing together the pelvis of each subject, that being the main area of distinction between the male and female skeletons. Women are structured so that babies can get out; men aren't. That's as far as I can go with identification, but I did manage to extract traces of marrow from the larger bones of each . . .' she hesitated, 'each person. I'll send them to Dorward in Gartcosh for analysis to see if it's possible to establish a DNA profile for the male, but with no great optimism. Your best hope is that when you find out who had it in for Ms McDaniels, there's a second name on their hit list.'

Forty-Four

'When did you discover this?' Alex asked, staring at him from her office chair. Her face was ashen beneath her summer tan.

'Yesterday afternoon,' her father replied. 'There's very little doubt that it's Carrie. I decided not to call you last night, because it's much better to break news like this in person.'

'God,' she whispered. 'The poor woman. Why would anyone . . .' She stopped mid sentence. 'It has to be connected to the work she was doing for me . . . hasn't it?'

'Ninety per cent, I'd say; maybe the whole ton.'

'They killed her? Those men? Then they did that with her body?' She shuddered, overwhelmed by a wave of dread. 'And they were in my home. Pops, I've had some sticky moments in my life, but I've never felt threatened the way I do right now. I feel safe at Dominic's, but even so, I lay awake last night thinking . . . and it dawned on me properly, for the first time, what might have happened if Griff hadn't been there. And if we both hadn't been at a loose end, he wouldn't have been.'

'That's why you stay with Dominic until they're apprehended. That's good, yes?'

She nodded. 'That's good,' she agreed. 'But I feel guilty now about not having been to visit Griff.'

'I have,' Bob revealed. 'I called in on him yesterday evening, on the way back from Lauder. I wanted to thank him. He's still in the Royal. They're keeping him for a couple of days,' he explained, 'to make sure there's no nerve damage. They don't think there is; they're just playing safe. It's as well; it'll give the wound more time to heal properly. It's in an awkward place – makes sitting very difficult.'

'Ah, poor boy,' Alex sighed. 'How was he, apart from the cut?'

'Angry. It's made him all the more determined to get out of uniform and back into CID.'

'Can you help with that?' she asked.

'I offered to put a word in, but he asked me not to; he wants to work his way back. He has a plan.'

'Not one he's shared with me.'

'Why should he? It's not as if the two of you are in a serious relationship . . . are you?'

'No. It's comfortable, no more than that. But I should still visit him in hospital. I owe him a very big thank you. Dominic's picking me up at five thirty. I'll try to talk him into taking me there.' She paused. 'Carrie's death is going to be all over the news, isn't it? Will my involvement become public knowledge?'

'No chance,' her father promised. 'One of the city freelances did file a report about a police incident at your address on Sunday morning, but the press office was told to describe it as a domestic incident, so nobody carried it. June Crampsey noticed it and asked me about it, knowing that you live in that block. I didn't lie to her; well, not exactly. I told her that

I was aware, but that it was not for publication.'

A half-smile crossed her face. 'Conflict of interest?' she suggested.

'No way, kid. Your best interests always come first with me.'

Forty-Five

Detective Constable Jackie Wright prided herself on being self-aware. She saw herself as a workhorse, and was comfortable with that. She had an eye on the promotion that she believed she deserved, but only for financial reasons. She was single, by choice rather than circumstance, and intended to remain so; she would always have to provide for herself.

She knew that she spent more time in the office than her colleagues, that she was seen as a reliable administrator and back-watcher. Those roles sat comfortably with her, and so when Sauce Haddock, Sammy Pye or Noele McClair went out on inquiries, she felt no resentment.

Every task was a challenge, some more than others. For example, tracking down the movements of the ill-fated Carrie McDaniels was likely to be essential to the investigation of her murder. She felt a buzz when she was able to report the use of her credit card in East Kilbride. That was her bit done, her part played; it was up to Sauce and Noele to establish why she had been there.

When Akram, the guy from BT, called her back, she felt an even greater surge of excitement. 'I have something for you,' he said. 'I've located all the material that the subject stored on our

Cloud facility, and I'm in a position to send it to you. To summarise, you were after updates over the last week; these all relate to her diary, appointments she made with times, locations and the people she was meeting. She didn't post anything else. If you were looking for more than that, you'll be disappointed, I'm afraid.'

'I'll be happy with anything you've got,' Wright replied, 'for I doubt we'll recover it from anywhere else, not now. Is there anything for Saturday in the material you've recovered?'

'I'd need to recheck to be sure, but I don't think so. Want me to?'

'No, just send it; and thanks for your help and co-operation.'

Wright leaned back, watching her computer screen, and waited. It was only a few seconds before an email with an attachment hit her inbox. She clicked on the file and found herself looking at the last week of Carrie McDaniels' diary, at the last entries she would ever make.

The first was on Sunday: *Dad, lunch. Drif t.* She thought the venue was misspelled until she remembered a beach-side café just past North Berwick on the East Lothian coast road.

Monday had two entries each, but Wright ignored them, focusing on the next two, the first on Tuesday, the second on Wednesday; the name on the first read *Alex Skinner*, while the second was *Alex, Brass.*

'Briefings,' she muttered, then moved on to the only Thursday entry. It read *12.00. Cedric Black, Millport!* She smiled at the exclamation point. Friday was more cryptic. Two meetings were listed; the first read *11.30. Saughton.*

'Saughton?' she repeated. 'What the hell does that mean?' She ran a very short list of potential meanings through her mind. 'Surely not,' she whispered.

She picked up her phone and ran a Google search for HMP Edinburgh; within seconds, she saw a number displayed. She held the cursor on it until it dialled automatically.

'Edinburgh Prison,' a gruff male voice said. *I don't suppose it wants to sound welcoming*, she thought.

'Morning,' she began as cheerfully as she could. 'Governor's office, please.'

'Who wants it?'

She let the friendly approach lapse. 'DC Jackie Wright, Serious Crimes, Edinburgh; I'm part of a homicide investigation.'

'Okay, hold on.'

She waited for half a minute as the call was transferred. 'Governor's secretary here,' a smoother female voice advised her. 'You're police, I'm told.'

Wright identified herself for a second time. 'We're investigating a murder; the victim's an Edinburgh woman, Ms Carrie McDaniels.'

'That's a murder now?' the secretary exclaimed. 'She's no longer missing?'

'Unfortunately that's the case. I have reason to believe that Ms McDaniels visited the prison on Friday morning, at half eleven. I'd like to know who she visited. Can you find out?'

'Mmm. It wasn't arranged through this office, I can tell you that. Does she have a friend among the prison population?'

'Not that I know of. My feeling is that it was part of an investigation she was carrying out.'

'Then leave it with me. I'll check with the assistant governors and come back to you.'

Wright thanked her and left her mobile number and direct landline, then turned to the second Friday entry. It was timed at 16.30, the location was Motherwell, and the entry showed three letters: WZB.

'Who the hell is WZB?' she pondered. Once again she picked up her phone and turned to Google. To her surprise, she found herself facing four options: a rare minerals mine in Western Australia, a legal practice in Los Angeles, a Bollywood actor, and finally, a steel stockholder in Motherwell, North Lanarkshire.

Wondering how Carrie McDaniels' search had led her into the steel industry, she dialled its number on her landline. Her call went straight to voicemail. 'This is Detective Constable Jackie Wright from the police in Edinburgh; I believe you may be able to help me with my inquiries.' She left both her numbers and hung up.

Returning to her computer, she clicked on the last page of the diary: Saturday, the day the woman had gone missing. 'Bugger!' she grunted.

There were only two entries; the first read *10.00 Terry Coats, Edinburgh Airport*. Wright peered at the name. 'Shit, the sarge's husband.' She moved on to the second entry: *19.00 GP. Sage, Newcastle. Malmaison*.

'Damn it,' she muttered. The afternoon was blank.

Forty-Six

'I think we've been given the vessel with the pestle, boss,' DS John Cotter observed.

Mann stared at him. 'Run that past me again.'

'I'm a movie geek,' he explained. 'More than that, actually,' he added, embarrassed. 'My degree was in film studies. There's a classic with Danny Kaye, *The Court Jester*, that's on every course for dialogue coaches. There's a scene about a pellet of poison that's put in a drinking vessel with the image of a pestle on it. He's not supposed to drink that; his is in a chalice with the sign of a palace on it.'

The DCI's eyes widened even more. 'And?'

'What I'm saying is that this investigation's a bit of a poisoned chalice?'

'You mean that was missed at the crime scene?'

'No, boss. I mean . . .' He stopped as he saw her grin.

'Sergeant, I can only imagine what Dan Provan would be saying if he was here. As he isn't, I'll do it for him – cleaned up a bit. Henceforth your official police nickname is "Hitchcock". Get used to it, live with it; it will follow you all through your career, just as "Sauce" follows DI Haddock through in Edinburgh . . . and everywhere else. As for the analogy,' she continued, 'if we play this right, we have definitely got the chalice with the palace with the brew that's true.'

'That's a misquotation, boss. It's "the chalice *from* the palace", not "with". Get it?'

She showed him a middle finger. 'Get this, Hitchcock?'

He drew a breath, then nodded. 'Loud and clear. It doesn't ease my worries, though. We've been landed with a murder investigation based on a flawed autopsy nine years ago, but with no supporting physical evidence. The body's long gone, so it can't be re-examined. Professor Scott might be an expert witness, but suppose we did find the person . . .'

'Or people.'

'. . . or people,' he conceded, 'who injected the victim with enough morphine to see off a Grand National winner; the only evidence against him – them – would be Scott's theory, and the defence would find another expert witness to say the opposite.'

'But we have got more than that,' she pointed out. 'From a single interview we now know that there was a second witness present during the post-mortem, and a third who tried to get in but wasn't allowed. Why was the second man there, and why was he talking to Banks before the examination? Who was the woman, and why was she so agitated? They're witnesses, and they need to be found and interviewed. Then there's the Oramorph itself. What happened to the capsules and the packaging? The suicide theory was underpinned by Marcia Brown's job. She was a hospital manager and the conclusion was that she used her position to acquire the drugs that killed her. Conclusion,' she repeated, 'but based on what? Was that supposition ever proved or even investigated? Lots of questions, Hitchcock, and one man might have the answers.'

'That being?'

'That being the one living person, other than Marguerite Swanson, we know was at the examination, and at the scene of the crime too. Detective Sergeant, as was, Terry Coats. We need to find him and interview him. He's our top priority.'

Forty-Seven

'Has Sir Robert always been so passionate about his coffee?' Noele McClair asked, walking into the Serious Crimes office.

'For as long as I've known him,' Haddock said. 'Have you always been so passionate about your eclairs? You had two! Is it something to do with the name?'

'Maybe you shouldn't start that one, Sauce,' she ventured.

'True.' He looked at DC Wright, who had risen from her chair as they entered. 'Jackie,' he exclaimed, 'you don't need to get up just because we come into a room.'

She looked back at him kindly. 'I didn't. I heard the sarge mention coffee and it flipped my switch; I've been at it non-stop while you two were on your break.'

'Fruitfully?'

'Oh yes, boss. If you'll let me fill up, I'll brief you.'

McClair went to her desk, which was next to that of the DC, and Haddock pulled up a chair alongside. They waited while she poured herself a mug of stewed coffee from the machine in the corner, returned to her station and looked through the notes on her desk.

'BT came good,' she announced. 'I've been able to confirm that Carrie visited Mr Cedric Black in Millport last Thursday morning. He was David Brass's family lawyer, but he's retired now. I've been in touch with him and he's willing to be reinterviewed. Can I do it?' she asked, tongue in cheek. 'On Friday, she had two appointments. The second was at a steel stockholder—'

'A what?' the DS asked.

'Wholesaler, basically,' Wright explained. 'That was in Motherwell. The business is called WZB. I've called them three times; I got voicemail each time, left a message each time, but so far none returned. Could the place be closed for the holidays?'

'That's unlikely,' McClair said. 'If there is still such a thing as the Fair Fortnight, it's in the second half of July.'

'Okay, I'll keep on trying. 'I've got some background on the business. It's a newish company; been trading successfully for five years. The owner is a company, RLIT Holdings Limited. It's registered in Scotland, but its only shareholder is RL Investment Trust, and that's based in Zurich, Switzerland.'

'What the hell has that got to do with a failed shoplifting in Kilmarnock nine years ago?' Haddock asked aloud. 'Only one way to find out,' he said, answering his own question. 'Find its owner and ask him. Keep trying, Jackie.' He winked at her. 'Maybe you can interview him while Noele and I are in Millport.'

'I might be busy somewhere else, sir,' she countered. 'Carrie's first meeting on Friday needs to be followed up too. It was in the morning, in Saughton Prison.'

The DI frowned. 'Why?' he exclaimed.

'I don't know,' the DC told him. 'But I know who she saw. His name is Jeffrey Morgan and he's doing eight years for corporate fraud. The visit was arranged at short notice, at her request. I've arranged another for three o'clock this afternoon.'

'Do you want to do it?'

'No, sir. I want to go to Millport. Black can see us at five; he has a Rotarians conference in Stirling tomorrow that he refuses to cancel.'

Haddock grinned. 'Okay,' he said. 'You've earned it. You and Noele can do that; I'll interview Morgan.'

Beside him, McClair made a hissing sound. 'Problem, sir,' she sighed. 'I'm a single parent, remember. It's too late for me to arrange cover for my Harry now.'

'How about her dad?'

'No fucking way, excuse my French.'

'Also, sir,' Wright volunteered, 'Noele should probably steer clear of Coats, at least until after he's been interviewed. He was Carrie's first appointment on Saturday morning.'

'Was he indeed?' Haddock said. 'I suppose that was inevitable, given that we now know of his involvement. You're right. No contact of any sort, Noele, until we've seen him. Jackie, you and I will pay him a visit tomorrow morning. This afternoon, Noele, you can see the prisoner Morgan. It's an informal interview, a fishing trip, so one officer will be enough.' He turned back to Wright. 'Cinderella, you shall go to Millport, with me. We'll leave sharpish. The route takes us close to Motherwell; it'll let us call in at WZB on the way, if we can find it.' He rubbed his hands together. 'Now I suggest that we all have an early lunch – that's assuming you still have room, Sergeant, after those eclairs.'

'Yes, boss,' the DC said, stopping him with a wave of her hand. 'But there's more. After I'd been through Carrie's diary, I had time on my hands, so I went looking for PC Parker, the officer you said was on the scene of the Marcia Brown shoplifting. The information I was given was that he and Vera Stephens, the person Brown accused of framing her, married and emigrated to Adelaide, where he joined the South Australia Police. I went on to its website, found a number for Human Resources and called it. Given the time difference, I didn't expect an answer, only voicemail, but by chance someone was working late. I told her what I was after, detail on a Peter Parker who I believed was a serving officer, and a contact number for him. She said she'd look into it and get back to me.'

Wright smiled. 'She must have been eager to please – that or bored with what she was doing – for I had an email five minutes before you got here. It said that our information was correct up to a point. Parker did join South Australia Police, seven years ago, same rank, constable. According to his annual reviews, he was an okay officer, conscientious and liked by his supervisors, but not outstanding and not regarded as promotion material. He was getting on fine until, just under a year ago, he resigned. He gave no reason at first, but the HR department didn't let it go at that. When they pressed him, he told them that he and his wife had split up. She'd met another bloke, a colleague at the clothing store where she worked, and she was pregnant by him. The police service offered to support him through his difficulties, but he declined and said that he intended to return to the UK once the divorce was finalised. The assumption was that he did, although they don't know for sure. He became an Australian citizen after three years on the force; he could still be there, but we'd need to run checks through the Aussie national social security department to find out for sure.'

'Can we find him if he is here?' McClair asked. 'Would there be a record of him returning to the UK?'

'Probably not directly,' Haddock guessed. 'Dual nationality is permitted between us and Australia. He could have, probably did, come back in using his British passport.'

'What about his National Insurance number? If that's active and he's been making contributions . . .'

'That's the obvious way. While we're seeing your ex tomorrow, see if you can track Parker down through the Department for Work and Pensions. For now, lunch, for we're all going to be busy this afternoon. You go and eat, while I give our mentor a call and bring him up to speed.'

Forty-Eight

'Do you think we've done the right thing, Mario?' Chief Constable Margaret Rose Steele asked her deputy, the man to whom she had once been married. 'Should we have integrated the Carrie McDaniels investigation and the inquiry into Marcia Brown's so-called suicide under a single command, rather than letting them run separately? I'm surprised nobody asked Perry Allsop that question when he did his press briefing announcing the identification of the remains.'

He peered at her, a double-decker sandwich paused halfway to his mouth. 'It was your idea,' he pointed out. 'Are you telling me you're having second thoughts? That would make a change,' he laughed. 'When you and I were together, you were always fucking right.'

'Someone had to be,' she shot back, 'for you were always wrong. No,' she continued. 'I'm conceding nothing, just asking for your opinion.'

'I think it's academic,' he told her. 'Effectively they are under a single commander, that being me. With Bob keeping an eye on both of them, that gives an added layer of assurance. By the way, that was a brilliant idea of yours, giving him a mentoring role. It sits comfortably with him and both teams.'

'Have you had any feedback from him?'

'Not much; there's been nothing to feed so far. He did say he likes Cotter, Lottie Mann's new DS.'

'That's good. She's taken over a high-profile job. Doing that and breaking in a new backup is asking a lot, especially after all those years she spent with Dan Provan. You're going to call me sexist, but I'm very aware that there are continuing pressures on female senior officers. We still have to prove ourselves.'

'Not in my eyes you don't.'

'I'm aware of that, Mario, or you wouldn't be my deputy. But there are still a few male supremacists left, even if they don't speak out loud these days, people like Greg Jay. Remember him?' she asked as he finished his sandwich.

'Very well. I was working for him when Bob hijacked me on to his team. Women PCs were for making the tea. That guy used to take pay-offs in kind from prostitutes for turning a blind eye. Everybody knew it but nobody said anything, as his Masonic connections helped him climb the ladder.'

Rose nodded. 'That's right, even in Jimmy Proud's day.'

'Jimmy was one.'

She gasped. 'You're joking.'

'No. You did his eulogy and yet you didn't know he was a Mason? That's another piece of male supremacy. I'm half Italian, half Irish Catholic, and that's as far away from a funny handshake as you can get in these parts, but even I knew.'

'Next you're going to tell me that Bob's one too.'

He shook his head firmly. 'No I'm not. His father was, but he didn't find out until after he was dead. He grew up in a heavily Masonic town, but he was never part of its culture.'

'I was his exec for a while,' she said, 'yet you're telling me stuff I never even suspected. Why wasn't he?'

'Because Bob Skinner, for all his camaraderie, for all his

multi-layered family, for all his charisma and his popularity, grew up as the ultimate loner. I reckon that if you scratch the surface deeply enough, he still is – just like his daughter.'

Rose smiled. 'Ask Andy Martin about that.'

'Andy was another, but he had the added complication of being a c—' He broke off in mid denunciation as his phone sounded. He picked it up from the table and took the call. 'McGuire.'

'Sir,' a female voice replied. 'Chief Superintendent Barbara Scott, divisional commander Ayrshire.'

'I know who you are, Barbara, go on.'

'Something's just landed on my desk that I thought should come straight to you. A traffic warden in Kilmarnock ticketed a car yesterday morning. When he went past today, it was still there, so he reported it to the police and the station commander ran a number check. The vehicle showed up as belonging to a restaurateur in Stevenson, reported stolen early on Saturday morning; the only problem was, it was supposed to be a Ford Mondeo. This car is a Renault. The station commander went out there himself, effected entry to the vehicle, and found the chassis number. When he checked that with the DVLA, he was told that the registered keeper is a Ms Carrie McDaniels, High Street, Edinburgh. Am I right in thinking . . .'

'Yes, you are, Barbara,' the DCC told her. 'Thank you for bringing this straight to me. I want you to put a security cordon round that car at once. Nobody touches it until a forensic team gets there from Gartcosh.' He ended the call, looking across at the chief constable.

'We've got Carrie's vehicle,' he told her. 'The bastards hid it in plain sight. Pray to God, or whoever else you believe in, that they've left something traceable behind.'

Forty-Nine

'Thanks for coming, sir,' Noele McClair said. 'I hope you didn't mind me calling.'

'Not at all; I don't blame you for wanting a witness to your meeting with this man. They don't allow phones in there, so you couldn't record it. It's okay with Sauce, and I had a gap in my diary, so all's well.' Skinner smiled. 'Apart from one thing: I'm not your line manager, our daughters go to school together, and they're best friends. It's Bob, not sir.'

'Noted.'

'So why are we here? Who is this guy Morgan and why is he important? Apart from him sharing my middle name, that is.'

'I don't know; I don't know who or what he is, only that Carrie McDaniels found it necessary to visit him here last week.'

Skinner was familiar with the entrance procedures at Her Majesty's Prison Edinburgh; he led them to the gate and into the security area, where the duty officer recognised him at once. 'I take it you'll be wanting to bypass the security gate, sir,' he said.

'I have a cardiac pacemaker,' Skinner explained to his companion. 'I'm advised not to go through those things. I'm not really sure why.'

268

On the other side of the barrier, a woman was waiting for them. 'Sir Robert,' she exclaimed, 'this is a surprise. I was only expecting DS McClair.'

'I'm a late inclusion, Bobbie. Noele, this is AG Forrest; she's been in here longer than most of the inmates.'

'Our friend Prisoner Skip is a popular man. Two visits in as many weeks. Are they connected?'

'Sadly, yes.' Her question surprised him. 'You do realise who last week's visitor was, don't you?'

'Her name was Daniels, that's all I know.'

'You missed a bit; her name was McDaniels.'

The assistant governor's hand flew to her mouth. 'Oh God! The woman who's gone missing?'

'No longer missing, I'm afraid. There was an announcement at midday: she was murdered.'

'Wow! Does that have anything to do with her visit to Morgan?'

'That's what we're here to find out, Ms Forrest,' McClair said. 'Can you establish for us whether he's had any visitors since then or been in contact with anyone outside the prison?'

'His lawyer came to see him yesterday, that I do know. It was to discuss his forthcoming application for parole.'

'We're thinking of last week,' Skinner told her.

'No other visitors that I know of, and I'm the responsible AG. As for outside contacts, phone calls are logged, so I should be able to find out. Come through to my office; I'll check before I take you to see him.'

Forrest's office was in an older part of the prison beyond the entrance block, which was a modern addition. They waited, watching her as she made an internal call and made a note on a pad. 'He called this number on Friday,' she announced as she hung up, tearing off a page and handing it to McClair. 'That was an hour after the visit from Ms Daniels . . . sorry, McDaniels.'

The DS thanked her. 'That's good; we can trace it back if we have to. Can we see Morgan now?'

'Of course. Follow me.'

She led them along a series of narrow corridors, interrupted by gates, each unlocked and locked as they passed through. As they walked, McClair whispered to Skinner, 'Now that we know about that phone call, I'm getting nervous about this interview. Should we be doing this informally? Shouldn't he be cautioned?'

'The same thought crossed my mind,' he admitted, 'but I'm okay with it for now. We've got no reason to suspect Morgan of this or any other crime. We may not even need to mention the phone call. Leave that in my hands; it might work to our advantage.'

Morgan was waiting for them in a small room, one that Skinner had been in several times before. He knew that prisoners met police there and that they were escorted to those sessions by governor ranks rather than prison officers. It was a piece of basic security that he found pointless; its purpose was to avoid the possibility of a loose-lipped officer putting his charge at risk, but the very fact that an AG was involved sent out a signal to the rest of the hall.

Nonetheless, he kept that thought to himself as he stepped through the door. Jeffrey 'Skip' Morgan did not cut a piratical figure or even close. He was a chubby man, advanced in middle age with a look in his eyes that told the former chief constable everything he needed to know. The man was afraid; he had survived his sentence, emotionally, by the skin of his teeth, and was terrified by the notion that his parole request might not be the automatic success that his lawyer had undoubtedly promised.

Bob kept silent as Roberta Forrest made the introductions, and then left. He waited as Noele McClair took a seat, but remained standing himself, fixing Morgan with a heavy stare. 'A woman came to see you last Friday,' he said coldly. 'The next day she was murdered. She had barely left you before you made an outside phone call. I'll give you two seconds to figure out how that looks for you. One, two. Time's up. Tell us, sunshine, who did you call and why?'

McClair stared at him, almost open-mouthed. *We may not even need to mention the phone call*, she thought.

'I called my wife, Eileen.' It was more of a squeal than an exclamation. 'I wanted to know what the hell had possessed her when she sent an investigator to talk to me about something that happened nine years ago, something I know nothing about. I've got a parole hearing coming up; the last bloody thing I need is to be implicated in a criminal investigation.'

'Criminal?' Skinner echoed. 'Did Carrie McDaniels suggest to you that there was criminality involved in what she was doing?'

'Not as such, no, but . . .' Morgan paused, gaining control of himself. 'Look, Marcia Brown screamed loud and long that she'd been framed. After she'd topped herself, her twin sister Joanie screamed even louder. She claimed that it was all part of a huge conspiracy to cover up something very dark, and that Marcia's death was part of it.'

'And was it?' McClair asked quietly.

'How the hell would I know? I knew nothing about any of it, other than what Joanie told me.'

'Why did she tell you?'

'Because I was the only bugger who would listen to her. She worked for me . . . and that was all, honestly,' he added. 'Whatever Eileen might have thought, there was never anything between me and Joanie but a desk.'

'Why did she send Carrie McDaniels to see you?' Skinner asked.

'She thought I could help her trace Joan.'

'Did you?'

'No,' Morgan replied. 'I fed her a line to get rid of her. I told her I had a number I could call to pass on a message; I said I would give Joanie her number, and it would be up to her whether she called. That was bullshit. I never had a number. I haven't seen Joanie since my company went bust.'

'Let's go back to this conspiracy that Marcia's sister spoke of. Did she give you any clue about it?'

'No. Only that it involved a woman called Gloria Stephens, a councillor. Joanie was off her face about that; she insisted that her sister hadn't killed herself, that she'd had help.'

'Did you believe that?'

'The woman Daniels—'

'McDaniels,' McClair interposed. 'Get her name right.'

'That's the name I was given,' Morgan snapped. 'She asked me the same thing. I told her there was nothing I'd rule out, but what I meant was that they were a pair of hysterics. Look, when Joanie came out with that stuff, as she did all the bloody time, I just wanted shot of her; and frankly, with my parole hearing in front of me, I just wanted shot of the McDaniels woman too. That's why I spun her a line.'

Fifty

Detective Sergeant Tarvil 'Wimpey' Singh had drawn what he regarded as the shortest of straws. He was in charge of the CCTV trawl across Edinburgh city centre, trying to plot the movements of two wanted men, the pair who had broken into Saltire House in Fountainbridge and stolen the Marcia Brown file from Alex Skinner's office; who had entered Carrie McDaniels' Royal Mile flat and taken her laptop and work papers; and who had found their way into Alex Skinner's duplex, attacking her and wounding Griff Montell.

Singh understood the reasoning behind the habit of assigning him to office-bound duties. His friend Jack McGurk, no midget himself, had declared in a crowded pub one evening, in mid celebration of the closure of a tricky investigation, 'Tarv, Wimpey build houses that are smaller than you.' The nickname had stuck, but his colleagues were careful not to use it in his presence. He was so conspicuously large that he could not be used on any operation where a stake-out might be necessary, and he did not fit comfortably into any car smaller than a seven-seater. Nevertheless, he had spent several years in what had then been known as Special Branch, in the old territorial force, in spite of what he regarded as his physical handicap. He would make the point on occasion, knowing all the while that in reality, most of what Special Branch had done was routine, and involved very little legwork.

His mind was dwelling on the state of the housing market when a young male constable called out to him. 'I might have something here, Sarge.'

Singh rose from his reinforced chair and lumbered ponderously across the room. 'Show me,' he said.

'Okay.' Constable Henry Devine, known as Sydney to both peers and seniors, faced an array of images on what seemed to be a split-screen monitor but was actually a series of screens mounted close together. He pointed to the one on the top left. 'There's nothing covered other than the entrance of Saltire House, and it goes without saying our subjects didn't break in the front door.'

'Why?' Singh demanded. 'Why does it?'

The constable sighed. 'Because I've checked, Sergeant. They didn't.'

'Fine. "Goes without saying" doesn't go down well in the witness box, Sid.'

'Noted, Sarge.' Devine continued, pointing to the image he had selected and frozen. 'The closest camera does give me those two individuals, back view, heading through Fountainbridge in the direction of Saltire House just after midnight. But they never get there, and that drew my attention.'

'Understood. Move on.'

'I will. About an hour and a half later,' Devine pointed to the bottom left of the four screens, 'in this camera, looking down St Mary's Street, we find another two men, same size, same general appearance as the Fountainbridge pair, but this time they're walking towards us. There's no facial identification, though, because they're wearing hoodies – think about that, Sarge, the hottest spell of weather in my lifetime and they're wearing hoodies. One of them appears to have something over his shoulder. When they pass this camera, and turn into the Royal Mile, bottom right image, we can see that it's a rucksack, and it looks empty.'

'Where do they go from there?' Singh asked.

'Immediately? Nowhere. The camera that covers the area where the entrance to the McDaniels flat is was out of action that evening. However,' he continued, 'later on, we pick them up again, top right, approaching and turning into the road that leads down to the Tun building, and on to Alex Skinner's block. See?' He pointed to the screen. 'The rucksack is gone, and this time one of the guys' hoods has slipped enough for us to have a look at him.'

The DS leaned forward and peered at the screen. The subject was taller than his companion, and wider in the shoulders. 'He's Asian,' Singh declared. 'Indian, Pakistani.'

'Sikh?'

'If he is, he's lapsed like me, for he isn't wearing a turban. This is a long shot from a single image, but if you asked me to guess, I'd say he's Pathan, Pashtun. He could be from the Punjab, Pakistan, Afghanistan – originally. Let's just assume operationally that he's Scottish. Can you do enough with that image to run it through facial recognition software?'

'Possibly.'

'Then do so, once we're finished here. Or are we finished here?'

'Not by a way, Sarge, and hold off on the photo enhancement. We don't see them again for a while, but when we do, they're legging it up Holyrood Road. The smaller guy's struggling to keep up, see, but he manages, as they go out of that shot.'

'Is that it?'

Sydney smiled. 'Oh no. They do disappear off the street cameras, and I did think I'd lost them, but then I thought, they stashed the rucksack somewhere. Where? A car, surely. Now they wouldn't want to be doing that on the street, so . . . The nearest covered car park is at the top of Holyrood Road, close to the lights. I got on to the operator. They have cameras on each floor. I asked them to start half an hour after the last street sighting, and they came up with the goods.'

He pushed a button and the screen array changed. 'Top left, they arrive, park and get out, carrying the empty rucksack; we can't see the car clearly, but we can make them out easily enough. Bottom left, they're back, the rucksack's full and they dump it. Top right, they're back for a second time, in a hurry; and bottom right, they're leaving, stopping at the ticket machine and raising the barrier. And this time, Sarge, we have an even better image of your Pashtun man as he inserts the ticket. We won't need to bother enhancing that first photograph. This one's much better; the computer can run facial recognition from it as it is.'

The huge DS beamed. 'Sid, that I would describe as a result; there are a few tiny bubbles coming your way. We might not know who he is yet, but we sure as hell know what he looks like. If our system doesn't recognise him, can you ask the Indian and Pakistani High Commissions if they can help us ID him?'

Devine shook his head. 'Not me, Sarge; it's above my pay grade. That one's down to you.'

'Fair enough. Now, the million-dollar question: did the car park camera pick up the registration?'

'It didn't need to. I've checked with the car park manager.

She told me the numbers are photographed on entry and printed on the tickets, which disappear into the machine on exit. There's very little activity through the night in that car park, even on Saturday night/ Sunday morning, so it was easy for her to find the right one from the time on the camera. That's the good news; the bad news is that it was Carrie McDaniels' number on the ticket.'

'It's not all bad. It's obvious they swapped the plates from one car to another; we now know they were driving the stolen Ford Mondeo.'

Fifty-One

'So this is Motherwell,' DC Jackie Wright murmured as they peeled off the roundabout. 'It's a place I only know from the football results,' she grinned, 'usually followed by the word "nil".'

'That's an old one,' Haddock snorted. 'They say that about all the teams in Fife; not without justification, I concede.'

'It's not the place I expected; I was still looking for big steel mills.'

'Those days are dead and gone. Gone to the Far East mostly, even though there are still a few relics in Britain. Nowadays Motherwell's best known, among a few of us, as the birthplace of Bob Skinner.'

'Really?'

'Really . . . and don't try the football joke on him, by the way. The frustration of being a Motherwell supporter is the only thing he didn't leave behind him. He doesn't talk about it much, but he was brought up here. His dad was a solicitor; the gaffer could have taken over his firm, but he didn't want to.'

'Why not?' Wright asked.

'You think I'm his confidant?'

'You're his blue-eyed boy; everybody knows that.'

'The gaffer has a few of those . . . and girls. One of them wears the chief constable's uniform.'

'And her predecessor was one too, wasn't he?'

'Don't go there with the Big Man,' Haddock warned her. 'Andy Martin's off limits as a subject these days.'

'Why? I know he was duff as chief constable, but . . .'

'He let Alex down, twice. The first time they got over it, but not the second. He's off the Skinner Christmas card list for good.'

'So why did Sir Robert leave Motherwell?'

'He wanted his kids to be brought up in a different atmosphere; that's all he ever said to me.'

Wright looked around. 'Seems reasonable; wanting your children to grow up at the seaside.'

'I don't think that's what he meant,' the DI said cryptically, as he turned into the car park of WZB Steel Stockholders.

'Nice car,' Wright observed as he parked alongside a Mercedes S Class with a WZB registration plate. 'Advertising on wheels.'

Haddock led her into a single-storey black building that fronted a big industrial warehouse. The interior confounded its nondescript appearance, with an expensive monogrammed carpet leading up to a modern reception desk that the DI surmised was of Scandinavian design but from somewhere more exclusive than IKEA. A girl sat behind it; she looked expensive also, until she spoke. 'Can I help yis?' Her accent reminded him of Bob Skinner, without the erosion of thirty years in the east of Scotland.

'We'd like to see whoever's in charge,' he told her.

'That would be Mr Butt, I suppose. Sorry, but I'm new here. I'm a temp,' she explained, 'but I'm hoping he'll keep me on.

Sandi, by the way, with an "i". Who will I tell him youse is?'

'Tell him we is the polis. I'm Detective Inspector Haddock, this is Detective Constable Wright.'

'One moment,' Sandi said. She rose from her chair, turned and knocked on a door behind her. She opened it after a muffled response and leaned inside for a few seconds before turning back to them. 'He wants to know what youse want, and why youse didn't make an appointment.'

'Tell him it's a murder investigation, Sandi. In these circumstances, we tend not to make appointments.'

He waited as she conveyed his response to the unseen man behind her. Eventually she turned back, opening the door wide and announcing, 'Youse may go in.'

'Thank you, Sandi,' Haddock said as he moved towards her. 'By the way, how long have you been working here?'

'I started yesterday. Why?'

'It means we don't need to talk to you as well, that's all.'

They stepped into a large office; its furniture looked to be from the same supplier as the reception desk, and the carpet was a continuation of the special order they had seen outside. However, the dominant feature of the room was none of that; it was a large picture window that displayed the activity in the warehouse, showing its machinery in action and keeping the workforce under constant management supervision. Haddock wondered how they felt about that, but it had nothing to do with his visit and so he determined to leave the question unspoken.

The man in charge of it all rose to greet them from a tan leather swivel chair. He was small, with grey hair and brown skin, and was dressed in a mix of European and Asian styles, a dark suit over a white collarless shirt, without a tie.

'Inspector, Constable,' he greeted them. His accent was peculiar, a mix of subcontinental and Scottish. 'I am Wasim Butt.' He paused, smiling. 'I can tell by the look on your faces that I'm not what you were expecting. You think of Pakistani businessmen, you think of corner shops and cash-and-carries, not the steel industry. We are everywhere, Officers, everywhere. How can I help you? My fairly useless new receptionist said there's been a murder. Can you tell me a little more?' The remnants of his smile vanished and were replaced by a frown. 'Is the victim someone I know? I hope not.'

'We're hoping you could tell us that, Mr Butt,' Haddock replied. 'The victim's name is Carrie McDaniels, and we believe she visited you last week, late on Friday afternoon to be specific.'

Butt leaned backwards, gazing at them, surprise in his eyes. 'She was here, you say? Who was she visiting?'

'Again, we don't know; we don't even know why.'

'Who was she, this unfortunate woman?'

'She was an investigator, looking into an old allegation of shoplifting.'

'You know that much, you must know why she came here,' Butt observed. 'If she came here,' he added. 'Do you know that for certain?'

'No,' Haddock admitted, 'we don't. All we have is a reconstruction of her diary; the original was stolen. Were you here yourself on Friday, Mr Butt?'

'No, I wasn't; I was back in Pakistan for a while. I only returned on Sunday. I can show you my passport if you like. It was stamped at the airport.'

'Then who was here?'

'Only the people on the shop floor; if you like, you can

speak to Steve O'Donnell, the foreman. He would know if a strange woman had been in the shed. Steve has an eye for the ladies.'

'Is there anyone else at management level?' Wright asked.

'No, only me. I have a son, Zaqib, who likes to preen and strut about the place . . . that's when he's here, which is not very often. But he's no use for anything serious; he has no business brain.'

'Where is he now?'

'Zaqib is in Pakistan; he has a wedding to arrange.'

'Whose?'

Butt gazed at the DC, his smile back in place. 'His own, my dear. Who else's?'

Fifty-Two

'I tried to raise Sauce, sir – er, DI Haddock,' Tarvil Singh said, 'but his phone was off. That being the case, I thought I'd better report to you direct.'

'You thought right, Sergeant. It doesn't tell us a lot we didn't already know, or couldn't have guessed, but it's confirmation. I'll put out a nationwide alert for the car. I've no doubt it'll turn up very soon.'

'You reckon, sir?' the DS exclaimed.

'Yeah, it's a near cert; we'll find it, maybe without the plates, but we'll find it . . . and when we do, it'll be burned to a fucking cinder. The footage you've been looking at was shot early on Sunday morning. I don't believe they broke into the pet crematorium on Saturday before they went to Edinburgh. That means – unless they had her stashed somewhere, and that just doesn't work – they had Carrie's body in that car, in the boot, all the time they were in that car park. Only an idiot would leave the forensic evidence for us to find, and whatever else these boys are, idiots they are not. It was good work by your lad Sydney, and he will get an acknowledgement for it, I promise, but you should prepare him for it all being in vain. I think the best we can hope for is that one of the tyres has survived, so that we can match the tracks we found at the crem and prove they were there. Thanks again, Wimpey; I'll brief Sauce myself when he contacts me at close of play today, as he's under orders to do.'

McGuire hung up, smiling at the knowledge that he was one of very few people who could use Singh's nickname without worrying about repercussions. The truth was, in fact, that nobody need worry. The DS was huge, but so big that the only way he could overcome anyone was by falling on them; he was given desk work because his line managers realised that he would fail any fitness test for operational duty that he was asked to take, and valued him too much to take that risk.

His smile widened as he dwelled on the nickname culture in the police service. They were a badge of distinction, and almost every officer acquired one at some stage. Maggie Rose was Red, because of her hair, and in her younger days, her politics. He himself was Cornetto, a nod to his Italian side, although he and his bosom pal Neil 'Nails' McIlhenney had gloried in their shared soubriquet, the Glimmer Twins. The old chief, Sir James, had always been Proud Jimmy. To McGuire, that had lacked imagination; privately he had called him PC Murdoch, after the beloved cartoon character. ACC Brian Mackie was known as Dick, after Deadeye, because he was reckoned to be the best shot on the force. In his early years, Skinner had been known in CID as Paton, because of his eulogising of the man he declared to be the greatest Motherwell player ever, even though he was too young to have seen him play. Later he had been simply the Big Man, not because of his size or the way he carried himself, but because he was the one to whom everybody deferred, whether he sought it or not. Andy Martin, on the other hand, had never acquired a nickname; to McGuire, that said it all.

'There's nothing more irritating than a guy who sits there smiling at a joke that nobody else has heard. You remind me of Phil Mickelson.'

The DCC turned to his newly arrived visitor.

'I'm sorry, Ginger,' he chuckled. 'I was miles away there.'

McGuire disliked the national force's command rank base in central Scotland – the Bunker, he and Maggie Rose called it – but its one advantage was that it lay within easy reach of the Crime Campus at Gartcosh.

'A personal visit?' he said to Arthur Dorward, who sat facing him, russet hair uncovered for once, and wearing a suit rather than a crime-scene onesie.

'It's always my choice in the biggest investigations, Mario,' the scientist replied. 'Sure, I could have phoned, and a written report will follow this, but I'm old-fashioned. I like to look the other person in the eye when I tell them something, just to make sure that it's all penetrated. Besides, you don't get a mug of tea over the phone.'

'The hint is taken.' The DCC rose, went to the door and issued a request to an unseen assistant.

'Do you never feel shame at not making it yourself?' Dorward asked him amiably.

'No more than you'll feel when you drink it,' McGuire retorted. 'I made my fair share, for Bob Skinner among many others. It's the custom.'

'A bit public-schoolish.'

'We don't cane them when they forget the sugar. Besides, it comes around. That young woman's out there for a reason. She beat off competition to get to make our tea; one day she'll be back here, in this chair,' he lowered himself into it, 'and someone else, maybe my wee lad, who knows, will be making it for her and her visitors.'

They waited until the tea arrived: a pot, a small milk jug and two mugs, carried on a tray by the DCC's assistant. McGuire thanked her and poured himself.

'Fuck me,' Dorward whispered as the door closed on her. 'The tips in this place are miserable.' He sipped from his mug, then put it down on a coaster on McGuire's desk. 'Gerry Heaney,' he said.

'Who?'

'Gerry Heaney, full name Gerard Francis Heaney, born in Coatbridge, Lanarkshire, thirty-three years ago, proud possessor of a string of convictions for extortion, assault and possession of a firearm, and three times a guest of the Mountbatten-Windsor Hotel Group.'

'He's one of the guys who killed Carrie McDaniels?'

'I'm not saying that, Mario . . . See, that's why I like to do this in person, even with you. All I'm saying is that his DNA was found inside her vehicle, and his fingerprints on the outside. I can't tell you when they were left there. It could have been on Saturday, it could have been a week ago. It was one of dozens of samples we found, but the only one that came up with a match when they were run through the national database. We've eliminated as many as we can – the victim herself, her father, the traffic warden who ticketed the car then called it in, a boyfriend the father told us about – but we're still left with a few we don't know.'

'Prints or DNA traces?' McGuire asked.

'Both.'

'Is your profiling good enough to indicate geographical or ethnic origin?'

'Up to a point; it's not something we focused on. Why?'

'Tarvil Singh's looking at CCTV of Carrie's abductors; we're certain one of them is Asian.'

Dorward nodded. 'I can review all the unidentified profiles for ethnicity. Asian, you said. Asia's a big multiracial place. Can you narrow it down?'

'He thinks the man might be Pashtun.'

'A good chunk of the British population's Pashtun these days. We might find it in more than one profile. Even if we do narrow it down to an individual, it won't take you far in terms of identifying him.'

'No, it won't, but maybe someone else can. If you can pin him down, we can ask other countries to check their databases.'

'You can ask, but will they?'

'Favours can be returned in the future.'

'Okay. I'll see what we can come up with; I'll include it in my formal report. Good luck with tracking down Gerry Heaney. He looks like a piece of work who's better off as one of Her Majesty's guests.'

Fifty-Three

'Is this weather ever going to break?' Jackie 'Always' Wright asked as she wiped melted ice cream from her wrist with a tissue. 'How hot is it?'

'Thirty-one degrees,' Haddock told her. 'Anyone who does not believe in global warming is an idiot, a politician, a fossil fuel industry lobbyist or all three rolled into one.'

'Then why are we not in our nice climate-controlled car rather than standing here failing to finish our Nardini's cones before they melt while waiting for a ferry?'

'If we were in our nice climate-controlled car we'd need the engine running to control the climate, and that would contribute to global warming.'

'Can we just sit in the shade with the engine switched off?'

'That I can live with.'

They returned to their saloon; after only a couple of minutes, Haddock relented and switched on the engine.

'You've been quiet ever since we left Motherwell,' Wright observed. 'Are you disappointed that we didn't wrap the case up there and then?'

'That would have been good,' he answered dryly. 'If they'd admitted that they dropped a slab of steel on her by accident then tried to cover it up by destroying the body.' He grinned. 'Maybe someone else was under it as well, hence the mystery of the second set of remains in the crematory.'

'How do we know that didn't happen?'

'I don't suppose we do for certain, nor will we until we find out whether she made it to her meeting with Noele's ex. But just for now, let's leave that thought in the "silly" box. Yes, I'm disappointed that we didn't come away with something, even if it was only confirmation she was there, without knowing why. Mr Butt offered to show us his passport, so we can take it as read that he really was in Pakistan. The foreman guy, O'Donnell, said categorically that he didn't see any strangers in the plant on Friday. Dunno about you, but my impression was that he isn't a practised liar.'

'I agree with that,' Wright said, watching the flatbed ferry approach its mooring. 'What about the son, the preening Zaqib, who his dad thinks is useless?'

'He's still in Pakistan, according to Wasim, who again doesn't strike me as a man to say anything he can't prove. Nevertheless,' he concluded, reaching for his phone. He found Tarvil Singh's number and called it. 'Sergeant, I have another task for you. I need you to check on the directors of the steel stockholder we've just visited. It's a limited company, WZB, and I'm assuming it's registered in Scotland. The man we saw is named Wasim Butt; he'll be one, I imagine. He has a son called Zaqib, and you may find him there also. Mr Butt is denying that Carrie McDaniels ever visited his premises. I'm not calling him a liar, but just to be sure, I'd like to know everything there is to know about him.'

'Got that, boss,' the DS said. 'Hot enough for you over there?' he added. There was a hint of laughter in his tone.

'And then some. Just for rubbing it in, here's another task. So far Jackie's come up with nothing in her attempts to find PC Spider-Man Parker, one of the key witnesses in the Marcia Brown shoplifting case. Have another go; I want you to ask the DWP whether he might have been issued with, or sought, a replacement National Insurance number. Check with the DVLA for anything noted on his driving licence – speeding convictions and the like; check with the passport office to see whether he's tried to renew his UK passport; and check with our own HR people in case he's made an attempt to rejoin the service here since his return to Britain. Finally, since he has dual British–Australian citizenship, ask the Aussie High Commission whether they've had any contact with him. Have a nice day in your nice climate-controlled office.'

Wright smiled as she ended the call. 'That's him told. Sir,' she murmured, 'that second body in the crematorium. I can't get my head round it. Where do we even start trying to trace him?'

'You were at the team briefing yesterday,' Haddock retorted. 'You heard what I said. It's a complete bolt from the blue, unfathomable, unpredictable; the only thing we can do is the obvious, and that means looking at the missing persons register for adult males.'

'You don't suppose the crematorium owners . . . what's their name?'

'McGough.'

'You don't suppose they have a business on the side? "Discreet disposals for the criminal underworld", the sort of thing you might advertise on the dark web?'

'Jackie, the heat's getting to you. The McGoughs called the police, remember.' He put the car in gear and moved it slowly forward towards the ferry.

Fifty-Four

'What do you know about this man Heaney?' Alex asked her father.

'Nothing more than I was told by Mario. He's a small-time professional thug, with no obvious talent for anything else. If you ask me to speculate, it wasn't him who broke into this building, and into your place. If the guy who did that has a record, given the sophistication of the systems he got through, he's more likely to be a safe-breaker . . . although there are damn few Johnny Ramenskys around these days.'

'Do they have any leads to the second man?'

'Thanks to various CCTV systems, they have a half-decent image. The probability is that he's ethnically Asian. Face recognition might pick him out of the database, but don't expect me to go blue in the face from holding my breath.'

'If it was Heaney who had the knife,' she said, 'as his criminal CV suggests, don't imagine that the other man isn't a threat too. I took Heaney down with a saucepan; the other one scared me more. If Griff hadn't come in when he did . . .' She shuddered.

'Hey, are you all right?' Bob asked anxiously.

She looked towards her office window, then shook her head. 'I can't say that I am, Pops,' she admitted. 'I've had some scrapes

– Griff bailed me out once before, remember – and not been bothered afterwards, but this is different. They were in my house, and after what they did to Carrie, I feel threatened in a way I never have before. Life was never like this when I was a corporate lawyer. It might have been boring and I might have questioned the ethics of some of it, but I slept well enough. I haven't done that since Sunday morning. I feel completely secure at Dominic's, but still I've barely closed my eyes. Even when these guys are caught and put away, I'm not sure I can get over this.'

He sighed, then smiled, trying to keep his own fear from showing. 'You will, I promise you. Post-traumatic stress doesn't just affect soldiers, you know. I'm a walking example; when I was a plod, I saw something so awful that I literally blocked it out of my mind for years.'

'In that case, you know what I'm saying.'

'Yes, and I'm promising you that you'll recover.'

'Pops, Carrie McDaniels took on an investigative job for me and wound up dead as a result. I'll always have to live with that.'

He held up a hand. 'Hold on, that has still to be established. It's possible that Carrie's murder was unrelated to the Marcia Brown investigation.'

'Are you holding your breath over that one?' she challenged.

He winced but did not answer.

'Exactly! Pops, this is a world where something like that can happen, and I chose to inhabit it. Maybe I should change my mind and switch back to corporate work. Mitch might even have me back at the firm.'

'He might indeed,' Bob agreed, 'but he'd have a sliver of doubt about you for ever more. You'd have the same.' He frowned, and his eyes seemed to go somewhere else. 'Alex, do you think I've never been scared? Twelve years ago, a bloke broke into my house. He was going to shoot me; he did fucking shoot me,' he exclaimed, 'but I got lucky and it was him who wound up dead.'

She stared at him. 'Pops, are you serious?'

'Never more so.'

'You never told me anything about that,' she said, her voice tremulous. 'You said that you'd been using a drill and the bit had broken and gone into your thigh! You were actually shot? And the man who shot you died? Who killed him?'

He looked at the ceiling. 'Who do you think?'

The silence hung between them like a barrier. 'How in God's name was that kept quiet?' she asked when she was able to break it.

'It was spook stuff,' he replied, 'and that's all I'll tell you. I woke up in a cold sweat for weeks after it. I was having a fucking PTS breakdown, but I couldn't tell anyone. It faded, though; I came through it. You will too, I promise you.'

She smiled weakly. He could tell that she was still shaken by his revelation; he regretted having made it, but it could not be taken back. 'I'll do it all the faster when these guys are caught and put away. How's the investigation going?'

'Slowly, because almost all traces of Carrie's movements have been erased. Sauce and his team are having to go back over the trail that she did leave behind her.'

'Why not revisit the Marcia Brown investigation?'

'They will in time. Once they've established that's all that she was doing. For example, they had her going to a steel warehouse in Motherwell. What's that got to do with a supermarket shoplifting?'

'It'll be connected,' she insisted, 'for sure. Carrie promised she'd work only on my brief. The whole thing started, according to Marcia, with a beef between her and the council leader, the Stephens woman. Has she been interviewed?'

'Her name wasn't in Carrie's diary. It's up to Sauce to determine if and when to interview her. She's a powerful woman, don't forget.'

'She's a small-time local politician and she should have no special treatment. She was Marcia's enemy. Marcia was framed, and now, God help us, you're overseeing a team investigating her murder. Stephens must be a suspect, given their history.'

'That's for the investigating officers to determine.'

'So fucking help them determine it!' she shouted.

Fifty-Five

'The first time I went on holiday to Spain,' Jackie Wright reminisced as Haddock drove slowly past a line of palm trees, 'there was a guy on the beach selling coconuts. If this weather keeps up, there'll be an opening for him here.'

'Give it a week and he'd be selling hot chestnuts. It's not exactly the Riviera, is it?'

'It'll do.'

'Oh yes? That ugly edifice on the mainland coast? That's a nuclear power station. You won't find many of those in Cap d'Antibes.'

'What's French for philistine?'

The DI was still smiling as his satnav told him they had reached their destination. He parked at the roadside, noting as he stepped out into the still searing heat that a tall, slender man was watching them from his doorway. 'Mr Black?' he called out as they approached him.

'That's me. You're prompt; come on inside.'

They made their way up the path that led to Black's imposing house, timing their approach to avoid the spray from the hose extension that was watering the lawn. 'I'm doing this while I can,' he explained. 'I'm expecting a hosepipe ban any time now.'

He ushered them indoors to a study that looked out onto a back garden. Its grassy area was burned beyond recovery.

'Can I offer you a drink, officers?' he asked. 'My partner's out this afternoon or she'd be plying us with coffee, but I do have sparkling water.'

'We're fine, thanks,' the DI replied. 'We have supplies in the car . . . although we may ask to use your toilet before we leave.'

The lawyer smiled. 'And if I refuse?'

'We'd probably have to arrest you. Obstruction, I reckon.'

'Well warned. Before we get to that stage, how can I help you? You were vague when you made the appointment. DC Wright is it?'

'Our investigation is very sensitive,' Haddock explained. 'I'm heading the inquiry into the abduction and murder of a woman named Carrie McDaniels. We've got reason to believe she visited you here on Friday.'

'That's right, she did, poor lass. I heard on the TV news that she'd been murdered; I wondered if that was behind your call. What a shocker that was! Identified from remains, the news bulletin said.'

'That's one way of putting it; her body was burned. It was the serial number on her watch that told us who she was.'

'I remember it: a Rolex, nice piece. Why would anybody want to kill her? Was it a random attack, or was she targeted?'

'That's what we need to establish, sir,' Wright declared. 'What did you discuss when she visited you?'

'She asked me about the Marcia Brown business,' he replied. 'You know about that?' Haddock nodded. 'She was working on the instructions of Alex Skinner . . . or so she told me. I took that at face value, but given what's happened, I begin to wonder if there was more to it.'

296

'You needn't wonder; it's true.'

'But that was just . . . Okay, it was a tragedy, but a storm in a teacup, no more than that.'

'What was your role?' Haddock asked. Seeing Black's quizzical look, he added, 'We're coming from a base of zero knowledge, just putting together a picture of Carrie and what she was doing, how far she'd got in her search.'

'There was nowhere for her to get to. It was a sordid episode with a very sad conclusion. My role, you ask? I was retained by Marcia after her arrest for theft from a Kilmarnock supermarket called LuxuMarket; a petty theft, I must say, one that other stores would have dismissed with a caution and a bar from the premises.'

'Why did she choose you?'

Black peered at the detective constable, surprised by her question. 'Why not?'

'Weren't you a family lawyer, sir?'

'Our practice was broad-based; we weren't strangers to the sheriff court. But yes, you're correct, our original relationship was as family solicitor and client; I helped Marcia and David Brass, her former husband, through their divorce. I don't think she knew any other lawyers, so she came to me when the trouble happened.'

'If she had lived,' Haddock asked, 'would you have got her off?'

'No, because the evidence was overwhelming; I told her as much. I made such a good job of persuading her that she killed herself.'

'Are you sure about that?'

'One hundred per cent.'

'What would her defence have been?'

'Non-existent. She claimed she was the victim of a conspiracy.'

'By whom?'

'Councillor Gloria Stephens, the leader of the West Coast Council. Marcia claimed she had evidence Stephens was up to no good. In fact she was implying she was guilty of criminal behaviour.'

'Did she have evidence to back that up?'

'I don't know; she refused to share it with me. I don't even know if it ever existed. She hated Stephens with a vengeance.'

'She sounds like the client from hell,' the DI observed.

'You can say that again; she certainly gave David Brass a terrible time during their marriage. Marcia could be a pain in the fundament. There was no end to the woman's obsessive behaviour.' He paused. 'Well, actually there was, when she took her own life. They said it was out of guilt and shame. That's bollocks. Marcia was a ball of disruptive energy. She had no friends on the council, only enemies. She had no shame either, not that I could detect. In life, her only allies were her sister Joan, who was as obsessive as her; David, even after their divorce; and Austin, their son. My suspicion is that she killed herself out of spite, out of sheer malice, out of guilt – not her own, but to inflict it on Gloria Stephens and everyone else who had crossed her.'

Fifty-Six

'Dominic, can I ask you something?'

He offered her the slow, languid smile that Alex had come to realise was not easily won. 'You just did, and the answer's yes.'

'I mean can I ask you something you might not want to talk about?'

'There's only one way to find out.'

'How does it feel to be a prisoner?' she ventured.

'I'm happy to talk about that; as a matter of fact, I do quite often, in my lectures. There are many answers, but it all begins with fear. I don't care who they are or what they've done, the first time a person is convicted and given a custodial sentence, the first time they walk through a door that they do not control and hear the key turn in the lock behind them, everyone is fearful.'

'Even you?'

'Even me. You might not realise it at the time, but the apprehension has more than one source. It took me a while to rationalise this. I never felt physically threatened in prison; I was who I was, and nobody questioned that, or me. At least that's what I thought. The more subtle truth was that I was never challenged because I never raised the question myself. I never offered or invited a threat. Through all the time I was inside, I was aloof. I made no friends; I rebuffed all efforts to befriend me.'

'So what were you afraid of?'

'I was afraid of myself and of what effect my sentence might have on me. There was always an intelligent person hiding inside Big Lennie the minder. I feared that he might disappear through being institutionalised; I feared his loss.'

'How did you conquer it?'

'It conquered itself when I discovered that prisons have libraries and that they actually do offer rehabilitation; more than that, they offer an education. During my first sentence, I did my Highers; I walked out of there with university entrance qualifications.'

'But you didn't use them,' Alex pointed out.

'I didn't have time,' her host countered. 'I got out, Tony Manson was murdered, and I went on my mission to take care of the people who did it.' He frowned. 'Your dad and I were in competition over that, but I was always a step ahead of him, until he caught up with me and we had our . . . discussion.'

'Didn't the intelligent man inside you tell you to leave it to him?'

A grin flashed across his face. 'He did,' Dominic chuckled, 'but Lennie told him to fuck off.'

Alex did not return his smile. 'When you and Pops had your . . . business meeting, if it had worked out the other way, would you – no, would Lennie have killed him?'

'Never!' he replied vehemently. 'At the time, I thought I'd subdued him; I was going to tie him up, hide him somewhere it would have taken a while to find, and make my getaway. It would have worked, too. If it had, I'd have been living in Argentina and been pretty much untraceable. Yes, I thought I'd subdued him, then he just exploded on me and wiped me out.'

She gazed at him. 'You guys,' she whispered. 'You have a friendship that even a top crime writer would do well to imagine, and yet it's for real, and I'm here.'

She winced, and lines appeared around her eyes; lines that she had been noticing in the mirror for a while and doing her best to disguise. 'I'm here because Carrie isn't. And the police aren't doing enough!' she exclaimed.

'They're doing their best, I'm sure.'

'That's what Pops says, but there's someone at the heart of it and they seem to be scared to confront her.'

'Who's that?' he asked.

'The woman Marcia was convinced had framed her, Gloria Stephens, the West Coast Council leader. Nobody's been to interview her, to put the right questions.'

Dominic fell silent; she watched him as he thought. 'I know that name,' he said eventually. 'I mentioned that I read the local paper when I was in HMP Kilmarnock, and she was never out of it. Plus, she visited the prison often, as an official visitor, but also as a councillor. There was a short-term population in there, guys and eventually some women, who were local people, and would be voting in the council elections when they were released. She's the only councillor I ever heard of who did surgeries in jail.'

'And Carrie didn't go to interview her?' Alex wondered. 'I find that hard to believe somehow.'

'Hey,' he retorted, 'didn't you say that Bob told you the last trace of Carrie was when her credit card was used to buy fuel in East Kilbride?'

'Just after midday; then nothing.'

'What if . . .' He pushed himself up from his chair on the deck. 'Come on.' He led her into the house, to the office area. 'Let's have a look . . .' He wakened his computer from sleep mode and searched for 'West Coast Council'. The official website was the top return; he clicked on it, then found the list of council members. Gloria Stephens was fourth from the top of the page. He selected her.

The image of a middle-aged woman appeared on screen. 'She's smiling,' Dominic observed, 'but not with her eyes. There's something predatory in them. She's a control freak; and not someone who takes well to being challenged.'

'You can tell that just by looking at her?'

'I looked at eyes like those every day for years of my life. Let's see what her page says.' He clicked on the arrow at the foot and it was refreshed. 'Well, well, well,' he whispered. 'On Saturday afternoon she had an open surgery in Newmilns. To get there from Edinburgh, avoiding Glasgow as you'd probably want to, you would go through East Kilbride. Would you bet against Newmilns as Carrie's destination?'

'No, I would not,' Alex declared. 'The only question is whether she reached it.'

'You should pass this on to your father, or to young Haddock directly.'

'I have a better idea. Let them go on at their own pace. That list says she has a surgery in Galston community centre at seven tomorrow evening. Why don't we ask her ourselves?'

Fifty-Seven

'Have you ever felt you were being used as a stalking horse, Hitch?' Lottie Mann asked her sergeant.

He considered the question for some time before replying. 'When I was sixteen, I had this Mackem girlfriend, a couple of years older than me. I won't go into detail, but she opened my eyes in all sorts of ways. Everybody but me wondered what she was doing playing around with a naïve Geordie twerp. Then the guy she'd fancied all along chucked his woman, turned up from Sunderland, kicked the shit out of me and carried her back across the Wear. Does that count?'

'I'd say it does,' the DCI conceded.

'The relevance being?'

'This investigation that Skinner and McGuire have set us on. Nine years ago an incompetent pathologist fucked up an autopsy and wrote a homicide off as a suicide. We've been tasked with finding out whether it was just that – incompetence – or something more sinister, and if so, who wanted the lady dead. But nobody gave us any backstory, just the name and the circumstances. I should have asked for more, but I didn't. I was so fucking star-struck at being picked out by those two that I asked no questions. I said as much to Dan last night.'

303

'What did he say?'

'You're too young to hear most of it,' she replied, 'but when he was finished, I googled our victim and found that she was high-profile – as high as your profile can be in Ayrshire at any rate – a public figure who was accused of shoplifting and couldn't face the consequences. That was the story.'

'You don't believe it?' John Cotter asked.

'It's not a matter of what I believe. It's why we weren't told, that's what I can't figure out. I've spent most of today trying to remember who it was that said he was only a prawn in the game, for that's how I feel.'

'Brian London.'

She stared at him from the passenger seat. 'Who?'

'Brian London,' the DS repeated. 'An old-time boxer; he said it after he was chinned by Muhammad Ali back in the sixties. Where I come from, Ali was an idol; my grandad met him when he visited Tyneside in 1977. He knew all about him and he told me that story.'

'In that case, I know how Mr London felt,' she declared as she took a ticket from the machine at the entrance to the Edinburgh Airport car park and watched the barrier rise.

After a fruitless ten-minute search for a free space in the open short-stay area, they headed for the multistorey; the only vacancies were on the top two floors. 'How do we find the security office?' Cotter asked as they stepped out of the lift. 'It won't be advertised, and this place is a maze.'

'Easy,' Mann replied.

As soon as they reached the main concourse, she headed for the first uniformed police officer in sight, holding her warrant card high. The sergeant seemed unimpressed; he nodded recognition but kept his eyes fixed on the milling crowds, and his Heckler & Koch carbine at the ready. 'We're looking for Terry Coats,' she told him. 'He works in security.'

'I know Terry,' he said. 'His office is airside. One floor up, go to fast-track and show your ID there. You'll probably have to go through the X-ray gates like everyone else, but you'll find him there. Does he know you're coming?'

'No, and keep it that way. I don't want you warning him.'

'I wouldn't dream of it. He's a popular man today.' He moved off to join his armed colleague.

'What did he mean by that?' Cotter wondered aloud as he followed his DCI towards the escalator.

Security was busy, but Mann had experienced worse on the one occasion she had flown through Edinburgh, taking her son Jakey for a week-long holiday in Turkey. As the sergeant had predicted, the staff member who inspected their credentials insisted that there were no exceptions to the rule. 'Everybody does it, going airside,' she said, 'even though Terry's office is just to the left of the baggage roller. You're not the first, but I expect you know that.'

The DS would have asked her what she meant, but he was hustled onwards and through the regimented security procedure. The unsmiling officer who watched them load their baggage containers raised an eyebrow when he saw their extendable batons. He picked up Cotter's and examined it. 'I don't think I can let you through with this,' he declared. 'You'll have to go back downstairs and check it into the hold.'

'You may be having a bad day,' Mann barked at him, pointing out the warrant card that lay in the tray beside the DS's phone, 'but if you try to obstruct us, trust me it will get a hell of a lot worse.' She thrust both containers onto the rollers and stalked off towards the metal-detector gate.

They retrieved their belongings and moved on. 'To the left of the roller,' the DCI murmured. She stepped past the area where baggage that had been singled out from the rest was being opened for closer inspection, and saw a corridor that had been hidden from view until then – a corridor where two figures stood, one of them very familiar. 'Hey,' she called out. 'Sauce Haddock! What the hell are you doing here?'

He turned towards her, taken by surprise. 'We're going to interview a potential witness in our investigation. Now I'll ask you the same thing. I know we're one big happy family now – or meant to be – but this is a fair way from Glasgow. What's your interest here?'

'The same as yours. We're investigating a murder, and we need to talk to someone.'

'What's your man's name?'

'Terry Coats. He used to be a DI until the force got too small for him, or he got too big for his boots, depending on what story you believe. Yours?'

'This is surreal,' Haddock said. 'What's your victim called?'

'Marcia Brown,' Mann replied. 'She died nine years ago; it was marked down as a suicide until new evidence came to light – or rather after old evidence was re-examined by someone competent. Yours?'

'You'll have read about her: Carrie McDaniels. She disappeared while looking into the criminal complaint against Marcia Brown that led to her death.'

'Then you're fucking right it's surreal, Sauce. Nobody told me that your investigation was linked.'

'And nobody told me about yours period. So what do we do here, Detective Chief Inspector? Will we take turns with Coats? Do we toss a coin to see who goes first?'

'Stuff that!' the DCI exclaimed. 'We see him together; we don't give him a bloody second to gather his thoughts. Come on.'

She led the way into the corridor, in which there were two doors, a little apart, the second bearing a name plate: *Mr T. Coats*. She rapped on it briefly, then opened it without waiting for a response and stepped into the room.

'Mr Coats,' she began, 'I'm DCI—' then stopped in mid stride and mid sentence. There were two men in the office. One she assumed was Terry Coats; the other she knew for certain was Bob Skinner. 'What the f . . .' she hissed as her colleagues gathered around her.

'Nicely timed,' their mentor said.

'What's going on here, gaffer?' Haddock asked him quietly.

'You could call it convergence,' Skinner replied. 'You and DCI Mann have been heading up entirely separate investigations, with the same person a factor in both; I was going to say at their heart, but that wouldn't be quite correct. Make no mistake, the murder of Carrie McDaniels is at the heart of yours.' He rose from his chair. 'Those at the highest level wanted nothing to get in the way of that, so when it was discovered that Marcia Brown's death wasn't the suicide it was deemed to be nine years ago, it was agreed that DCI Mann would pursue it without knowledge of or interaction with you . . . and *vice versa*. I was asked to assume informal oversight of both of you.'

'But how could you separate the two?' Mann protested.

'Why would you not?' Skinner countered. 'There was no evidence that Councillor Brown's death was linked to the charge against her, nor is there yet. There's only one existing link between your cases, one living witness, and he's here. So when each of you told me separately that you were planning to interview Mr Coats, unannounced, I decided that was the moment of convergence. When I suggested to each of you separately that ten thirty was always a good time to catch him, I did so because I told him to be here.'

Jackie Wright felt like a spectator rather than a participant. She looked at Haddock, then at Mann, wondering if one of them would erupt at having been set up. Neither did, but the DI's voice had a chill in it when he spoke.

'Now that he is, and we are, are you going to leave us to get on with it . . . gaffer?'

'No, I am not, Detective Inspector.' Skinner smiled. 'Don't swing the other leg over that high horse, son. You wouldn't stay on it and the fall might hurt you. Informal oversight, I said earlier, but I've got a warrant card too – yes, I still have; I'm officially a special – and it says that I do what the chief constable asks me to do. Yours says you do what she orders you to do. I'm staying, Sauce, because I believe it's the constructive thing to do, and also because I want to ensure that this unusual situation plays out in the proper manner. Myself and Mr Coats here, who has probably never been silent for so long in his entire life, have baggage; his kid's my kid's best pal, even if he and Noele are no longer together. That apart, he is a former police officer, of equivalent rank to you; he isn't a suspect, or a person of interest, he's a witness, and I intend to see that he's treated with appropriate courtesy. Think of this not as an interview, but as a general discussion of circumstances and events.' He looked Haddock in the eye, then Mann. 'Are we square with that?'

The DCI allowed him a faint smile. 'This takes me back, sir,' she said. 'I'm clear.'

'What she said,' Haddock muttered.

'That's good. Now, this room's just about big enough for all of us, but we need three more chairs.' He looked at Cotter. 'Hitch, you and Always fetch them from the security area, please. I saw some there when I came in.'

'How does he know my nickname?' the DS whispered to Wright.

'He knows everything,' she murmured in return, 'even mine, which I don't like at all, as it has another context.'

'If anyone tries to stop you,' Coats called out, breaking his silence, 'tell them I sent you.'

'What do you do here?' Mann asked him.

'Mostly I manage the people out there, and I'm responsible for perimeter security. It's a big site, so it's a big job.'

'Mostly? What else?'

'I'm on the lookout for scams, security of goods, stuff being smuggled into and out of airside. Also money laundering; that's not an official function, but as an ex-cop I keep an eye out for situations where it might be happening.'

'Illegal immigration?'

'No, that's Border Force; they're a very tight crew.' He stopped as Cotter and Wright returned with the chairs and the detectives arranged themselves round his desk. 'Okay,' he resumed, 'who wants first crack?' As he spoke, he took out his phone and set it to voice memo mode. 'I assume you want to record this; I certainly do.'

'As long as it remains confidential,' Skinner cautioned him.

'For my own protection, that's all. Fire away.'

'Carrie McDaniels,' Haddock said. 'We know that she had a meeting with you scheduled for Saturday morning, but we don't know what you discussed.'

'That surprises me,' Coats exclaimed. He tapped his phone. 'She recorded all of it.'

'You didn't?'

'No. I didn't take it too seriously, to be honest; a nine-year-old investigation that never reached a conclusion . . . not in court, that is. It's annoying that it's never gone away, but it's history. Why haven't you got McDaniels' recording?'

'All her data, her files, and the fiscal's report that was the basis of her investigation were stolen in two thefts early on Sunday morning.'

'That's why you're certain her death is linked to this investigation?'

'That's right,' the DI confirmed.

'I don't see how it can be. It was small-time stuff. Brown was as guilty as sin. She was advised to plead that way for her own good, but she was insisting on going to trial until the negative publicity in the local press, which was always in the Labour council's pocket, got to her and she took an overdose.'

'Can you run through your discussion with Carrie McDaniels, as far as you can remember it?'

Coats nodded. 'Sure. I told her I got involved because I was asked to by Shereen Mason, the station commander. She'd been called by a PC called Parker, known as Spider-Man, also Spidey, not just for the name but because his mates said he was so fucking ugly he needed a mask; he'd been asked to go to her directly because the store manager was bricking it about Brown being a local councillor. Mason promised me that if I did it she'd sign off on the report, although in the end she never did, left me twisting in the wind. I went there, interviewed everyone involved – store manager, security guards – then confronted Councillor Brown back at the station. I interviewed her, inspected the goods and charged her. In those days,' he added, 'she didn't need to have a lawyer present.'

'Anything else come back to mind?'

'There was something about a discount sticker. McDaniels said the security boy had mentioned it, the one who stopped her; an Asian kid on a summer job.'

'Did she mention his name?'

'She did, in fact: Butt, Zaqib Butt.'

'Are you sure about that?' the DI asked.

'Certain. There was a kid in my class at school called Zaqib, and the name stuck with me. Why, is that significant?'

'It might be. We recovered Carrie's diary from the Cloud; there was an entry about a visit to a steel stockholder called WZB. It's owned by a Wasim Butt, and he has a son named Zaqib. Butt senior said she never arrived there, but at last we now have the connection. What could Zaqib have told her about that discount ticket? Any idea?'

'Not very much. He told her it was there when he stopped the woman, then it disappeared.'

'Boss,' Jackie Wright exclaimed, tugging lightly on Haddock's sleeve. 'Surely that confirms that Carrie was at WZB last Friday. Wasim wasn't there, the temp hadn't started, and Steve O'Donnell wouldn't necessarily have seen her if she'd never been on the shop floor. When we spoke to him out there, I noticed that the viewing window in the office was one-way glass; you can't see through it.'

'Agreed,' he said. 'But Zaqib's gone to Pakistan to plan his wedding. Is that convenient or just a coincidence? We need to follow up on that; wherever he is, we need to contact him and interview him.'

'So,' Skinner said, 'progress. Terry, is there anything else you remember about your meeting with Carrie?'

'Only that she was looking hard into the conspiracy angle. That was Brown's defence, and I included it when I typed up her statement for the report to the fiscal. McDaniels will have seen that if she had a copy. Brown had Spidey setting the whole thing up with his girlfriend, because of some spat between her and the girlfriend's mother.'

'Could that have happened?'

'Bob, my notes are long gone, but from what I can remember, there was no evidence to back it up. As I said, the store manager crapped herself when she realised who'd been arrested, Spidey advised her to phone Mason directly, and that was that. The girlfriend, Vera Stephens, was never interviewed, because she wasn't a witness. As for the person named Adrian who Brown claimed had distracted her while the goods were being planted, I went over the store looking for a trace of him, but there was no sign. Marcia wasn't the only one to float that conspiracy theory. Her sister Joan, she bent my ear about it.'

'When did you meet her?' Haddock asked.

'She ID-ed the body. And she turned up for the post-mortem; she was in a right state. I had to chuck her out. She said the conspiracy had something to do with a planning application that Stephens was rubber-stamping quietly because people would lose their jobs. She was raving; that was understandable, because Marcia was her twin. Later on, the son bought into that too, but he had to be careful not to cross the line of defamation in that fucking blog of his.'

'You had reason to dislike that blog, Mr Coats, didn't you?'

'Too right I did, mate, but it didn't exist at the time of his mother's arrest so it couldn't have affected my judgement. I did my job, played it by the book, and in no way did I stitch her up.'

'Fair enough,' Mann said. 'Now, can I turn to Councillor Brown's death?'

'Fire away.'

'You were the investigating officer in the theft case and you attended the scene. Wasn't that unusual?'

'I agree, it was, but blame Mason again.'

'Who found the body?'

'The postman; he had a recorded delivery letter that needed signing for. He rang her bell; there was no reply, but he knew her car and saw it parked outside. He took a look through her letter box. The way it was positioned, it had a view of her bedroom door. It was open, and he could see an arm hanging off the side of the bed. He battered the door, couldn't rouse her. Just then, by sheer chance, a patrol car passed by; he stopped it, the officers effected an entrance and found her dead. They called it in to Mason, who hit her personal panic button again and rang me. She didn't tell me who the victim was, just that it was a sudden death and she'd take it as a personal favour if I could follow it up.'

'Were you and she close?' Cotter asked, for no reason other than to register his presence.

Coats glared at him. 'What's that supposed to mean?' he snapped. 'Are you asking if I was shagging her? She was fifty-one, plug-ugly and she had a moustache. Grow up, son.'

'In that case, I'll ask it in another way,' Mann said. 'Did Chief Inspector Mason, a very nice woman I knew well in my first uniformed posting, but who was, as you suggest, a bit of a panic merchant, have any expectation that you would cover up inconvenient facts or findings? In other words, did she have something on you?'

'No, she did not; there was never anything to have,' he added firmly. 'She didn't trust anyone else in the station with a sensitive inquiry, simple as that.'

'Okay. Can you tell us what you found when you arrived at the scene?'

'A dead woman, aged around fifty, lying on a bed; two uniforms, one of them very green, literally and metaphorically; a doctor who had certified death and would have fucked right off had I not told him to examine the victim again in my presence.'

'What was your immediate reaction?' the DCI continued. 'Did you recognise her at once?'

'Of course I did!' Coats snapped. 'I'd interviewed and charged her a couple of weeks before. I was shocked; I hadn't prepared myself for that or been given the chance.'

'Was the nature of the death obvious?'

'If you mean was my immediate conclusion that she had committed suicide, no, it wasn't. She was lying on top of the bed rather than under the duvet, but she was wearing pyjamas. I'd seen a few sudden death victims in my career, and she looked like any one of them. She looked like my dad,' he murmured, his eyes softening. 'He had a cerebral haemorrhage in his armchair while he was reading the *Glasgow Herald*. He just looked as if he'd fallen asleep. So did Marcia Brown.'

Mann paused for a second, giving Coats time to come back to them. 'When did you first realise that she might have topped herself?'

'When I found the capsules in the pedal bin in her *en suite*; a lot of them, and their boxes. The labels said they were Oramorph, morphine by mouth.'

'What made you look there?'

'Training, and years of experience. You'd have done the same . . . I hope.'

'Was there anything on the boxes to indicate their origin? The belief was that she'd stolen them from the hospital where she was manager.'

'There was nothing that I saw, and I did look for it. I did a proper job; I searched the whole house carefully.' He looked at Mann, then at Skinner. 'I know you guys are going to ask whether I read any significance into that. The fact is, I didn't; I knew from my previous encounter with the victim that she was a hospital manager. In the absence of labelling, you're right, Chief Inspector, my presumption was that she had stolen the drugs she used from her work, probably on the day she died so that the theft wouldn't be discovered until after she was gone.'

'Did you make any attempt to verify that?'

'Personally, no. I did what I was asked to do by Mason, and reported back to her. Look, Lottie,' He paused. 'I know your first name; I've heard of you, and you can take that as a compliment . . . Whatever that bitch Toni Field, our late chief constable in Strathclyde, might have thought, I was very good at my job. If I had thought for one second that there was any possibility of the death being other than natural, accidental or self-inflicted, I would have called for backup and forensics and got everybody out of the place until they arrived. But I didn't, because I looked; I went over the flat room by room, window by window, and there was no sign of intrusion anywhere. There were no extra glasses in the sink or anywhere else, just the one at the side of the bed, with the dregs of red wine in it. There was a single plate, one cup, one fork and two teaspoons in the dishwasher. In the kitchen bin I found the box for a ready-made curry, and a yoghurt cup. The wine bottle was on the work surface with not much left in it. Merlot. I remember that because I hate fucking merlot.'

'The uniforms broke in,' Skinner reminded him. 'If there had been signs of intrusion, they'd have been destroyed.'

'Nevertheless, I looked for them, as you do, and I didn't see anything. There were two locks, Bob, a night latch and a mortice. I asked the plods about that. The older one was a big bloke; he said they were both engaged, and he'd had a hell of a problem kicking the door in.'

'Was there a chain in place?'

'That I don't know.'

'Can I move on to the post-mortem examination, Terry?' Mann continued. 'You attended it, I believe.'

'I did. Again, it was at Chief Inspector Mason's request; she felt that since I'd attended the scene, it would be best if I carried on. That was reasonable; I couldn't argue with it. Well, I could have,' he acknowledged. 'I might have suggested that as Ms Brown's arresting officer there might be a conflict of interest, given that she'd protested her innocence right up to the day she died. But I didn't; I was upset by her death and just wanted the business over and done with, so I did as I was asked.'

'I don't have an issue with that,' the DCI told him. 'Personally, I fucking hate autopsies; once they're over, I try to put them out of my mind. So I will understand if your recollection's hazy, but how much do you remember about it?'

'Quite a lot, as it happens. For starters, I thought the pathologist was a wanker. He wasn't one of the people I knew. They were all busy elsewhere, so they'd pulled this bloke in, from Edinburgh I think, on a sort of locum basis. He was disinterested; he'd a student assisting him, and I remember thinking it would have been better if she'd done the job. As it was, all he let her do was the photography, probably because he didn't know how to use the camera in that mortuary. My impression was that he'd been told it was a suicide, and all he was interested in was joining the dots, because it was a very short examination. When the blood analysis came back, he said "Eureka!" like he was fucking Aristotle, and pretty much closed her up.'

'Who else was present? Hitch and I were told there was another man.'

'That's right. Cedric Black, Marcia's lawyer when she was arrested.'

'Why was he there?'

'He didn't say, but I didn't find it unusual that he should be. It never occurred to me to query it.'

'Did you hear him speak to the pathologist?'

'No, but I saw them talking. I asked him why, and he said they'd met years before when the man – Banks, that was his name – was an expert witness in a case where he was instructing solicitor.'

'You said earlier that Joan Brown was there,' Mann reminded him.

'Was she ever. It was fucking scary to look at her. She and Marcia were identical twins, so she was the living image, literally, of the woman on the examination table. She was hysterical, yelling at Black. It was entirely inappropriate for her to be there, considering what Banks was about to do to her sister, so I took her right out of there; all the time she was shouting about the so-called conspiracy. Eventually I quietened her down, bollocked the people who'd let her in and made sure she was off the premises.'

'What happened to the empty Oramorph capsules and boxes?' Mann asked.

'I put them in an evidence bag at the scene and gave them to Mason with my report.'

'I take it you wore gloves as you searched Marcia Brown's place,' Skinner murmured.

Coats looked offended. 'Standard procedure, Bob.'

'You didn't ask for the capsules to be fingerprinted?'

'How often do I have to say this? The C in CID stands for Criminal: this was a uniform branch procedure that I did as a favour.'

'Fair enough. One last question. Did you see a syringe anywhere in the apartment?'

'Absolutely not. If there had been, I would have found it, believe me.'

'I do, but I had to ask.'

'Is that what they're saying now? That she was injected with the Oramorph?'

'That's the theory. Is it possible that the officers who were there when you arrived might have removed one?'

'Anything's possible, but tell me why they would.'

'Should we interview Chief Inspector Mason?' Cotter asked.

'She died last year,' the DCI told him. 'Skype doesn't reach that far.'

Fifty-Eight

'If any one of you,' Skinner focused on Haddock, but Mann was in his field of vision, 'still feels that you were set up at that meeting, I apologise.' Then he grinned. 'But it was priceless to see the expressions on your faces when you walked through that door.'

They were still in Coats' office, but he had gone, 'on my rounds', leaving them to have a debrief.

'The day you stop surprising me, gaffer,' Haddock replied, 'I'll know that I'm taking the job for granted. But why don't you just rejoin, FFS?'

'I don't want to. I put in my time, and I'm not coming back to what I was. Okay, I have experience and maybe skills that are still of value, but I want to do other things with my life. When Andy Martin was chief, he didn't want me around; that suited me, for I didn't want to be around him either, not by that time.'

'Hmph,' Mann grunted. 'Why do I think of Manchester United after Fergie retired?'

Skinner peered at her over the spectacles that he wore very rarely. 'Not quite, Lottie. The Police Authority did get it right at the second attempt. This mentoring role was his successor's idea, and it suits me. I have no rank; my warrant card does give me a degree of authority, but my oversight is no more than that, and any views I express are suggestions, not orders.'

'What are you going to suggest now, gaffer?' Haddock asked.

'I wouldn't be so presumptuous; you're all good officers. I'm a mentor, remember, no more. Sauce, you have clear lines of inquiry. Lottie, you and John were tasked with investigating Marcia Brown's homicide, and you still are. Graham Scott will go into the witness box and swear that she was murdered, but you still need physical evidence to find the perpetrators and convict them.'

'Them?'

'That's what Graham thinks; two people at least, given the way she was restrained.'

Cotter raised a hand. 'Sir?'

'Yes, Hitch?'

'Isn't DI Haddock's team looking for the same person?' he asked. 'If Marcia Brown was murdered to stop her from going to trial, and Carrie McDaniels was killed to stop her investigating her death, surely those crimes must be linked?'

'Surely? In what way is it sure? The methodology in the two crimes was completely different. Brown's death was staged to make it appear self-inflicted, and that went unchallenged for nine years. Carrie started to look into the events that preceded it, and a couple of days later she was abducted, killed, and her body disposed of in a cruel and unsubtle way, along with that of someone else, whose role in the business we still don't understand. The bodies were burned so that the investigators couldn't be sure whose they were. I don't believe that was an attempt to conceal a crime, as with Marcia; I suspect it was a tactic to hinder the inevitable investigation. If they hadn't forgotten about her watch, it would have worked too.'

'So you're saying we're looking for two separate killers?' Haddock asked.

'Until you can prove otherwise, yes. Four, actually. Two men took Carrie and attacked Alex, and the belief is that two people killed Marcia. The most effective way to find them is to run two separate investigations, surely? That's my view, but I wouldn't force it on you, even if I could.' He looked from one senior officer to the other. 'What do you two say?'

The young DI looked at Mann; they made eye contact for a couple of seconds. 'Like Sir Robert says, Sauce,' she murmured, 'you do your thing, we do ours; maybe we'll meet in the middle again, maybe not. Anything else?' she added, turning back to Skinner.

'One more thing,' he responded. 'We've heard lots about Joan Brown, but why aren't either of you talking to her?'

'Because she's walking the Camino de Santiago,' Haddock explained. 'You know Spain; it means she's virtually untraceable among the crowds. We did ask the Spanish Policía Nacional for help, but we've had nothing back.'

'No,' he replied. 'It means we know where she is. Nobody's untraceable, Sauce, and nobody goes on the Camino without planning. There are ATMs in Spain too, and cash is needed for a journey like that. Lottie, she's your witness, I'd say, rather than Sauce's. I suggest . . .' he paused for emphasis, 'that you find out where and when she last used her bank card and take it from there.'

Fifty-Nine

Tarvil Singh was a lifelong fan of the Walker Brothers; he was also proud of his voice, a fine baritone, he believed. The second of these truths he kept to himself. For all his Sikh heritage, his wife was a committed Scottish Presbyterian; they had been married in her church and he often accompanied her and her parents to services. He had never understood why song was a fundamental part of Christian worship, but he did not question it. Instead he went along with it, up to a point. Surrounded by reedy voices, some singing in tune, most slightly off key, invariably Tarvil would mime.

There were no constraints, however, in an empty CID suite. He was halfway through the second verse of 'The Sun Ain't Gonna Shine (Anymore)', when the door behind him opened and Sauce Haddock and Jackie Wright stepped silently into the room. They waited until the echoes of the last chorus had faded before applauding. He spun round, feeling the hot flush of embarrassment spread across his face.

'Not bad, Tarvil,' the DI said, 'not bad. Me, I prefer "No Regrets". Mostly, though, I prefer anything other than the Walker Brothers. Have you ever thought about "The Laughing

322

Policeman" as your signature tune? That would go down well at smokers.'

'There are no smokers any more,' Wright pointed out, 'since the law changed.'

Haddock nodded. 'Exactly.'

'How did it go with Coats?' Singh asked, desperate to move on before the talk turned to *Britain's Got Talent*.

'It was interesting. He didn't tell us much that we hadn't figured out about Carrie, but guess what? Two of our friends from the west were there, and Bob Skinner, who's been running us all like P. T. fucking Barnum. And if you break out into "A Million Dreams",' he warned, 'you're in uniform at Easter Road for the next Hearts game.'

'Too bad. That's my encore number.'

'Save it for the next time we're out. What's been happening?'

Singh smiled. 'Something very interesting,' he replied. 'I did a Companies House search like you asked for WZB. Found it no problem. The directors are Wasim Butt and Zaqib Butt, no surprise there. Wasim's on the board of a few companies, but Zaqib only shows up on the WZB board.'

'Are there any personal details about him?'

'Not on the website, but that's the thing. I did a social media search for him, starting with Facebook, as you do, and up he popped, with a list of all the places he's worked.'

'And one of them was LuxuMarket,' the DI said. 'Carrie McDaniels was on to that; Terry Coats told us. It's good that we know, but it's of no immediate help. Wasim Butt told us that Zaqib's in Pakistan, organising his wedding.'

'Is that right?' Singh mused. 'I thought Scottish Muslims restricted themselves to one wife, to comply with the law.'

'They do,' Haddock agreed. 'Why do you say that?'

'Because according to his Facebook page, he's married already, with two kids, and he lives in Carluke. I've verified that with the electoral register. His wife's name's Krystle, and they live in Station Road.' He beamed, and broke out into the opening verse of 'Get Me to the Church on Time'.

Sixty

'Are you sure you're okay in that seat?' Alex asked her out-sized passenger. 'We've been on the road for over an hour. When I bought this thing, I didn't envisage ever carrying someone who was two metres tall.'

'I'll be fine as long as the weather doesn't break,' Dominic Jackson assured her. 'If it rains and you have to put the roof up, then I'd have a problem.'

'I don't think there's any chance of that. According to the forecasters, this weather's going to stay with us for another week at least.'

'Then God help the prison population; those places aren't designed to adapt to these conditions, not even the modern ones. As for Barlinnie and the rest of the older estate, that doesn't bear thinking about.'

'What can the Justice Department do?' she wondered aloud.

'Bring in portable air-con units, I guess, if they can source enough of them.'

'Have you ever thought about writing a book about prison life, Dominic?'

'Yes,' he replied. 'For about five seconds, then I binned the idea. I want to spend the rest of my life in anonymity, Alex. I did bad things for what I hoped were good reasons, knowing that if I was caught, society would exact a price. I've paid my tab and I'm happy with that; if I wrote a memoir, one, I'd blow my cover, so to speak, and two, I'd be accused of cashing in on crime.'

'I wasn't thinking of an autobiography,' she countered. 'The book I have in mind would be a self-help guide for prisoners: how to survive long sentences, and how to find rehabilitation. You told me that you've counselled prisoners already. This would take those sessions to a wider audience.'

'And me with it.'

'You could use a pseudonym.'

'Mmm,' he murmured, 'like "the Secret Footballer", you mean? "The Secret Lifer". Trust me, he wouldn't stay secret for long. The media would out me inside forty-eight hours. And lest you forget,' he added, 'the media includes your father. He's the supervising director of the *Saltire*, and of the other InterMedia outlets that they're opening up in Britain. Nice idea, but I will pass.'

She drove on; the evening traffic had lessened by the time she took the exit signposted for East Kilbride. 'This is the route Carrie took, poor girl.' She shuddered and gnawed at her lip. 'It's dreadful, Dominic, what happened to her. I can't get my head round it. Pops says I'm experiencing PTSD. Does psychology offer a cure for that?'

'I'd prefer to say that you're experiencing survivor guilt,' he told her. 'You're thinking that if you'd done your own investigative work, Carrie would still be alive and you'd have wound up in that crematory. But you didn't, she's dead, and there's a voice in your head that you can't still that's thanking God it wasn't you, and that it's Peter McDaniels mourning his daughter and not Bob Skinner. You don't want to hear that voice or to acknowledge its existence, but you have to, and you have to accept what it's telling you without taking the burden of blame on yourself. What you did for Carrie was provide her with employment, no more. You didn't ask her to take a risk, you had no way of knowing that a low-grade historic investigation would have such consequences . . . if it even did, for nobody has yet proved a link between the Marcia Brown case and Carrie's murder.'

'You're telling me to get over it?'

'I'm telling you to accept it, and to realise that it wasn't your fault. As for the feeling of relief, every soldier who has ever lost a comrade in action has felt it. "Wow, that was a close one!" You know what I'm feeling?' he asked her, sharply. 'I didn't know Carrie and I've never met her father. But I do know yours, and I'm feeling relief that it's not him figuring out how you give a proper funeral to a pile of charred bone fragments. That's life, and that's death.'

'Shit happens?'

'No, that's callous; own the grief, disown the guilt, that's what I'm saying.'

She looked at the road ahead as she approached a junction, then glanced at him. 'You're a wise man, Dr Jackson, I'm glad you're my friend.'

They carried on to and through East Kilbride, then found the motorway that headed south-west to Ayrshire. 'Have you decided what you're going to say to Stephens?' Dominic asked her as they reached the exit that led to their destination.

'You probably know the lawyer's maxim: never ask a witness a question unless you know the answer already. I don't know any of the answers, so I'm going to have to busk it. I don't intend to ask her anything unless I can't avoid it.'

Galston community centre was easy to find; it was a squat white-painted building that had never won any architectural awards, but there was a bustle of activity about it indicating that it served its purpose. As they stepped inside, they were faced by a noticeboard; at its centre was the same smiling image of Gloria Stephens that had featured on the council website, with an arrow pointing to a stairway and advice that the surgery was being held in rooms 10 and 11. Constituents only: no press.

Dominic shrugged. 'I used to be a constituent, of sorts,' he said.

They climbed the stairs. Room 10 was the first on their left and its door was open, revealing a burly, surly man in jeans and a black T-shirt, but nobody else. He stared at them as they entered; Alex could see puzzlement in his eyes as he studied her companion. 'Surgery?' he grunted.

'We'd like to see the councillor, yes.'

'Ye'll need tae fill in a form,' he snapped.

'No, Ronnie, we won't,' Jackson replied. 'We'll just be going straight in.'

The connection was made. Ronnie switched from aggressive to subservient in an instant. 'Very good, Lennie. How're ye doing, like? Is this your bird?'

'Lennie's no more; now I'm Dr Dominic Jackson. No, this is not my bird, this is my colleague. Before we see Mrs Stephens, were you at the surgery in Newmilns on Saturday?'

'Aye.'

From the pocket of his pale-blue cotton jacket, which was marked by the corpses of a few doomed insects that it had picked up on the drive from Edinburgh, he produced a folded copy of the *Saltire*, the edition that had confirmed the death of

Carrie McDaniels. He held it up, showing her image. 'This woman was there, yes? My colleague's investigator? The one who was abducted and murdered shortly after leaving?'

'Aye, but . . . The councillor . . .'

'The councillor can tell us herself, Ronnie. You wait here, and don't think about doing an Elvis. We have the police on speed-dial, and if you leave the building, they'll be called.'

The man nodded. 'Aye, Lennie. Ah mean, aye, Doctor. Ah'll go naewhere. Will I announce yis?'

Jackson displayed the faintest smile. 'I don't think so.'

He closed the door of Room 10 behind them. 'Ronnie was one of the local constituents that Councillor Gloria visited in prison. I think he's her cousin.'

'He certainly respects you,' Alex observed.

'No he doesn't. He fears me; he doesn't know why, only that he does. In prison, fear is always a safer bet than respect.'

Alex knocked lightly on the door of Room 11, then, without waiting for a response, opened it and stepped inside. Taken by surprise, Gloria Stephens stared up at her from her seat at a small table, slightly open-mouthed. 'Who the hell are—' She stopped abruptly as Jackson's bulk blocked the light from the hall outside. 'Ronnie!' she shouted.

'He won't be joining us,' Alex informed her.

'In that case, I hope he's calling the police.'

'That's the last thing he'll be doing. At the moment, he's working out how he can avoid going back inside.'

Stephens focused on Jackson. 'That's where I've seen you before,' she murmured. 'Kilmarnock Prison; you were always in the bloody library when I visited there. What the hell are you doing here?'

'I'm supporting Ms Skinner, Councillor, that's all. The

person who came to visit you on Saturday on her behalf never made it back home. I might be harder to get rid of than Carrie McDaniels.'

'I have no idea what you're talking about.'

'Let's have no cowshit, Mrs Stephens,' Alex snapped. She took the *Saltire* from Jackson and slammed it on the table. 'I know that she visited your Newmilns surgery on Saturday. I know that was the last place she was seen alive. I know that after she left you, she was rattled, for she dropped a message on my voicemail asking me for an urgent meeting, one she never made. None of that's speculation, nor is the fact that you and cousin Ronnie knew she was dead before we showed you that page. Her name is on every billboard and her face has been on every front page since she went missing. People like you read the papers every day, so no way did you not know she was dead. What you need to persuade me now, and after that the police, is that you didn't kill her yourself, or order her death.'

'Why the fuck would I do that?' Stephens barked, her voice loud, rough and rasping. 'She was just a nosy snooper for a nosy fucking lawyer, looking into something that's been dead and buried for nine years and was never fucking important anyway.'

'Then tell me about it,' Alex counter-challenged. 'When you do, be aware that I'm an officer of the court, and as such I have a duty to report anything that may be criminal behaviour to the Crown. Withholding evidence from a murder investigation is a serious offence; you've done that, so tell me why I shouldn't report it.'

'Do you know who you're talking to?'

Alex nodded. 'Yes, I'm talking to a small-time local politician who's head of a minority Labour administration on her council, one that relies for its survival on the support of her natural enemies, the Conservative group. But I'm done talking to you, Mrs Stephens. Now I'm going to listen to you tell me what happened when my investigator came to your Newmilns surgery on Saturday. If you don't, I will call Deputy Chief Constable McGuire and advise him of an obstruction of the course of justice. Then I'll make sure that your arrest gets front-page coverage, just as my friend Carrie's murder did. If you don't believe that, fucking google me: Alexis Skinner, LLB, solicitor advocate; you'll find that I have a profile.'

Stephens took her phone from the table; she tapped in an entry, then studied it, scrolling occasionally. Finally she nodded. 'You have, haven't you. And I know who your father is.' She stared up at Jackson. 'Funny company you're keeping, I must say.'

'Both my father and I are comfortable with Dominic.'

'I know who he really is, though.'

'He gained his doctorate as Dominic Jackson. Most people have forgotten who he was, and those who haven't don't care. Are you going to talk to us?'

'Aye, okay,' Stephens sighed. 'Sit down.' She waited as Alex seated herself; Jackson remained standing, his back against the wall. 'She came here, just like you,' she began, 'but she tried to be smart. She filled in a constituent form with a phoney name that I saw through in half a second. Daniella fucking Carrington,' she snorted. 'Who was she trying tae kid? When I challenged her, she owned up. She told me who she was, and she gave me this.' She delved into her handbag and produced a business card, sliding it across the table towards Alex, who left it untouched. 'She told me she was working for you and that she was digging up the old Marcia Brown LuxuMarket shop-lifting case. She did more than that; she accused our Vera, my daughter, of setting the whole thing up, her and her boyfriend, a polis called Parker, spotty bastard. She based all this on a story she'd been fed about me and Marcia having a blazing row in the council offices. Then she threatened me.'

'Threatened you with what?' Alex asked.

'With you,' Stephens retorted. 'The same guff about you being an officer of the court and reporting me to the polis. Nonsense, all fucking nonsense. That was when I really lost my rag.'

'And assaulted her? Is that how she died?' Alex challenged. As she did so, she was aware of the first law of cross-examination. She knew that her investigator had left Stephens' office alive, because of the timing of her voicemail, but she wanted to provoke the woman, wanted to see the Stephens who had confronted Carrie and inspired the alarm that had been in her voice.

'No!' she yelled. 'For fuck's sake! I told her it was all crap. Marcia Brown and I had blazing fucking rows all the time, because that was the sort of woman she was. She was a fucking shit-stirrer by nature, just like that son of hers, Austin, and he came to a bad end too. And you know what? None of it meant a fucking thing to me. To me, Marcia Brown was a gnat . . . and I don't mean a fucking Nationalist; a wee insect like the big man's got splattered on his lapel. She was nothing, she had no power on the council, for I had an absolute majority at the time; all she was was a nuisance, and no' a very big one either. She had a down on me, sure; I got the same old guff every council leader gets about being in property developers' back pockets, brown envelopes, all that shite. So when your woman Carrie came in and started throwing it at me as well, and quoting it at me, yes, I went ballistic. I told her to get the fuck

out of my office, before I had big Ronnie do it the hard way.'
She paused, realising what she had said. 'Not that I would
have,' she added. 'I was just so bloody angry. Get Ronnie in
here if you want, he'll confirm it.'

'I'm sure he will,' Alex agreed. 'Before I do that, did you
have one of your frequent blazing rows with Marcia just before
the shoplifting allegation?'

'We did,' Stephens admitted, 'in my room; it was just the
two of us in there, but you could have heard us out in the
street. She was really worked up.'

'What was her complaint?'

'She was on about a planning application for a change of
use; her argument was that it was going to cost dozens of people
their jobs. Maybe she had a point, as it turned out, but we were
nowhere near that stage. The application was only in principle,
not for full consent; we were a long way short of that, but she
never made a distinction between types of application; I don't
think she actually understood the difference. It was from a
third-party developer as well, not from the owner of the
premises, so it was completely speculative. Marcia had no time
for that argument; she had no time for anybody's case other
than her own. As far as she was concerned, it was cut and dried,
and as usual the Labour group were in cahoots with the
developer. I couldnae shout her down – I never could, truth be
told; she'd lungs like a blast furnace; fucking unpleasant woman
– so I just let her blow herself out. Eventually she stormed out,
yelling "Criminal!" as she went.'

'That was the end of the matter as far as you were concerned?'

'And as far as she was; we had the numbers and there were
no grounds for refusal. That's something else Marcia never
understood. The planning laws and regulations aren't about

job creation, or even preservation. The area in question was zoned for commercial use, and that was the end of the matter.'

'Who was the applicant?'

'I can't remember, honestly.'

'What were the premises?'

'LuxuMarket; it was for alterations to the building rather than a change of use. It happened, eventually; the supermarket closed and became something else.'

'Who owns it now?'

'There was a company name on the planning applications, but the guy behind it's called Butt, Wasim Butt. Household Supplies and Services, it's called. Nothing controversial there, so really what's the fucking fuss about? Are you seriously trying to suggest that somebody would get killed over that?'

'I don't know, Councillor,' Alex replied. 'That's for the police to determine, and it's why you should have called them as soon as you became aware of Carrie McDaniels' death.'

Stephens sagged into herself, a dumpy, unattractive middle-aged woman, stripped of her authority. 'Maybe, but do you know what happened after Marcia did herself in? Her twin sister turned up at a council meeting. She didn't say anything, just sat in the public gallery staring at me. I didn't know of her existence until then, and I was utterly terrified. I've never been as scared in my entire fucking life. When your woman brought it up again, that all came back. I just wanted the whole fucking thing to go away.'

'Speak to the police, and maybe it will,' Alex said. 'I'll check with DCC McGuire at ten tomorrow morning. If he hasn't heard from you, I'll tell him myself, and the consequences will be down to you. Goodbye, Mrs Stephens.' She rose and left the room, with Dominic following her.

'Did you get all that?' she asked him in the corridor.

He took his phone from his breast pocket and held it to his ear as he played back a voice recording. 'Sounds okay,' he told her.

'What did you think of her?'

'What I thought before we went in there: a little woman puffed up by aggression and spurious authority. Her act's okay for the West Coast Council, but it's no wonder she's never looked at national politics. She'd be eaten alive at that level.'

'And Carrie? Could Stephens have had a hand in her death, and in the attack on me?'

'Not a prayer,' he assured her. 'She has her hands full staying alive herself, figuratively speaking.'

Sixty-One

'I've got it!'

Sauce Haddock looked up from his paperwork at Tarvil Singh's shout.

'The Passport Agency have come up with Zaqib Butt's photo,' the DS continued.

'Are we sure it's our Zaqib?'

'Yes, boss, the address matches. It's him, no question.'

The DI moved from the cubicle that he had borrowed from the absent DCI Sammy Pye to stand behind Singh and view his computer monitor. He saw a clean-shaven young man, managing to look engaging and friendly even while posing unsmiling as the purpose required. 'When was it taken?'

'His last renewal was five years ago, when he was twenty-four.'

'The big question: does he match the image you recovered from the car park camera?'

'Let's find out.' Singh parked the photograph in a corner of the screen and went into his library. He made a selection, clicked, and a second image appeared. With a deft movement of his trackpad, he laid them side by side. 'You reckon?'

'I'm not sure,' Haddock admitted. 'The resolution on the

car park pic isn't good enough to be absolutely certain. Can you boost it?'

'That's as good as it gets. It could be, I suppose, if you allow for ageing since the passport mug shot was taken. If only he'd been arrested recently,' the DS grunted, 'we'd have something more definitive.'

'You have checked that?'

'Do me a favour, Sauce.'

'Sorry, of course you have.'

'I've done a general search too, in case there's been a photo in the local press: Chamber of Commerce do, that sort of thing. No luck, though. There was a story about WZB in the *Motherwell Times*, about Zaqib collecting an award for steel company of the year from a trade organisation, but it didn't have a photograph.'

'What about the father?' Haddock asked.

'It can't be him. The image might be iffy, but it's a younger man than Wasim.'

'I didn't mean that. Was he mentioned in that story?'

'No, he wasn't; only Zaqib. "Well-known local businessman", it called him.'

'Is that right?' Haddock observed. 'His dad said he was no fucking use; that he was no more than a poser, or words to that effect. You'd have thought he'd be more proud of him than that, winning awards and all. You know what, Tarvil, there's something wrong with Wasim. I can't put my finger on it, but he's not square.'

'It looks as if he lied to you about Zaqib being in Pakistan to arrange his wedding.'

'Maybe he lied about him being in Pakistan at all. If that was him in the car, he'd have good reason. Noele,' he called out to the other sergeant, who was sitting a few feet away, 'you and me, we're off to Carluke to pay a call on Zaqib's wife.'

'What about me?' Singh asked. 'I'm sitting on my hands now, and it's getting fucking painful.'

'Then do everything again, and a wee bit more. Everyone who's a witness in the investigation, everyone we've interviewed, everyone who's been mentioned, right back to the moment Marcia Brown was nicked in LuxuMarket. Background checks on them all, as far back as you can.' He paused. 'And one more thing: find bloody Spider-Man.'

Haddock was heading for the door, with McClair following, when his phone chimed. 'Lottie,' he said as he took the call. 'What can I do for you, ma'am?'

'Lay off the "ma'am" for a start, and maybe I won't have to call you "sir" when you make detective super in a few years. I thought I'd let you know: we've pinned down Joan Brown through her bank card to a town in Spain called Burgos. She stayed there last night in a tourist apartment; I'll ask the Spanish police to check it out. If she's still there, great; if not, she won't be very far away, since the point of the trail is that you do it on foot, like St James did himself. They'll find her and ask her to call me.'

'Is there any guarantee that she will?'

'When she hears I'm investigating her sister's murder? What do you think? I have one small problem, though, and I need your help. Dan's got tickets for a Fleetwood Mac concert in the Hydro tonight; personally I can't fucking stand wrinkly rock, but I can't let the wee soul down. For the time it lasts, can I put my phone on divert to yours?'

Sixty-Two

'I suppose you could argue that the national police service has improved things,' Noele McClair suggested, as Haddock turned into Station Road. 'Before, we'd have needed to tell Strathclyde we were coming to see this woman, maybe even had to bring one of their people along with us.'

'Don't let Bob Skinner hear you suggest that,' the DI told her. 'He'd argue that he never had a territorial problem, and that all unification did was make people feel remote from their police service and with it more vulnerable. He did argue it, loud and long, but the politicians didn't listen to him.'

'What do you think? Or are you automatically in his camp?'

'I think they should have listened to each other. Bob's right: people do feel less secure in their homes; they feel that the butter's spread too thin in the national service. But you make a good point too: CID works better as part of a single organisation, so maybe that's what should have happened. Public order and safeguarding should have been kept as it was, and criminal investigation should have been made national. If it was down to me, I'd have a dozen assistant chiefs, pretty much autonomous, running the uniform section on a regional basis, and big Mario at the head of a single crime-fighting organisation, with everybody under the supervision of Maggie Rose or somebody like her. But I'm only a simple foot soldier. Nobody listens to the likes of me. Is this it?' He slowed to a crawl to allow McClair to read the name burned onto a varnished board at the entrance to a drive leading up to a detached bungalow. Green moss on its roof tiles suggested that it was older than some of the neighbouring houses.

'Yes, Russell Court,' she replied. 'That's the address Tarvil gave us. And there are two cars in the drive. It looks as if the chance we took not calling her in advance has paid off.'

'She and the kids were unlikely to have gone to Pakistan on holiday with Daddy.'

'Indeed not. Look.'

The front door of Russell Court had opened and a young woman wearing a halter top and shorts emerged, carrying a boy child on her hip, with another, older, by her side, and tugging at a stroller with her free hand.

Haddock turned their car into the driveway, switched off the engine and stepped out. 'Mrs Butt?' he called as she stopped to stare at him. 'Krystle Butt? Police. We're wondering if we can have a word.'

'Why? What's it about? Has the yard been broken into or something?' Sudden fear crossed her face. 'Is it my husband?' she asked anxiously. 'Has something happened to him?'

'No, he's fine,' the DI assured her. 'It has to do with a visitor he had at WZB last Friday.'

'The woman? He told me about her.' Releasing the stroller, she hitched her younger child higher and patted his brother on the shoulder. 'Go back indoors, Rashid; we'll go to the pool in a wee minute, but Mummy needs to talk to these people.' The child obeyed without protest. 'Come inside,' she said. 'This might be a big plot, but our neighbours can hear our budgie fart.'

The house was spacious, with a welcoming hall and a wooden staircase whose banisters reminded Haddock of his boyhood home, a late-fifties villa. In contrast, the furnishings were modern, and European in style. There was no hint of the absent Zaqib's ethnic origins, in either his home or the dress of his children as their mother deposited both in the middle of an array of toys on the living room floor.

'What about this woman?' she asked, once she was free to give them her complete attention. 'Why are you after her?'

'We're not,' the DI replied. 'We're after the people who killed her.'

Krystle Butt's eyes widened. 'You're joking,' she gasped.

'I wish I was. Her name was Carrie McDaniels; her remains were found on Monday morning. We had information that she visited your husband on Friday afternoon at the WZB warehouse, but when we spoke to your father-in-law and his foreman, we were told that nobody had any knowledge of her being there.'

'Rubbish!' she snapped. 'How would they know? Wasim wasn't even there, and as for Steve O'Donnell, he never leaves the shop floor. I've been in Zaki's office half a dozen times and not bumped into him. Last time I saw him was at the Christmas lunch. Zaki never mentioned her name, but if it's the woman you're talking about, the one that was murdered, she was definitely there.'

'Which makes us wonder, Mrs Butt,' McClair ventured, 'why he left the country so suddenly. Can I ask you something? Are you and Zaqib formally married? Are you legally husband

and wife? Bear in mind we can check it out.'

'You don't need to; it's not a secret. We call ourselves Mr and Mrs, but we aren't. Zaki's Muslim by birth and upbringing, but he's non-practising. The truth is he's an atheist, but that's a dangerous thing to say within his community. It's seen as blasphemy, and they have the death penalty for that in Pakistan. We've never married because I'd have to convert to Islam, and I'm not prepared to do that. As for Rash and Ally, the kids, we're putting off the evil hour, so to speak, but the hints have begun to drop.'

'Does that mean that when his father told us he's gone back to Pakistan to arrange his wedding, he might have been telling the truth?'

She paled beneath her summer tan. 'The old bastard!' she hissed. 'He told you that?'

McClair nodded.

'He's a . . .' She stopped in mid sentence as she realised that Rashid was looking at her, distracted from his toys. 'He might wish that, but it's not true. He can't really do anything about it, for he needs Zaqib to run the business. He might have invested the start-up money, but he knows nothing about it. Zaqib is managing director in every respect; he runs sales, distribution and the financial side. He's an accountant,' she added, 'as am I. We met at uni and graduated on the same day.'

'Is your husband really in Pakistan?'

'Oh yes, that much is true. His father called on Friday evening, left him a voicemail while he was playing golf at Lanark. He said he had to go to Rawalpindi because Wasim had to come back to Scotland on business, and because Imran, Zaki's uncle, is dying. Wedding indeed! Unless . . . Imran's got a daughter, Benazir, and I think Wasim's always had an eye on pairing them off. He's an evil old sod really. He's never seen his grandchildren, you know.'

'When did Zaqib leave?' Haddock asked.

'Saturday morning, from Glasgow Airport. I drove him there, with the kids in the back. I had to take them; there was no time to find a sitter.'

'Have you heard from him since?'

'No, but . . .' She paused. 'To hell with this! I'm going to FaceTime him now; you can ask him these questions yourself.'

She picked up an iPad from a sideboard that was just within reach, turned it on and tapped the screen several times. The detectives watched her, listening to a ringtone until it ended abruptly.

'Krys,' a male voice said. 'Baby, I'm sorry, I meant to call you earlier. I've been out for supper and it went on for longer than I'd imagined.' The accent was almost pure Glaswegian.

'How's your uncle?' she asked.

'Imran's fine; that's who I was with. I don't know what my dad was playing at sending me out here. Imran's cancer's in remission, and his consultant expects him to make a full recovery. He's in no danger at all and hasn't been for a while. I'd come home tomorrow, but I haven't seen him recently, so I'll stay for another few days, if that's all right with you.'

'How's your cousin?' she asked pointedly.

Haddock and McClair heard a laugh. 'Benny's good too. She's waiting for the results of her finals, but she's on track for an honours degree. Yes, Imran drops the odd hint, but he's not serious any more. Benny just rolls her eyes. The fact is, she's got a bloke, another medical student; he's from a good family and Imran likes him, so I think that's the way it'll go.'

'Have you been to the mosque?'

'This is Pakistan; of course I have. Appearances have to be maintained. Don't worry, it won't become a habit. Hey, kid, I love—'

'Zaki,' Krystle said, cutting him off, 'I have people with me. They're police officers, and they need to speak to you. Detective Inspector . . .' She looked up from the screen.

'Haddock,' he called out, loud enough to be picked up, 'and Detective Sergeant McClair.'

'What can I do for you?' Butt asked as his partner passed the tablet across.

'Your Friday-afternoon visitor,' the DI began, nodding involuntarily to the smooth, youthful face on screen.

'Yes, the investigator. Carrie something; a bit predatory, I thought.'

'Why?' McClair spoke off camera.

'Quick glance at my left hand for a gold band. I'm not being sexist; it's a sign of a single person on the prowl.'

'Was she wearing any jewellery?'

'Not that I recall, but her Rolex was impressive.'

'Who did you tell about her visit apart from your partner?' Haddock asked.

'My father.'

'Why?'

'I thought he'd be curious, that's all. She asked me about an incident that happened around ten years ago, in a supermarket called LuxuMarket. The old man had got me a summer job there on the security staff.'

'How did he do that?'

'He'd an interest in the business; only about twenty per cent – the majority shareholder was an alleged gangster from Dundee – but Dad could pull the odd string.'

'When did you tell him about the visit?'

'I called him from the car while I was driving to the golf club.'

'I see,' the DI murmured. 'If I read it right, he called you back not long after that and said he needed you to go to Pakistan.'

'That's right. I don't know why he didn't tell me there and then.' He paused, looking at the screen of his device. 'Look, mate, what's this about? Was this woman on some sort of con? Because if so, it didn't work.'

'No, Mr Butt, she was legitimate. I'm sorry to have to tell you but the day after she visited you, she was abducted and murdered. When it happened, you were travelling to Pakistan on a scheduled flight. That's as good an alibi as we've ever encountered.'

'Hold on a minute!' The face on the iPad twisted; calmness was replaced by protestation and anger. 'I don't know what you're talking about. I'd never met the woman before, and I hadn't given her a thought since speaking to my father.'

'Then you might want to think about it now. I know roughly why she visited you, but what did you tell her?'

'Nothing much. She was asking me for details of something that happened when I was a kid and that was over in an after-noon. She was working on a theory that a woman I stopped for shoplifting had been set up by people in the store, people I didn't even know. I never got to know them either,' he added. 'I chucked the job as soon as I heard that she had died.'

'Was leaving your own decision? Did your father play any part in it?'

'I didn't even tell him!'

'Even though he'd got you the job?'

'Even though.' Butt made a visible effort to calm himself. 'Inspector, what is this? What can I do? Where the hell do I stand?'

'If you think about the circumstances, you may realise why we're viewing you as a person of interest. Be clear,' Haddock emphasised, 'I'm not calling you a suspect, and I hope I never have to, but I would like you to return to Scotland for more formal questioning. Will you do that voluntarily?'

'Mate,' the man replied, 'I'm on the first flight home. If that woman was murdered, and I didn't do everything I could to help you, I'd never be able to look my kids in the eye again. That's not the sort of man their father is. As for mine,' he added, 'that's another matter.'

Sixty-Three

'They're on the way back to Edinburgh now,' Mario McGuire said, 'and hopefully Zaqib Butt's on his way to the airport. If he isn't, I'll ask for a warrant.'

'Gut tells me he is,' Bob Skinner said to his phone. It was on speaker mode, lying on his desk in Saltire House. 'From what you say, he volunteered everything he could over FaceTime. Sauce believes him, and that's good enough for me. Whether that's everything Butt knows, time will tell. If he isn't on the first plane home, I don't think your warrant will ever be served.'

'Why wouldn't it?'

'You used to be a detective; work it out.'

'I still am, just like you. And just like you, I will bask in the work of my juniors. I had a call from Tarvil Singh while Sauce and McClair were off air. You're going to love this one. He ran deep background checks on all the players in the original investigation, right back to birth certificates, more or less, and came up with a beauty. Marcia Brown's claim was that she was set up by Gloria Stephens' daughter and her cop boyfriend, who just happened to be in the store at the time, conveniently visiting. Maybe it was convenient, but it wasn't necessarily his girlfriend that PC Spider-Man was visiting; it was just as likely

347

to have been his sister. The store manager, Mrs Hazel Delaney, who's now running Grandpa McCullough's radio station in Dundee, her maiden name was Parker. I called Sauce once he was clear of Butt's wife and told him. He practically did cartwheels in his car. When he saw Delaney at the radio station, there was a bloke working in reception. There's more than that: Terry Coats said something about him being called Spider-Man not just because of his name, but because he needed a mask. The man at the radio station had acne scars so bad that he wore cosmetics.'

Bob laughed. 'Be sure your skin will find you out. Is Sauce going up there to reinterview them?'

'No, bugger that; they had a chance to own up, and they didn't take it. I've had them lifted for withholding; they're on their way down to Fettes now. They might even be there before he gets back. Things are falling into place, Bob.'

'Are they? How do the Parkers tie into Wasim Butt, and how does he tie into Carrie McDaniels being murdered?'

'That I don't know,' the DCC admitted, 'but I do know a bit more about the background. I had a call this morning from a solicitor acting for Mrs Stephens. He said that she now realises she was visited by Carrie on Friday and wants to make a full statement.'

'Well, well, my daughter will be pleased.'

'What's Alex got to do with it?'

She was sitting across from her father. 'Carrie was working for her, remember?'

'True. The lawyer also says that Stephens has no knowledge of what happened to McDaniels after she left her.'

'If she had, she wouldn't be phoning you,' Skinner pointed out.

'The one thing I don't get is why she had her brief call me and not the SIO on the case.'

'She's been a council leader for years. Going to the top probably comes naturally to her.'

'Maybe,' he conceded. 'Anyway, that's us up to speed. Will you make that other call like I asked? The way things are, it might be awkward for Sauce.'

'Yes, sure, I'll do it now.'

'Any other bright ideas before I go?' McGuire asked.

'Yes, one. Ask Lottie to set up observation on Wasim Butt's other business; the one that used to be LuxuMarket and is now called Household Supplies and Services, or something similar.'

'Will do. You gonna tell me why?'

'I don't know myself yet. Cheers.'

'You gonna tell *me* why?' Alex asked, as the phone fell silent.

'Same answer,' Bob said. 'Sometimes you just have to give the tree a bloody good shake to see if anything falls out. Not unlike your entirely unauthorised trip with Dominic to confront Stephens. I could have saved you the bother, by the way.' He smiled broadly.

'How would that have been? You're at your worst when you're smug,' she added.

He laughed and nodded. 'Probably. Did it never occur to you that I might have known all about her? Aileen, my former wife, your former stepmother, was the leader of the Labour Party in Scotland, before she foresaw its collapse and fucked off to London to play among the big folk. She marked my card about quite a few people, and Gloria Stephens was one of them. "A small-time, small-town bully, full of wind and vinegar, lacking the courage or vision to take any risky action, content just to sit on her hands and survive election after election."

That was her verdict, and her judgement is always spot on, as she's proving in London by positioning herself behind an ageing, unelectable leader and quietly building a power base on the left.'

'That's pretty much what Dominic said about Stephens,' Alex conceded.

'I know; he told me. If he'd thought for a second that she was capable of having Carrie murdered, he wouldn't have let you near her.'

'Hmph,' she snorted. 'I'll be having a word with him.'

'Don't be doing that; he promised me he'd look after you, remember.' He paused, seeing something in her eyes. 'Here,' he murmured, 'are you . . .'

'What if I was?' she retorted defensively. 'He's an attractive man. Very serious, but charismatic, and I like him. Maybe I wouldn't have when he was Lennie Plenderleith, but I do now.' She winked. 'But not in that way, so you can stop worrying. Dominic is happy in himself; the surprising thing is that he's making me feel that way too. Living with him is giving me a break from myself, and I'm enjoying it. It's more satisfying long term than phoning Montell for a quick shag, know what I mean?' She rose and left him gazing after her, shaking his head and smiling.

After a few moments' contemplation, he reached for his phone and called up a number from his directory.

'Bob,' Cameron McCullough responded. 'What are they saying I've done now? This isn't still about LuxuMarket, is it? I thought Sauce and I had squared that away.'

'I hope you have, but it hasn't gone away completely. There are more questions to be asked, and the powers think it might be less awkward if they come from me rather than him. When you owned that business, you had a minority shareholder, right?'

'Correct. The shares were held by an investment vehicle, but the beneficial owner's name was Wasim Butt.'

'How did he come to be involved?'

'I bought him out . . . or most of him. Before the site became a supermarket, it was a cash-and-carry booze warehouse, selling in bulk at heavy discount to trade customers and to punters if you had a special ticket. There were quite a few of them in the cities, you remember. They started to fall by the wayside, though; the rise of online trading and the arrival of mega stores like Costco ate into the customer base and they fell like dominos. Wasim owned one of those businesses, in Kilmarnock. It was going the same way when I was approached by a lawyer on his behalf and asked if I would be interested in buying it. He had planning consent from the local council to convert it into a supermarket, but he didn't have, or possibly didn't want to risk, the capital required to bring that about.'

'Why you?'

'Why not? I'm an entrepreneur; people bring deals to me all the time. Anyway, I thought about it, I had some money lying about doing nothing, and so I agreed. The way we structured it, a new holding company was set up; I had eighty per cent and Butt kept twenty. End of story.'

'Not quite, Cameron,' Skinner said. 'You don't own it any more.'

'No, I don't, you're correct. The conversion was successful and LuxuMarket made money, though not enough to meet my expectations on that level of investment. A few years back, I was approached, indirectly through my lawyer, by someone who was interested in buying me out. The terms were acceptable; I did the deal and made a nice profit, which I used to buy Black Shield Lodge, the hotel complex. LuxuMarket closed and became something else.'

'Who was the buyer?'

'It was yet another venture capital outfit; I can't recall the name, but I can find out if necessary.'

'It isn't. I know already; the owner of the vehicle is Wasim Butt.'

'He bought it back?' McCullough exclaimed. 'Where did he get that sort of dough?'

'Good question,' Skinner conceded. 'Around the same time, he also set his son up as a steel stockholder. Sometime soon, people might be looking for the source of those funds.'

'They can't touch me!' McCullough protested. 'I acted in good faith.'

'Relax. Nobody doubts that. I'm keeping you informed, that's all. I'll pass on what you told me about Butt to Sauce, and to a second officer who's looking into another aspect of the case.'

'Do that; also, when you speak to my acting grandson-in-law, or whatever the hell he is, ask him how I'm supposed to run a radio station when my manager and receptionist have been arrested by his team and carted off to Edinburgh. When am I getting them back?'

'That depends on how co-operative they are. Might be tomorrow, might not. What are you going to do? Is it a major hassle?'

'I can handle it,' McCullough admitted. 'Mia effectively runs the station, and Ignacio's been sweating buckets in the restaurant. He'll be delighted to step in front of house; he might even have an idea about following in his mother's footsteps on air.'

'Don't push that one!' Skinner warned. 'He's got a degree to finish.'

'I'm with you on that one; after that, it's his choice. Nothing you or I can do about.'

'Agreed. One last thing, Cameron: the lawyers you mentioned in the LuxuMarket deal, buying and selling; the police might need their names.'

'Same bloke both times; the man who approached me originally on Wasim's behalf. He was local, he was competent and frankly he was cheap; the deal wasn't big enough for me to involve my serious advisers. His name was Black, Cedric Black.'

Sixty-Four

'Are they ready for us?' Haddock asked Singh.

'Their solicitor wants five minutes with them, then five with you before the interview starts.' Singh smiled as the DI's eyebrows rose. 'Humour him,' he said. 'He's a new boy. His name's Simkins. I explained to him that it doesn't work that way, that he's there to ensure his clients' legal rights are protected and to advise them against self-incrimination if he thinks it's necessary. They're in Room 1.'

'His clock's ticking,' McClair observed, checking her watch.

'Before you go down there,' her fellow DS said, 'something of interest. I've been running checks of the national DNA database for everyone involved in the case, so they're on hand for checking against findings at Carrie's apartment and on her car. Wasim Butt's on it.'

'Is he?' Haddock exclaimed. 'Does that mean he has convictions?'

'No, it doesn't. He has the rarest blood group, AB negative, and he's on the donor list. His DNA is on file through that.'

'Okay. Have you told Dorward?' Singh threw him a silent snarl. 'Aye, okay, sorry again. Noele, let's go.'

Haddock led the way from the Serious Crimes suite and

down one flight of stairs; as they turned into a corridor, they saw a uniformed constable standing outside the interview room door. He looked uncomfortable in the heat.

'Is it baking in there?' Haddock asked. The PC nodded. 'Is there enough water so they don't have an excuse for an interruption?'

'Plenty, sir.'

'Fine, let's be at them.' He thrust the door open and led McClair into the room.

A burly young man who had been seated at the table facing them jumped to his feet. He had thick tousled hair, his left ear was misshapen and his nose was twisted off the straight. *Prop forward*, the DI thought. *Not quite good enough.*

'I didn't say I was ready for you, Officers,' the solicitor protested.

'That's not the issue,' Haddock replied quietly. 'We're ready for you, and that's what matters. You're on our side of the table, Mr Simkins; move round, please, and sit behind your clients. We're interviewing them, not you.' He looked at the pair as he and his DS took their places opposite them. 'Mrs Delaney, Mr Parker,' he said, switching on a recording device, 'you know us, Detective Inspector Harold Haddock and Detective Sergeant Noele McClair. I assume you were cautioned when you were arrested, but I will repeat it for the tape and for the benefit of Mr Simkins.' He recited the standard form of words and asked if they understood.

'My clients—' Simkins began.

'I'll say this once, sir. You are not a party in this interview; you are a professional adviser to your clients. Don't interrupt me again on anything other than a matter of law.' He looked at the woman opposite him; her eyes betrayed her anxiety, and she was perspiring in the stifling heat of the room. Her brother looked beaten before the game had even begun. His acne was uncovered; his face was pitted so badly that Haddock felt a pang of sympathy. 'This needn't have been necessary, Mrs Delaney, if you'd been open and honest with us in Dundee. You weren't, and now you've laid yourselves open to charges.'

She gnawed at her lip. 'I know,' she said, 'and I'm sorry. I was only trying to protect Peter.'

'From what?' He looked at the disfigured man. 'Are you prepared to admit to a conspiracy against Mrs Marcia Brown?'

'Fuck no!' he cried.

'Peter's more or less in hiding,' Hazel Delaney explained. 'His ex-wife, Vera, she's trying to find him so she can take him to court. They split up after she got herself knocked up by another bloke, a car dealer, and went off with him. The guy is minted, but Vera's still after Pete for a bigger share of their joint property than he reckons she deserves. Plus, she wants rights to his pension.'

'If those are her rights—' McClair began.

'They're not,' Parker protested. 'She's inflated the value of everything we had. I gave her a fair share, after expenses were deducted. It's all accounted for, but she's hired her own legal clowns and they're saying I could have got more. If she'd been reasonable, I'd still be in Australia and in the police service there. As it was, I had to get out.'

'Without leaving a forwarding address, even for your ex-employers?'

'TFR, lady. Her mother was bad enough, but Vera's twice as venomous. She's like that big spider in *Lord of the Rings*.'

'Ungoliant,' Simkins volunteered.

'No, ya twat!' Parker snapped. 'Shelob.'

Haddock stifled a smile. 'How long have you been back?' he asked.

'For the best part of a year,' his sister said.

'Where has he been living?'

'With me. I'm a widow, as you might know. The neighbours probably think he's a bidey-in and I've never made them any the wiser. Look, it's not just Vera and her constant hassling; he was crushed by her desertion, by the divorce. He's been having a continuous breakdown ever since. If you'd been through something like that, you'd understand.'

'I have been, and I do,' McClair responded. 'But Mrs Delaney, there's no record of your brother anywhere.'

'Does there need to be?'

'I'm afraid there does. He's employed at your radio station. The DWP and the taxman have an interest in that.'

'Pin money,' Delaney countered. 'I pay him out of the petty cash; the station expenses account.'

'Does Cameron McCullough know?' Haddock asked.

Her face was flushed, but she reddened even more. 'No.' She looked at him. 'Shit,' she whispered, 'you and he are related.'

'We're not, but even if we were,' he glanced at Simkins, whose eyes had widened, 'I wouldn't discuss details of an active investigation with him. He won't be hearing it from me, but you might want to think seriously about setting things straight.'

'I will. Mr McCullough's been good to me over the years; he offered me a move to Dundee to be nearer my husband's base, and then he supported me when Ron was killed. I should have told him.'

'Make sure you do, but now can we go back to the thing that started all this: the theft charge against Marcia Brown. You were both there and you played a part in her arrest and the prosecution. She made allegations at the time that were never followed up after her death. She claimed conspiracy, and said that you, Mr Parker, were a part of it with your girlfriend, Vera Stephens.'

The ex-policeman wiped a hand across his face, as if he was trying to eradicate his blemishes, an unconscious gesture that he had made half a dozen times during the interview. 'Rubbish, all of it,' he said. 'There never was a conspiracy; Marcia Brown stole that stuff, pure and simple. When she realised it was discounted, she ripped the ticket off herself. Christ, there was footage of her doing it, in the car park, when the security boy's back was turned.'

'She claimed that she was distracted by someone, a constituent she called Adrian, after she'd cleared the checkout, and that's when the stolen goods were planted on her trolley.'

'No,' Parker declared firmly. 'She wasn't. She was clever enough to leave her trolley in an area that wasn't covered by the security cameras, but she didn't notice the one that actually recorded her stealing the clothes.'

'That's right,' Hazel Delaney confirmed. 'I reviewed the footage myself afterwards. I found both of the clips Pete's talking about.'

'Terry Coats never mentioned them.'

'He wouldn't,' her brother said. 'I gave them to Chief Inspector Mason, my boss. She didn't like to be in the witness chain for anything, so she told me to take them straight to Bobby Hough, the fiscal. Ask him; he'll confirm it.'

'That's unlikely,' Haddock replied. 'He has Alzheimer's. What about Vera?' he continued. 'What was her part in this?'

The hunted man threw back his head and laughed out loud,

almost maniacally, his eyes rolling upwards. 'That's the biggest joke of all,' he exclaimed. 'Vera couldn't stand her mother; they barely spoke to each other, and when they did, it always ended in an argument. That's the reason she and I went to Australia: to get away from the vicious wee cow.'

Sixty-Five

'It's great being a hived-off specialist service,' Arthur Dorward told Tarvil Singh as he took his call. 'I get to be called "sir" by all the plods and newbie detectives. That never happened back in the old days when I was a DS like you.'

'That's very good . . . sir,' Singh replied. 'Now what precisely the fuck can I do for you?'

'You? Nothing, but is your gaffer in?'

'Sauce? As it happens, he's walking through the door right now; he's smiling, so it must have gone well downstairs.'

'I'd better speak to him then, not that it isn't always a pleasure dealing with your good self. By the way, when's the other half of the Menu due back?'

'DCI Pye? His paternity leave's up the week after next.'

'Paternity leave,' Dorward grunted. 'There was enough fornication went on in the police service before you were rewarded for it. Now? Jesus. Let's have Haddock.'

Singh put a hand over the mouthpiece and called out to the DI. 'Arthur Dorward. Like a dog with two cocks in a forest.'

Haddock grinned, went into the small office and took the call. 'Arthur,' he said, 'I'm told you're giving away free sunshine this morning. Don't you think we've got enough?'

'Take it while it's going, son,' the veteran retorted. 'Take the good news as well. My people have finished checking the database for matches to all the DNA samples we were able to recover from Carrie McDaniels' car. One direct match showed up, for Mr Gerard Heaney, muscle for hire, but we know about him.'

'Correct,' Haddock agreed, 'so why the jollity?'

'That's because I ran them all – personally, you understand – against a profile that was passed on to me for a man named Wasim Butt, who's a witness, I gather. I didn't get a direct match for him, but I did find one that's very close. Wasim hasn't been in contact with the victim's vehicle, but his son has.'

'Nice one, Ginger,' the DI exclaimed, only for his elation to evaporate as quickly as it had arisen. 'But . . .'

'Are you going to let the air out of my balloon?' Dorward asked.

'Maybe. Do you have any way of determining when or how that sample got there?'

'No,' he admitted with a sigh. 'Go on.'

'Thing is, we know that Carrie met with Wasim's son last Friday at his business premises.'

'Bugger. It was nice while it lasted.'

'I'll get you another sample, and prints, just for elimination, but that'll be him, I'm afraid.'

'Ah well,' Dorward said. 'At least I can go back to being my usual miserable bastard self.'

'That you can, Arthur, that you can.'

Sixty-Six

'That's a shame,' Cheeky Davis said. 'I've known Hazel since she went to work at the radio station, and I like her. I saw the brother too, last time I was there, but I thought no more of him other than noticing his make-up. Poor guy.'

'That was the second reason for him being called Spider-Man in the force,' Sauce told her. 'His less sympathetic colleagues ribbed him about needing to wear a mask.'

'Bastards.'

'Agreed. A strong station commander would have known about that and come down on it hard, but everything we're hearing about the late Chief Inspector Mason suggests that she was the opposite. How do you think your grandpa will react when he finds out Hazel's been hiding her brother in plain sight?'

'That's not the question. How will Mia react? That's what you should be asking. The station's her toy, really. She's a director.'

'And you're not. Are you jealous?' He was teasing, but she took him seriously.

'I can't be a director of anything that my accountancy firm audits. You know that, Sauce. I'm not jealous of Mia in any way; if anything, it's the other way around. Before Grandpa married her, he took me out for dinner and promised me that it wouldn't affect my inheritance in any significant way. He had a trust fund established to look after my mum when he's gone. Under his new will, that passes to Mia.'

'You never told me that before,' Sauce said. 'What about your mum?'

'She becomes my responsibility. I'm good with that. As I've told you often enough, she's an idiot, so it'll be better all round that she's under my control. Mia? It's not jealousy. I don't like the woman, plain and simple.'

'Does she know what's in the will?'

'Yes. She's never said anything to me, but I wouldn't be surprised if she contests it after Grandpa dies.'

'Given that he's only in his sixties, and he's one of the fittest guys of that age I know, she'll have a long time to wait for that . . . as long as he's careful to check the sugar bowl for ground glass.' He winked at her. 'Bob Skinner told me about her family background and it's fucking horrifi—'

The Z-Cars ringtone of his work phone stopped him in mid description. He looked at the screen; the number was unknown to him, but he answered, a simple 'Yes?'

'Is that Detective Chief Inspector Mann?' a woman's voice enquired. He read the accent as west of Scotland.

'No, it isn't. I'm Detective Inspector Haddock, a colleague of DCI Mann's.'

'My name's Joan Brown,' the caller said. 'I'm in Spain and I've been asked by the police to call Chief Inspector Mann as a matter of urgency.'

'Okay. DCI Mann's busy tonight, but she briefed me about a potential call and put her phone on divert.'

'She? Oh, sorry, I just assumed . . .'

'Nobody makes that mistake twice,' Haddock chuckled.

'The Spanish police officer who approached me said she wanted to talk to me about the murder of my sister. That's what I thought he said, but his English wasn't at all good. He couldn't have meant that, could he?'

'He did, Ms Brown. Her post-mortem has been reviewed by a senior pathologist, and his conclusion is that she couldn't have committed suicide. There had to be third-party involvement.'

'Assisted suicide? Is that what he's saying?'

'He doesn't believe so.'

'Why has this come up now? Does it have to do with David Brass, my former brother-in-law?'

'In a way,' the DI admitted. 'Mr Brass instructed a lawyer to re-examine your sister's prosecution for theft. That led, indirectly, to the re-examination of what had been classified as her suicide. However, there's been another death. The solicitor hired a private investigator to look into the case. She conducted a number of interviews, but on Saturday afternoon she vanished . . . until Monday morning, when her remains were found.'

'Are you telling me that the two are connected?'

'I can't tell you that, because we don't know for sure. DCI Mann is looking into it; I'm leading the investigation into the death of Carrie McDaniels, the investigator. We're not ruling out a connection, that's all I'll say.'

'I knew it,' Brown hissed. 'I always knew she didn't kill herself. She phoned me, you know, a couple of days before she died. She'd been drinking, something she did a bit too much. She told me she was looking forward to going to court, for she was planning to use it to expose corruption within the council.'

'What kind of corruption?'

'She didn't tell me; the only hint she dropped was that it involved a planning application by a man who wanted to take over LuxuMarket and put loads of people out of work. She had information from a source, a boyfriend who'd worked for this man in his cash-and-carry business. I've got to confess, Mr Haddock, that I didn't take her seriously. My sister saw conspiracy everywhere. If someone spent too long in the pub toilet, they were snorting cocaine, not . . . whatever they were really doing. No, I didn't take her seriously, not until Cedric Black, her lawyer, called me and said the police needed me to identify her body. After that, oh yes, I believed her.'

'You went to the autopsy, didn't you? You made a fuss there?'

'I did. I'd asked Black to tell me when it was happening. He didn't, but I found out from the chief inspector at the station handling Marcia's death. I turned up and I lost my temper, because I felt convinced that Black just wanted the whole business to go away, that he wanted everything covered up. I shouldn't have, I know. There was a policeman present, the same man who was there when I identified Marcia; he was very understanding, but he made it clear that I couldn't stay.'

'The boyfriend,' the DI asked, making notes, 'did she give you a name?'

'No, only that he was Asian, and younger than Marcia; they were always younger than her and they were usually Asian. They were always respectful, she said, and they never wanted to marry her.'

'Afterwards, how closely were you involved with your nephew Austin in his protests, if I can call them that?'

'I supported him, of course, encouraged him. He went as far as he could until he was threatened with legal action and went down another route with Brass Rubbings.'

'Who threatened him?'

'The man, of course; the man behind the planning application that got Marcia so excited and may have got her killed. He was Asian too, but not her type; too old. His name was Butt, Wasim Butt. She was convinced he had the council leader in his pocket, and that she was behind the shoplifting conspiracy, to shut her up . . . as if it would have!' She paused. 'There was a conspiracy, Detective Inspector,' she asked, anxious for the first time, 'wasn't there?'

Sixty-Seven

Tarvil Singh smiled as he countersigned the statement. For him it had been the rarest of rare days, and he was a happy man. He saw it as a reward for his sterling desk work that Sauce Haddock had sent him to pick up Zaqib Butt from the morning Emirates flight at Glasgow Airport, and take him to the Crime Campus at Gartcosh. If he had known that it had only happened because there was nobody else available, Jackie Wright being on a day's leave, he would have been only marginally less pleased.

Arthur Dorward had taken Butt's DNA sample and fingerprints, personally rather than sending a junior, then the detective sergeant had taken a full statement about his meeting with Carrie McDaniels.

'When she left,' he had asked, on Haddock's instruction, 'did you see her off? Did you go to the car park with her?'

'Yes. I had to. I was really tight for time for my golf match; the guy I was playing, I know him and if I'd been one minute late on the tee, he'd have claimed the tie. It was the club championship too.'

'Did you win?'

'Easy, six and five; I'm in the semi-final, a week on Sunday.'

'You couldn't have stayed much longer in Pakistan, in that case.'

'No, but that was no worry to me. It was good to see that Uncle Imran's on the mend, for all my father's pessimism, but I really don't like the place. How about you? You're a Sikh, going by your name. Do you ever go back to the land of your birth?'

'I pass by the old Simpson Maternity in Edinburgh every so often, but I don't make pilgrimages. My grandfather was from the Punjab, but a package holiday in Turkey's as close as I've got.'

'I'm the same, almost. I'm a Weegie, born if not bred; I was brought up in Eastwood, went to Hutchie Grammar, and learned my golf at Williamwood. I was twelve the first time my dad took me to Rawalpindi. I caught a bug the first day there, spent a week sat on the toilet and have hated the place ever since.'

'How about your father?'

'Oh, he's old school. He was born there, did some time in the army when he was young – he says he still has connections – then came over here and got into the cash-and-carry business.'

'Has he ever been in any other business?' Another Haddock question.

'Hah! Fuck no! Other than the sectors he's comfortable in, and that's big sheds really, Dad is basically clueless. Funny, he never wanted me in the household supplies company; I thought he would, I assumed it almost, but he said he had bigger ambitions for me. WZB is my inheritance in advance, that's what he told me; he's on the board, but it's mine, all of it.'

'You're not involved in his company at all, not even as a director?'

'Not at all. Sergeant, my father feels a duty towards me because I'm his son, but I don't believe he likes me too much. He'd like me to be a good Pakistani Muslim and marry my cousin Benny. He doesn't acknowledge Krystle as my partner, and his grandchildren don't even know him. If I had any siblings, I doubt I'd have had a penny off him.'

'Thanks,' Singh said, as he passed Butt a copy of the signed statement. 'Is the jet lag starting to get to you?'

'Not really; I wasn't there long enough. My circadian clock was still struggling to readjust from UK time, so I don't expect to miss too much sleep.'

'Still, you'll want to get home. I've got to hang around here for a while, so I've arranged for a car to take you; unmarked, by the way. You wouldn't want to be dropped off by something with a blue light on top.'

Butt smiled; his relief was mostly about being spared another car journey with a driver of Singh's size, but he thanked him for his thoughtfulness.

The DS watched him depart, then, feeling peckish, headed for the canteen. He was finishing his second tuna mayonnaise roll when Arthur Dorward dropped into a seat beside him, a mug of tea in his right hand.

'I thought I'd find you here, Wimpey.'

'You were right then, Ginger. Am I that good company, or do you have news for me?'

'Both, and for that DI of yours. I do love rattling that boy's cage, and this will, for sure.'

Singh finished his roll and reached for a four-finger Kit Kat. 'Do tell.'

'I've done a quick analysis of Zaqib's DNA sample. He's his father's son all right, no doubt about it. But . . .' he paused to take a mouthful from his mug, and for effect, 'his profile doesn't match the one we found on Carrie's Renault. Wasim Butt has another son.'

'Eh,' the DS gasped. 'Zaqib's just after telling me he's an only child, and I believed him.'

'He might believe it too. The sons have different mothers. Zaqib's sample shows European influences on his maternal side. The other one is pure Indo-Pakistani.' Dorward beamed. 'Have a nice day, Detective Inspector Haddock.'

'Fuck!' Singh hissed. 'I'd better tell him.'

He reached for his phone, but Dorward put a hand on his arm to stop him. 'Before you do, I have some more glory to bask in. It took a lot of effort, and I've probably broken some ground in forensic science, but . . . the second body in the crematory; I know whose it is.'

Sixty-Eight

'Gerry Heaney?' Alex stared at Haddock, wide-eyed with shock and surprise. 'The man I hit with the Le Creuset.'

'That's what we believe,' he replied. 'Arthur was able to extract viable matter from the thickest of the bone samples, sufficient for him to construct enough of a DNA profile to get a match with Heaney.'

'Are you saying that I killed him?' she asked. 'If I did, that can't be swept under the carpet. It'll become public and there'll be pressure on the Crown Office to consider a culpable homicide charge.'

'No way,' Griff Montell exclaimed as he lay on his hospital bed in a green and orange robe, tied at the waist. 'That wouldn't hold up for a minute. You didn't hit him that hard. He was strong enough to get up and slice me open as I was restraining his mate.'

'That's why I asked if I could meet you both here,' Haddock said. 'The events are covered by your statements, yours and Alex's, but we've moved on from there.'

'You're close to nailing them?' Montell frowned. 'Him, rather, since Heaney's out of the picture.'

'Closer, Griff, closer. But to ease your worries, Alex, you

371

didn't kill Heaney, not unless you shot him in the head as well as slugging him with your pan. What's it made of?'

'Cast iron, enamelled.'

'I can vouch for that,' Montell volunteered. 'My sister gave me one like it last Christmas. I use it all the time,' he added.

'Lucky you,' the DI said. 'We like our Tefal stuff. But neither of them contains copper or lead, melted traces of which were found in a skull fragment that it's now been determined belonged to Heaney. They were from the bullet that killed him.'

'What about Carrie?' Alex asked quietly. 'Was Sarah, or Arthur, able to determine how she died?'

'No, and I doubt they ever will.'

'There's something that's been concerning me,' she said. 'Carrie didn't know where I live. She couldn't have told them.'

'They broke into your office, remember. Do you keep anything there with your address on it?'

She winced. 'Lots of stuff. I tend not to think of security within a secure building. Idiot.'

'No you're not, no more than any other person.'

'Well I feel as if I am. Sauce, why was Heaney killed?'

'Best guess,' the DI replied, 'with things going wrong at your place, and with Carrie dead in the boot of their car, his partner decided he was too big a risk. Alex, this is organised crime we're dealing with. These people are ruthless.'

'Then why did we survive?' Montell asked. 'If Heaney was shot, it meant his mate had a firearm, so why not just shoot the two of us?'

'Two or more gunshots, seven floors up, with you two having yelled your heads off already? The neighbours would have been disturbed for certain. What would their chances have been of making it out of there?'

'True. Then there's the other possibility: that they knew who Alex's father is and didn't fancy the consequences.'

'Maybe all of the above,' Haddock conceded, 'but once they were out of there, our mystery man made a decision, and it was goodbye, Heaney; he was a Crown witness waiting to happen, so he had to go. The other guy,' he continued, 'the one you took down, Griff. Did you have time to form any impressions?'

'Not much, but he was a strong bastard. I had him in a proper hold, the kind we use as restraint, but he knew how to get out of it. I was holding him by pure strength, but not for much longer, even without Heaney cutting me.'

'Anything else? Did you see or sense anything? We think he was Asian, but we're not sure about his age.'

Montell drew a breath, shifted on the bed and winced with pain at the movement. 'Sauce,' he said, 'after that guy sliced my arse half off, he could have been a fucking Martian, for all I knew or cared.'

Sixty-Nine

'Bloody hell,' Jackie Wright whispered as she read the email on her screen. 'Sarge,' she called out to Tarvil Singh, 'come and have a look at this.'

'What's so exciting?' he asked, rising from his chair and lumbering across the room.

'I asked the Border Force to co-ordinate a check of arrivals and departures from Scottish airports last weekend, looking for the names Wasim and Zaqib Butt. Look what they came back with.' As he leaned over her, a mix of deodorant and cologne brought her almost to gagging point, but she fought it off. 'Start with Saturday,' she told him.

He did as she suggested. 'Okay, there's Zaqib, heading out on Saturday morning, on British Airways connecting at Heathrow with a Qatar Airways flight to Doha and on to Rawalpindi. We knew that.'

'Next day?'

He peered at the screen, reading. 'Next day we have Wasim Butt getting off an Emirates flight at Glasgow at thirteen fifteen hours. Fine, but only confirmation.'

She scrolled on to another page. 'And here?'

Singh sighed, then his eyes narrowed. 'What the fu—

Wasim gets back on an Emirates flight that same evening, heading for Rawalpindi via Dubai. But hold on! Wait! Oh shit! That's Arthur Dorward's mystery DNA profile. That's not old Wasim; that's got to be his other son, Zaqib's half-brother. So how come we've never heard of him?'

'Because,' Wright replied, 'he's not a British national. He has a Pakistani passport, which the Border Force scanned as he left the country. Scanned and copied,' she added. 'Now look at this.' She clicked, and a passport photograph appeared, magnified, on screen. 'Does that match the image you got off the car park camera, or does it not?'

Seventy

The whispers of nepotism were a thing of the almost distant past. Assistant Chief Constable Lowell Payne had proved himself to his team and to his senior officers, of whom there were only two, the chief and her deputy. His meteoric rise during the second half of his career had culminated in his appointment as head of Special Branch in the defunct Strathclyde police force. At the time, there were a few insiders who suggested that it owed much to the fact that he was married to Bob Skinner's former sister-in-law, but the only one who had been reckless enough to say so to the service's last chief constable had been told in a loud voice that it owed far more to the factionalism and prejudice of his predecessors in not spotting the man's talents in organisation, analysis and leadership.

And yet, when he was faced with a tricky situation on a Saturday morning, it was Skinner he called. 'This is only for advice, you understand,' he said.

'It's all I'm in a position to give you, Lowell.'

'Come off it, Bob. The deputy chief told me about your role in mentoring young SIOs. I know you're involved in something right now, because one of those young SIOs told me: DCI Charlotte Mann.'

'How did you come to be speaking to Lottie?'

'Because she stood on the toes of a couple of my people. I've got an operation going; it's international, but we're at the sharp end.'

'Terrorism?'

'No,' Payne replied. 'People trafficking and human slavery. There's an operation called Household Supplies and Services, in Kilmarnock; it's a shed, a warehouse selling anything for the home, from bog rolls to Brasso, in bulk, to the public and the trade, from the premises and through eBay and Amazon. That side of it probably breaks even at best; it's the services bit that we're interested in. Our information is that most of those are provided by illegals who are here against their will, from eastern Europe and the Middle East, refugees who've been sucked in and are too afraid to break free. Some of them go out as cleaners, to wealthy householders, shops and factories. Those ones have papers and go through the books. Those who don't provide other services. Prostitutes, male and female, young and younger; drug mules who bring the stuff in and are then made to cut and distribute it. Fucking horrible business, Bob, and we thought we had them.'

'But now you don't?'

'Only the other ranks; the commanding officer has disappeared. The frontman in this organisation is Wasim Butt, a British citizen of Pakistani origin. He owns the shed and the legitimate business; he's been in Scotland for over thirty years, and lives in the Newton Mearns area on the west side of Glasgow. One son, name of Zaqib, who runs a steel stockholder business in Motherwell. We believe it was set up with money laundered from the human slavery trade, but we can't prove it.'

'Zaqib?' Skinner asked. 'What about him?'

'He has no connection with his father's business; at least none that we can find. He's twenty-nine, has two kids with a girl he met at uni, lives in Carluke, plays golf at Lanark off a handicap of two, lucky bastard.'

'So why aren't you picking up Wasim and shutting the whole thing down?'

'Because Wasim isn't the main player; like I said, he's the frontman for the legitimate business. There's somebody else, a younger man, giving the orders as far as we can see and running what we'll call the import side; in fact, the Importer is our name for him. He's the trafficker, the slaver; we've had sight of him, but the bugger is we don't know who he is.'

'Haven't you followed him? Kept him under continuous observation?'

'We've tried,' Payne told him, 'but he's too good. In my opinion, the guy has been trained in counter-surveillance techniques; he's a pro. However,' he continued, 'in the last month, he's been here and he's been active. We had a tip-off from Poland that there's another shipment on the move, and this time, my Europol colleagues have managed to infiltrate it. They have a female officer undercover among the traffickees. Through her we hope to tie down all the details of the operation, including how they make landfall here. Most importantly, we hope that she'll finally put a name to the Importer.'

'Good for you,' Skinner said, 'but how does Lottie tie in with this?'

'She ties in because this morning, my guys found her and her DS on surveillance of the same premises as us. They braced her about it. She told them to fuck off and tried to pull rank. They called me and I ordered her to come to my office without informing anyone. She and I had a long conversation, in the course of which she told me that if I wasn't sharing – which I can't – neither was she. Her operation was confidential, she said, and under your supervision.'

'I wouldn't quite put it like that, but I have a degree of knowledge. You want advice, you said?'

'Yes,' Payne agreed. 'I want you to tell me whether I should go straight to the DCC and put Mann on a disciplinary.'

'You shouldn't,' Skinner retorted. 'How much of this does Mario know? He's mentioned nothing to me.'

'Only the nature of the operation. He told me to report when I have results . . . which I'll never get now, because it appears to be fucking blown. I had further word from Poland a couple of hours ago. The human cargo, their UCO included, were dumped on a beach in Denmark and left there. It happened yesterday; it took them hours to get to the nearest town. And worse, the Importer has disappeared; nobody's seen the prick since Friday. Mann and Cotter show up, and the show's over. You still don't think I should have Mann's guts for garters?'

'I still don't think so. What she did . . . I don't give orders, but my suggestions are usually acted upon. If I'd known about your op, or if Mario had, I'd have spoken to you, of course. But neither of us did, which makes Mann innocent.'

'Shit,' the ACC sighed. 'What am I going to tell the Poles, the Germans, all the rest of them?'

'Search me,' Skinner replied. Then he chuckled. 'That's what I'd have told you an hour ago,' he said, 'before I had a call from another team. Now? You can tell all your friends you're a fucking hero, because you know who the Importer is. Before you do that, though, I want you to use your international contacts and find out everything there is to know about him. I have a very personal interest in this man, Lowell, and so do you. He killed someone I know, and he almost did the same to your niece, my daughter. I don't expect you'll be able to put me in a room with him, but if you can, he's fucking dead.'

Seventy-One

'I promise you, Detective Inspector,' Zaqib Butt insisted, 'I have never heard of this man, and I have never seen him. What the fuck's going on here? You ask me to leave my Sunday at home with my kids, you bring me through to Edinburgh and you start to treat me as if I'm a suspect. I've done nothing wrong; I've done everything you've asked of me. I even came home early from visiting my family in Pakistan. Now you throw this shit at me.'

'Bear with us please, Mr Butt,' Haddock said. 'Look at the name on the passport: Wasim Butt.'

'I'm looking. I'm looking. There's fuck knows how many Wasim Butts in Pakistan. You're telling me this one's my brother? Are you serious, mate?'

'Half-brother,' Noele McClair told him. 'He's ten years older than you, to the month. The intelligence that our colleagues received from Pakistan this morning confirms that he was born in Hyderabad, to your father and Azra Khawaja.'

'That's not my mother,' he exclaimed. 'Her maiden name's Rachel Mazari. She and my father met and married over here. Her grandmother was Scottish. That's where the Rachel came from. My dad worked for her father when he arrived and

381

eventually took over the business. Are you suggesting that she and my father might not be legally married?'

'No, we're not,' Haddock assured him. 'Our information is that your father dissolved his first marriage before he came to Scotland. Wasim junior remained with his mother and her father. He was educated in Hyderabad and went to university in Lahore.'

Zaqib shook his head, then rubbed his face in his hands. 'My father has never so much as hinted that I had a brother,' he said. 'Uncle Imran's never mentioned him either. Neither has my cousin Benny. They would know about him, surely?'

'Not necessarily; Wasim junior was born and raised in Hyderabad, remember. My geography's crap, but that's not exactly next door to Rawalpindi, is it?'

'No, it's not,' he conceded. 'Pakistan's a place it's easy to get lost in, I suppose. Bloody hell, you're turning my life upside down; you realise that, don't you?'

'We hope we are,' Noele McClair told him. 'If not, you could be implicated in very serious crimes.'

He gasped. 'What the fuck are you talking about?'

Haddock looked him in the eye. 'We believe that your brother murdered Carrie McDaniels, on your father's orders.'

'This gets even crazier. The only thing my dad could murder is a fucking curry.'

The DI slid the car park photo across the table, placing the passport image beside it. 'The same man, yes?'

Zaqib studied them, moving from one to the other and back again. 'Yes,' he conceded after a while.

'The second photo was taken in a car park in Edinburgh early on Sunday morning; this was just after your half-brother and an accomplice attacked Alex Skinner, the solicitor who engaged Carrie McDaniels, in her flat. She was unhurt, but a police officer who was there was seriously wounded before they left the scene. We are fairly certain that when they drove out of that car park, in a stolen vehicle, Carrie's body was in the boot. They took it to a pet crematorium south of Edinburgh, broke in and put it in the furnace. Once that was done, we think Wasim Butt shot his accomplice and put him in there as well.'

'Fuck! If he knows I'm with you . . . Are my family safe?'

'Your half-brother flew to Pakistan that same day, and we're fairly sure he's still there. God only knows where. As you said, it's an easy place to lose yourself.'

'Are they safe from my father? In case he sends somebody else. They mean nothing to him.'

'Yes, they are. He's not going to do that, but we're keeping an eye on them, don't worry. You've been asked before, but I need to hear it again. Are you involved with his company in any way?'

'No, not at all. He doesn't want me to be; he says it's too mundane for me. The truth is, the only time I've been to the site was when it was LuxuMarket and I worked there, when the Marcia Brown business happened. You're not going to tell me my father had her killed as well, are you?'

'We're not ruling it out,' Haddock admitted. 'Others are looking into that. Meantime, the money your father gave you to start WZB came from an investment trust registered in Zurich. Did he tell you anything about its history?'

'No, and I didn't ask. It wasn't a hell of a lot, in business terms: five hundred thousand. The company was heavily indebted at the beginning; my father arranged a loan that was guaranteed by his company. I was given five years to clear it, and I did it with two to spare. Once I'd done that, the ownership was transferred legally to my name. What is it that my father's done?' he asked. 'What is it that's so bad that people were killed for it?'

'We can't tell you that, not yet. For now, I'd like you to stay with us for an hour or so, then I'll have a car take you back to Carluke.'

'Why wait for an hour?'

'By then I should have heard that your father's been arrested. There's no point in us putting temptation in your way, Zaqib, by giving you a chance to phone him and tip him off.'

'He's gone thirty years without tipping me off that I had a brother, Inspector; you'd have no worries on that score.'

Seventy-Two

'What do you think?' McGuire asked as he switched off the TV monitor in his office on which he and his companions had watched the interview. 'Is he on the level or did he know all along?'

Skinner grinned. 'The boy's okay,' he said. 'He plays off a two handicap at Lanark. People off two always want to get down to scratch; that wouldn't leave enough time to be part of an organised crime group as well. Seriously, though,' he added, 'you and I have both been around long enough to know when someone's faking it, and he seemed genuinely shocked when Sauce told him about his brother.'

'Do we trust Lowell's information from Pakistan? Could they be protecting one of their own?'

'Would you trust criminal intelligence from Italy, Cornetto? Or from Ireland, for that matter?'

The DCC grunted an acknowledgement. 'Granted. What else did they tell us, Lowell, other than what Sauce quoted there?'

'According to them, Wasim junior has quite a background,' ACC Payne responded. 'He graduated from Lahore in physics, then joined the army. He served there until he was twenty-eight, then transferred to the Federal Investigation Agency; that's part of the Pakistani state security machine. He was placed in the immigration wing and worked there for four years until he quit, saying that he was going into the family business.'

'The immigration wing?' Skinner repeated.

Payne nodded. 'Tasked with preventing illegal immigration; laugh if you will, Bob, but it's an issue, especially with the Taliban active in Afghanistan, hiding out across the border, and being a presence in Pakistan too.'

'I get that. Was his job active, or desk-bound?'

'Very active.'

'Then he must have seen a lot of inventive ways to move people across borders.'

'Will they find him for us?' McGuire asked.

'They will try, I'm assured.'

'What's the extradition situation?'

'We don't have a treaty with Pakistan. It's not impossible, but we'd have to present a case through the UK Justice Department, one that gave a strong likelihood of conviction. Can be done, but it'll take time. So, Mario,' Payne continued, 'are we go? Can I arrest Wasim senior and execute the warrant for a search of his premises?'

'Have we got enough to hold him?'

'Enough to arrest, for sure. My team can place his son in Scotland last week, on the premises. Then there was his knowledge of Carrie's visit to Zaqib.'

'Okay,' the DCC declared. 'Proceed. That still worries me, though.'

'What?' Skinner asked.

'Zaqib, letting him go. He's still in the chain. He told his father about Carrie, and his father ordered the killing.'

His friend smiled. 'Ah, but was old Wasim hearing it for the first time? There's someone else you should lift, but as subtly as you can manage, and not until tomorrow morning, because there isn't enough to hold him overnight. Also,' he added, 'I want to be there when he's interviewed.'

Seventy-Three

'What's all this about?' Cedric Black asked angrily in the interview room in the Clyde Gateway police office. 'I've gone along with this so far, from the call by the deputy chief constable, no less, asking me if I can advise you on a couple of points in an ongoing investigation. I even went along with the request that I come to the mainland. But I do object to being picked up by uniformed officers in a patrol car and blue-lighted all the way up to Glasgow.'

'Sorry about that.' The man facing him settled himself into a chair that was more comfortable than he had known in any similar room in any other station. 'It makes me wonder, though. We thought we were giving you VIP treatment, but you seem to be interpreting it in the opposite way, as if we were treating you like a suspect, a criminal even. Trust me, your average suspect doesn't get a call from Mario McGuire asking for his assistance; he gets a heavy knock on the door at first light. Mario sends his apologies by the way; he's been caught up in other things.'

He paused, glancing to his left. 'Before we go any further, we should introduce ourselves. This is Detective Sergeant Noele McClair, and I'm Sir Robert Skinner. I'm no longer a full-time police officer, but I do have advisory status, and the deputy chief has asked me to sit in for him. As you're aware from an earlier visit by Detective Inspector Haddock and DC Wright, they and DS McClair are investigating the abduction and death of Ms Carrie McDaniels.'

'Yes, I am,' Black retorted, 'and I told them everything I know about it, which is exactly nothing.'

'Be that as it may, you were acquainted with Ms McDaniels, yes?' McClair asked.

'Yes, I was, but only briefly. She visited me in Millport about ten days ago; a week last Friday, in fact.'

'And you discussed what?'

'She asked me about an old business I was peripherally involved with, a shoplifting allegation against a woman I'd represented in the past . . . in a manner of speaking, that is. She and her husband had divorced a few years before that, and I acted for him in the property split.'

'You acted for *him*,' the DS repeated.

'Yes.'

'And yet you defended her in the theft charge?'

'I know,' Black said. 'It sounds odd, but I was the only lawyer Marcia Brown knew. She called me and told me that I'd been an arsehole – her words – in the property matter, and that she hoped I'd be the same in her defence.'

'And were you?'

'Detective Sergeant, she didn't have a defence. I told her as much, and as you undoubtedly know, she killed herself.'

Skinner leaned forward. 'That's what you told Ms McDaniels?'

'That's it; nothing more, because I knew nothing more. Marcia claimed conspiracy; that was going to be her defence. I suppose I mentioned that as well.'

'Did you believe her?'

'I believed that's what she believed.'

'Well, you were wrong. She invented the whole thing.' He laid both palms on the table, as if he was pushing it away. 'Leaving that aside, I'd like to ask you about LuxuMarket, the premises on which the theft took place. The majority shareholder was another client of yours, wasn't he?'

Black looked at him, surprised by the change of direction.

'Mr McCullough? Yes, he was,' he confirmed. 'He was offered the property by the previous owner; his business was failing and he wanted out.'

'But he didn't get out completely, that previous owner, did he?'

The solicitor's gaze fell to the table, and he took a deep breath. 'No, he didn't. He retained a twenty per cent share in LuxuMarket.'

'At whose request?'

'His own.'

'Who acted for him?'

He looked away, towards the window. 'My firm did.'

'Didn't you have an ethical problem with that? Representing both the seller and the buyer in the same commercial transaction?'

'My partner acted for the vendor.'

'And that's ethical? Come on, man,' Skinner laughed. 'Stop pulling my chain. When the deal was completed, did the two parties, buyer and seller, meet? Be careful how you answer this, otherwise I'll have to switch on that recording device over there and make this a formal interview. I know Cameron McCullough, and I know that he used you because it was a small deal by his standards. Answer my question so I don't have to ask him. Did he and the vendor meet?'

'Yes, they did.'

'Did you and your partner disclose to Cameron that you were from the same law firm?'

'No, we did not.'

'In effect, what happened is that you went out and found a buyer for the vendor, your original client. When he asked you to act for him in the purchase, you got greedy and trousered two fees for the same deal.'

The lawyer sniffed. 'If you want to put it that way, Sir Robert.'

'I do. Why Cameron?' he asked.

'At that time, if you were looking for a venture capital investor, he was one of very few people with cash. It was in the middle of the recession, remember.'

'A few years down the line, when your original client wanted to buy him out, who made that approach?'

'I did. I set out the terms and Mr McCullough accepted. The second time, they didn't meet; there was no need.'

'What was the name of your other client?'

'Mr Butt,' Black replied. 'Mr Wasim Butt.'

'When he told you that he wanted to buy Mr McCullough out, did you ask him where the money was coming from?'

'No, but I'm sure you know anyway. The funds came from the RL Investment Trust, based in Zurich.'

'Who was behind that?'

'Mr Butt, I assumed.'

Skinner nodded. 'Let's go back to Carrie McDaniels, and her visit to you. After she left you, did you call anyone to tell them about her visit? Before you lie to me, you should understand that if you do, I will know. I have your professional reputation in the palm of my hand, mate, so don't make me crush it.'

'I called Wasim Butt,' the lawyer confessed.

'I thought you were retired from practice.'

'I am, but not from my business with him.' He glared at Skinner. 'Do what you have to,' he snapped, 'but I have had enough of this. I want to leave, so please arrange for a car to take me back to Millport. I don't care how many blue lights it has on top, I don't even care if the sirens blare all the way there; I just want to go home.'

'You will,' McClair said, 'when you've answered one more question. Which Wasim Butt did you call? Father or son?'

Seventy-Four

'No comment,' Wasim Butt whispered.

'I put it to you, sir,' Sauce Haddock said, 'that the first you knew about Carrie McDaniels' investigation of the Marcia Brown case was when you were told by your son. Not Zaqib, but your older son, your namesake, Wasim, the boy you left behind in Pakistan when you ended your marriage to his mother.'

Butt's solicitor murmured in his ear. 'No comment,' he repeated.

The DI sighed and looked at the lawyer. 'I suppose you think you're doing a good job for your client. Wrong. He can "no comment" all he likes, but it won't make any difference. He will be charged with conspiracy to murder, with complicity in human slavery and aiding and abetting prostitution, some of it involving minors. My colleagues in our specialist crimes unit have enough on him to put him away just about for ever, and the Crown Office has authorised me to charge him. The best you can do for him is to shut the hell up and allow him to decide for himself how long he wants to spend inside.

'Mr Butt, let me spell a couple of things out to you. We

have a witness, a very scared witness, who will swear that as soon as Carrie McDaniels left his house, he called your son, Wasim junior, on a mobile number. I have no doubt at all that when we gain access to your phone records, as we will very soon, we'll find that you received a call from that same mobile number. When Zaqib called you later on to tell you about Carrie's visit to him, it wasn't the first time you'd heard her name.'

He paused to allow his words to sink in; the solicitor opened his mouth, but Haddock silenced him with a look and a raised hand. 'This part is speculation,' he continued, 'and not too relevant to the situation you're in now, but I am expecting your phone records to show that as soon as Zaqib's call to you was over, you called Wasim back. It'll be for the jury to decide who actually ordered the execution of the young woman, but it was one of the two of you, and as the senior figure, you're where they'll look first. Maybe if you were standing side by side in the dock, they might decide differently, but your son won't be there. The Crown has less than four months from the date of your remand to bring you to trial. Even if he was arrested in Pakistan tomorrow, if his former colleagues in the Federal Investigation Agency turned against him, no way could he be extradited within that time frame. I have to tell you, Mr Butt, that when Detective Constable Wright and I look across this table at you, we don't see a cold-blooded killer; we see a man who's been sucked into something and is shitting himself, maybe even literally. So that's it: you either talk to us, or we end this interview right now and charge you with everything the Crown Office has authorised.'

The solicitor, who was also of Pakistani origin, leaned towards Butt again, murmuring in a language neither Haddock nor Wright understood. His client pushed him away, shaking his head and shouting, 'Enough!' He buried his face in his hands for a few seconds. The lawyer persisted, but again he was rebuffed, with a volley of words in a tone that would have been angry in any language.

At last Butt turned back to the detectives. 'You are asking me to betray my son,' he said.

'No,' the DI replied. 'Betrayal isn't an issue. We know your son is guilty of everything you'll be charged with, and we have enough to prove it. We're offering you a chance to help yourself. Do you confirm what I've just put to you?'

Yet again the solicitor tried to intervene, and again his client pushed him away. 'Get out of here,' he hissed in English.

'No,' Haddock said. 'He stays here; I am not taking the chance of you claiming that we infringed your right to legal advice. Please carry on.'

'Yes,' Butt said. 'I confirm it. My son Wasim did call me to tell me that the investigator had been to see Mr Black.'

'What did he say? What was his tone?'

'He was angry. He told me that anyone who even scratched the surface of that issue might uncover things that could not be seen. He blamed me for warning the woman's son to stop persecuting us, and so exposing myself. He even blamed Zaqib for stopping her at the supermarket in the first place. He said that any attention that was drawn to the place, and what is done there now, would jeopardise both of us.'

'To be clear, when he called you, he was in Scotland and you were in Pakistan, visiting your brother.'

He nodded. 'For the recorder, please, Mr Butt,' Jackie Wright requested. 'We need to hear you say it.'

'Yes, that is correct.'

'When Wasim is in Scotland, where does he live?' the DI asked.

'In the warehouse; there is a room there, and a cooker. He comes and goes at night. People shop for him during the day.'

'Back to that Friday: you had heard from Wasim junior, then Zaqib called you?'

'Not straight away, but a few hours later. He wasn't angry, more curious about the questions she had asked, but I was anxious.'

'So you called Wasim junior back?'

'Yes, and this time he was different; he had decided what to do. He told me to get myself back from Rawalpindi straight away, and to get Zaqib out there. He said that he wanted him as far away as possible for a week or so.'

'Did he tell you what he was going to do?'

'No he did not, that I promise.'

The DI paused. 'If he had, would you have prevented him?'

'Not would I, could I. No, I could not. Make no mistake, Officers, I was a figurehead. My son was in charge from the very beginning.'

Haddock stared him down, a technique he had learned from Bob Skinner. 'Do you expect me to believe that?' he said coldly.

'Not really. But it is the truth.'

'Tell it to the jury,' the DI snapped, then moved on. 'Can you confirm that Zaqib never knew he had an older brother?'

Butt nodded, then remembered the recorder. 'Yes, I can. I never told him, nor did I ever tell Rachel, my wife, that I had been married before I left Pakistan.'

'But Wasim knows about Zaqib?'

'Yes.'

'Were you always in contact with him?'

'No, not always. His mother and I, obviously we did not part on good terms when I decided that I was going to leave her behind and go to Britain. Her father, he was part of the reason. He was a very strong man, and a very powerful man in Hyderabad. He was involved in business that was not entirely legal, and he insisted that I work in it, for him. I could not take that, so I left my wife and my son. I heard nothing from Wasim until he had left Hyderabad himself to go to Lahore University. Then he got in touch. It was a shock, I can tell you. I had put him out of my mind.'

'When was the first time you met after that?' Haddock asked.

'After he joined the army, when he was twenty-four or twenty-five. I went to visit my brother Imran, and when I was there, I flew to Karachi to meet with my son.'

'Did you ever tell Imran about him?'

'No,' Butt replied. 'Imran is older than me. He had left Hyderabad for Rawalpindi before I married Azra. He is a very proper man, and I didn't want him to think badly of me.'

'So how did you and Wasim junior get involved in the human slavery business?' Wright asked, unable to keep the anger from her tone.

'He came to me ten years ago and told me that he had joined the FIA, the intelligence police. His work there had shown him how easy it was to move people around, and he had got involved in sending people to Glasgow and other places. He said there was money in it, but it was the tip of the iceberg. He asked me about my cash-and-carry business. I told him that I had sold most of it to Cameron McCullough. He said that if I bought him out, we could turn it into something else and move people through it, not just from Pakistan, from parts of Europe as well. I said that if I had that kind of money I wouldn't have sold it in the first place. He said, don't worry about that, I'll provide the cash. And he did.'

Haddock held his gaze. 'What about the money to set Zaqib up in WZB? Was that his too?'

'No,' he said firmly. 'That was mine. It was what I had left from the original sale to Mr McCullough. I did it for Zaqib's safety,' he insisted. 'Wasim made it clear that he could never know what we were doing. Zaqib is a straight-up guy; he would not have accepted it. If he had found out . . . well, they might have been brothers, but he was nothing to Wasim.'

'And Cedric Black? His call to Wasim was instant; was he complicit?'

Wasim Butt senior drew a breath, and a half-smile came to his lips. 'Mr Black? He is one of those lawyers who does not want to know what his clients are doing. But he did, he did.'

Seventy-Five

'What about Black?' Lottie Mann exclaimed. 'Is he under arrest?'

'No, no,' Mario McGuire replied. 'We have to be careful with him. He's on his way back to Millport, maybe with a slightly raised heart rate but thinking that he's free and clear. He knows we can't hold him on the basis of a single phone call to a non-contract mobile that was probably melted along with Carrie McDaniels and Gerry Heaney. We have to prove that Wasim junior was on the other end and we have to get beyond reasonable doubt that Black told him about Carrie's visit. Wasim senior's confession takes us part of the way there, but we need more, much more, before the Crown Office will authorise charges. We might have enough for the Law Society to remove his practising certificate, but he's retired anyway, so that's hardly a sanction.'

'Will we ever get him?'

'Is he guilty of anything, Lottie?' Skinner looked at her as he posed the question. 'Did he have knowledge of what went on behind the scenes at Household Supplies and Services? Old Wasim says yes; Black'll say no. And even if a miracle occurs and we – sorry, you, me not being officially a polis any more – have Wasim the younger in your custody this time next week, that will not be a tie-breaker, for he is going to say precisely bugger all.'

'Will we ever?' John Cotter asked.

'We can always hope,' Lowell Payne told him. 'But the cynic in me says we'll never see him again. He's become a major embarrassment to the Federal Intelligence Agency, one of their own going into private practice, so to speak. They may well be reluctant to look too hard for him. They may even take the pragmatic way out.'

The young DS stared at him. 'What's that, sir?'

'One behind the ear,' Skinner retorted. 'Murky world, intelligence; it has its own rules.'

Lottie Mann shuddered. 'I suppose that's it for our investigation,' she sighed. 'Wasim junior heard about Marcia Brown and took care of her before she became trouble.'

'Not quite,' Payne told her. 'The FIA did cough up Wasim's service record. When Marcia died, he was on an operation in Pakistan.'

'This too,' Skinner added. 'If it had been him, I doubt she'd have been killed by an overdose of Oramorph injected by an invisible syringe; nothing so subtle. She'd just have vanished. No, you two still have an active investigation on your hands.'

'But not a single lead,' Cotter complained.

His mentor grinned. 'That's when it gets really interesting, Hitch. You might have no leads as such, but I'm going to give you a shopping list. Given that you're a film buff, did you ever see *Raiders of the Lost Ark?*'

'My third-ever favourite film, sir, after *The Godfather* and *It's a Wonderful Life.*'

'I thought it might be. It's my number two, after *Con Air*. When you start to work through my list, I want you to be thinking of the very last scene.'

Seventy-Six

'He's quite certain about that?' Dominic Jackson asked.

'Do you think he'd have given me the green light to go home if he wasn't?' Alex countered. 'Lowell Payne had word today that Wasim Butt the younger was killed in a shootout with police when they went to arrest him at his grandfather's home in Hyderabad.'

'Are they sure it was him?'

'They are now. Uncle Lowell is a world-class sceptic, just like my father, but the Pakistani police showed him photographs of the body, and sent him a DNA profile that matches the one Arthur Dorward produced in Gartcosh. That leaves Butt senior up against it, with nothing to establish that he didn't order Carrie's killing himself.'

Dominic raised an eyebrow and showed her a tiny smile. 'Will you defend him if he instructs you?'

She grinned back at him from her chair on the deck. 'Even if he had the vision to do that, I'd be disqualified because I'd be a prosecution witness in any trial, but I don't actually believe there will be one. The Crown will accept a plea to the human trafficking and prosecution charges and be content to make a statement at sentencing hanging the murders of

Carrie and Heaney firmly round the son's neck.'

'So that's it? My peace is restored?'

'As I'm sure you'll be relieved to hear.'

'Are you moving back tonight?' She nodded but avoided his gaze; he seized on it. 'Are you all right about that?'

'I don't have any choice; I have to go back there sooner or later. And why not tonight? I've had a more secure lock fitted, and a deadbolt, and the bastards who broke in are both dead. It's just that . . .' She hesitated. 'Dominic, I've never been really scared before. I've been in trouble a couple of times, but I always had absolute faith that my father would be there to get me out. This time he wasn't. Those two guys were facing me; I actually did believe that I was going to die, and I was terrified. It undermined everything I thought I was. That was bad enough; hearing that Carrie had been murdered added another layer. I can't shake this feeling of being threatened. Look at my job. I mix with bad bastards for a living. What if another of them decides that I know too much?'

'Alex, kid, that's not going to happen.'

'I know,' she said. 'The sensible, rational part of me knows.' She tapped her head. 'But there's a scared woman in here who's never been there before.'

'Then let me exorcise you,' he replied. 'I promised Bob I would keep you safe, and I will, physically and psychologically. You've lived with me for the last week; now you can return the hospitality. You'll move back to your place, maybe tomorrow, not tonight, and I'll come with you. I'll stay for as long as you need me, and I'll work with you until the scared woman's gone for good.' He looked at her unblinking. 'Deal?'

'Deal.' She held out a hand and they shook. 'You'll miss your deck, though.'

'You've got a balcony, haven't you?'

'With barely room for you, let alone both of us. Still, the view's good.' She paused. 'Maybe it's just as well I'm staying tonight,' she conceded. 'I have an important meeting tomorrow with David Brass, the client Carrie and I were acting for. I need to brief him on the outcome of the investigation, including the fact that his ex-wife was a fucking thief all along. He's due in my office at eleven tomorrow, and since he knows him, my father says he wants to come too.'

Seventy-Seven

'M r Brass, welcome, I'm glad you could join us. You remember Clarice Meadows, my PA, don't you? She'll be sitting in on the briefing taking notes as necessary. Also, my father thought it would be appropriate for him to be here too, since he started this ball rolling by sending you to me. He's in his office above; I'll let him know you're here.'

As Clarice ushered her client to a seat at the small table, Alex fired off a text. She was distributing mugs of coffee when her father arrived.

'David,' he exclaimed heartily. 'Good to see you again.'

Pleasantries over, everyone seated, Alex began. 'I have to report a definite conclusion, Mr Brass. I briefed an investigator to look into the file you left me and follow up on it as necessary. She, and others, spoke to the principal players in the event, and I'm afraid that it's been established quite clearly that Marcia was guilty as charged. She staged her own arrest and tried to make it look like a set-up by Councillor Stephens, her enemy on the council. Her reason for this? She was concerned that a planning application for a change of use of the LuxuMarket premises was going to put many people out of work. Spurious, because it was only an application in principle, nothing to get excited about, but she wanted her day in court where she could level accusations against Councillor Stephens in what she thought were privileged circumstances that would guarantee them being reported. She never did get that opportunity, though, because she was found dead in advance of proceedings, a death that was subsequently determined to have been suicide. That's probably not what you wanted to hear, Mr Brass, given your own concerns about the case, and also those of your late son and his aunt, Joan Brown, Marcia's twin, the pair of them being determined to prove her innocence. Sorry, but that's the position.'

Brass sat for almost a minute, looking away from the table, taking in what he had been told, nodding occasionally. Finally he turned to face her. 'You know what, Ms Skinner,' he said. 'None of that surprises me. What I told you before about Marcia and me wasn't completely true. We didn't stay friends after the divorce. I tried to tell Austin, God bless him, that his mother was a nutcase. If your investigation has proved it, well, it's a shame it's too late, but at least it'll finally shut up Marcia's bloody sister. Thank you, Ms Skinner, you've done well. And thank you, Bob, for introducing me to your very capable daughter.'

Skinner smiled. 'My pleasure, David.'

'Mine too, Mr Brass,' Alex added. 'I wish I could stop there, but unfortunately, although the original incident was nothing to get excited about, when we started to look into it, a couple of people did. My investigator's name was Carrie McDaniels; unless you've been completely cocooned and isolated from newspapers, radio and TV news bulletins, you'll know that she was found dead just over a week ago.'

The elderly dentist's mouth fell open. 'Yes,' he sighed,

visibly shaken. 'I feel terrible guilt that she was working on my behalf. What happ—'

'It's better that my dad explains. He knows the details better than I do.'

Skinner nodded. 'That in-principle planning application, David: Marcia was right to be leery about it, but not for any reason she ever suspected. When LuxuMarket closed, it became a household supplies warehouse that traded respectably but was in fact a front for organised crime. When Carrie started asking questions, the people in the background panicked. They feared that she would draw attention to a very nasty business, and so they killed her. They also broke into Alex's home and threatened to kill her too.' Brass was blinking rapidly, his eyes moving from one Skinner to the other. 'I say "they", but it was really one man, a Pakistani intelligence officer gone rogue, a man named Wasim Butt. Wasim Butt junior, I should say, for he was the son of the guy who approached Austin and threatened him into temporary silence. Junior didn't want any witnesses, so he killed his accomplice as well as Carrie, and disposed of their bodies together. Then he escaped to Pakistan, where subsequently, we've been told, he died himself. The Pakistani police reported to my former colleague this morning that he was killed resisting arrest. That's a version I choose to accept, although I don't believe a fucking word of it. All I care about is that he's as dead as Carrie.'

Brass seemed to have shrunk into his chair. 'That's awful,' he whispered. 'That poor woman; if I had known it would lead to this, I'd never have dug up that piece of ancient history.'

'However hard your ex-sister-in-law pressed you?'

'What? Yes, no,' he muttered, confused.

'No, you wouldn't,' Skinner said. 'But if you hadn't done that, the police would never have discovered that Marcia didn't kill herself at all, that she was murdered. So you did justice a favour, for all the tragedy that followed.'

Looking across at Brass, Clarice Meadows experienced a sudden fear that his eyes were about to pop out of their sockets. 'What . . .' He shook himself. 'Are you saying that this Wasim man killed Marcia too?' he asked.

'That would be a neat conclusion, but . . .' Skinner rose, opened the door and called out, 'Lottie, Hitch, it's time for you to join us.'

'Pops?' Alex said.

'Sorry, kid. I felt it best not to mention this in advance. DCI Mann and DS Cotter need to interview Mr Brass, and since I knew he'd be here . . .'

'Interview him? About what?'

'About the murder of his former wife. It'll be under caution, and he's your client, so it's as well we're meeting here.'

David Brass was staring at him, and past him at the looming presence of Lottie Mann. 'Murder?' he exclaimed. 'Bob, I don't understand. What lunacy is this? What does it mean, that I'm to be interviewed under caution?'

'It means as a suspect; as the prime suspect, in fact. It means you have the right to legal advice while you're being questioned. Alex can offer you that, being a criminal specialist, or we take things elsewhere and you can instruct another solicitor. Your choice.'

'Would I find anyone better?'

'No.'

'You've set this up, clearly. Would she be influenced by you?' he asked, frowning.

'She hasn't been since she was fourteen years old.'

'Maybe not,' his daughter intervened, 'but I don't think it's appropriate that I continue. Wait one minute.' She left the room. Its five occupants waited in silence, watching two minutes tick away on the wall clock, then three, until she returned, accompanied by another woman, younger than she was by a year or two. 'This is my associate, Johanna DaCosta,' she announced. 'She hasn't been involved in the Marcia Brown investigation at all, so it would be far better if she advised Mr Brass, if he's agreeable.' She looked at him. 'Yes?'

'I'd prefer you,' he murmured. 'But if that can't be, yes, I will instruct her.'

'Thank you,' Johanna said. 'Alex, it's best if you withdraw, and Clarice too. I doubt the police will want either of you here.' She turned to the officers. 'If you prefer to do this at your place with your own recorders, it's understood, but we have a smaller version here.'

'That'll do,' Mann conceded, then looked down at Cotter. 'We're here, so let's do it. Hitch, I'd like you to video this as well on your phone.'

'We have a stand for that too,' DaCosta volunteered.

'Fine. We'll set up if you'd like a couple of minutes alone with your client.'

Brass shook his head. 'I have nothing to tell her. Let's get on with it.' He scowled. 'I want to get home. My wife killed herself; it was proved, so this is nonsense.'

DaCosta left the room with her two colleagues, returning with the equipment. As she did, her eyes found Skinner standing quietly in a corner. 'Sir Robert,' she ventured, 'shouldn't you be leaving us too, since this is a formal police interview, with my client under caution?'

'I have a role, Johanna; oversight, let's call it. Look on me as the deputy chief constable's eyes and ears.'

'And voice?'

'Only when appropriate; DCI Mann is the senior investigating officer. It's her show.'

'Thank you, sir,' Mann murmured as she and Cotter took seats facing Brass and DaCosta, Skinner remaining in his corner, leaning against the wall. She introduced herself and her colleague for the tape and administered the formal caution.

'Mr Brass,' she began, 'nine years ago, your former wife Marcia Brown, an elected independent member of the West Coast Council, was found dead in her home. At the time she was due to face trial on a shoplifting charge, and an assumption seems to have been made that she took the easy way out. A postmortem examination was carried out, performed by a locum pathologist with a student assistant. A lethal quantity of morphine was found in her bloodstream, Oramorph capsules were found in her flat, and on the recommendation of the pathologist, the procurator fiscal, Mr Robert Hough, determined that she had taken her own life. The case was closed.'

'Why was it ever reopened?' Brass asked angrily. 'It was clear that that was what happened.'

'You can blame yourself for that,' the DCI retorted. 'If you hadn't asked Ms Skinner to look into the shoplifting complaint, it never would have been. If you hadn't done that, Mr Brass, lots of things wouldn't have happened and a couple of people would still be alive. But sad as that is, it's the subject of a separate investigation, now concluded, and not relevant to mine. Why was this case reopened? you ask. You can blame the guy standing in the corner for that. It was plain innate curiosity that led Sir Robert Skinner to ask Professor Graham Scott to

410

take another look at the autopsy report. He did so, and came to a very different conclusion than the examining pathologist. He believes that the morphine that killed Ms Brown was not self-administered, but forcibly injected into her bloodstream, while she was being restrained. His view originally was that it would have taken two people to do that, one to hold her, the other to inject her, but since then he's conceded that one person could have done it, if he was strong enough in the hands and forearms and experienced in using a syringe. As a dentist would be, for example.' She paused, leaning back. 'Sir Robert said earlier that this is my show. Maybe it is, but it's not a solo performance. Detective Sergeant Cotter, you did most of the legwork; you should carry on.'

The little DS sat straighter, coughed and began. 'When your wife . . . sorry, sir, your ex-wife died, you and she had been divorced for several years.' His Tyneside accent sounded out of place among the lowland Scots; the atmosphere in the room seemed to change subtly.

'About five, actually,' Brass replied briskly.

'That's right. That meant you weren't her next of kin.'

'No, my son was.'

'Along with her twin sister. I'm not sure who takes precedence in Scots law, but when they need a formal identification, the police tend to go for who's handiest. In this case, it was her sister, wasn't it?'

'I suppose it must have been. Actually,' he murmured calmly, 'now that I think about it, Austin was away on a course at the time.'

'Noted, sir. Fact is, we know that her sister did the identification.' Cotter paused and took a tablet from the document case he had brought with him. He set it on its folding cover and switched it on. 'I got in touch with her myself, just to confirm that; it wasn't easy, but I was able to set up a video call and our technical people helped me record it. Just as well, eh? I'm rubbish at that stuff, me. This is it.'

He hit a button and the screen image vanished, replaced by the face of a middle-aged woman, and in a small box in the corner, that of Cotter himself. 'Are you ready, Ms Brown?' His voice sounded metallic, but the Tyneside twang was still there.

'Yes, Sergeant. I'm fine. Two police interviews in as many days. Have you found out who killed that woman?'

'I'm on another team, but I believe that's progressing. I want to ask you specifically about your sister's death, and about you identifying her body.'

'Something I will never forget. Nor the autopsy. I went there to make sure it was done properly, but the policeman said I couldn't stay. Black was there, though, the lawyer who did the settlement. I'm afraid I had a go at him.'

'Going back a step, what did you do after you made the formal identification? Did you try to contact your nephew?'

'I did, but without success. He was away. The police had to locate him.'

'You didn't think of calling his father?'

She frowned at the camera. 'Not for one second! David and Marcia had been at daggers drawn, Sergeant. Relations between them were never great, not even when they were married – he liked a drink after work – but by then they were very bad. Marcia had learned that he was selling his dental practice. She realised that its value hadn't been included in her divorce settlement – that's what happens when you're stupid enough to let your husband's lawyer act for both of you – and she told him in no uncertain terms that she'd be expecting fifty per cent of the proceeds. I know this because she called him from my house.'

'You're sure about that?'

'I'm certain, Mr Cotter; she put the phone on speaker mode. He called her words I didn't know he knew.'

'Was her claim realistic?'

'Oh yes. She hadn't taken legal advice at that stage, but I consulted my solicitor on her behalf; she told me it was a sure thing. A claim to an equal share would be successful, for there had either been negligence or deliberate deception at the time of the divorce settlement. The latter more likely, in my book, although it couldn't have occurred to Marcia. When she was arrested for the shoplifting, she actually called the same man, the one who'd stitched her up over the settlement. She was bloody naïve when it came to lawyers. I don't know what she was thinking.'

'Could she have been thinking that it didn't matter who she called?' Cotter suggested, from his onscreen box. 'Wasn't it the case that her sole purpose was to use her court appearance to release the bees in her bonnet over that planning application? From what I've heard, Ms Brown, your sister was a volatile woman, and very determined.'

'She was all of that,' she admitted. 'It was never diagnosed, but with hindsight I'd say she could have been bipolar. There was the respected, capable hospital manager and there was the Marcia who beat off all opposition to win and hold her council seat as an independent, fearless, unquenchable champion of the underdog against the system. That was her at home too: always confrontational. David's never been my favourite man, but I must admit she gave him a hell of a time, during their marriage and after it. The claim to a share of the practice sale was the latest in a . . .' She stopped and took a breath, 'Oh, I suppose you'd call it harassment. After the divorce, she broke up at least two of his relationships that I know of, by calling the women involved and spilling what she called the truth about him. I've no idea whether it was the truth or not, and maybe she hadn't either. She could be vindictive.'

'Hold on a minute,' Cotter intervened. 'If Marcia gave Mr Brass all that trouble, why did he engage a solicitor to take another look at the theft allegation, years after the event?'

'Because I insisted. David still had the folder that Austin's friend in the fiscal's office gave him. With poor Austin dead, there was no one fighting for his mother. I told David I wasn't having that, and that I wanted the case reopened. Marcia might have been all the things I just told you, but she was still my crazy twin, and I didn't believe she was a thief. It seems I might have been wrong about that, but now it's been established that she didn't kill herself, if what you're telling me is right, that's actually more important to me than the theft charge. It's daft, but I'm grateful to David. I hope he can find some peace after this and that he can mourn his son properly, even if he never shed a tear over Marcia's death.'

'How kind of her,' Brass whispered as the recording ended.

'Yes, that's what I thought,' Cotter agreed. 'And then I spoke to Cedric Black, your solicitor friend. You've known him for a long time, haven't you?'

'I suppose I have.'

'He was your patient, wasn't he, in your practice in Stewarton in Ayrshire?'

'That's right, he was. We went right back to the early days of my career; his too.'

'It was a substantial practice, am I right?'

414

Brass frowned. 'I wouldn't say so; how does one measure these things?'

'By turnover, I believe,' the DS retorted. 'I've checked with NHS Scotland: in the three years before the sale, yours averaged four hundred and thirty-seven thousand pounds. That would give it a marketplace valuation of around half a million. A quarter of a million: that's what a successful claim by your ex-wife would have cost you. I'm relatively new at this job, sir, but I've seen people killed for a hell of a lot less than that.'

'I dare say you have, Detective Sergeant Cotter, but I'm not that kind of man. You're jumping to a ridiculous and frankly offensive conclusion.'

'Mmm,' the DS murmured. 'If you say so, sir.' He paused, shifting in his chair. 'Going back to Mr Black,' he continued. 'When I spoke to him, it was to ask why he'd been at the post-mortem; he said he'd felt a duty as Marcia's defence lawyer. But he also told me – he volunteered it in fact – that on the day after she died, you'd asked him to be there, on behalf of you and your son, "to see that things were done right", as he put it to me.'

'That's right, I did.'

The DS pursed his lips. 'See,' he said, 'the problem I have wi' that, sir, is at that point, how did you know that Marcia was dead?'

Brass gave a tiny but perceptible gasp. 'I suppose Cedric must have told me. It's nine years ago, and my memory's no longer perfect.'

'Mr Black says that he didn't. I asked him. He swore blind that he didn't. We've just heard Joan say that she didn't tell you either. And it wasn't reported in the local media until five days after her death. I confirmed that with the editor of the local paper. He felt very guilty about their coverage of the arrest; he still does, because he thinks it contributed to her killing herself. I haven't bothered to tell him it wasn't suicide, by the way. He can live with his bloody guilt for a little longer. So who did tell you, Mr Brass, that your former wife was dead?'

Brass shifted in his seat, glancing up at the clock. 'It must have been the police,' he snapped.

'It wasn't. I've spoken to the man who handled the case. He never called you. Why should he? You weren't the next of kin. So if none of them told you, and yet you knew, well, there's only one way, sir, isn't there? You were there when she died: just you and you alone.'

Brass's eyes flashed fear signals as he stared at the man he had thought of as his ally. 'Bob, help me here.'

'You're beyond help,' Skinner told him coldly. 'Mine or anyone else's.'

The old dentist pushed his chair away from the table, turning to Johanna DaCosta. 'What should I do?'

'My advice to you would be to make no further comment.' She looked across the table at Mann. 'I haven't heard enough, Chief Inspector. You can't accuse my client on the basis of that alone.'

'I'm aware of that,' she replied. 'But there's more. Go on, Hitch.'

'Yes, pet, there is,' Cotter said, lapsing into patronising Geordie as he glanced at the solicitor. 'Sorry,' he murmured as her glare hit him. 'I went on the hunt, you see,' he continued, recovering himself, 'into the deepest of the deep, the dust-covered, the long-forgotten, the Crown Office archives. I looked for the year in question, and there, to my surprise, I found the evidence from the case – productions, you lawyers call them, don't you – hidden away in a crate like the Ark of the Covenant,' he glanced at Skinner, 'at the end of my second most favourite movie. There wasn't a lot: a wine glass still wi' the dregs in it, more than a dozen empty Oramorph capsules, and their boxes. There were bar codes on those. When I showed them to the manufacturer, they were able to tell me, even from that far back, that they'd been issued to a pharmacy in Stewarton, Ayrshire. When I checked there, I was told that they had been sold on to a local dentist who kept a stock for patients who suffered extreme dental pain. The pharmacist admitted he probably shouldn't have done it, but he said that Mr Brass was a persuasive bloke, and that an Oramorph capsule wasn't going to kill anyone.' Cotter frowned. 'No,' he said, 'but upwards of a dozen of them did the job. We found something else on two of the capsules as well: usable fingerprints that were missed when an attempt was made to wipe them clean. There's no doubt whose they'll match, is there, sir?'

As David Brass sank back into his chair, gazing at the wall, tight-lipped and stone-faced, Skinner straightened himself and stepped out of his corner. 'And all you had to do,' he sighed, 'was take the capsules with you and just leave the syringe hanging out of her arm with her thumbprint on it. You're no fucking mastermind, David, are you?'

. . . And now

There's rarely a night when I don't feel endangered. Not now. Not since Carrie.

Dominic stayed with me for a full week; he watched me, talked to me, tried to convince me that I was the safest person in the city, living seven storeys high, in an apartment with a door so thick that it would take Mario McGuire, armed with a battering ram the size of Tarvil Singh, to break it down.

At the end of that week, I told him that I was persuaded, that I was good, and that it was okay for him to go back to his deck, on which the first rain in a month had just fallen, in great golf-ball-sized lumps.

I didn't sleep a wink that night, or the next. On the third, I took one of the zopiclone pills that my online GP had prescribed for me; it worked, but left me feeling hung-over next morning, unable to concentrate or function properly until around midday. That made me change my medication: red wine did the business after a while, and didn't have such damaging after-effects. I ate very little; I had hardly any appetite, plus I couldn't be arsed to cook for myself. After a couple of weeks, I realised as I stepped out of the shower and caught a glimpse of my naked self in the mirror that I could see my ribs, for the first time in several years.

I longed for the weekends, when I could escape down to Gullane to chill out with my young siblings, especially James Andrew. I know now that I'll never have a kid, and that might be just as well, because if I did, I would spend all of its childhood watching it and comparing it with its exceptional young uncle. One weekend I went to Dundee to catch up with Ignacio, but he was so completely taken up with being the gofer at the radio station, and doing the sports headlines, that I went home earlier than I had intended.

Dominic called me every day; he didn't ask me how I was because he knew damn well I would say I was good. He talked to me, that was all, and I talked to him, feeling relaxed for the first time since I had awakened that morning, usually dry-mouthed and bleary-eyed. I could have phoned Griff; he was mobile by then and he'd have come if I'd asked, but it would have involved casual sex, and to my surprise, I'd lost my taste for that too.

It was Tuesday and I had opened my first bottle of the evening when the buzzer sounded from the street below. I went to my locked and bolted door, looked at the video display and saw Dominic, crouching down so that the camera could see his face. 'Let's go eat,' he called out. 'Don't dress up, nothing fancy; come as you are.'

I threw on a light jacket and went downstairs; his car was outside, his big high-roofed SUV, the only type of vehicle that could make him close to comfortable. As I climbed in, I saw two pizza boxes in the back, two plastic-encased salads, and a six-pack of Irn-Bru. Rather than driving into town, he took us into Holyrood Park, past the playing fields and up the narrow road until we came to Dunsapie Loch.

The heatwave was gone, and the inevitable storm that had followed it; the weather was back to normal for August: mild, not too hot, nothing approaching cold. He parked, found a place beside the water, threw a travel rug on the ground and unpacked our meal.

'So tell me,' he said as we were approaching the end, 'how are you?'

'I'm good.'

'You're not, and we both know it. You sit up in that tower of yours, locked in, probably with a Taser that your father gave you when nobody was looking; you drink too much and you're anxious, because what happened there and its association with what was done to your friend has made the place untenable for you.'

'Wow!' I exclaimed. 'Now I know why you prefer real tea to tea bags; it's so you can read the fucking leaves.'

He laughed, more freely than I'd ever heard him. 'If that's so, I've got a fucking doctorate in it.'

'And how are both of you?' I asked. 'You and your doctorate.'

The smile faded; he looked at me and then away. For a moment I thought he was nervous, but I banished the thought.

'The doctorate is doing very well. The police are giving me serious consultancy work. Imagine that: not just our lot, but a couple of agencies in England as well. Me? I'm lonely.'

I stared at him, my breath truly taken away.

'Don't be alarmed,' he said.

'I wasn't; flattered more like.'

'Don't be that either. I'm not going down on one knee, I'm just telling it like it is.' He looked sideways and up, and pointed towards Arthur's Seat. 'If the old king ever existed and really did sit up there, he must have been fucking lonely. I know this because I've been lonely too, without realising it, for all my life. When I was in prison, it was a virtue; it helped me isolate myself, focus on my studies and become who I am now. When I began my new life, my new career, I thought it would always be like that, and I was content. Then you came to stay with me, and everything changed. I'd never before appreciated what company really is, never had anyone to share my space with. I'd been married, sure, but there was no companionship there; she came to me having been one of Tony Manson's hookers, and that's what she went back to when I went away. Sex is overrated, Alex, and it complicates your life. I have no interest in it any more.'

'I can't quite go that far,' I admitted, made to feel awkward by his frankness, 'but I'm with you on the overrated.'

'Thing is,' he continued, as awkwardly as I, 'when you left, when you went away, I discovered in that moment what loneliness really is. And I have to tell you, I don't like it. Alex,' he gulped, 'would you consider flat-sharing with an oversized doctor of psychology with a terrible past but a promising future, who wants nothing more than somebody to keep him company?'

I couldn't turn him down. No, it didn't occur to me for one second to turn him down. I rented my place to an independent financial adviser and moved back in with Dominic. Now I am more content than I have ever been; with my celibate friend, I have found true peace.

But even there, in my dreams, every night, that fearful sense of endangerment visits me and haunts me, as I remember Carrie, and that bad, bad fire.

XTREME
SPORTS

by Matt Barr

ticktock

Matt Barr, 31, is from Manchester in England and did his first snowboard season straight after finishing a degree in English Literature at the University of Sheffield.

He went on to become Senior Editor of White Lines Snowboarding Magazine before co-founding ACM in 1999, giving him the freedom to explore the world. As a journalist Matt is happiest going off the beaten track, and his dispatches from some of the world's more unusual corners (recent trips have included Iran, Russia, Uzbekistan and Lebanon) makes him a favourite among the UK's more discerning national travel editors.

Copyright © ticktock Entertainment Ltd 2008

First published in Great Britain in 2008 by ticktock Media Ltd,
2 Orchard Business Centre, North Farm Road, Tunbridge Wells, Kent, TN2 3XF

ticktock project editor: Julia Adams
ticktock project designer: Sara Greasley
ticktock picture researcher: Lizzie Knowles

With thanks to: Diana LeCore, Marc Adams

ISBN 978 1 84696 522 7 pbk

Printed in China

Picture credits (t=top; b=bottom; c=centre; l=left; r=right):
ACM Group: 4/5, 9cl, 22/23t, 22cr, 31cl, 33b, 34b, 35bl, 54. AFP/ Getty Images: 48/49. A Snowboards: 11t. Abelboden Tourism: 7t. Matt Barr: 1, 2, 3, 34t, 61b. Mike Basich: 56. Blickwinkel/ Alamy: 57b. Blotto/ Burton Snowboards: 6t, 8/9t, 23b, 43t, 51b, 55tl, 55tr. Breckenridge: 40. Burton Snowboards: 8b, 9b, 11c, 17 all, 18b, 20b, 21t, 21c, 29t, 35t, 35bc, 35br, 58t, 59c, 59b. Rita Cami: 28. Canadian Press/ Rex Features: 50. Jess Curtes/ Burton Snowboards: 59t, 61t. Dakine: 18c inset. Nick Hamilton: 30t. Martin Harvey/ Corbis: 33t. Jackson Hole Mountain Resort: 27t. Jupier Images/ Image Source Black: 22bl. Lech Tourism: 31t. Eddie Lee/ thirtytwo snowboards: 47b. James McPhail: 13b, 14/15, 16, 18t, 18c, 20/21 main, 27b, 29b, 32, 38/39, 41b, 42, 44, 45b, 46b, 57c. Chris Moran: 26, 45t, 58c. Silvretta Nova: 46/47t. Oakley: 21b, 55. Ortovox: 37t. Damien Poullenot: 57t. Shutterstock: 12, 19, 24/25, 36. Sipa Press/ Rex Features: 52/53t, 52b, 53b. Squaw: 13t. Solomon Snowboards: 60. STL/ ICON/ Actionplus: 51b. Ticktock Media Archive: 37b, 41t. Treble Cone: 7b. www.explore.co.uk: 57c.

Contents

chapter 1: introduction

Pro rider Chris Moran pushes snowboarding to a new level by seeking out the impressive slopes in East Greenland, with temperatures of down to -65°C!

Snowboarding is one of the world's most dynamic young sports and is set to become even more popular. Snowboarding means travel, the outdoors, adventure and having a fun, healthy time with your friends.

It's no wonder so many people are taking up this great sport. Fun and totally addictive, snowboarding offers endless self-expression and gives you the opportunity to explore one of the most beautiful and adventurous environments on the planet: the mountains. Like its close cousins skateboarding and surfing, snowboarding is attractive for many reasons, but most people enjoy it because it gives them a sense of freedom.

In this book, we will be introducing you to the exciting world of snowboarding – how it all started, some of the crazy fashions and the amazing mountains that are home to snowboarders. We will also be explaining the snowboarding-speak and finding out just what a Roast Beef trick is!

SNOWBOARDING

Lake Louise mountain resort, Canada

For most people, snowboarding involves travelling to the mountains to get to the snow. This means it's a great way of exploring the world and some of the amazing places out there.

And if after all that, you decide you want to master the board yourself, the best way is to get out there and get riding!

To get started, take a few lessons with a qualified instructor at your nearest slope, or learn from friends who are more advanced than you. After all, that is what snowboarding is all about!

Nobody really knows when the first snowboarder took that all-important sideways step. We do know that in 1914, Toni Lenhardt invented the mono-glider, a primitive snowboard. He was followed in 1939 by Vern Wicklund, who filmed himself riding in Chicago on an early prototype. Look at these old boards to get an idea of the type of equipment snowboarders were riding back then!

Although these pioneers invented variations of the snowboard in the early twentieth century, it wasn't until an American called Sherman Poppen invented a stand up sledge for his daughter in the 1960s that the sport really took off. It didn't sell very well, but it did inspire a generation of young skateboarders and surfers to design their own boards.

These are some of the first snowboards. With no bindings, a few of them were a tricky ride!

Snowboarding became skiing's cooler younger brother

The first commercial snowboard – 'The Snurfer' by Brunswick Manufacturing – came off the press in 1965. Although marketed as a child's toy, it was followed by a second wave of adult boards manufactured by surfer Dimitrije Milovich who started Winterstick Snowboards in 1972.

The two main innovators in the 1970s were Tom Sims and Jake Burton Carpenter. By 1977, they had set up the influential Sims and Burton companies and were making the sport popular in America.

Tom Sims (far right) and Jake Burton Carpenter (far left) in 1983, preparing for one of the first snowboarding races

The monoski, an invention of the 1960s, consists of one ski; unlike a snowboard, the rider faces forwards

By 1984, snowboarding was also becoming popular in Europe, thanks to a man called Régis Rolland. Régis was a ski instructor from Les Arcs in France who made Europe's first snowboarding film 'Apocalypse Snow'. The film was made in the winter of 1983, and then released around the world. It helped to bring the sport to another level of popularity, outside the US. In Europe, the monoski – a popular variation on the "classic" skis involving just one ski – was still rising in popularity. But by the late 80s, it started giving way to the snowboard.

From the early 90s onwards, the world knew about snowboarding. Winter sports enthusiasts were grappling for a piece of the action as the sport doubled in size nearly every year. People like Jake Burton Carpenter, who started off constructing snowboards in a barn in Vermont, US, in 1977, suddenly found themselves expanding to huge companies in order to meet the demands of the the world's snowboarders.

SNOWBOARDING

A scene from 'Apocalypse Snow'

Apocalypse Snow

All in all, Régis Rolland made three 'Apocalypse Snow' films. Régis was introduced to snowboarding in 1981, when a couple of American pro riders visited France and gave him a board. With his friends, he began to film them riding their local resort and ended up making the legendary 'Apocalypse Snow' series. The films featured some incredible costumes and images and are a great example of how colourful snowboarding can be. They are rated as classic snowboarding films by today's riders.

Jake Burton Carpenter constructing an early snowboard

Today, snowboarding is the world's most popular winter sport. Estimates vary, but according to the industry there are somewhere between eight and fourteen million riders out there today, and it is increasing every year.

In reality, the term 'snowboarding' covers a lot of different meanings. Today it's possible to be a 'freerider', a 'freestyler', and even a 'jibber'! Confused? Allow us to explain.

Freeriding

While most snowboarders tend to stick to marked trails (known as 'pistes' in Europe) when they are on the mountain, 'freeriding' is the art of using the whole mountain as your playground. Freeriders like to ride in deep powder snow, find the steepest parts of the mountain and even jump off cliffs! It can be extremely dangerous, and some pro riders have been known to launch themselves off 35 metre-high cliffs. But it is also one of the things that makes snowboarding so much fun.

A half pipe gets its name from the shape – it is literally half a pipe!

Freestyle

'freestyle' is where snowboarding copies the tricks of skateboarding and surfing and performs them on the snow. Today, resorts build big snow jumps and obstacles so that freestylers can perform their tricks properly, 'half pipes' are especially popular.

Jibbing

'Jibbing' is a great example of how snowboarding constantly evolves as people try to learn new things. Jibbing has its roots in skateboarding, where people ride urban obstacles such as handrails and concrete ledges on their boards. Snowboarders quickly copied skateboarding, and an entirely new kind of snowboarder was born. Today jibbing is very popular among young riders.

13

chapter 2: gear and fashion

There may be a standard set of gear for snowboarding, but who's to say you can't have your individual style?

Without snow, there
can be no snowboarding!
But it means that riders
need to protect themselves
from the cold and snow and
the many different weather
conditions you find in the
mountains. Not to mention
all the gear that riders need,
depending on the different
types of snow...

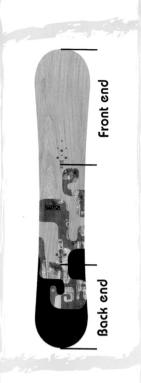

Front end

Back end

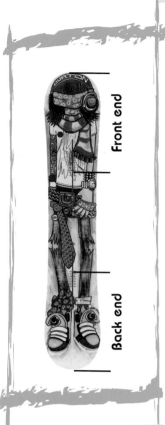

Front end

Back end

Front end

Back end

Freeride board

When most people think of snowboarding, they probably think of freeriding — big long descents, lots of snow and no crowds. Freeride boards are wider, so that they 'float' better on top of deep snow. They are longer too, so that they can go faster. The board will also tend to be longer at the front than at the back, so that rider is able to 'surf' the snow

Freestyle board

If freestyle is all about performing spectacular tricks, then a freestyle board needs to enable the rider to jump and spin with ease. Freestyle boards tend to be shorter and have a nose and tail that are the same length, so that you can ride the board backwards and forwards. They are also lighter.

Powder board

Sometimes, when pro riders are going into really extreme conditions, they will take a special powder board. Powder boards are extremely long. They are designed to be ridden as quickly as possible, in steep and deep snow. If the board has a shorter or lighter tail, the rider's weight is at the back of the board. This makes the board glide better on the snow. One type of powder board is called 'The Fish' because it floats so well!

E ven though there are many different types of board, they all have the same basic elements. These are the most important ones:

Deck and base

Deck   Base

The upper surface of the snowboard is the deck. This is the surface that the rider's feet are strapped to. The part that is in contact with the snow is called the base. Riders regularly put wax on the base of their boards to make sure they slide well.

Metal edges

Snow can be icy, soft, squashy or slushy, so probably the most important parts of the board are the metal edges. They help the board turn by cutting into the snow and are normally very sharp. Early snowboards didn't have any edges, which made it very difficult to grip on the snow and ice.

Bindings

These are the bits that attach the rider to the board by their feet. Bindings are usually made out of plastic and metal and clamp the feet into place securely. They can be very stiff.

Metal edges were first used in snowboard construction on the Sims 1500 FE and the Burton Performer in 1985. Until then, ice was much more interesting!

Being exposed to the elements means that snowboarders have to make sure they wear the right clothing. This will shield them from the harmful effects of the sun and snow and protect their body from the impact of a fall.

A snowboarder in typical gear

Boots:

The boots are the most important item of kit for any rider. They are designed to fit the bindings of the board and keep the rider securely attached to it. They also offer support and protection.

Gloves:

Essential, as snowboarders spend most of the day with their hands in the snow. As a result, snow gloves are hard-wearing, waterproof and cosy inside.

Helmet:

A lot of smart riders today wear a helmet when they go snowboarding. If you're freeriding, cracking your head on a hidden rock is a real possibility. Plenty of riders have landed on their head while hitting the jumps in the fun park. In the worst cases, riders have lost their lives due to head-injuries.

Goggles:

These protect the eyes from spraying snow when going down slopes. They also guard eyes from the sun, and the danger of snow blindness.

Snow blindness Snow blindness occurs when the light of the sun reflects off the snow. The UV rays in the reflected sunlight cause a similar effect to a sunburn on the eye. Symptoms can run from eyes being bloodshot and teary to permanent vision loss.

Although it is important for the clothing to protect the rider, it doesn't mean it can't look good as well. In snowboarding, like skateboarding, fashion has always had an important role. Much of this is to do with the fact that they are exciting and dynamic sports that allow people to express themselves easily.

The 1980s – The Neon Years

In the 80s, snow fashion was influenced by the bright neon colours of the surf world. As you can see in this picture, this meant bright yellows and orange neons, with patterns.

The 1990s – The Baggy Revolution

By the 90s, the surf influence was being left behind. Skateboarding and hip hop influences became very important. This meant riders began to wear really baggy clothes and sport dreadlocks and wacky coloured gear.

Today – Fashion and Function

These days snowboarding is still a highly fashion-conscious sport. People like to make sure that the clothes they wear are going to keep them warm and dry, as well as being very individual. As a result, clothing brands now make high-quality gear that is more visually striking each year.

the mountain

With peaks of up to 4,809 metres and guaranteed snowfall all year round, the Alps are one of the most popular winter sport destinations in the world.

There are many amazing mountains out there, and riders are spoilt for choice. Towering peaks, steep and blindingly fast runs, or huge jumps are all on offer at some of the world's best resorts. Here are a few of the top-ten choices where you can get their kicks.

✿ Courchevel 1850
LAC BLEU

✿ Courchevel 1850
LOZE EST

La Tania ✿ Le Praz
LANCHES

La Tania
CRETES

MERIBEL
COL de la LOZE

✿ Le Praz

✿ Courchevel 1850
CHENUS

Central Europe

Countries in the Alpine area, such as Austria, France and Italy have long been known for their excellent resorts. They are popular with snowboarders from around the world. The Alpine slopes are especially famous among snowboarders, as this is where the world speed snowboarding record was set. Riders with the need for speed will definitely seek out some of these incredibly steep runs.

Slope signpost, Méribel resort, French Alps

SNOWBOARDING

Breckenridge, Colorado, USA

USA

America is the home of snowboarding. It has some of the world's best riders, the biggest resorts and a huge variety of riding within its borders. Riders who are seeking the best pipes and trickiest jumps will travel here to get their thrills on gravity-defying airs and tough tricks.

Mount Tasman, NZ

New Zealand

New Zealand has incredible conditions to offer riders when it is summer in the northern hemisphere. It has some of the steepest cliffs and biggest drops, which is why so many freeriders spend whole seasons in this amazing environment.

Atypical resort has different types of terrain, which snowboarders make their own. Here is what most riders can find in the resort of their choice.

Piste

Pistes/Trails

These are roads that lead the skiing and snowboarding traffic all over the resort. They can be narrow, wide, steep, mellow or bumpy, but they are usually the safest way of getting around. They get groomed each night by huge machines called piste bashers.

Off-piste

Basically, every part of the in-resort area that isn't a piste! When there is fresh snow, riding the bits between the pistes on your snowboard is about as good as life gets. It ranges from tree runs to big open powder field. Yes, it's a playground, but it can also be dangerous, as we shall see later. Off-piste sections of the mountain are within the resort boundaries.

Backcountry

The areas on the mountain that are outside the resort boundaries, and that are the most dangerous. The backcountry is basically the mountain wilderness. It has huge appeal for most riders, but it is very dangerous due to avalanche danger and unpredictable weather changes. Being stuck in a far-flung region of the mountains in a raging blizzard can be life-threatening.

Pistes (or 'trails' in North America) are ranked according to colour. This is because some are steeper than others, and are trickier to ride as a result. The easiest runs are green and blue, with red being intermediate. Black is the hardest, with double black for experts only!

The weather in the mountains can change very quickly, which any snowboarder can be caught out by if they aren't careful. Snow is a lot more versatile and destructive than you might think. As a rider, the more you know about snow, the more you'll be at home on the mountain. Here are some facts and figures you probably never knew about snow.

Temperature

People often say, "It's too cold to snow". This idea is false. As long as there is moisture in the air and a way for it to rise and form clouds, there can be snow — even in temperatures well below zero. Most heavy snowfalls occur in temperatures of -9°C or above.

Blizzards

While snowfall is essential for riders, and fresh snow is fantastic to ride, it can also turn into a huge threat for them. As soon as the temperatures hit less than -7°C and winds of greater than 55 km/h, heavy snowfall is considered a blizzard. At this stage, snow will be falling or blowing in the wind for at least three hours, reducing visibility to 400 metres or less.

SNOWBOARDING

A rider enjoying fresh powder

Types of snow

Snow is different all around the world. This is because individual snow crystals contain different amounts of liquid. This gives snow from different areas their differing consistencies. For example, snow in New England, USA, may contain 10 centimietres of water for every 25 centimetres on the ground; whereas dryer snow such as that found in the Pyrenees (Spain/France), may have about a centimetre of water for every 25 centimetres. This is snow that most riders favour, and is called 'powder'. Fresh powder is any rider's dream. It is very dry, so the board glides a lot faster and turns become extremely spectacular.

The slopes are
empty as a blizzard rages

A severe blizzard is one with temperatures near or below -12°C, winds of more than 70 km/h, and visibility near zero. Blizzards are extremely destructive, and are something riders will avoid being caught up in at all costs.

In the early days of snowboarding, it was easy to choose where to go riding as so few resorts actually allowed it. Today, snowboarders are welcome everywhere and have never had more choice when it comes to booking a trip away. Believe it or not, you can now go riding in the following areas:

Iran

The average temperature in Iran is around 40°C, with a large desert region dominating the country. It might not be the most obvious country to go snowboarding, but, the resorts of Dizin and Shemshak (an hour north of the capital Tehran) have great snow, empty slopes, friendly locals and fantastic food. Famous American pro and former world champion Craig Kelly used to rate Iran as his favourite place to go snowboarding.

Atlas Mountains, Morocco

Morocco

Yes, you can go riding in Morocco, a hot country on the north west coast of Africa. It makes it one of the only places in the world where you can go surfing in great conditions one day and then go snowboarding the next.

Where next?

As snowboarding becomes more popular, intrepid shredders head further afield to find less crowded slopes. It means that exotic places like Greenland, Russia, and even Antarctica have been explored by riders looking for the next best thing. With peaks of up to 4,897 metres minimum temperatures of -90°C, and winds of up to 160 kilometres per hour, this is an incredible challenge for even the most experienced pro!

Mountains in Greenland

Avalanches are terrifying forces of nature that can destroy whole towns, as well as single snow slopes. An avalanche is a very large and sudden rush of snow down a mountain. Sometimes known as 'slides', avalanches are difficult to predict and extremely frightening. Pro riders must know what to do when faced with this danger. Sometimes, experienced riders simply turn away from a slope that looks unstable. At the very least, they ALWAYS carry the following kit:

Transceiver

Sometimes known as a 'beeper', this is a rider's lifeline. They give out a signal so that the buried rider can be found. This reduces the amount of time a victim is submerged by the avalanche. Essential!

Legends we've lost

Even the best, with many years of experience, succumb to the deadly power of the avalanche. In recent years, four-time world freeriding champion Craig Kelly (36, above) and Tommy Brunner (35), one of Europe's most experienced backcountry riders, have been killed by avalanches.

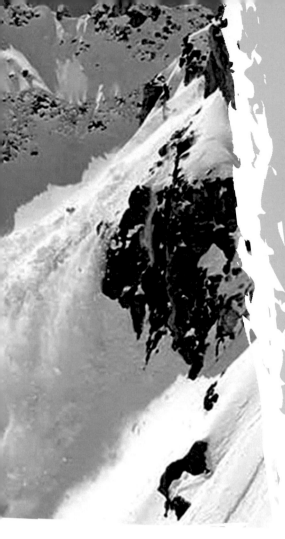

Probe

A probe is a fold-away marker that is placed in the snow above the buried victim to pinpoint their position.

Shovel

Essential to dig out a victim. Pros and serious backcountry riders always carry a shovel.

Backpack

Riders carry a backpack in which to store their shovel, probe and other essentials such as food and a medical kit.

35

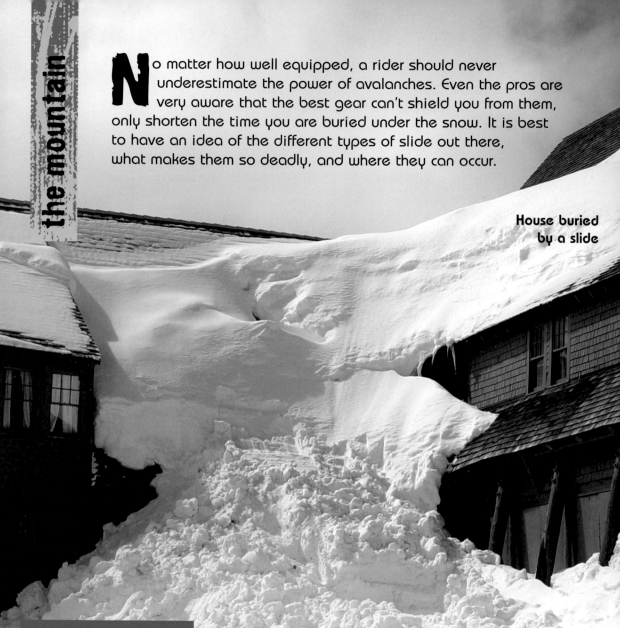

No matter how well equipped, a rider should never underestimate the power of avalanches. Even the pros are very aware that the best gear can't shield you from them, only shorten the time you are buried under the snow. It is best to have an idea of the different types of slide out there, what makes them so deadly, and where they can occur.

House buried by a slide

How?

Settled snow is made up of many layers, a new one forms every time it snows. Some of these layers gradually join together and from a 'snow cover'. Others remain separated from those above and below. An avalanche occurs when the force of gravity trying to pull the snow downhill is greater than the strength of the bonds between these snow layers. In order to set an avalanche off, some kind of trigger is usually required to set the snow sliding — for example the weight of a snowboarder or skier.

When?

The most common months for avalanches in the northern hemisphere are, in order: February, March and January, due to the heavy snowfall. Although 80% of avalanches occur after major snowfall, a large number also occur in periods of thaw. Most of these take place in April.

Locating an avalanche victim with a probe and shovel

A powder avalanche tearing down a slope

Where?

Avalanches can occur on gradients of as little as 25 degrees. About 98% of all avalanches occur on slopes of 25-50 degrees, and roughly 90% of all avalanches start on slopes of 30-45 degrees. Most skiing and snowboarding slopes are between 25 and 50 degrees.

Avalanches There are different types of avalanches. Powder avalanches, consisting of very dry snow, can reach speeds of over 300 km/h. Flowing avalanches are made up of wet snow, which is much heavier. They can reach speeds of 50-80 km/h.

chapter 4: tricks and stunts

Japanese rider Sinsuke Saitou performing an Indie grab at a hight of about 4 metres.

For many riders, powder is one thing, but snowboarding is really all about jumping and leaving the ground. As we've seen, snowboarding takes its roots from skateboarding, so it was always very likely that tricks using purpose-built jumps would follow in the quest for new thrills.

Riders use quarter pipes to gain particularly high airs and perform elaborate tricks

Quarter pipe

As the name suggests, a quarter pipe is basically half a half pipe. Riders aim straight at the fearsome wall of the quarter pipe and are shot into the air. They then land on the same wall, creating a graceful arc in the air.

Jump A jump is basically a purpose-built pile of snow that riders use to get air. Today, resorts spend lots of money making sure riders have enough jumps to keep them entertained.

Funparks

Designed to mimic the skate parks of the 70s and 80s, any good resort will have a fun park these days. They include handrails, a huge variety of imaginative jumps and often quirky obstacles such as picnic benches and even cars!

Half Pipe

Riders use a half pipe to reach for the skies and perform complicated stunts. If you've seen the Olympics, then you'll know what to expect – death-defying leaps in front of huge crowds. The world's first snowboard halfpipe was shaped by skateboarder Mark Anolik near Tahoe City, California, US, in 1979. It became a training ground for early American freestylers such as Terry Kidwell and Keith Kimmel.

International freestyling pro Quentin Robbins (NZ)

As we've seen, jibbing came about when riders began to copy skateboarding tricks on handrails and concrete ledges. Jibbing became an underground movement that gave riders a new buzz and a growing number of followers.

Why would snowboarding, a mountain sport, suddenly look towards inner city handrails for inspiration? Back in the 1980s, snowboarding was looking for its own identity. Freestyle was beginning to become popular, but the pipes were poor and jumps were small. Suddenly, jibbing opened up a new area to explore. This was in the late 80s and early 90s.

Pioneering freestyle snowboarder and jibber Jeremy Jones

18-year-old US rider Jake Blauvelt at the Winter X Games finals (2005)

By the mid 90s, jibbing had died out and it took a group of riders from Salt Lake City in America to reignite the flame. Kids all over the world realised that they didn't need to go to resorts to get their kicks – all they needed was a patch of snow, a handrail and their imaginations. Companies began to make jib specific boards, and pros could make a career doing nothing but handrails. Jibbing was back, and it was big business.

Today, jibbers practise tricks that they then perform on snow or in urban areas. Some jibbers just ride rails though – and rarely bother riding the rest of the resort itself!

What is a trick?

A trick is basically anything a rider does that involves them leaving the ground or using an obstacle to perform a stunt. Snowboarding takes many of its fashion and trick influences from skateboarding, a sport with a very rich and unique culture. One of the strangest things about both sports is the way the tricks are named. Whoever makes up the trick gets to pick the name, and it means there are some very odd trick names out there. For instance, some skateboarders name new tricks after their favourite food. As a result, there is a whole group of 'food grabs' with names ranging from 'Roast Beef' to 'Canadian Bacon'.

British pro Adam Gendle performs the Indie grab

Grabs

Most of the strange names refer to grabs, which are the basis of all snowboarding freestyle. As skateboards don't have bindings, skaters grab their boards to stabilise themselves in the air. It became clear that by grabbing in different places you could make up new tricks. Soon there were more grabs than anyone could keep track of – and snowboarders began to steal them.

Method

Probably the most coveted grab of all is the Method grab. This is basically grabbing the heel edge of the board between your feet with your front hand and pushing your back leg out. It is very difficult and is a good measure of a rider's skill and natural style.

Indie

The easiest grab – the Indie is just grabbing the board between your toes with your back hand, so it is very natural. It is still a very stylish trick though (see image opposite).

Roast Beef

The Roast Beef is a classic 'food' grab, and is grabbing the toe edge of the board with your back hand after having put it through your legs from the back. Sounds tricky – and it can be!

For most people, it is the death defying stunts and spins that make snowboarding so compelling. Since the beginning riders have been trying to outdo each other in their hardest tricks. Spins are basically multiples of one complete (360 degrees) rotation. So a '360' means one full spin, and a 720 is two complete spins. Then it gets complicated!

One of the first skate tricks to cross over to the snow world was the McTwist, invented by skateboarder Mike McGill in 1985. It is an upside down 540 degree rotation. This means the rider completes 1 ½ full spins in mid-air before touching down on the snow again.

World freestyle champion Terje Håkonsen performing a McTwist

A frontside 360

Finnish rider Markku Koski landed the first ever backwards 1440 (four full rotations) in competition. He did it during the halfpipe competition at the US Open in 2002, which he went on to take second place in.

Markku Koski performing a 1440

In 1998, when the video game '1080 Snowboarding' was introduced, actually doing a 1080 (three full rotations) on a snowboard was more of a concept than a reality. The trick is now commonplace. This year German pro David Benedek was famously captured on film doing a trick called a 'double-corked 1080' – three full rotations spun like a corkscrew!

World-renowned US gold medalist Hannah Teter performing in the half pipe at the Winter Olympics 2006 in Turin, Italy.

Although for most snowboarders the sport has nothing to do with competition, it is still a very exciting sport to watch and there are plenty of national and international contests around the world.

Top pros battle it out for supremacy in fun parks, half pipes and over big air jumps and are usually judged by a panel of experts. The judges are looking for how well the tricks are executed, how high the riders go and how unique the riders' performances are. The following contests are all international, and see riders from all over the world taking part.

Air and Style

One of snowboarding's most prestigious comps, the Air and Style is also one of the oldest. It is held in the Olympic stadium in Munich, Germany. The world's best freestyle riders compete on huge ramps, performing some of the most amazing and record-breaking tricks.

Travice Rice on his way to winning the Air and Style 2006

Sponsorship at contests

A lot of pros can only afford to snowboard for a living because they are sponsored. This means they get money in return for advertising for a company at contests and winning them. Top-earning US pro Shawn White has sponsorship deals with the snowboarding company Burton, Sony PlayStation and 14 other companies. He is said to have earned US$ 1million in 2006. This is not the norm, though. Most pros earn around US$ 400 per contest won.

Winter X Games

Usually held in one of the big American resorts in January each year, the Winter X-Games hold competitions for skiing, snowboarding, snowmobiling and snowskating. It often features never before seen stunts. Competitors can win gold, silver and bronze medals as well as big prize money. The grand total of prize money is US$ 1 million.

Martin Cernik (Czech Republic) performing a backside 360 at the 2002 Winter X Games

The fact that snowboarding is now an Olympic sport is a sign that the sport is becoming more and more mainstream. As we have seen, early snowboarders took their cues from skateboarding, yet skateboarding is a long, long way from being an Olympic sport. In contrast, snowboarding is growing in popularity at the Games. At the 2006 Olympic Games, there were 62 competitors, whose amazing performances were watched by 30,000 spectators.

Disciplines

Today, snowboarders compete in half pipe, parallel giant slalom (basically a race) and snowboard cross — an exciting race between a field of many competitors with jumps, banks and other obstacles. Top experts judge their skill, speed and style, and men and women compete separately.

Men's Parallel Giant Slalom, Winter Olympics 2006

SNOWBOARDING

Men's snowboard cross competition at the Winter Olympics 2006

Snowboarding debuted at the 1998 Winter Olympics Nagano, Japan, with giant slalom and halfpipe events. Canada's Ross Rabliagati was the first snowboarder to win gold in the giant slalom event, while France's Karine Ruby won the women's event. Switzerland's Gian Simmen won the first halfpipe gold medal, and keeps his prized possession in the safe at his local bank in Arosa.

Men's snowboard cross competition, Winter Olympics 2006

When snowboarding appeared in the 1998 Olympics in Japan, the resort of Nagano (which hosted the halfpipe event) still hadn't opened its lift to regular snowboarders! It finally lifted the ban two seasons later, which is a further example of how young the sport still is, and how quickly it is being accepted all over the world.

Ingemar's Air

Swedish snowboarder Ingemar Backman smashed the record for the world's highest quarter pipe air in Riksgransen in 1996. He was measured at 7.5 metres out of the coping and the feat became so legendary that it is still simply known as 'Ingemar's Air'.

Every few years, someone comes along and breaks the height barrier.

54

Heikki 'The Flying' Sorsa

Finland's Heikki Sorsa recorded the highest ever quarter pipe air when he styled an amazing method over Holmenkollen Stadium in Oslo, Norway at the 2001 Arctic Challenge. The air measured at 9.5 metres and earned him the title 'The Flying Sorsa'.

Sorsa performing his trademark soaringly high method grab.

Terje

Terje Håkonsen added to his legendary status in March 2007 when he broke Sorsa's record at the Oakley Arctic Challenge event. Terje hit an incredible 9.8 metres in height – and performed a 360 while he was at it!

Terje Håkonsen was the first ever rider to have a snowboarding movie made exclusively about himself. The movie 'Subjekt Haakonsen' was released in 1996 and featured the riding of Terje and friends.

Highest airs are not the only way to measure snowboarding greatness. But who else has played their part in setting some of the many milestones in the history of snowboarding? These are some of the most astounding contributions to the development of the sport:

The largest drop from an aircraft on a snowboard was performed by USA's Mike Basich in 2003 when he jumped out of a helicopter at around 34 metres He is currently the only pro to specialise in this extreme stunt.

SNOWBOARDING

Legendary pro Terje Håkonsen recently became the first known person to ride a wave on a snowboard. He was towed into a wave by a jet ski in Hossegor, France, wearing his full snowboarding garb: boots, bindings, goggles, waterproof pants and all!

Think you've been to the top of the hill? On May 24th 2001 Marco Siffredi became the first person to climb and ride down Mt Everest. Siffredi rode from the summit to Advanced Base Camp recording a total vertical drop of 2.5 kilometres! On a second attempt in 2002 to ride down the steeper north face of the mountain, Marco disappeared never to be seen again.

The North Face, Mount Everest (8,850 metres)

Need for Speed

The fastest snowboarder in the world is Australia's Darren Powell. He rode his board at an eye-wateringly scary 201.907 km/h at the 'Flying Kilometre' championships in Les Arcs (France) on 2nd May 1999. The 7 times world speed snowboard champ wears gear that is designed to be extremely aerodynamic, including a streamlined helmet.

Who are snowboarding's most influential riders? As you might imagine, this is something that snow lovers have endlessly debated over the years. As in every sport, some people have more of an impact than others and in reality the debate is endless. Here are some of the true greats:

Jake Burton

In 1977, Jake Burton Carpenter started Burton Snowboards from a workshop on his farm in Vermont (US). Today, it is estimated that half the snowboards sold in the world have his name on them. And he still rides 100 days a year!

Shaun White

Shaun started off as one of the youngest snowboarding pros, gaining sponsorship from the snowboarding manufacturer Burton at the age of six. He has gone on to win a gold medal in at least one international championship each year since 2003, including the Winter Olympic Games 2006. Having started his professional sport in career in skateboarding, Shaun has been winning medals since the age of 15.

US pro Craig was the first freeriding professional. He quit the contest scene to ride powder and is referred to as the 'Godfather of freeriding'. He was sadly killed in 2003, but his influence looms large.

SNOWBOARDING

Terje Håkonsen

Without doubt, Terje is the most legendary rider of them all. The quiet Norwegian has won every type of contest, and has also made some of the best films. He topped a 2004 poll as the most influential snowboarder on the planet. His name has been lent to two snowboard tricks: the Håkonflip and the J-Tear, which is his first name partially reversed.

Hannah Teter

Hannah Teter, Olympic gold winner in 2006, is a master of the half pipe. The American is probably best know for being the first woman to land a 900 in a half pipe competition in 2002 (aged 15).

Tom Sims

This Snowboarding pioneer from the US was a keen skateboarder. He had originally attempted to recreate the feeling of skating on snow by sliding down a hill on a board he had built as a high school project in 1963. In 1977 he started producing snowboards in his garage under the Sims name.

David Benedek

So what actually got today's pros hooked on snowboarding in the first place, and what have their scariest moments been on a board?

" I can't believe how hard the first couple of days snowboarding were in the very beginning. I don't think anyone really gets a break from those, no matter how talented they turn out to be! From then on it's all fun and or at least a very good progression that keep you motivated - and that's one thing which is really great about snowboarding: the fun and challenge of progressing never stop. "

David Benedek, Germany

60

Terje Håkonsen

" I've had some really scary situations in Alaska... we were hiking along the ridge with cornices on either side. It's really dangerous. The guy was about four metres in front of me, and I said 'On the left here, there's a cornice' and as he took one step to the side, the whole cornice just went. It wasn't humungous, but it was big. If he'd have gone, he'd ... maybe not have been killed, but he'd have been scared. And I think that was about as scared as I've been. I've been in one avalanche. It was scary because it happened so quick. I got to a tree as well, and I felt pretty confident holding that tree. That was in Mount Baker, about 15 years ago. "

Terje Håkonsen, Norway

" Snowboarding is fun to me because you get to travel all the time...which I think is why I still do it so much. I've been to places that I never would have been to without snowboarding and I always go with my friends. There's also something extra special about doing an activity that's in nature. You get so exhilarated by just being in the mountains that it makes snowboarding even better. "

Adam Gendle, UK

Adam Gendle

Glossary

Aerodynamic Of or having a shape that reduces the air drag and therefore enhances speed.

Air The passage of time a rider spends off the ground.

Boardercross An exciting race between a group of snowboarders over a course with jumps, steep corners and other obstacles. The one who stays on their feet usually wins!

Coping The top edge of a half pipe or quarter pipe.

Frontside and Backside Basically this refers to which the way the spin goes – left or right! If the rider spins so that the front of their body faces outwards, it is called a 'frontside' spin. If they spin so their back faces outwards, it is a backside spin.

Gradient This refers to the angle of a slope – in other words, how steep it is!

Monoski A kind of forerunner to the snowboard. The rider stands on the middle of the board with his feet together facing forwards, and wiggles their hips to turn.

Nose and Tail The front (nose) and back (tail) of a snowboard, relating to the direction the rider travels in.

Powder Deep, bottomless fluffy snow is what all snowboarders want to ride in. It is soft, forgiving and gives you a feeling like no other when you ride it. It is known as powder.

Regular and Goofy Refers to which way a rider stands on the snowboard. If the riders has his left foot forward, he is known as a 'regular' rider. If it is with right foot forward, they are a 'goofy' rider. Nobody really knows where these terms came from.

Shredders/shredding One nickname for snowboarding is 'shredding', while snowboarders are sometimes called 'shredders'.

Skate Park As skateboarding became more popular in the 70s, people began to build concrete and wooden parks so skaters would have places to skate. Snowboarders copied the idea at resorts, and called them fun parks.

Skateboarding A hugely popular urban sport that in many ways provides snowboarding with a lot of its roots and culture.

Snow Cover Or 'snow pack'. This basically means the many layers of snow that have fallen over the course of the winter, and then settled to cause one thick layer.

Spins The 'spin' is what most tricks are based on. Because riders are strapped to their boards, they cannot perform the same flips as skateboarders. So they jump and spin 360 degrees or more in the air.

Streamlined Offering very little wind-resistance.

Surfing The original board sport, and is where skateboarding and snowboarding come from. It is thought to have first been practised in Hawaii, and is now one of the world's most popular extreme sports.

Thaw The thaw comes when the snow melts as spring arrives. In western Europe, this is usually at the end of April and the beginning of May. The winter season usually runs from December to May.

Toe edge/Heel edge The edges of a snowboard bordering on the heels/toes of the rider.

Wax Snowboarders apply wax to the base of their board to make sure it glides smoothly on the snow. It is melted onto the base using an iron and then scraped off for a smooth finish.

Index